THE LAST CRUSADERS
IVAN THE TERRIBLE

THE LAST CRUSADERS

IVAN THE TERRIBLE

William Napier

First published in Great Britain in 2014 by Orion Books,
an imprint of The Orion Publishing Group Ltd
Orion House, 5 Upper Saint Martin's Lane
London WC2H 9EA

An Hachette UK Company

5 7 9 10 8 6 4

A CIP catalogue record for this book
is available from the British Library.

ISBN (Hardback) 978 1 4091 0537 4
ISBN (Trade Paperback) 978 1 4091 0538 1
ISBN (Ebook) 978 1 4091 0539 8

Typeset by Deltatype Ltd, Birkenhead, Merseyside

Printed in Great Britain by Clays Ltd, St Ives plc

The Orion Publishing Group's policy is to use papers
that are natural, renewable and recyclable products and
made from wood grown in sustainable forests. The logging
and manufacturing processes are expected to conform to
the environmental regulations of the country of origin.

www.orionbooks.co.uk

To Susanna,
Rachel and Verity

BALTIC SEA

LAKE LADOGA

NOVGOROD

POLAND

R U S S I A

MOSCOW

R. MOSKVA

R. OKA

KAZAN

CHERNIGOV

SAMARA

KIEV

VORONEZH

SARATOV

R. DNIESTER

BORYSTHENES

R. DNIEPER (BORYSTHENES)

R. VOLGA

ASTRAKHAN

AZOV

R. DON (TANAIS)

CRIMEA

SEA

B L A C K   S E A

O T T O M A N

T U R K E Y

C A U C A S U S   M T S

HEMESH ALLES

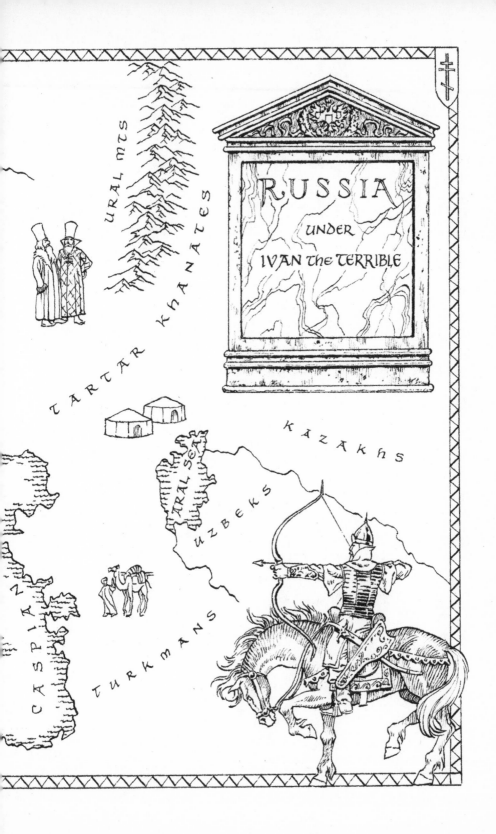

RUSSIA

UNDER

IVAN THE TERRIBLE

URAL MTS

TARTAR KHANATES

CASPIAN

URAL SEA

UZBEKS

KAZAKHS

TURKMANS

PROLOGUE
Moscow, 1541

His family were killing each other again.

Crouching in his chamber, the boy stared up towards the window and grey daylight and prayed and shook with terror. He seemed to have been shaking with terror all the few years of his life, praying desperately to God for mercy and safekeeping as long as he could remember.

There were screams, shouts, the ring of steel, the sounds of heavy-booted running men. An animal howl. The boy crouched lower, gripping the embroidered curtain that hung around his bed for thin comfort. He was petrified, unable even to crawl under the bed to hide. The curtain trembled as he clutched it. The embroidered figures of noble huntsmen and their ladies rippled and waved mockingly at him from their golden otherworld. Something thumped at his chamber door. He could not move. The shouting men ran on.

Another day, another round of bloodletting and vengeance in the gaunt palace of the Grand Duchy of Muscovy, called simply the Kremlin: the Fortress.

At last he unclenched his bunched fists from the curtain and stepped slowly over to the door. Something was pushing gently against it from the other side, but he could hear nothing, no breathing. Bathed again in the icy sweat of fear, he slowly drew the door open. A body lay just outside, head lolling across the threshold, tongue out, throat cut, blood oozing in a dark swathe across the polished wooden floor towards him. He stepped back in disgust so as not to soil his soft sheepskin boots. But he felt another emotion

I

too: triumph at seeing another slain, another dead, another rendered this stupid, lolling corpse, so helpless at his chamber door – and he still alive, so alive. There was a strange sweetness to it. A power.

He did not recognize the corpse. A thick-set man, eyes puffy and closed. Some henchman who chose the wrong side. In life he could have picked the boy up and hugged him to death like a bear, but now he was just dead weight. The boy kicked him gently in the ribs. Dead, dead as a dead hog at Martinmas. The boy smiled faintly. And he himself alive. Life was cruel, but God had made it thus.

Was the dead man at his door a warning to him, a murderous threat? Or was it merely by chance that it was at his chamber door this particular thug had fumbled his weapon and lost his life? He would never know.

His heart still racing, mind in a whirl of God and dread and triumph, he pushed the door closed again. Shot the bolt. Went carefully over to the window, trying to calm his breathing, stepping slow and stately as if the Duke himself in a cathedral procession. To be a Duke, said his father, you must act a Duke.

He stood at the tall window of the chamber and looked out upon one of the Kremlin's inner courtyards. There came another distant scream, and he laid his hands flat on the cool stone ledge. He was Ivan, son of Vasily, Grand Duke of Moscow, and of Elena, of Lithuanian descent. Surely his father would soon have restored order, taken red revenge on these barbaric boyars running murderous riot. But both his parents were dead now, his father when he was just six, his beautiful mother when he was eight, surely poisoned, the palace gossip said. He was a pitiful orphan in a young, unstable city racked by rivalry, hatred and the relentless struggle for dominance. He had once seen a pack of street dogs erupt into a mass brawl, ripping into each other with slavering jaws.

As in the street, so in the palace. As amongst dogs, so amongst men.

More screams, sounding far off. But the boy was already retreating from the sordid world around him into dreams of power and grandeur. He prayed to God Almighty and God heard his prayers. He would survive, by the grace of God, Creator and Destroyer of men. He would conquer, and one day he too would be Grand Duke.

One scream rose above the others. It was the scream of a woman, driven out onto a high balcony across the courtyard from where he stood and watched. Again he felt a tranquillity. It was her they were about to kill, not him. The tranquillity of relief and curiosity. The men behind had stripped her half-naked and driven her at swordpoint onto this cruel public promontory. Perhaps she was the wife or the whore of the man butchered at his door. If the boy glanced back now, he thought he would see the man's blood seeping under the door towards him, a spreading crimson lake ...

He did not look round. He stared across at the woman about to die, feeling more intensely that calm and vicarious power. Kill her, he found himself thinking. Yes, kill her! And he did not even know who she was. Again a faint smile.

The men behind her stabbed her three or four times in the back and she arched and howled once more and crawled up desperately onto the parapet and one gave her a last sharp stab in the arm and she was over and falling and hitting the ground below with a leaden thump. Her limbs spasmed briefly and she was still.

One day ... One day all this would be his. And the whole world would feel his power. The boy lowered his gaze and thanked God and was at peace.

1

Shropshire, England, 1574

The early spring sunshine fell on the fields bright with young green wheat and spangled with dew, and the bell of the manor house chapel was calling its summons to the field workers. Sir Nicholas Ingoldsby, aged twenty-five, baronet in the County of Shropshire, had been up since before dawn, bent over his desk. He laid down his pen and rubbed his eyes, and gazed out of the lead-paned window into the enchanted country beyond. He had always preferred being out of doors – on his feet, on a horse, even up a tree. Then he gave a deep sigh and read what he had written.

Three horses, £6 10s; six pigs, £2; a hundred and fifty sheep, £37; nineteen acres of wheat, £27; thirty-two acres of barley, £32; two acres of beans, £1 10s.

He smiled ruefully. He had become a bean counter, the dutiful son of his late father, old Sir John Ingoldsby, managing the ancestral estate that had been in the family of the Ingoldsbys for three hundred years. But was this really the duty he owed his father? When he was younger, and still a naïve boy, he had felt differently. He glanced up at the ancient sword that still hung above the fireplace – the sword with which his father had fought against the Ottoman Turks, at the desperate, heroic and doomed Siege of Rhodes in 1522, when he was still a Knight of St John.

But when the Order of St John was abolished in England by order of the State, Sir John had had to choose between his loyalty to that strange, antique, ferocious brotherhood of warrior-monks, or his country. He had chosen his country, and returned to England to marry, to raise his children, and live as a quiet, obedient, unobtrusive old Catholic family of the shires.

Now Nicholas seemed set on a similar life. Was he old before his time? He flexed his aching shoulders. No, his heart still burned within him. Just like at sixteen, when he had seen his beloved father killed in a stupid accident before his eyes, and in a fit of youthful idealism, had set off with his faithful old friend, Matthew Hodgkin, for the island of Malta, to serve with his father's old Order, in some confused dream of a Noble Crusade ... What a trial by fire that had been!

And an unexpectedly long one too. The Great Siege itself, all that deadly summer of 1565 – the young girl Maddalena, his first true love, his first heartbreak – the sorrowful departure from Malta, and then the fate of so many Christian voyagers on that sea: capture and enslavement by Barbary pirates. The galleys.

And Algiers jail. Years passed. He grimaced. Even now he could smell the dungeons he and Hodge had lain in, hear the scuttle of rats, picture their sharp, inquisitive muzzles nosing the fetid air, one forepaw raised, searching out any fresh corpses to feed on in that hellhole. Their escape.

Drunken quayside brawls, whorehouses, knife fights – the feckless life of any nationless vagabond. And then the Cyprus campaign with the Knights once more, quite unexpectedly, and that epic, destructive naval battle of Lepanto.

And then home – and this. Peace. Domesticity. He who had come back from the front line of the Turkish wars with a still restless heart, who still awoke from nightmares of Malta and Lepanto – strange nightmares that comprised exhilaration as well as terror – he who had for seven wild years lived in the heart of history!

Another sigh arose from deep within him, and he stared again at his estate accounts. Hereditary baronet he might be, but in terms of income, no more than a country yeoman. He had taken back the old family servants, the estate workers, he had cared for his sisters, married them off one by one to suitable husbands round about. He had even started to look around for a wife himself, to continue the ancient, noble, though distinctly impoverished, lineage of Ingoldsby. And to cool his restless heart with yet more dutifulness.

He ran his tongue over the pit in his gum where a tooth had

been only yesterday. He refused to pay a professional tooth drawer, a damnable expense, so he had resorted – in traditional peasant style – to the services of the blacksmith, with his iron tongs and his strong right arm. Still cost him threepence. And that was the most bloodshed he wanted to see nowadays. No more wild travels and adventures for him. Not any more. He was, he told himself, perfectly content. He must be.

Now then. There were eight gallons of wheat to a bushel, and eight pounds of wheat to a gallon. But he was buying in grain from Cornwall where it was counted eighteen to the bushel – unless you were buying directly off a boat, in which case it was sixteen ... And he was buying in Cornish grain unlading from the Severn. Did that mean ...?

There came a knock at the door.

'Enter.'

It was Jenkyn, the old steward. He looked anxious.

'What is it, man?'

'Sire – they've took Master Hodgkin.'

'Took?'

'Bandits, sire. Holding 'im up in Hound Wood. Demanding a ransom for him they are and all, or they say they'll cut his throat by midnight.'

He was on his feet and reaching for his cloak already. 'How many of 'em?'

'I don't know, sire. The lad come running saying they was great brutes of men, with faces all snarled up like the gargoyles round the church porch.'

'He has a vivid turn of phrase.'

He took down that venerable sword from over the fireplace and unsheathed it and eyed the blade. Still notched by Ottoman scimitars. 'Get me Will Rooker and saddle up two horses. We don't truckle with bandits in Shropshire.'

As he turned and strode from the room, his flaring cloak brushed the inkpot and overturned it. Black gall seeped over all the good work he had done, but he never even noticed.

2

He and his bailiff, sturdy Will Rooker, mounted up in the yard. Will had some old long beaten sword that might have seen service in the Wars of the Roses a century ago, and along with his sword, Nicholas carried a hunting crossbow across his back, and half a dozen bolts.

He felt the familiar excitement arise, all his good resolutions about sober duty and the quiet life already forgotten. One thing fighting the Turk had taught him: never negotiate, never surrender. And if he could face the Grand Turk, he could certainly face a band of impertinent Border bandits. They would have to fight. He had no choice. And assuming a band of twenty or so, they would have to attack with all aggression, hope to put a dent in one or two, and send the rest fleeing in confusion before they could put a knife to Hodge's throat.

The night was growing dark, the moon too thin to give much light. They tied up their horses three fields away, downwind, and spoke to them to calm them and allay their fears, their harrumphs and whickers. Nicholas winched up the crossbow and loaded a bolt, and then they crept along the field's edge under the darkness of the high old hedge, moving slow, until they came to Hound Wood. They crouched.

Nicholas glanced sourly at Will. Sneered in the dark. The fools of bandits had actually lit a fire to warm themselves and to cook whatever game they'd poached from his woods. Rank amateurs.

They went as silently as they could, knowing the bandits would see nothing, gazing sottishly into the orange heart of the fire, awaiting their ransom money. Patience was all. At last Nicholas was up behind a broad old oak not twenty feet off, crossbow readied, feet positioned carefully on soft ground free of twigs. He could have chuckled to himself. There were two of them. Two bandits. Hulking brutes, to be sure, from the hunched back of the one sitting, but no great number – the second of them lay wrapped in his cloak on the ground, probably dead drunk already. Hodge himself sat opposite, staring into the fire with an expression so untroubled Nicholas could have laughed again.

He lined up his crossbow and took aim at the head of the brute sitting on the log. Head the size of a cannonball from an Ottoman siege gun. At this distance it was too easy. Like potting apples at a May fair. He lowered the bow a little and aimed to take out his right arm. Hesitated. Something about the shape of the fellow ...

He felt a presence just behind him, and then something cold at his throat. The touch of bright steel. He kept very, very still.

And then the brute at the fireside spoke, without turning round. A deep, rumbling, bearlike voice as if out of a cave.

'Greetings, Master Ingoldsby. Fine hospitality you show us.'

The cold steel was removed from his throat and he lowered his bow to the ground, speechless with astonishment. He turned and there beside him stood a giant of a man with a broad, ruddy face and a mop of tow-coloured hair. For the first time he noticed another very serious sword indeed hanging in its scabbard from a nearby branch.

'Ned Stanley! John Smith!' he gasped. 'If I knew any blasphemies I'd swear them now!'

'Rubbish ambuscade of yours there, young Ingoldsby,' said Stanley. 'Brother Smith here said he smelt your horses coming ten minutes ago.'

'And this hare's tough too,' grumbled Smith.

Hodge stood. 'That's because you've over-roasted it,' he said. 'You never could cook, you.'

After effusive greetings and embraces, Nicholas stood back, trying to make sense of their presence. Sir John Smith and Sir Edward Stanley, Knights Commander of the Order of St John, both old enough to be his father, both in their fifth decades, yet as he knew from fighting alongside them, as tough and as dangerous as any soldiers under the sun. They were the elite. The Turks called them the Mad Dogs of Christendom.

Nicholas grinned. Things always happened when these two appeared. Sir John Smith, a bear of a man with black hair and beard now increasingly grizzled, his deep rumbling voice, his eyes red and bloodshot when angered, like an enraged bull. He could knock any man senseless with a single, casual blow, and was seemingly indestructible. When he stripped to bathe, his tree-trunk torso had more scars than skin. And he took a grim delight in always predicting the worst.

And Sir Edward Stanley, of an old English family, of similar build to Smith but even taller, like a Norse giant, with tousled fair hair, ruddy cheeks, dancing blue eyes and laughing disposition. As Nicholas knew, he always seemed most cheerful when facing desperate odds, in the heat of a battle, with death staring him in the face. He was never happier.

And the pair were certainly in great danger in Protestant England, as well as being feared and hated throughout the Mohammedan world, just as much as the Knights Templar had ever been. Now the Knights Templar were destroyed, by corrupt kings without and their own corruption within. But the Knights of St John fought on, the greatest warriors of Christendom, against a Mohammedan tide that was once more sweeping westwards. Palestine was again in the hands of the Caliphate, and that old medieval dream of a Christian Holy Land seemed more distant than ever.

The Knights of St John had been driven from Rhodes, and finally besieged on their island home of Malta: an Ottoman siege that went spectacularly wrong, and became one of Christendom's most heroic victories. And he had been there. Even now he could hardly believe it. All four of them had been there, comrades-in-arms; even the home-loving Hodge.

Nicholas waved at the two knights and explained to Will Rooker as best he could, 'Old friends of mine. I can say no more. On your life, Will, mention this to no one.'

'Not till Doomsday, sire,' said Rooker stoutly.

Nicholas told him to head back to the house. He would return presently.

'Last time we came direct to your door,' said Stanley, solemn again, 'tragedy ensued, and your father lost his life. As you well know. We needed to come and find you, but without risk of discovery or household tittle-tattle.' He looked after the departing Rooker. 'Less risk, at any rate.'

'Rooker's a good man.' Nicholas looked them over. Two Catholic knights, travelling *sub rosa* and under cover of night in Elizabeth's Protestant England. The danger was immense.

He said, 'If you're caught, you'll be beheaded within a day. And Hodge and I will probably be racked till we stretch from here to Shrewsbury.'

Stanley looked evasive. 'Our being here is not without risk, it is true. But we do carry a letter of *passe-par-tout*, a sealed letter direct to Elizabeth's secretary from our Grand Master, and new information of great value to London. Tidings from the East, you might say. Though not exactly glad tidings.'

'But the Pope, your Holy Father, has virtually ordered her assassination. Four years ago he declared her excommunicated and a heretic – which is as good as ordering her removal from the English throne.'

'Is the Pope not your Holy Father too?' said Smith sharply.

Nicholas hesitated. 'My Catholic faith is blurring with the years. This new Church of England is a broad church. Our parson here still has a crucifix on the wall, still reads the Psalms in Latin. And no, I most certainly have no interest in assassinating my Queen. Have you? Why are you here?'

Smith and Stanley exchanged glances. They would not be telling their old comrade Ingoldsby everything tonight. It was not possible. But they needed him. Stanley said, 'We want access that you can get us. How is your account of your travels to Malta and the Battle of Lepanto that you were writing for the Court? Is the Queen not impatient for it? It will be excellent foreign intelligence for her and her secretary Lord Cecil.'

'How do you know ...?' Then Nicholas shook his head. The spy network of the Knights of St John was legendary. It spread across all of Christendom and well beyond, to the court of Constantinople, to Persia even ...

'Nearly done,' he said. 'I will go to London later this summer.'

'Finish it in three days.'

He snorted. 'Out of the question, Stanley. It's a busy time of year, seed to sow, animals to get out into the fields, endless accounts ...'

'Three days,' said Stanley. 'We need to move by then.'

'Brazen cheek,' muttered Nicholas. 'Every time I encounter you afresh, I know there's going to be trouble. It's out of the question.'

3

It was with ink still on his fingers and bleared eyes that Nicholas rode out at the head of the four along the London road, three days later. There was much to do on the estate – not least the late lambing – but he had promised good reward to Will Rooker and his brother for managing it all while he was gone, and they were sound men. He would only be gone a short while, he said, just a few weeks. Back before May Day at the latest.

Hodge looked gloomy at his words. He felt a terrible foreboding that they would be gone a lot, lot longer.

They slept one night in the melancholy shadows of a ruined monastery, without any fire to warm their bones or cheer their hearts. Bare ruined choirs where late the sweet birds sang. Was it possible – Nicholas lay awake wondering, the dew settling on his face towards dawn – was it possible that only four decades ago, when his father was a boy, this was one of the great monasteries of England, a place of prayer and worship, unspeakably beautiful choirs of heavenly voices? Rest and hospitality for any pilgrim that asked, healing for any sick that came? Surely when that oaf Henry destroyed the monasteries he destroyed part of England's own soul.

And now his Protestant daughter sat on the throne. Nicholas's Queen, whom he now served, now rode to London for. He rolled on his side. Truly the world was out of joint.

They found rooms at an unwholesome inn at Wapping, the Mermaid. Hodge squinted up at the worm-eaten sign-board of the fair fish-maiden. 'Looks like she's got a bad dose of the clap.'

The first thing the landlord said was it was sixpence for half an hour upstairs with his daughter, or a shilling for a quarter ounce of this new nicotiana. 'Fresh from the Americas.'

They politely declined both.

Leaving his comrades to talk over old times in a private chamber, Nicholas rode over to Whitehall Palace to lodge his account of his travels with an uninterested clerk. Smudged and hurriedly written as it was, it would have to do. He stressed that it was commanded expressly by Her Majesty some three years ago. The clerk, sickly and pockmarked, seemed even more uninterested. He went back the next day to see if there was any response. Nothing. Dealing with government was often trying.

In the meantime they waited at Wapping and kept low. Smith and Stanley felt it was too risky to stay with Nicholas and Hodge and found lodgings somewhere else unspecified. 'A safe house,' said Stanley vaguely. Old Catholic families still abounded. Yet Nicholas already feared they were being watched. The landlord eyed them suspiciously from the start. No one could help but notice the two knights' deep un-English colour, cheeks burned brown by the Mediterranean sun, and yet their gentlemanly demeanour, and their aura of martial power.

At night the Mermaid was filled with mariners of the roughest sort, all flashing gold earrings and ribbons in their pigtails and gleaming daggers at their belts, and some very tall tales indeed. They disbursed their hard-won earnings as fast as they could drink them, as did their brazen shouting whores.

Hodge and Nicholas tried to keep inconspicuous and drank small beer as long as they could. The noise and stench grew worse and the fetid reek of this new-fangled tobacco in every mariner's clay pipebowl made the eyes sting and the stomach sicken. It would never catch on. Then a drunken whore fell across their table quite bare-breasted and eyed them with a stupid, feigned lasciviousness, before rolling onto the sawdust floor and lying there half asleep. Feeling rather ridiculous, Nicholas leaned down and covered her modesty with a kerchief.

'Quite the gentleman,' said Hodge. 'What's this inn's name again, The Devil's Whore?'

Nicholas grinned. The reechy stew of humanity in all its rumbustious shamelessness. He checked the dagger at his waist. Might be needed before this night was out. Yet he felt the thrill of it all as well, the hum of the great capital. Though he loved his native countryside with a love too deep for words, there was another kind of pleasure here. But please God, let him not be tempted tonight by a whore. Another blowsy wench was pouting at them across the room, though sitting in a mariner's lap. One night with Venus, a lifetime with Mercury. One onion-breathed kiss on the lips, and a month later, a body of welted sores. Or the mariner's own jealous dagger in your back, for that matter.

All was talk of foreign voyages and ventures. Even in darkest Shropshire they had eventually heard tell of Sir Francis Drake's extraordinary voyage to the Indies, the looted Spanish treasures he brought back with him.

'Four thousand seven hundred per cent!' murmured an older man, more sober suited. A maritime investor, perhaps, listening for tips. 'Four thousand seven hundred per cent on every guinea invested.'

'What's that in plain English?' said a blear-eyed sailor, leaning towards him.

'Invest a guinea,' said the older man, 'and you'll get back forty-seven.'

The sailor gaped.

'If Drake's not shot, hanged, drowned, burned or devoured by cannibals on his next voyage!' said another.

There was talk of other great travellers, of Giles Fletcher, of Anthony Jenkinson and his marvellous map of the East, and this new Empire of the Russias. A mariner sunburnt and muscled sat beside them, jovial and well soused, and showed them a bangle squeezed round his powerful wrist.

'Pure gold,' he said. He had a Devon accent, like Drake himself. 'Pure African gold. Got from a woman there for a mere bit of cloth. And the women there,' he waved his hands sinuously, 'got rumps on 'em good enough to eat.'

''Pon my faith,' said Nicholas politely.

'Now I like to think there's half a dozen pied coloured bastards o' mine running about the jungle, naked as Adam!' He roared with laughter. 'Look. This bangle here. African gold.' Why did drunkards always repeat themselves? 'Come from the ancient kingdoms inland. Come by camel across the desert. Remarkable beasts. They call it the Gold Coast, 'tis so common.'

'That's nothing,' said another mariner. 'There are isles in the southern seas, about the Portugal islands and the East Indies, where gold is so common they reckon it worthless entirely.'

'That's lies,' said the first.

Daggers would be out soon. A drunken mariner would quarrel with his own shadow. Nicholas had his dagger loosened in its sheath, Hodge likewise, but that hefty three-legged stool there might prove more useful if things should get lively.

The world travellers and gold connoisseurs talked of lands beyond the equinoctial sun where the natives were burnt quite black but gold was as common as clay, and though they were only naked and unchristened savages they dined off trenchers of pure gold. Gold knives, gold beds, everything. Gold gold gold. Nicholas began to sicken of the word.

'You mean,' he said, 'you could sail back with a dozen shiploads of gold?'

'Aye, lad, just so. For a few fardels of Hampshire kersey. Nice bit of cloth but not worth that much. And jacinths, rubies, emeralds ...'

Hodge nudged Nicholas sharply under the table but he pressed on. 'But then wouldn't gold be worth less in England? If you came back with hundreds of tons of it? Like it is in these fabled islands of yours?'

The mariner snapped, 'Gold is gold, you fool. Gold is precious wherever it is.'

'But you just said it wasn't. In these fabled islands. Because there's so much of it. It's only precious where it's rare.'

'You call me a liar?'

'No, I just question your grasp of economics.'

'Oh bloody hell,' sighed Hodge.

'Don't get smart with me, Master Wordy Quickwits,' snapped the mariner, 'or I'll kick your arse down Wapping Stairs and give you a bellyful of sweet Thames water to sup on.'

A fight was a gnat's breath away, but Nicholas just grinned

broadly and gave the mariner a mighty slap on the back and ordered him up another mug of ale. 'Here's a man after my own heart, Hodge. Do you have a ship or work one?'

The mariner scowled. 'Not I. My captain does.'

'We might need to take ship soon. We have a journey to go.'

'Aye,' said Hodge. 'Back to Shropshire. By horse.'

Nicholas said, a little heady, musing, 'I feel there's something in the air.' Thoughts of returning home by May Day were already receding. The world was so rich, so wide ...

'You got an estate to run,' said Hodge. 'The lambing, spring crops to sort. And abroad's a bloody awful place anyhow. I know, I've been there. Full of people who want to rob you or kill you or both.'

Nicholas gazed into the middle distance. 'Something with the taste of far-off adventure ...'

'Don't you dare. I don't have a sense of adventure.'

'It'll come back to you,' said Nicholas.

'I'm not going up to Hull again and that coast,' said the mariner. 'Grim old coast, that is.'

'Not Hull,' said Nicholas. 'Possibly further. Possibly Constantinople.'

The mariner laughed. 'Go and visit the Turk? Now who's the teller of tall tales?'

Hodge gripped Nicholas's shoulder. 'What else have those devious knights been telling you?'

Nicholas looked evasive. Then he said in a low, serious tone, 'They admitted to me when we were on the road that the Order has intercepted a message from the heart of the Sublime Porte itself. One of their trusted agents came back to Malta with a letter in fearsome code, but marked from the Sultan's own secretariat. The agent said that two men had already been murdered for possession of the letter, and he only narrowly escaped with his own life. After poring over it many days, the Knights understood it to read, *The Black Sea is flooding north, through summer meadows.*'

'Very pretty. What the devil does that mean?'

'They're not sure. But if two men died for it, it must matter.'

'Tell me what they *think* it means.' Hodge was exasperated. 'For the love of God, Nick, have I ever betrayed you?'

Of course he had not. For all that they were still officially master and man, they were two equals in every other respect. 'It may mean,' he said quietly, 'that the Ottoman Empire is about to march north and attack Russia. To wipe it off the map.'

4

On the third day a messenger came to them with commandment to attend the First Secretary himself at Greenwich in the instant. Lord Cecil.

'Mother Mary,' muttered Nicholas, 'what did they make of my account of Malta and Lepanto? This is like going to see the head-master back at grammar school.'

They waited for hours, were given more wine than they wanted, were moved from chamber into grander and grander chamber, listened to the stately ticking of a fine Italian wall-clock and sighed away most of the afternoon. At last, after it had struck six, they were summoned before William Cecil himself. The most powerful man in the kingdom, perhaps, after the Archbishop of Canterbury.

A small man, hunched, beady-eyed, pallid. Her Majesty was sup-posed to call him 'My little elf'. And a brain as elfin and cunning, nimble and far-seeing as any in Christendom. If a ruler's first duty was to choose his counsellors wisely, then Elizabeth had certainly fulfilled it.

He greeted them abruptly, voice thin and sharp, and asked where they were staying.

'The Mermaid, at Wapping.'

'Wapping?' said Cecil with distaste. 'That's where we hang pirates.'

'Just nearby,' said Hodge. 'Can smell 'em hangin' there in an east wind, I shouldn't wonder.' Cecil looked at him sourly. Hodge had already taken a strong dislike to the First Secretary, for keeping them waiting three hours or more, so he pressed on, just to annoy him, 'And the doxy upstairs is only sixpence for half an hour, he says she's his daughter but I shouldn't wonder if she isn't just the same age as he is!'

Cecil winced. 'You are ...?'

'Master Matthew Hodgkin of the County of Shropshire, Gentleman, and Queen's Pension of Five Pounds for Life for services at the Great and Gallant Battle of Lepanto against the Wicked Turk.'

Cecil eyed him with eyes as cold as a fish on a marble slab. 'Fascinating. But would you mind waiting outside? It's Ingoldsby here I must talk with.'

Hodge was guided firmly to an outer chamber. Seeing his expression as he went, Nicholas had to suppress a smile.

The door shut again and Cecil talked with the precise rapidity of the highly intelligent and highly pragmatic.

'Your report of your travels, which the Queen perceived might prove so useful to us.' He glanced down at it on his desk. 'Excellent. Valuable material. Only occasionally over-written.'

'Over ...?'

'Extraneous detail. We in government are not interested in Maltese flora or Cypriot fauna.' He smiled bleakly. 'But information on winds, tides, coasts, fortifications, armaments, all useful. The account of the flaying and murder of this Bragadino at Famagusta, before the Battle of Lepanto ... shocking, shocking.' He did not sound remotely shocked. 'We will want you to work for us again.'

'I, I ... I am not a ... I do not work for you, I am a simple Shropshire farmer.'

'And baronet.'

'And baronet, yes.'

'Who travelled widely in the Mediterranean when younger – on some kind of idealistic pilgrimage or crusade in memory of his late father, Sir John Ingoldsby, former Knight of St John – and who ended up at both the Siege of Malta and the Battle of Lepanto.'

'Yes, but—'

'Who has seen much, therefore, of manners and men abroad, and whose knowledge and experience would be useful to us.'

'Yes, but—'

'And you are a Catholic, are you not?'

19

Nicholas hesitated. 'I am devoted to Her Majesty, and a loyal churchgoer in her church.'

'You are a Catholic. You have even fought alongside Spaniards and Italians at Malta and Lepanto – Spaniards who are rapidly becoming our gravest enemies. Or do you deny Rome, deny Peter?'

He froze. No, he could not.

'You are a Catholic,' repeated Cecil, voice like a scalpel. 'Things can be difficult for Catholics. Increasingly so nowadays. Unless they demonstrate clear loyalty and service to our State.'

His mind reeled. This he had not expected. Cecil wanted him to be a spy.

'You have travelled widely, have fought well in the Turkish wars, you speak some languages – French, Italian, Spanish, passing Turkish – am I right?'

He must be honest. Cecil would see through everything. 'And a little Arabic, yes, and Greek. Traveller's Greek, not scholar's.'

'You'll not be translating Homer.' Cecil switched abruptly, the seasoned interrogator. 'Your two companions – they are safely lodged?'

Be non-committal. 'I believe so.'

'In London?'

'Yes.'

'You do not know where?'

'I do not.'

Cecil came round from behind his desk and very close to him: almost a head shorter, but radiating a kind of power. 'You do not,' he agreed softly. 'But we do.' He turned away. 'We see their every move.'

He ordered Nicholas to sit. He walked about, small neat hands clasped behind him. 'A delicate matter has arisen. Unusual, to say the least. Unusual, too, for such a matter to be entrusted to a Catholic – of however wavering a sort,' he added sarcastically. 'But I know you have told the truth so far. There are a number of things in your account which the intelligence of this kingdom knew already. For example, you have merely corroborated for us the details of Nicosia's defences in Cyprus.

'We know very well you attend your church regularly, you foment no dissent, you talk no religion. Within your household there is still a Catholic missal on your bookshelf in your study, that belonged to your father – his name is on the flyleaf – but you do not look at it regularly, and you have no priest visiting in secret.'

How Cecil loved such knowledge, and the look in this Ingoldsby's eyes, the alarm and the helpless admiration! Intelligence was everything in this brave new world. Knowledge was power. 'Yes, it pays to keep watch on one's subjects – especially the more wandering sort.'

He turned over Nicholas's account on his desk and laid it face down, as if the matter was closed. 'Tomorrow,' he said. 'Whitehall Palace, ten o'clock in the morning. Her Majesty will see you then. And – leave your friend behind.'

He grasped Hodge's hand in the outer chamber.

'Cheek,' muttered Hodge. 'Well?'

'I need a drink. And more than small beer. That man knows everything.'

The second time in his life he had come before Her Majesty, Queen Elizabeth, daughter of Henry, Enemy of Rome.

Today she was wearing a gown of old gold, embroidered with pearls and gold beads and the shapes of aged oak leaves. Nicholas wasn't quite sure it matched her red hair but he thought it wiser not to say. He bowed low.

Cecil stood close by her. She feigned forgetfulness. 'Remind me who you are.' He explained as clearly as he could. She waved a slim white hand. 'You have taken a long time to complete the account we asked you for.'

'Alas, yes, there was an estate to run, and my sisters—'

'You have taken a very long time.'

He bowed low again, teeth clenched. 'I have taken a very long time.' Much as he revered his monarch, it angered him to grovel. 'Yes, Majesty. My regrets.'

'As well I did not command an account of your entire life, or it would have taken you a lifetime to complete.'

He laughed gracefully. 'I am not a fast writer, Majesty.'

'Evidently. Fortunately I am a somewhat swifter reader, and read your account in a single night.'

Three hundred pages? Quite possibly. She was a woman of awesome intellect, as powerful as any man's – more powerful than many men's, indeed.

'You are with your … friends at Wapping?'

Nothing was named directly in this world. She would never use the phrase 'Knights of St John'. All was double talk and allusion.

'I am with my old comrade Hodge. The others lodge elsewhere.'

'Your old friends have experience of the court of Constantinople which will be invaluable. We have had some communication with them. The family of one, the Stanleys, are an old family, largely Protestant, loyal servants. But you do not need to trouble yourself with the complex business of high politics, you a simple, slow-witted yeoman farmer.' She smiled. 'So you are under new command from us, firstly to sail for Constantinople.'

'As spies?'

'As ambassadors and merchants,' said Cecil sharply. 'Merchandise and money are welcome the world over, regardless of religion.'

So it was true, what Smith and Stanley had hinted before to him. They were bound for Constantinople! The heart of the enemy itself. Fabled city of minarets and bazaars, palaces and fountains, negro slaves, sherbet, secret assignations in dark streets under the crescent moon …

'You will take gifts from us, to the Sultana Safiye herself,' said the Queen. 'You know of her?'

'I have some idea – she is Italian by birth, is she not?'

Elizabeth eyed Cecil, and he spoke in a voice like an encyclopaedia. 'She was born Sofia Bellicui Baffo, in Venice, about 1550. Her father was governor of Corfu. The romantic tale goes that she was captured by Mohammedan pirates, forced into concubinage, earned the favour of the Sultan Murad, the third of that name, and by great good fortune became the mother of his first-born son, the future Sultan Mehmet. So now she has become Sultana, most powerful woman in the Ottoman Empire. She is still only some twenty-four years of age, and reputed a great beauty—'

Elizabeth, over thirty years of age and no great beauty, though often flattered as such, interrupted sharply. 'Or perhaps she is just a common Venetian whore who has crawled to the top with her usual harlot's bag of bedroom tricks. What matters is that she has written us a letter, requesting friendship and sending gifts. She writes to us in most eloquent terms, sends us – as I recall – "so honourable and sweet a salutation that a choir of Nightingales could not attain the like, for the love we have for each other is like garden of pleasant birds …"'

'She's been out East too long,' he muttered.

Her Majesty heard him and smiled. 'You are merchants, but also our ambassadors. We wish to know all about this Sultana Safiye – her new Turkish name. You know what Safiye means in Turkish?'

Nicholas struggled to remember.

Elizabeth smiled a thin smile. 'It means The Pure. Very amusing. So you will have an audience with this Pure Whore, charm her, do whatever you need. You have good looks, modesty and courtliness. Our agent there tells us she has information useful to us. She is now a Mohammedan convert – for the furtherance of her career – but was born a Christian. You will cement our alliance – for though the religion of Islam is assuredly the enemy of Christendom, yet we both in England and the Ottoman Empire have an enemy in Rome. Perhaps this makes us unlikely temporary allies, of a sort.'

Politics was always complicated, compromised. And how on earth could Smith and Stanley be going on this mission too?

She read his thoughts. 'Your friends – from Malta – are at much greater risk than you are. But that is their affair. We have their assurance that their Order, at least, feels no special duty to fight against fellow Christians, or assassinate Protestant rulers.'

'I believe this is true,' said Nicholas.

'Then comes a more delicate mission,' said Elizabeth. 'You will sail on over the Pontine Sea to Russia, and up to the Grand Duchy of Muscovy.'

The Black Sea is flooding north, through summer meadows. 'Russia?'

'Just so. Increasingly a great and powerful enemy of the Ottomans.'

'So – our enemy?'

Her thin smile. 'Not so naive, Master Ingoldsby. Very much our friends, and esteemed trading partners. Christian, but not of Rome. And, potentially, very, very wealthy. How on earth could this combination make them our enemies?'

He felt quite lost. Bowed again, for good measure.

'The journey up to Muscovy alone will, I am sure, be ... interesting. You will have to pass through Tatar lands, and vast, lawless plains ruled by mounted bandits called the Cossacks. But I am sure you will cope admirably, and again you will gather all information useful to us. We already have the good maps and the reports of our loyal servant Anthony Jenkinson, Captain-General of the Russia Company. Here. See.'

She indicated and a steward unrolled a magnificent illustrated map: a work of cartographic art. In the bottom left was the image of a memorial stone that read, *Russiae, Moscoviae et Tartariae Descriptio.*

It showed a country of many rivers and exotic creatures. In the far north was a land, Samoyeda, where Jenkinson had pictured men in furs kneeling down before stone idols or squares of hide suspended from long poles. Beyond the last city to the east was an empty land called Sibir. There was a Cassac, and Colmack, and Kirgessi praying to trees, and from some of the trees were hanging corpses.

There were camels and conical tents among the Tumen, wild leaping horsemen at Astrakhan and in the Crimea, a great river called the Don, known to the Greeks as the Tanais, and the Neper, or anciently, Borysthenes ... It was a lot to take in. And towards the north was a small city on a small river, called Moskva.

'In Russian,' said Cecil, 'Moskva means dark or troubled waters.'

'But Master Jenkinson is a merchant to his soul,' snapped the Queen. 'Much fanciful illustration, and reports of crops and timber and beeswax, less about armies and fortifications, in which your eye is more experienced.'

'Truly, Majesty, I was only ever a soldier by accident—'

He was going to remind her that he really was only a yeoman farmer, even if he had inherited a baronetcy from his father; that he had only gone to Malta as a naive, vainglorious boy, imagining himself on some noble crusade in his father's name, had only become caught up in the battles of Cyprus and Lepanto as little more than a vagabond, along with his faithful friend Hodge. But she ignored him entirely.

'In addition you have a sharp eye and an agreeable style in prose. You were tutored in Cicero?'

'My father was a great admirer of Tacitus. He said Cicero's sentences were too long.'

'Ah yes, perhaps your style is Tacitan. "They make a wasteland and they call it peace," yes?'

He bowed. Her Majesty was known to be a very fine scholar – and not chary of displaying her scholarship either.

'And then in Muscovy itself – this delicate matter.'

If we get there alive in our own skins, thought Nicholas sourly. Cecil coughed. Elizabeth let him go on.

'The Grand Duke of Muscovy, Ivan by name' – even Cecil hesitated – 'has sent our beloved Queen a Proposal of Marriage.'

Elizabeth touched a kerchief to her mouth in amusement. 'Notwithstanding that he is married already.'

A little like your own father, thought Nicholas. But silence now, traitorous thoughts.

Cecil said, 'What do you know of this Ivan yourself, as a travelled, somewhat educated gentleman of England?'

Nicholas racked his brains, found little but tall tales there. 'Tales of a Grand Prince of the East,' he murmured, 'who moves about with a horde who live in tents, or hibernates like a bear in a far northern fastness of ice and snow, in a gold palace set with jewels.'

'Ye-es,' said Cecil. 'Exaggerations to some degree, perhaps.' His humour was drier than Arabian sand. 'Nevertheless, this Proposal is in earnest, and this Muscovy is a great and rising power. This Caesar of Muscovy, Ivan – Caesar becomes Czar in their barbarous tongue – was a mere tribal chieftain only four decades ago. His kingdom no more than a huddle of wooden houses and churches on the River Moskva, deep in the heart of this great unknown land.'

He waved his hand over Jenkinson's map.

'Now, suddenly, he has risen to rule from the icy wastes of the White Sea and the Baltic in the north, all the way down to the desert sands of the Caspian Sea in the south. He has twice conquered the Mohammedan hordes in great battle, these Tatars – warriors of Turkic custom, Turkic blood and Turkic ferocity. Kinsmen and of course powerful allies of the Ottomans. We believe the Tatars are descendants of Ghenghiz Khan, who terrorized all the world. The Russians call them the Golden Horde, their most ancient and bitter enemies.

'Now Ivan has already taken the city of Kazan from the Khanate to the east, and the important port of Astrakhan on the Caspian. With Russia's great, broad rivers flowing through flat lands without mountain passes, Czar Ivan rules over trade routes of unimaginable reach, from the Baltic to the shores of Persia across the Caspian Sea. From there lies a land route straight to India and China. He could sell German salt herrings to the Shah in Isfahan if he wanted, in straight exchange for Eastern silk and spices. Imagine the profit in that.'

Nicholas's eyes roved over the map, struggling to picture the scale of this vast empire risen so suddenly from obscurity.

Cecil said, 'He can only wax wealthier and more powerful still with such a kingdom.'

'And become a greater threat to the Turks,' said Elizabeth. 'What are his intentions? Where will he turn next? If he turns against the Khanate of the Crimea, and conquers, he will then have access to the Black Sea, and the Mediterranean beyond. Then his reach will be beyond all other empires of the world.'

'And so you see,' said Cecil, his hands clasped as if in prayer, 'negotiations regarding this Proposal of Marriage will have to be delicate. We are playing for time, but not refusing. You will take Ivan a fine oil portrait of Her Majesty, and other gifts.'

'You are not ...' at last Nicholas could not help himself, and against all court etiquette he blurted out, 'you are not going to accept his Proposal?'

But Elizabeth only smiled tolerantly and said with softened voice, 'Of course we are not. But that is not why you are going.'

He bowed out of her presence, greatly relieved. Only later did he reflect that he still wasn't exactly sure why he was going. As a kind of freelance spy?

5

'Tell me the bad news,' said Hodge, already dark of temper.

'We're commanded to go to Constantinople.'

'Turkey!'

'Just so. By royal command. So you can't even say no.'

Hodge's scowl deepened still further.

'It gets worse,' said Nicholas.

'How could it get worse?'

'We then go on to Russia.'

'Russia!'

'The Caesar of all the Russias, Ivan, has proposed marriage to our Queen.'

'The villain. And what are we supposed to do about it? I'm not marrying the bugger in her stead.'

Nicholas slapped him on the shoulder and said cheerfully, 'We're going as emissaries, ambassadors, with gifts, and also as spies. With no experience, no support, and no escape if things go wrong.'

'When things go wrong.' Hodge raised his eyes to heaven. 'Why us, O Lord, why us?'

'And also, I think, to make friends with this Czar Ivan of Russia.'

'How quaint.'

They spent the afternoon at the duelling school in the Artillery Gardens north of the city, near Moorfields. Nicholas felt they should exercise their sword arms. 'Just in case.' The Italian master there said they were clumsy and out of practice, but by the end of two hours' hard exercise he grudgingly admitted they had some skill.

'You will need thees skill too,' he said. 'London full of bad men, bad men. Wild men. Terrible. Worse than Italy.'

'What about Russia?' said Nicholas.

Things moved rapidly. Nicholas negotiated with his belligerent new mariner friend back at the Mermaid, who gave him word of a sea captain sailing for Spain with a load of Suffolk cloth in two days' time. Smith and Stanley reappeared from their unknown lodgings and he told them Cecil knew where they were. Smith grunted, 'We know where he is too.'

'Russia?' said Stanley. 'Interesting.'

They found the captain at Wapping Stairs, looked over the plump little merchantman going to Cadiz, agreed a price. Bought some provisions. Sent word to Cecil, had two precious crates loaded on board, one bound for the court of Constantinople, one for Muscovy.

'This is unreal,' said Hodge. 'Pinch me.'

'Business of State,' said Nicholas. 'Not ours to question it.'

And a day after that they sailed down a gilded Thames at dawn into the rising sun. Nicholas looked back on the slowly awakening city, and pictured the green shires of England beyond. He had no idea when they would return, but it would not be by Michaelmas now, and he felt that familiar thrill and ache of traveller's joy, traveller's sorrow.

Tacking down the Channel they passed the new St Catherine's lighthouse on the Isle of Wight. Mercifully God sent them clear weather for rounding the dreaded Eddystone, sixteen miles off the Devon coast.

'Sixteen miles out to sea,' said Hodge wonderingly. 'A huge mountain arising from the seabed miles below, its peak just breaking the waves. Beggars imagination.'

Nicholas stared down into the black depths. If you took away all the sea it would stand a huge lonely mountain, higher than any in Wales or Scotland perhaps. Everywhere the fearful grandeur, the illimitable power of the Creator. There was no reckoning it.

*

'Tell us what you know of Russia,' said Nicholas. Already he dreamed of the place, he had seen woodcuts. Carriages on huge sledges, men in long fur coats and outlandish conical hats, monstrous bears ...

Stanley said, 'Her River Volga makes our Thames look like a stream. As she nears the sea you cannot see one shore from the other.'

'Travellers' exaggeration,' said Hodge scornfully.

'Truth,' said Stanley. 'It was a while back now, nearly twenty years ago. We were very young knights then.'

'You have – been in Russia?'

'He's a born liar,' said Hodge.

Stanley grinned. 'Oh, it was cold when we washed up on the shores of the White Sea with the noble Richard Chancellor! There were whale bones littering that shore like the bleached roofbeams of a great church.'

Hodge yawned. But Nicholas wondered if it was possible. Perhaps they worked as special agents, stirring up this nascent Muscovy to attack Turkey's Tatar allies? If so, they had succeeded. Thrilling to think what tales Smith and Stanley had to tell of their travels and secret missions. They had murmured also of the Yemen, of India, he remembered, when they sailed from England that first time, he and Hodge but skinny, shivering, innocent boys of sixteen. So long ago, yet less than a decade. How Stanley had teased them with his travels and marvels. But was it only teasing?

The Knight Commander claimed to have sat beside the Great Mughal, riding into battle on an elephant dressed in scarlet silk. Ascended the High Kashmirs, met with holy men who could fly. Seen the very flower of Austrian chivalry fall beneath the curved blades of the Turk, seen Christian skulls whitening on the great Hungarian plain. Gazed upon the ruins of Antioch, of Heliopolis, and the wondrous pagan temples of Isfahan. Slipped unseen through the Straits of Bab-el-Mandeb beneath the bright Arabian moon. And now, yes, walked in thick furs along the banks of the frozen Moskva, and set eyes on the Czar of all the Russias himself, whom they call Ivan the Terrible.

'He's just read a lot of travelling books,' said Hodge, 'and has no reverence for the truth.'

'But the Russians have their own way of doing things,' said Stanley. 'They are not of the West. You will learn this for yourselves. You will encounter before long Ivan's own special forces. The Oprichnina.'

Nicholas had never heard the word before, but something in Stanley's tone made him shiver. 'Like our constables of the watch?'

Stanley smiled an uncomforting smile. 'Yes, if our constables of the watch rode about on black horses, dressed like black monks, armed with whips and spears and with severed dogs' heads tied to their saddles—'

'Severed dogs' heads?' cried Hodge indignantly. He was always a great dog-lover.

Stanley nodded.

'The savage, sick-hearted villains!'

'Of all the barbarous bastards I ever met,' put in Smith softly, 'they are the most bastardly of them all.'

'The people of Russia might agree with you there, Brother Smith,' said Stanley. 'But they have to keep quiet about it. The Oprichnina are great favourites of the Czar.'

'Why are they tolerated though?' said Nicholas. 'What of the law?'

'In Russia,' said Stanley, 'Czar Ivan's word is the law. And Czar Ivan, our supposed Christian ally now, may prove the most dangerous threat of all.'

'Why?'

'Because—'

'Because he's a mad dog,' said Smith curtly. 'Because he's a bloody loon. All the cruelty he suffered as a boy has multiplied in him tenfold, a hundredfold, and now comes out like poison. We have heard that he roasted a warlord of the Finns on a spear over an open fire – roasted him alive, himself. We have heard he murdered his own chancellor – tore him limb from limb – and had his own State treasurer skinned in front of him. We have heard he had Leonid, Archbishop of Novgorod, sewn into a bearskin and thrown to ravenous hounds. Doubtless,' he added sarcastically, 'for some deep symbolic reason.'

Nicholas gaped. 'Exaggerations, surely?'

'You think? Ask the people of Novgorod. He slaughtered them

in their thousands. Men, women, children ... The streets ran with innocent blood. Ivan rejoiced to see it.'

'And the people of Moscow admired him for his strength,' said Stanley. 'It is very hard to understand why one country follows one path, another country another. But England, for all its troubles, is a green and gentle country compared to most. Ideas like Magna Carta, or the King-in-Parliament, do not flourish in Russia. Perhaps they cannot afford such civilized luxuries. They need a tyrant to rule them, to keep order. They have spent centuries just struggling to survive, fighting off the Tatars.

'And the Tatars, believe me, know how to fight.'

They caught a good west wind over a bad sea and pitched and rolled across Biscay. Retched and spewed, lay groaning, wrapped in blankets on a soaking deck, already wondering why they came. Smith refused to spew. Just refused. Said it weakened your sinews. Stood at the stern with a face the colour of the green sea itself and held it in. Stood for twenty-four hours solid, mighty hands strangling the taffrail.

'He's not human,' groaned Hodge.

The seamen's curses would have set the Devil's own ears burning and all had seaweed flies crawling in their matted hair. But the captain knew his business, and there was no drink but weak beer aboard. They rounded Cape Finisterre and Galicia's fanged coastline and followed the Portugal coast down and then rounded Cape St Vincent and passed a low-lying marshy Spanish shore and so came to the bright white city of Cadiz.

They took on fresh water, anchovies, oranges, almonds and fig cake. Nicholas said, 'I know a good tavern on the quayside. Surely just a cup or two of sweet Spanish wine ...?'

Stanley shook his head. 'No chance.'

'Why the hurry? Such vulgar haste does not befit our ambassadorial dignity.'

Smith snorted with derision at this new-found status of his scruffy young Shropshire friends. Then he said, grim and curt, 'We hurry because they hurry. They will be riding soon.'

*

The good west wind was holding and the captain open to the persuasion of gold. He would sail on to Malta for a fee.

'And any Barbary pirates,' said Stanley, 'we will deal with ourselves.'

None came. The great Christian victory of Lepanto did indeed seem to have brought some peace to the bloody saltwater battleline of the Mediterranean. For now.

'That's just why we're puzzled,' said Stanley.

'Why so?'

'Because the Turks are surely still too exhausted after Lepanto to fight again in the Mediterranean. Yet something great is stirring. We can feel it. And we need to find out what.'

They took on water in the Balearics and three days later dropped anchor in the magnificent harbour of Malta beneath the majestic new city of Valletta. The two Knights sent word to their Grand Master. Nicholas and Hodge did not step ashore. Though they could have gone to visit old friends, and more than old friends – the beloved family of Franco Briffa, whom they had lodged with and fought for, and the grave of Maddalena, the first girl Nicholas had ever loved – yet they chose not to. Many tales, many tears. Sometimes it is better never to go back. He and Hodge would be greeted with open arms by the people of the old city – had he not been christened, embarrassingly, the English Hero, for one or two accidents of foolhardy gallantry that long hot summer? Nicholas smiled sadly to himself. Nine years ago, yet it all seemed so long ago, when he was sixteen, barely more than a schoolboy. And now already they were saying it was the Greatest Siege in History – and he and Hodge had been there, alongside Smith and Stanley and all the other knights, so many of them slain. And when victory came at last, victory scarcely believable against such odds – nine hundred knights fought and defeated an Ottoman army of thirty thousand or more – it was a mixed victory, a tainted triumph, as perhaps all victories are. For the girl Maddalena, the daughter of the house, whom he had fallen in love with, was among the many fallen. He thought then he would never love again. She would always be young, beautiful, ageless, perfect.

*

32

The English captain was pleased enough to offload his bales of woollen cloth and kersey, Cornish tin, pewter, lead and rabbit skins, and bring home raw silk, indigo, currants, oil, wine, camel-hair cloth and angora wool, and make a fine profit for both himself and his employers back at the London Exchange.

Word came from the Grand Master that afternoon. Stanley listened, nodded, turned and said, 'There's a Sicily merchantman leaving for Constantinople within the hour. Ship out.'

They sailed at sunset over the Ionian Sea and fell asleep on deck with the warm breezes in their hair. They rounded Cape Matapan and passed between Cythera and Crete, the last Christian land in the east, and then north among the Cyclades and into the waters of the Turks. Dreamlike it seemed, to be sailing into the heart of the enemy's world, an enemy that they had fought so bitterly at Malta and Lepanto. Now they took them gifts. Such was the way of things.

They passed Chios to starboard and Lemnos to larboard, and entered the Dardanelles Strait preceded by a school of curvetting porpoises. The Sea of Marmara lay sunlit and calm and the breeze dropped off as they sailed with slow and stately dignity into the capital of the Mohammedan world, and stepped ashore near Seraglio Point, below the Palace of Hormisdas.

6

Nicholas could not believe it was so simple to step ashore into the heart of this great enemy Mohammedan empire – yet merchants, travellers and ambassadors did it all the time. He gazed around in awe upon the dusty, crowded, deafeningly noisy quayside of the most populous city on earth. Above rose the great towers and minarets like giant candle-snuffers, banners in the breeze, and above them all, the green banner of Islam.

They were accosted immediately by a multitude of helpful voices offering guidance, tobacco, coffee, girls and boys.

'Inglisz!' they soon surmised. 'Inglisz always welcome! You do not worship idols like the filthy Greeks,' spit, 'you are Protestants, yeas, you are brothers of Islam, People of the Book, Inglisz brothers!'

It was one point of view.

'You want a boy? I know a sweet boy, behind like a peach.'

Crowds began to gather and stare, without hostility but with inexhaustible curiosity. Smith was already feeling uncomfortable. 'I've no interest in your peachy-arsed catamites,' he growled, 'we're making for the English embassy in Pera.'

'Yeas please, come, Sir Inglisz, come, I take.'

Smith knew his way round the ancient city of the enemy all too well, but Stanley had given him firm orders to feign ignorance. 'And be courteous, Brother John, and docile, though I know it makes your guts writhe within you. And for the love of God, no mention of Malta now.'

Two quayside guards with long pikes were already coming over. They busied themselves with paying the captain, and making their farewells. The captain bellowed for porters, gangplanks slammed down, wooden barrows appeared and unlading began. The four travellers agreed to one small man in ballooning red pantaloons guiding them, and made their way into the crowd. The guards watched them go with narrowed eyes.

At the gates into the city everything was searched.

'Gifts,' said Stanley at his sternest. 'From the Queen of England to the Sultan himself. First they must be lodged at the English embassy.'

They were immediately provided with an additional escort of six armed soldiers.

Word spread fast. The crowd made way, staring, entranced. 'Inglisz merchants! Come for the Sultan himself with Inglisz gold and jewels!'

Even with armed escort, progress through the Grand Bazaar was a battle. The soldiers struck out left and right with heavy wooden pikes, but the recipients of the blows took it all without complaint. Nicholas had never imagined such a scene. The Grand Bazaar of Constantinople had eighteen gates and sixty-seven main streets. London's Cheapside seemed like a toy market in comparison.

'And four thousand shops,' said their guide. 'Many, many. Here you can buy anything you desire. It is the Bazaar of the World.'

The mingled odours were indescribable: drains and camel dung and fresh red camel-meat hanging from butchers' hooks, and frankincense, rose-petal jam, huge steaming cauldrons of tripe soup reeking of garlic, reckoned the perfect cure for a hangover. For the Turks, though Mohammedans, were still great lovers of wine.

'I feel sick,' said Hodge, already dreaming of damp woods and green fields.

More sickly perfumes: attar of roses from Adrianople, essence of hyacinth, almond and cypress oil, then the streets of the tailors, caftans of heavily brocaded Bursa velvet, then the coppersmiths, the ceaseless tink of their delicate hammers, the charcoal fires fanned by negro slaves with goose wings, a sheep being butchered with cleavers in the middle of the street. Brains gathered in a bowl for soup.

'A fine gentlemanly thing it is,' said Nicholas, 'to travel the world and see other men and manners.'

Hodge regarded him sourly.

They passed through a huge dusty square, surrounded by a wooden portico. The slave market. Negresses black as night and stark naked, standing on a raised stage as if for hanging. Prospective buyers examining their long ebony limbs, pulling open their mouths with rough fingers, examining their perfect white teeth as you would a horse. Even Smith muttered, 'Poor heathen bitches.'

On other platforms, diaphanously draped, the most expensive Georgian and Circassian slave girls, famed for their beauty, bound for the harems of only the wealthiest merchants of all, if not taken by the Sultan's own buyers for the Imperial harem itself. Nicholas could not help but look.

'Forget it, lad,' said Stanley. 'You couldn't afford one of them for your whole estate in Shropshire.'

'I am looking with pity, not lust,' said Nicholas.

Stanley grunted sceptically.

The owner of the slave farm out in Anatolia was saying as they passed by, 'Now a melon may take only one summer to grow from seed, whereas one of these beauties takes fourteen, fifteen summers. But then the reward, the reward!'

A strange thing, thought Nicholas, to farm human beings. Yet other lands, other customs. Then again, was he not in some sense a helpless slave to his Queen, taking orders he could not disobey? He suppressed the thought for his peace of mind.

At last they came to Pera and the cool English Embassy with its enclosed and shady garden, and were made welcome. And a message had already come for them. They would be expected to dine at the Palace tonight.

'It seems,' said the consul, 'that there is already considerable curiosity about the English visitors.'

'Excellent,' said Stanley, 'excellent.'

A seneschal received them at the palace gate, and conducted them with elaborate commentary past the Gate of Felicity leading into the extensive gardens and many pavilions and villas beyond, where lived in luxurious captivity the Sultan's numberless wives and concubines. The passageway between the male and female quarters was called the Golden Road, he explained, and guarded by

Nubian eunuchs more strictly than any other in the Sultan's vast domain.

They waited on low divans in a sweet-scented chamber of gilt and velvet, and were brought coffee and sweet sherbet.

'I need an ale,' said Hodge.

Next they were admitted into a greater chamber lined with a dozen or more palace guards, and there, to their great surprise, in this country where women were kept virtually invisible, they were greeted by a woman: a strikingly beautiful dark-eyed girl in her twenties, eyes heavily outlined with kohl like an ancient Egyptian.

She introduced herself as one Esperanza Malachi. 'And as you may be wondering,' she said, 'I am not Muslim but a Jewess, hence my being allowed to go unveiled about the palace, as well as ... other freedoms.' Her eyes rested on Nicholas as she said this, and her voice was gently lilting, faintly mocking. He felt they were being seduced already. Careful now.

She explained that as *kira* to the Sultana, she was her closest adviser and financial agent. 'The Sultana is Venetian by birth, as you know,' she said. 'A great lover of fine dresses, but very extravagant.'

Her freedom was surprising, but charming. Stanley said he would be delighted to make the Sultana's acquaintance.

They passed on into a still grander chamber, where they finally met the celebrated Venetian Sultana Safiye herself, formerly Sophia Bellicui Baffo. Rather than receiving them stiffly on a throne, she came towards them with the light, dancing steps of a young girl. Tall, fair-haired, slender, a young mother in her mid-twenties with laughing eyes, consort of Sultan Murad III, and one of the most powerful women in the world.

Esperanza Malachi curtsied very low with head bowed, pretty neck as graceful as a swan's beneath her dark ringlets, and then introduced the Sultana. 'Our beloved guests, I give you the Sultana Devletlu İsmetlu Malika Safiyā Valida Aliyyetü'ş-şân Hazretleri.'

All vainglorious heads of State loved long titles and numerous names, but the Sultana smiled ironically at her own. Despite her fairness and Esperanza's dark-eyed beauty, thought Nicholas, they were almost like two sisters in their teasing manner. Their audience with the Sultan would have a little more formality. This was like some unexpected enclave of Venetian femininity and flirtation in a palace otherwise ruled by the strictest, most masculine Ottoman hierarchy.

'You may address me simply as the Sultana Safiye,' she said. 'My Esperanza is teasing you with too much ... information.' She fixed Stanley's eye. 'One cannot take in too much information at once, can one?'

Her manner was captivating, yet ...

Stanley bowed his head and said nothing.

'How was your voyage?'

'A fair one, Your Majesty.'

'You came by way of, let me think, Cadiz, and Sicily?'

'Cadiz, the Balearics, Malta, and north of Crete,' he replied rapidly.

'Malta?'

'Aye.'

She smiled, then took Smith's hands in hers. 'My,' she said, 'what mighty hands you have for an ambassador of court. You could bend a horseshoe, Brother. And these scars!'

Brother? Why was she calling him Brother? She certainly knew how to discompose John Smith. He huffed and tried to answer, but she interrupted, 'Yet could you undo a pretty lady's pearl necklace, do you think?'

This was too much for Smith and he snatched his hands away. She laughed lightly; Nicholas was beginning to think this was the most dangerous interrogation they had ever faced. Like an evening at the Court of Paris with King Francis and his gaily dancing whores. But very, very dangerous.

'Come,' she said. 'The Sultan awaits us.'

They were specially robed for the occasion in a side chamber, valets fussing about tying them into garments of cloth of gold. Smith growled throughout.

'Patience, dear John,' said Stanley. 'Count yourself lucky. Many a visitor before the Sultan has his arms pinioned behind his back throughout the audience, for fear of assassination.'

'You could still kill a man with arms pinioned,' objected Smith. 'Butt him to the ground and a sharp stomp to the windpipe.'

Stanley gave him a warning look and Smith fell silent.

The Sultan Murad sat on a golden throne surrounded by a green satin carpet sewn with silver and pearls. A man of medium height but slim build, with a henna-red beard and mild, scholarly features. They said he was fond of opium, wine and women, painting and clock-making, and for an Ottoman Sultan, shockingly uninterested in waging war on Christendom. Bookish and eccentric, he preferred to pore over his exquisite collection of Persian miniatures, plundered from the Palace of the Seven Heavens at Tabriz by his grandfather, Sultan Selim the Grim. And one night he wandered in the bazaar in disguise and heard a cook named Ferhat holding forth about the mismanagement of State finances. Murad promptly gave him a top job in government.

Nicholas could see at once that this was no Suleiman the Magnificent. So why this sense of threat? What was to be the next move in the eternal war between Islam and Christendom?

Each of them kissed his gently proffered hand, and then the gifts of the great English Queen were brought forth. Twelve pieces of gilt plate, thirty-six garments of fine cloth, ten of satin, and six pieces of finest Holland. There was also an exchange of elaborately sealed letters. Then they dined, the Sultan still high upon his lonely throne, conversing with none, while the rest sat cross-legged below him on long carpets, eating from exquisite porcelain bowls set before them.

After days and weeks of ship's fare, it was truly a feast: saffron rice with raisins, roasted kid, candied apricots, cherries, a sallet of almonds, grated apple and wild greens, roast quail, partridge, baby camel in camel's milk ... though sadly no wine. The Sultan was delicate enough only to drink in private. Throughout it all was low, polite, empty conversation. Nicholas felt intensely that there was more to come, more going on behind the scenes. The entire Sublime Porte worked in that way, politics and plots busily conducted behind this serene and jewelled façade.

After they had dined they stood and filed out of the chamber, while the black slaves scrambled over the carpets for the scraps.

'Look at them blackamoors,' said Hodge. 'Like animals.'

'Perhaps because they are treated like animals,' said Nicholas.

Hodge harrumphed.

Unrobing again, Stanley had calculated that no valet spoke English, and he said softly to them all, 'Trust no one. They are trying to sow division amongst us.' They looked questioningly at him, but he simply repeated, 'Trust no one.'

They were just on the point of departing to sleep again at the English Embassy, when they were stopped by a richly dressed vizier, glittering eyes and sharp forked beard.

'Please,' he said, 'the night is advanced and the streets are dark. We insist that you sleep in our guest quarters. There is wine in your rooms and the beds are of the softest.'

Stanley said, 'I, we, really need to return—'

'Please,' repeated the Vizier. Guards moved a little behind him, and his gaze was fixed and unblinking. 'We insist.'

Stanley hesitated, knowing they were not being offered a choice. 'But of course. We are flattered at your kindness.'

The Vizier smiled.

7

Nicholas could almost have laughed at the unreality of it all. They were not only in Constantinople, but now passing the night in the Sultan's Palace, under his very roof! They who had fought at Malta and Lepanto! If only it was known. Then he sobered. Someone did know. So much more was known than spoken. He felt it in his bones.

His chamber had high ceilings for coolness in summer, damask hangings, elaborately carved wooden screens, and a huge white bed with sheets that might have been white silk. Probably the only time in his life. His hand slithered over them. Preferred linen.

A silver ewer full of dark red wine stood by his bedside and ... two olivewood cups. He poured a cup and drained half of it – decent enough – and was stripped down to the waist when there came the softest tap at his door. He went over and unlatched it, opened it wide, expecting Hodge or one of the knights. Before he could even react, a slim figure in a face veil had slipped into the room behind him. He closed the door. So they had sent him a concubine. True hospitality.

He turned and she had already drawn off her veil.

'You,' he said. 'I didn't think you wore a veil.'

'Depends,' she said.

'And if you're the only woman roving about on her own, every-one will know who you are anyway.'

Esperanza Malachi smiled her infuriating, teasing smile and tossed the scrap of muslin onto the bed. 'Pour me a cup of that wine, and let us give thanks that we are Christian and Jew, and our

God heartily approves of such things. This is new red from Greece, apparently.'

'Is it?' He sounded testy, even to himself.

'From the Peloponnese. Overlooking the sea where that great battle of the galleys was fought three years ago. Lepanto.'

He didn't react, poured her wine. 'How would you know that so precisely?'

She laughed again. He already knew this one would never answer a single direct question. He observed quietly that Islam and Christendom were now at peace, weren't they? Handed her the cup. She sipped it, looking over the rim at him like – he swallowed – like the most skilled courtesan. Why were huge dark eyes so attractive anyway? What was the point of that?

She said, 'Let us drink to peace, you and I. Sir Nicholas Ingoldsby and the Jewess.' They knocked cups. 'Though some are friendlier towards the West than others. Some of the imams hold that no unbeliever should be allowed in Constantinople at all. Others, even within the palace, believe in much closer connections. My, look at your scars!' She touched his elbow. 'This looks like a musket ball.'

'Tough being a court ambassador,' he said. 'Always in the wars.'

'And this,' she said, touching his chest with feathersoft fingertips.

He stepped back and reached for his shirt and pulled it back on. 'Yes, all very manly I'm sure.'

She sat on the side of his bed and stretched out her legs, baring slim brown feet, thin sandals decorated with mother-of-pearl.

He drank more slowly. 'The Sultan does not seem such a man of war.'

'He is not,' she agreed. 'He prefers the company of artists, musicians, dancing girls ... Do you know the ritual of how he chooses a girl for the night?'

He sighed. 'I do not. I am sure it is all very alluring and will inflame my helpless, lust-driven masculine flesh so much that I cannot resist your charms. And then we will lie together, and then in helpless thrall to you, I will tell you all the most important State secrets of England. Isn't that how it's supposed to go?'

She drained her cup and kissed her pretty mouth to the back of her hand, red wine and lipstick kiss. 'The Sultan first has to process along the Golden Road to the women's quarters and bow low to his Mother and request entrance. Then the girls are paraded before him, and he signals his choice for the night. Then there are many hours of preparation as the girl is scrubbed and bathed by virgins, painted and perfumed, dusted with henna ... Can you imagine how it must vex a man of hot blood and impatience?'

'I'm sure.'

'At last she is brought to his room by two of the older ladies and he takes her hand and draws her inside. The rest we can perhaps imagine. She must submit to his every wish. And in the morning, any money that is left in the chamber is hers by right.'

'So she is a whore?'

'Is she? Or a kept wife? After that night, the girl may never see the Sultan again. He may be the only man she ever lies with. The date is carefully registered, in case she falls pregnant. If not, she may merely grow old in the prison of the women's quarters, and eventually be exiled to the Palace of Tears.' She was becoming too melancholy. 'Sit beside me,' she said.

'I prefer to stand.'

'Do you think, if you were Sultan, you would choose a girl like me?'

'I think it's unlikely I'll ever be Sultan.'

'Are all Englishmen so reserved as you?'

'We try.'

'If you were Italian you'd be on top of me by now.'

'I prefer to be English, thank you.'

She regarded this lean, handsome, mysterious, drily humorous emissary of the Queen Elizabeth with curiosity. It was time to be more plain-spoken then. They said that was the English way. 'Have no fear. You are in no danger here.'

He looked puzzled. 'I didn't think we were especially – though there is much I am uneasy about.'

'Then know this. The Sultana, but no one else, knows that your companions are Knights of St John, and that you all fought at Malta and Lepanto.'

He was already on his feet. 'How the devil—' They were in greatest danger here, as good as dead. The Turks regarded the Knights of St John as their bitterest, most implacable enemies. At Lepanto, had they not made straight for the Flagship of the Order, specifically to destroy it at any cost?

Esperanza Malachi soothed him. 'The Sultana loves to tease and to taunt, but you are in no danger. It was she who arranged for you to be kept here tonight. The Sultana knows much, and some of what she knows, I know – but she is very discreet. And my mistress' – she bit her lip – 'she would not be displeased, she would take no action – if word were to come to you and your companions that there is a secret pact between the Ottoman throne and the Tatar nations of the Asian steppes.'

Now he sat beside her, so that she might speak as quietly as possible. They could both die for this. 'Go on.'

'Sultan Murad himself wants peace. He dislikes war, not least the expense of it. But others in the Divan require it – perpetual jihad against the Cross – so an alliance with the Tatars suits all. It is a kind of a balance. And the Tatars, not the Turks, can do the fighting. Yet my mistress feels this might be more widely known. She has distaste at the idea of the Tatar nations riding against any Christian power, as in the days of Ghenghiz Khan. Her Catholic birth, her Venetian loyalties—'

'Yes yes,' he cut in. 'Where are they riding, and when?'

'The Tatars are riding against Moscow.'

He nodded slowly, thinking fast. 'So much was guessed. Is that all?'

'But all the Tatar nations. The Crimea Tatars led by their great warlord Devlet Giray, the Nogai Tatars, the Kuban under his banner too, perhaps those from further east as well.'

'They have raided before. The Russians and Tatars have always fought. The nomads of the steppes raided north the same summer as Lepanto. It is no surprise they will again.'

'This time it is no mere raid. It is a full-scale invasion, a war of extermination.'

It was a terrible phrase. 'How many?'

'Perhaps one hundred thousand.'

The Black Sea is flowing north, through summer meadows. The Knights had been right in their guesswork.

She said, 'You must know that they will cross the Oka river at the ford, close by the Russian defensive line, by night. And they

44

have been gifted with many of the finest Ottoman muskets, given military and siege advice. It may even be that some companies of Janizaries ride with them.'

'No field guns?'

She shook her head. 'I do not know.'

'They have no siegecraft.'

Again she shook her head. 'They are the finest, most ferocious horsemen in the world.'

Now Nicholas understood. This upstart Christian power of Muscovy to the Ottoman north was to be snuffed out like a candle. No mere nomad cattle raid, taking what animals you could round up and then disappearing away south over those measureless Scythian plains ... The Tatar armies, with Ottoman support, meant to raze Moscow to the ground. And then perhaps establish a new Tatar khanate in the Kremlin – was that possible? All the Russias had been under the foreign yoke before, for many hundreds of years. A powerful new Mohammedan Tatar empire, loyal to the Ottomans, with a hundred thousand mounted warriors under arms, on the very borders of Europe ...

'When?'

She shrugged. 'This summer.'

'Then we are already too late.' His voice rose. 'Why are we even being told this? What can we do about it now?'

'My mistress has only recently learned of it herself. You too are going to Moscow. And an army so large rides slowly. You may yet arrive first. And you are English. Allies of Czar Ivan.'

'I'm not sure if we're allies exactly ...'

'You might send urgent word back to your Queen. She might send English reinforcements for Moscow via the north, over the White Sea.'

'Very unlikely.' He shook his head. 'Queen Elizabeth knows well how expensive foreign wars are. And this Sultana plays a dangerous game.'

'I, too, am in danger, telling you this. I know it.'

He took her hand.

'You cannot depart tonight,' she said. 'You cannot even get past the guard.'

'You'd be surprised what my companions can do.'

All her flirtation was gone now. She saw visions of war, ransacked cities, burning and desolation.

He saw her sadness and kissed her. She pulled him towards her. 'Lie with me.'

'It will still avail you nothing. Politically, I mean. I'll be telling you no pillow secrets afterwards.'

'Just lie with me,' she said, thinking of the girls in the harem who slept with the Sultan only once in a lifetime, draping slim arms around his neck and pulling him close.

8

He woke to early morning sunshine streaming through the latticed wooden shutters and patterning the bed, and nothing but the lingering scent of her dark hair on the pillow beside him. He felt desolate and afraid. The old familiar cloud of danger rising up once more over him, his comrades and all those he loved.

He murmured the intelligence to Smith and Stanley as they walked down a corridor. They nodded and said nothing. It seemed to come as grim confirmation rather than startling revelation.

'More later,' muttered Stanley. 'Not safe here. Walls have ears.'

'Even the steaming teapots have listeners in 'em,' added Smith bitterly.

There was a long, slow, elaborate breakfast that was agony. Nicholas wasn't even hungry. No Sultan appeared, but still the meal lasted half the morning. Already Nicholas wondered if it was deliberate – to delay them. The atmosphere of this gilded, secretive court was fraying his nerves, no matter how lavish the ostentatious hospitality. There was no sign of Esperanza Malachi, vanished like a dream.

And then they were bid farewell and returned to the English House. They laded up the baggage and made straight for the quayside. Smith felt unwell. Stanley feared they may have been poisoned, or come close to it. They were in a hurry to be gone.

A Turkish galley was departing for the Greek coast. The captain espied them with their several barrows of baggage and crates, and immediately began haggling. A crowd appeared from nowhere and seemed to close in around them. It felt bad. At the back of the crowd, Nicholas saw a man in dark robes speaking with members of the crowd, low and confidential, and then stepping away again to watch. This was very bad. A babel of voices drowned out every other sound except the seabirds crying overhead, but some inner voice told him they were in immediate and extreme danger. And as ambassadors and merchants, they were unarmoured and unarmed but for the swords at their sides, which all gentlemen carried, and small daggers at their belts. A crate aboard carried their precious firearms, well nailed and secure.

Stanley had already come to an agreement with the captain. The captain smiled. He had no teeth at all. The crowd seemed to be pushing them aboard. Nicholas glanced round one last time, feeling he was missing something. And then up on a wall overlooking the quayside he saw a woman in a veil. On her own, must be a whore. Yet ... Then she lifted her veil and it was her, Esperanza. She was looking for him. He dared not signal to her, it might be her death. He stared intently back. Then she saw him. He was being pushed and jostled but he kept his eyes on her. She made to raise her hand as if stroking back her hair, shielding her eyes from the brilliant Mediterranean sun, but it was as if she was indicating the galley by the quay before them. And then, very clearly and deliberately, he saw her shake her head.

He glanced round. Smith and Stanley were already aboard, and calling back to him with impatience. He looked around once more, and thought he glimpsed a figure step up beside her – a man in a dark robe. No. But he couldn't be sure. And then she was gone.

Their baggage and the crates were stacked at the back of the galley, a fine boat of the grander sort, and they collapsed against them feeling strangely exhausted. Faces to the sun. The galley moved out across the water.

When no mariner was near, Nicholas murmured, 'Stanley, I think we are in danger on this galley.'

'We are in danger everywhere. Comes with the job.'

'But – particular danger.' And he told him of Esperanza Malachi on the quayside. Smith listened too.

Hodge said, 'What? What? What is it now? Don't tell me, it's getting worse and all going proper dungheap. There was something wrong with that lamb last night, I tell you, and—'

'This new ... friend of yours has already put herself in great danger,' said Smith. 'So perhaps we can trust her word. She must be fond of you.'

'She was only doing her mistress's bidding. The Sultana does not like this planned campaign of the Tatars.'

'We suspected it was coming. But it is useful to have it confirmed, and some numbers, daunting as they are. We thought it was just Devlet Giray and the Tatars of the Crimea, but if he has joined with the Nogai also, the Kuban and the Kalmyks from further East ... But we will never get through now if other forces have their way.'

They looked casually around. Other forces. They would never know who. You never knew who was really on your side, who betrayed you, even why. But Stanley trusted Nicholas with his life, after all they had endured together; he trusted his judgement of this Jewish girl, despite her easy ways, and he trusted that Nicholas had correctly interpreted her signal from the quayside. This galley was a trap, and the moment they were out of sight of land, the captain and his crew would be on them to cut their throats. Probably they'd get to keep their victims' baggage as their reward. But Stanley judged they were better off aboard than going back on land. They were in danger everywhere, but here they might have a chance.

The galley was now half a mile from shore. Casually he went aft and relieved himself off the stern, taking in everything. Strolled back, greeting the brawny boatswain himself in fluent Turkish that the man found oddly alarming. His steady drumbeat slowed momentarily.

'Fine morning, old shipmate!' cried Stanley. 'Praise Allah and his Prophet, eh?' The boatswain tried to smile. As if he had only just now noticed the size and swagger of this blond infidel they were supposed to deal with soon, and the evident quality of his fine sword. The boatswain's fingers splayed and then gripped the whipstaff the tighter. He wished he'd sharpened his dagger this morning.

'Fine morning!' he replied with forced cheer.

'A shallow sea, the Sea of Marmara?'

'That it is, sire.'

'Blows up quite a storm.'

'Aye, sire.'

'One must be ready for it.'

'That's so.' The boatswain was moving from foot to foot uneasily, eyeing him, fixed smile. Guilty as hell.

'But we Englishmen – we know how to handle storms.' Stanley rested his hand on the pommel of his sword and smiled pleasantly. Returned to his companions by the baggage. 'Keep 'em jumpy,' he murmured, still grinning broadly. 'Anxious. The warfare of the mind begins here.'

'So few of them,' said Smith. 'Captain, boatswain, half a dozen mariners. We've no guns about us, but we can handle this much, surely.'

Stanley said, 'Look down below. The slaves on the rear four benches are only pretending to wear their manacles. They're unlocked.'

'They're soldiers?'

'Could be the best Janizaries, for all I know.'

'No Janizary would sit on a rowing bench, even in deceit.' Then he touched his fist to his mouth. 'Damn.'

They were in trouble.

'Four benches. Some sixteen of 'em?'

'Thereabouts. All ready to jump up and join in the scrap.'

Scrap, thought Nicholas. Our lives are hanging by a thread, and soon we'll be no more than four corpses with gaping throats, sinking silently down through clouds of our own blood into the saltwater depths ... And he talks of a scrap, as if it was a schoolboys' fight in a field, instead of a ruthless, covert assassination of four suspected spies. They'd slice open their gizzards and dump them overboard. If the English court enquired of them a month or two hence, the Sublime Porte could send a letter from the Sultan himself, expressing the most flowery condolences and suggesting that they must have been lost at sea.

'But only one way up from below,' murmured Stanley. 'A narrow stair. You can hold that pass, Leonidas.'

Smith growled. He couldn't wait. Let them attack him, he'd skewer them as they came. Despite the heat, both he and Stanley drew their doublets on over their linen shirts.

'And the rest of us, keep close and back to back. Use every rail and mast you can.'

A mariner, a young skinny lad who looked Greek himself, came by and offered them a scoop of water from a pail. They all said no. The lad looked oddly disappointed. Smith watched him go back aft. He set the pail back down and had a quiet word with the captain. The captain looked uneasy.

'Drugged,' muttered Smith. 'Opium, valerian … Lazy beggars. They want to cut our throats as we doze.'

'I'm parched though,' said Nicholas.

'Did you think our breakfast was heavily salted this morning?' said Stanley.

Nicholas frowned. 'A little.'

'To keep us a-thirsting, so we'd not refuse water once aboard.'

'You really think they're that cunning?'

'I know they are.'

He fidgeted. His father's old sword at his side. God knew if it would hold in a straight encounter with a new Ottoman blade. What had the soldiers down below hidden under their benches? A few good crossbows and all four of them were done for. They'd be stuck like pigs before they got close. He stood to his feet. 'When are they going to set about us?'

The rest stood. It was too nerve-racking to stay seated. Stanley wondered if they should head straight overboard themselves and make for the shore and safety that way. Still only a mile off. At night they might have made it, but now under a full sun the galley would only come after them and stick them in the water. And he didn't think they would make it to nightfall. It was coming soon. Their guardedness was obvious, they knew it was coming, and the captain knew they knew.

'Only one thing for it,' said Smith. 'Old trick from Alexander onwards. We start this ourselves.'

Without another word Stanley went back and approached the captain.

'I hope you kept your blades oiled, boys,' said Smith softly. 'Now loosen them in their sheaths.'

9

Even as Stanley came near, the captain, fear apparent in his eyes, started to back away from this approaching giant whilst raising his left hand. The boatswain immediately began a double-drumbeat. It was the signal. From below came a noise of unmanacled chains thrown off, Turks rising up from the rowing benches, heading for the stairs ...

Stanley moved like a big cat, pure pace and concentration. The captain had already drawn his sword but the knight closed in on him and batted the flat of the blade aside with his doubleted arm. Like a panther irritably batting aside a pygmy's spear. Then he seized the captain around the waist, tipped him aside as he might a large water vessel, slammed his head sharply down on the heavy wooden rail and rolled him senseless overboard. He still had not drawn his own blade.

The boatswain had abandoned his drum already and was coming at Stanley furiously, dagger flailing. Nicholas stepped out and ran him through, placed his boot against his belly and immediately pulled the long blade free again. The boatswain collapsed to the ground, knelt, whooping horribly, his grubby djellaba staining deep red. Nicholas had not even time to do the chivalrous thing and finish him. He turned and flanked Stanley, Hodge the other side. He had not killed a man since Lepanto, but he felt nothing except the burning blood inside him, and the furious animal desperation to stay alive, no matter what. Shame and disgust would follow after. That was when you drank to oblivion.

Smith made for the top of the short ladder coming up from

below. A Turk was already halfway up. Smith booted him hard in the chest, tumbling him back, then swung his leg down and kicked the ladder aside. But the soldiers were lithe and well trained, and others were quick to scramble along the benches to the bulwarks of the galley and swing up over the boards and the awnings. They came running at the doomed quartet along the catwalk, daggers in their hands, or swinging poles, hooks on ropes, anything they could find. Like a slave revolt. But mercifully no pistols or crossbows that Nicholas could see, or they'd have been finished. Matchlocks took too long to prepare, and powder and bowstrings never liked sea air for long.

'Back! Back!' cried Stanley desperately. 'Hold together! Hand to hand!'

Smith stepped in beside them and they backed up against the stern cabin, no more than a rough plank shack for shade from the midday sun. The only way, the last stand, as they were surrounded by a mob of mariners and soldiers, yelling for their blood.

'Your captain's drowned,' roared Smith, thrusting forward long and low and slicing through a bare leg at the knee, a man falling screaming to the deck, 'your boatswain's dead,' pulling back sharp, on guard, parry, parry, 'and soon the rest of you villains will be fishfood! Come on, boys, step closer!'

The deck was slick with blood, the leather soles of Nicholas's boots were slippery with it. The galley floundered and gently rolled as the furious skirmish was fought, the cries carrying over the Sea of Marmara not a mile off from the city shore. Other boats were starting to slow and their captains to look over. They must finish this fast.

There was a slim figure up on the roof of the shack behind them. Stanley glanced back. 'Take him!' Nicholas was up in a trice, knocking him down. He rose up again. Both staggered. It was the young mariner, the Greek water-boy, no more than fourteen. He reached for his dagger, shaking all over. 'Kneel!' said Nicholas, swordpoint already at the boy's throat. 'Do not draw. If you draw I will kill you.' The shack shuddered beneath them as another body crashed into it. The boy knelt and bowed his head in utter misery. 'Lie flat down,' said Nicholas. 'Do not stir until this is done.'

Then he jumped back alongside and ran a soldier through from behind. Ducked under another flailing blow that cruelly caught the wounded soldier again and finished him, a home strike. Several bodies already lay stretched out about the deck and he saw Stanley with a long blade in each hand, one his own, one Turkish, thrust out laterally and cut two at once. Hodge had lost his blade altogether and taken up a polehook, bringing it down heavily on a soldier's skull and then rapidly pulling it back and driving it forward again full into another's face. A horrible soft, sinking feel to it. The Turk reeling and screaming in agony, covering his face with his hands, his eyes ...

Suddenly it was over. Though determined fighters, the Turkish soldiers were no opium-crazed jihadis longing for martyrdom and the Mohammedan paradise, and this ferocious resistance was entirely unexpected. No one had said it would be like this ... The last few threw down their weapons and knelt, but for one, a big, round-bellied, black-bearded fellow who remained standing, though weaponless, bloodied at the neck but quite calm. Hardly even out of breath. He was thinking bitterly, whoever had sent them out on this galley to despatch a few enemies of the Sultan – mere lackeys and tittle-tattles, as they were told, mere vagabond spies – had been speaking out of his pampered court arse.

He said gruffly, 'You're no ordinary spies.'

Stanley nodded to him curtly. 'Kneel.'

'I suppose that was why we were sent to kill you.'

Stanley laid a huge hand on the fellow's shoulder, repeated 'Kneel!' and shoved him to his knees.

There were four dead, along with the slain boatswain and the captain overboard – the worst deceiver, in the knights' view. Soldiers were soldiers, born for war, but a captain who turns against his own passengers ... There were several others wounded, some badly.

'Are we hurt?' he asked.

Nicholas had an embarrassing sprain to his ankle and kept quiet. Maybe later. Hodge had been hit on the head, making his vision flutter disconcertingly awhile, but his skull was famously thick, as he liked to boast. Smith had a sword cut to his upper arm that bled a fair bit. Stanley eyed it. Nothing serious. He had seen his old comrade-in-arms bleed a deal more than that and fight on regardless. He must have left several firkins of blood on the rocks of Fort St Elmo at Malta.

Stanley went below and looked over the terrified slaves. They had no idea what had happened, or whose hands they were in now. One thing they knew for certain: life for a galley slave rarely got any better. He merely passed from one savage slave-driver to another. One of the wretched oarsmen sat manacled at the ankle, unmoving, his shaven head bowed, with blood actually dripping through the planks from the deck above and spotting his helpless white pate.

Stanley roared back up, 'Smith! Have the prisoners swab the deck will you, and sharpish!' Then he tore off a strip of linen from his ripped and frayed shirt and gave it to the poor fellow, who mopped himself silently.

Stanley called out over the rest of them, these forty or so emaciated, despairing stinkards, now in their hands, 'Christians?' He walked forward along the gangway, bent almost double, sick with the stench. '*Christianoi?*'

Some of them nodded, though all of them in this beshitten and sweating dungeon of creaking timber walls looked like the worst criminals of the Ottoman Empire: murderers and rapists of the foulest sort. Any that claimed to be Christian captives, he demanded of them the Lord's Prayer. Our Father, who art in heaven – in Greek – was enough. He got Nicholas and Hodge unmanacling them with a crowbar. The eight freed Christians, starved as they were, embraced each other and gave three cheers and scrambled up the ladder into the sunlight as if escaping from Hades itself. The sun blinded them for several minutes.

In their place, Smith herded the surviving captives down below and had them manacled.

'How the wheel of fortune turns,' said the black-bearded fellow equably.

Stanley couldn't help but like him, though he had been trying to kill him but ten minutes before. 'Your name, philosopher?'

'Ibrahim.'

'Ibrahim. Get used to it now.'

'Where are we headed? Italy?'

Stanley shook his head. 'North.'

'North?'

Stanley grinned. 'East, then north. So spit on your palms, friend, and take up the oar. We have a way to go.'

Still in sight of the minarets of Constantinople. Nicholas scanned the nearest boats of this busy waterway between east and west. Thank God no shots had been fired. But for some shouts, it had been a quiet if murderous fray. On one nearby dhow a moustachioed seaman looked curiously over to them, but Nicholas shouted back cheerfully, 'All good here, brother! Just a couple of unruly slaves needing a good beating!'

The seaman raised his hand in acknowledgement.

They laid the corpses of the four dead alongside each other – like pickled herrings, as Hodge put it. They would roll them overboard after dark. The Dead Man's Splash by moonlight. Some of the injured were in a bad way, one barely breathing, the one with a caved-in skull jabbering ceaselessly in Arabic ... In desperate straits they might have pushed them into the longboat and let them fend for themselves, but now was the time for forgiveness.

They hove to until dusk and then brought the galley in as close as they dared to the southern shore on the Chalcedon side. Smith himself rowed them in. They left them stumbling through the shallows in single file, arms on each other's shoulders. All men, Smith reflected, the fire of battle now gone from even his bellicose heart – all men when walking wounded, limping, heads bandaged and bowed, looked much the same.

They rowed after dark. Hodge took up the drumstick, an old mutton bone. 'Always wanted to do this,' he said.

Smith squatted down at the hatch as the drumbeat began and said to the wretched below, 'We are Christians and soldiers, not ambassadors, and damn finer soldiers than you'll ever be. The rest of you are not even soldiers but the scum of the criminal earth. We are your deadliest enemies. My brothers have been fighting both Arab and Turk for five long centuries now. Twenty generations. Nevertheless, you may find we are not the harshest of slavers. Row well, do not stint, and you will see no sign of the whip.'

And with that supreme insouciance which often comes good, they rowed back east under an Orient moon, its cold light silvering the small waves of the Bosphorus. They passed beneath the very nose of Seraglio Point and through the twenty miles or so of the narrow straits, and after they had disposed of the corpses and sluiced the decks once more, Nicholas and Hodge fell asleep. They dreamt disturbed and violent dreams.

They awoke at dawn to the sun coming up over the vastness of a sun-beaten inland sea. The Euxine, the Black Sea, Kara Deniz.

'Next stop,' said Stanley, 'the mouth of a mighty river called the Dnieper, and a coast the ancient Greeks called the Chersonese.'

To a land called Russia, and a king who called himself Czar.

'So remind me,' said Hodge, rubbing his head. 'What was our Royal Command in Constantinople? To look after this English alliance with the Turks, tread delicately and find out what more we could. Yes?'

Nicholas looked at him sourly.

'Well,' he sniffed. 'We fairly buggered that one up.'

It was true. Though they'd discovered important intelligence in the city, and escaped with their lives, it was not a glorious success. They'd better charm Muscovy or they'd have hell to pay back home.

The Black Sea was flooding north through summer meadows. Nicholas closed his eyes again to the early morning sun, and saw the Tatar Horde riding, almost hidden in the long steppe grass, the whispering feathergrass that could hide a whole army. Ancient nomad horsemen with their bows and blades, broad Asiatic faces painted for war, riding in revenge, revenge for Kazan and Astrakhan, so recently fallen to the armies of Ivan the Terrible. Passing along the old black roads of the steppe, resting overnight in shallow valleys studded with their campfires or in the thin birch forests, passing over river fords they knew of old, the wide ford of the Oka river, slipping through Muscovy's poor defensive line, approaching the wooden city itself while the city still dreamed its restless dreams ...

10

They stopped only once, a week later, to row to the Thracian shore and take on fresh water and food. The galley had been ill-provisioned, and they needed the rowing slaves well fed and strong. No whip was used but they made a good pace.

'When we come to the mouth of the great river,' Smith said, 'there are slave fairs there. We may sell you to worse masters than ourselves – or we may simply turn you loose. Depends how you row.'

It worked better than any whip. The galley surged north over the inland sea, a hundred miles or more from dawn till dawn.

They came close to a broad flat country of plains and low pale hills and winding waters, and Nicholas had an overwhelming sense of a vast land spreading away on every side. The next sea was the frozen Arctic, many thousands of miles north.

There was a scattering of fishing boats and some smoke arising from a few homesteads along the shore, but no sign of any major settlement. Then a fair-haired boy came across to them in a bob-bing wooden boat and back-rowed in the small waves, calling up to them in Russian.

'He's no Tatar,' muttered Hodge.

'Maybe Russian, or maybe Germanic,' said Stanley. 'There re-main old villages of the Goths hereabouts. From a thousand years ago.' He called down. 'We don't want your fish, boy! But find us a pilot for the river and you'll have a silver penny.'

'I can pilot you,' said the boy. 'It's my river. Where are you from?'

'And if we turn over on a sandbank?' said Stanley.

'Then you can beat the devil out of me,' said the boy cheerfully. 'You won't though. I'm the best pilot for miles.'

'Proud little beggar,' said Smith with grudging admiration.

Stanley scanned the shore, glanced down at the slaves, considered. It might be good to deal with no one else but a boy for now. Keep low. He called back, 'Very well! We're sending you two more rowers. You go ahead, we follow. How many days can we go upstream?'

'Three days. Then you come to the market. Saturday's the fair!'

'Perfect.'

It was no exaggeration. This great river made the Thames look like a stripling stream. In the morning mist, keeping close to the east bank, the far west bank was several miles away and barely visible. Nicholas felt almost humiliated. England was so small. But Hodge sneered, 'No safe anchorage here. Might as well still be at sea. And I don't see any Greenwich Palace neither, nor Whitehall, nor St Paul's. Lot of barbarians they must be here.'

Just green shores, sandbanks, smoky huts. Just a thin growth of alder and willow and then beyond, the limitless steppe.

The further upriver they rowed, the further they left the cooling sea breezes behind them, the hotter it got. They all felt a growing oppression. The vastness. The wide slow river. The loneliness under this boundless sky.

It was with relief they came to habitation three days later, just as their young pilot had said. A huge, motley slave fair on the right bank of the river. They anchored two hundred yards off in the lee of an island and rowed ashore in the longboat. The boy came as their interpreter.

'Keep your eyes skinned,' said Stanley. 'And answer no questions. We are here only to find horses and move on.'

They walled up a wooden jetty and into the mêlée, by no means exotic in that haggling, money-changing, hard-drinking hubbub of humanity. They walked between stalls fluttering with colourful banners, and the pony carts of fur sellers and sellers of sheepskins. Pushing through the crowds they saw all the races of Asia, not at cut-throat war but simply buying and selling. There was a round-faced, yellow-skinned fellow with a topknot and a long belted gown ...

'There's your first Tatar,' said Smith.

'Shall we ask him if he knows of the planned attack on Muscovy?'

'Perhaps not.'

There were Kipchaks and Uighurs, Russians and Germans and Ukrainians, Greeks and Armenians, Bulgars and even a white-robed desert Arab with a camel train of four. How on earth did he get here? But he well knew how much profit he might make from selling Damascus dates and decorated daggers and slim rolls of the finest watered silk in this country. He could then increase his gains tenfold, twentyfold, by buying a fair-skinned Circassian maiden here, long flowing hair the colour of spring sunshine, to auction in the souq of Damascus ... If he made it safely back home with her untarnished, virgin, untouched by any robbers and bandits along the perilous way, and kept his own hands off her himself all that time – though the Prophet knew what continence that would take – he might sell her to a rich merchant of his native city for enough gold to keep him for life.

After a time he ceased to haggle over his wares and pulled out a small prayer rug and laid it down facing east and knelt and prayed to Allah. No one even commented. All mingled without enmity, amid barter and exchange. Money was a great healer of tribal differences.

There was a German soldier, or rather mercenary, called Heinrich von Staten. He had a booming voice and greeted them as fellow Protestants without asking. He had done well in the Polish Wars, and was also at the Sack of Novgorod, fighting for Ivan himself. Now he was shipping out and home via Italy. He had a troop of men under him and several wagons.

'I went into Novgorod empty-handed, and came out with forty fine horses and twenty-two wagonloads of plunder!' he roared, red face and beery breath. 'A man can get rich in Russia – if he knows how to steal, and quits early. Once he has made his fortune, it is better to get away, abroad. Enrich yourself, then leave.' He headed for his barge, calling back to them, 'That is my advice, my friends! This is a shitheap of a country for anything but plunder!'

'What of Czar Ivan?' Smith called after the brute. 'What was it like to fight for him?'

The mercenary looked back and there was an evil light in his eye. He rubbed his beard. 'What was it like to fight for Czar Ivan? Well, put it like this. He does not mind how you treat his enemies. He does not protest at any ... *entertainments* you may wish to have with the women you capture or the men you put to the sword.' He laughed. 'Oh, you will have a fine old time fighting for Czar Ivan, my comrades! But I say again – do not stay here too long.' And then with a laugh he was gone.

'What barbarians have we come amongst?' murmured Hodge.

'Christian barbarians,' said Stanley bitterly. 'As opposed to Mohammedan barbarians.'

There were hunched old fortune tellers outside tents embroidered with supposedly mystical runes of great power, dancing bears moving slow and lumbering to strange wooden pipes, slaves of every age and colour in wooden holding pens – Smith asked for some prices. There were fine-featured Armenian girls selling needles, knives, hatchets, ironwork. The huge fair spread right across a slow, winding tributary of the great river; you could walk from bank to bank over rafts and luggers. And everywhere were hastily built sheds and shadowy taverns, watchful merchants and black-robed priests drinking out of sight.

There was the spectacle of dogs attacking a wolverine, old blind ballad singers, a cripple on crutches singing as he went ... A woman bartered a pot of sturgeon's roe for some Tatar deerskin boots and a honeycomb. Another, a peasant, gambled away his precious furs, drank away the rest, finally sold the clothes off his back – Nicholas watched these transactions in wonder – then crossed himself three times, spat on the ground for good luck, and set off to walk back home, naked but for a loincloth.

Nicholas asked how far. The peasant muttered some slurred Russian. The boy translated. 'He says thirty *versts*.'

'Twenty miles,' said Stanley.

'He's going to get sunstroke,' said Hodge.

'Doubtless,' said Stanley. 'But they say the Russian peasant is indestructible. Only God can take his life.'

61

The naked peasant called back one more time. 'It's not the sun I fear. It's the wife.'

They saw only the crudest coins, no printed books, and not a soul you might call a fine lady or a nobleman. Nicholas felt he had stepped back in time, into a scene before the Conquest, in the Dark Ages, or even before the Greeks and Romans. A scene from the ancient world, before cities were built, when it was just villages and barter and drunkenness and no sign of kings or governments anywhere. He ought to feel scorn, yet he felt a mounting excitement. This was a wild country still.

'Beyond here it becomes difficult,' said the boy. 'Many sandbanks, strong currents. Your galley will run aground and roll sooner or later. But there are other smaller boats to take you north, though it is slow, upstream.'

'How many *versts* a day?'

The boy shrugged. 'Ten. Twenty at most.'

Smith said, 'Too slow. We need to take to the land then, and move fast.'

'The land is much more dangerous.'

Smith hardly heard him. 'We need horses. The best.'

'You'll find the best here.'

They brought the galley slaves ashore, with their sores and their blistered hands and their backs and shoulders burned chestnut brown even through the awning, yet in good shape for that. Powerfully muscled, well watered and well fed. They found a barber to shave their heads afresh.

'You said you'd set us free if we rowed hard,' snarled the black-bearded Ibrahim. 'And we did. Now you're sprucing us up for sale.'

Smith said nothing.

He spat. 'Seed of the Devil.'

Smith grinned at him wolfishly.

Once shaven, they were led to a forge and the chains knocked from their ankles. They stood and stared, stupefied.

'We are free?'

'Aye,' said Smith. 'You rowed well.'

'So why the barber?'

62

'We just thought head lice did not become free men,' said Stanley.

They shook their shaven heads, then smiled, then laughed. Several shook the knights' hands, some even said, 'Go with God.' Then they were gone.

'Back to their rapes and their thievery,' muttered Smith.

'You never know,' said Stanley.

There followed hard haggling as they tested buyers for a sea-going galley, no crew, as seen. Buyers saw they were in a hurry and had no more use for it, and it was an absurd exchange, an entire galley for just four riding horses and four packhorses. But necessity demanded it. They also got saddles and kit, blanket rolls, millet flour, beans, pork fat, dried fruit, and some new fire flints, and were left with a few age-blackened coins of Ottoman stamp.

'Here,' said Stanley to their young guide. 'These will only weigh us down.'

A man came over, greeted them cautiously. It was the boy's father.

'You are riding north?'

'Aye, fast. To Moscow.'

He smiled, a very discomforting smile. 'To Moscow?'

'Aye.'

''Tis a good way to Moscow. Many days and weeks. And dangerous country all the way. There are just the four of you?'

'Aye.'

'You are riding through Cossack lands, Tatar lands. Debatable country. The land of the empty steppe, day after day.'

'So we understand.'

'And these cases and crates you carry with you. Gifts for the court of Moscow? Weapons?'

'Nothing but empty air in 'em,' said Stanley. 'We like to carry empty crates.'

'You are cracked in your wits.' The man shook his head. 'You will never arrive in Moscow. And if you do get there . . .'

'What?' said Nicholas, getting irritated. 'What if – when – we do get there?'

His blood ran cold at the answer that came.

'Moscow will destroy you,' said the man. 'Her Czar Ivan will destroy you. As he destroys everything.' The man wiped his mouth and looked around and then looked back and fixed Nicholas with his eyes. He was smiling no longer and spoke with absolute conviction. 'He is the Devil Incarnate, come to Earth to torment men for their sins.'

Smith spurred his horse with sudden violence. 'Hah!' And they left dust behind them.

11

After an hour they had left the fair far behind them and their horses tired so they slowed to a walk along a trail through a sea of tall and sighing feathergrass. Mile upon mile it stretched away, as far as the eye could see.

Hodge muttered to Nicholas, 'I did think of having my fortune told back there, in one of those old crones' tents. But there was no point. I can see it already. We'll soon get our throats cut out in this grassy wilderness, and be left for one of these savages' sky burials. Supper for buzzards.'

'Hodge,' said Nicholas. 'It's always a great comfort to have you with me.'

The trail faded soon and they rode on over grassland. Though the market was only a few miles back, they neither saw nor heard a mule train, not a living soul. Only the swish-swish of the tall grass against their leather boots, grass seeds lodging within, shaken out at eve by firelight.

They broke open the crate with the firearms in it and shouldered them. A wheel-lock musket for Stanley, Smith's treasured Persian jezail, and squat matchlock arquebuses for Nicholas and Hodge. They freed the horses of their gear and watered them, then left them half-hobbled to forage. Campfire sunk in a shallow pit, a little millet paste and pork fat to silence their grumbling bellies. Did they dare hunt game with their muskets? They put up game birds from time to time, partridges and great ungainly fowl they could not name. But the report of a shot would carry for miles over the plains. They would wait awhile.

The dry wind, tongues parched, water rationed. They spoke little. Days in the saddle blurred into days, evenings stiff and weary, staring silently into the fire. The Queen's Ambassadors indeed, a sorry and travel-stained troupe. They took water at every river or watercourse they came to, the horses drinking so greedily they had to prevent them from taking too much or they would swell and sicken. Nights under the open sky, the sigh of the grass, overhead a sea of brilliant stars and God's own utter silence. Not a nightbird called. Occasionally by day a huge crane flapped leisurely across the vast sky, or they heard a waterbird's lonesome call from a river and followed it down. The land parched, the grass shorter and paler now. Pale shallow hills on the horizon, treeless steppe. Once, far off, a herd of antelope, saiga antelope. Too distant to hunt. Their mouths watered, hearts ached, they could not say why. It was hard and bitter journeying.

Somewhere to the east, moving through the feathergrass of the parched summer steppe, the Tatars too were riding.

Late afternoon, and riding a faint trampled trail through tall grass again. Nicholas riding at the front, drowsing in the saddle, sun going down in the west and burning his left cheek, his left hand. He sat up. Something ...

He reined in. His horse nickered, he stroked her neck.

The other three reined in behind, Hodge leading the packhorses.

'I thought I heard something in the grass. Yonder.'

'Some beast.'

'No. Sound of a horseman.'

Smith said, 'You were dreaming.'

'I think someone's coming.'

They waited in silence. The grass was so tall, the steppe rolling in shallow hills and swales, even a mounted horseman might be hidden from them. But nothing. Smith was about to grunt and ride on when he too heard it. A swish through the grass just a little too regular to be the wind.

'Dismount,' he said, rapidly doing so himself. 'Behind your horses. Brother Stanley, fire up the matchcord.' Then he was wadding his own firearm, ramming in powder and ball, resting it across his horse's back.

A whinny. A single horseman, his horse catching the scent of other horses and wanting to be with them. They would surprise him.

And then he appeared on the faint trail ahead of them. An exotic creature in a pointed kalpak hat and a belted coat, riding a small dark pony. No saddle, not even stirrups, just a rope hackamore in the pony's mouth. He stopped in an instant and pulled his pony restively round and stared down the trail at these unearthly intruders in his empty land. He had a narrow moustache and thin beard, and bright gold earrings gleamed through long shaggy hair, but most of all they noticed how he was festooned with weaponry: recurved bow, quiver and musket over his shoulders, leather belt carrying a knife, a broad-bladed sword curved like a Saracen's, another pistol or two. A one-man arsenal.

Looking utterly unafraid of these alien horsemen facing him, not fifty yards off, weapons readied, he looked easily over their four-horse baggage train, eyes glittering. Then he astonished them outright by grinning at them hugely, yanking his pony around and, breaking into an instant gallop, vanishing away into the wilderness of the grass.

Smith rested his weapon. 'Well,' he said. 'They know we're here now.'

'Evil-looking type,' said Hodge. 'He'll be back, I suppose?'

'Oh yes, he'll be back,' said Stanley with his usual good cheer. 'With fifty of his fellows, I don't doubt, anxious for us to show them the contents of our cases. We will just have to be polite. For that, my dear friends and gentlemen-at-arms – that was our first steppe Cossack.'

They made camp just half an hour later as usual. Even lit a fire. But kept their weapons always at the ready. It all depended on how badly this fellow and his comrades wanted to see what was in their baggage cases – or wanted them dead, said Hodge pleasantly. Stanley said he still thought a few well-aimed shots might startle them off for good. 'All bandits are cowards.'

'Some hope,' said Hodge.

Nicholas slept for a couple of hours before he was shaken awake.

'Nick. Nick. Wake up.'

'Uh?'

'We have company.'

Stanley himself had been keeping first watch, musket across his knees, but even he hadn't heard a thing. The first he knew was a gentle tap on his shoulder and he froze. Around the back of his neck was a circlet of sharp blades held steady, like some strange floating ruff.

'Lean forward, guest of mine,' said a gravelly voice, 'and lay your musket down in the dust.'

He did so.

The owner of the voice stepped before him. 'Welcome,' he said, bowing extravagantly, 'to my country.'

12

A fellow of medium height but very broad chest, in baggy breeches, scuffed leather boots and a fine embroidered blue shirt. A white scar where a nostril had once been torn open in a knife fight, yet handsome with his neat beard and laughing eyes.

Then even he was taken by surprise when Smith stepped out of the shadows behind, a sword clenched in each huge fist. The Cossacks stopped and stared at him, but he remained very calm and still.

The leader smiled. 'Thank you, yes, we will take your weapons from you for now.'

'I'm not offering you my weapons.'

'Please. It is better this way. If you fight, all four of you will die.'

'And so will half of you.'

'You will kill ten of us, single-handed?'

'He will, in truth,' said Stanley, still sitting ignominiously in the dust. 'Smith, don't. Hand 'em over.'

Smith growled and fought inwardly, eyes burning, mouth working furiously beneath his grizzled black beard. Eventually he mastered himself enough to raise both swords and hurl them forward so they stuck quivering in the ground, perilously near the leader's feet. But the Cossack chief only grinned. He already liked this brute.

'Now,' he said, 'bind them.'

Smith roared and fought but he was soon crushed and held down by sheer weight of numbers – though he blacked several eyes and bloodied several noses before his arms were finally roped hard behind his back. His speech was nothing but the richest obscenities, unbecoming, thought Nicholas – as Smith was at last thrown down in the dust beside him – unbecoming of a man who was, strange to recall, a lifelong member of a monastic order. Just as well Smith hadn't joined the Franciscans. Not his style.

Of the bandits there were at least twenty. They stoked up the fire with more dung and sat companionably around, swilling some evil-smelling spirit from a leather flask. There in the fire's glow was the small moustachioed rider in his pointed kalpak hat they had met earlier, hardly distinguishable from a full-blood Tatar. Beyond the firelight, others were busy going through the baggage cases – snorting with disgust over the beautifully wrapped porcelain dining plates and lengths of finest Bruges lace that the Queen had sent for the Court of Moscow. Yet the noiseless expertise with which they had ambushed them had to be admired. And all four felt that though these were dangerous and lawless men, if they had wanted to kill them, they would have done so already.

The gravel-voiced chieftain with the extravagant manners introduced himself. 'Stenka, son of Timofey, that is Timofeivitch. At your service, and delighted to carry your baggage for you a little way.'

His men laughed.

Amongst their lost baggage was Smith's precious Persian jezail, the finest musket he had ever known, its barrel unusually rifled for accuracy like a short-range fowling piece, yet so beautifully crafted that it still had the power of a smooth-bore firearm. All he could think of was how to retrieve it. Stanley said Smith loved that gun more than most men loved their wives.

The four of them sat at swordpoint in the dust, an outward-facing circle. Yet Smith still argued with their captors. 'We have no need of you. We are going to Moscow.'

'To Moscow? Ah, to the Court of our beloved Father the Czar? As long as he doesn't start thinking he actually rules over us free men of the steppe. We rule ourselves down here, do we not, comrades?'

Noisy, half-drunk agreement.

Stenka Timofeivitch grinned broadly. 'Now, tell me where you are from. You are not Turks.'

'No, we are not Turks!' said Smith.

'Indeed,' nodded Stenka. 'Or we should already have had your intestines out to restring our bows. Perhaps you are Germans? They get everywhere.'

'Not Germans,' said Stanley. 'English.'

'Ah, English,' said Stenka pleasantly. 'I have never met English before. Nor killed one, for that matter.'

'Nor have I yet killed a Coss—' began Smith with his usual diplomacy. Stanley swiftly intervened.

'No need for that,' he said. 'We are delighted to be here, enjoying your hospitality.'

'Why else are you here?'

'Simply in embassy to the Court. That alone.'

'Don't take me for an illiterate fool,' snapped Stenka. 'English merchants and ambassadors round the North Cape and sail into Archangel in the white north, coming to Moscow by river portage. This is no ordinary way to Moscow. A very long way round from England. You are well sunburned. What business had you in the Mediterranean?'

'None of your business.'

'If you do not tell us, we will torture you.'

'You amaze me.'

'Or we torture your friends, until you yourself answer.'

'A tired old trick.'

'It tends to work.'

'If you say so. Try it now.'

Stenka Timofeivitch wavered then smiled. These were tough strangers after all. And they had one virtue he could not ignore. They were fellow Christians, even if not of the true Orthodox Church of Mother Russia. He cursed jovially, then said, 'Let us eat. Maybe torture later, yes?'

All the Cossacks laughed very much at that.

And so, bound and aching in the dust, they ate morsels fed to them at dagger-point by these wild men of the steppe – morsels of meat and game better than anything they had tasted for days, though still starvation rations. Only Smith refused.

'Eat, Brother. Keep your strength up.'

Smith just sneered.

They awoke with a start to the sound of pistol fire. Stared blearily about. But it was only Stenka Timofeivitch, using their priceless porcelain plates for target practice. He had wedged them upright amid balls of horsedung some fifty yards off, and was shooting at each of them with two pistols at once, with typical buccaneer disregard for preserving gunpowder. He hit home every time. His men looked on admiring.

When he stopped to have them reloaded, Stanley called out, 'Those make costly targets!'

'These trinkets? Made for women!' He took another loaded pair of pistols and blasted another one. Then he paused and looked back at Stanley, eyes narrowed. 'How costly?'

'In England,' said Stanley, 'one of these plates would cost as much as a decent horse.'

'A horse?'

Stanley nodded.

'Savages,' muttered Hodge. 'They can only think in terms of 'orses, look.'

Stenka considered. Then he bawled, 'Get these trinkets wrapped up again! God damn you, Englishman, why did you not say so before?'

'I didn't know you were going to start shooting them.'

Stenka growled and strode away over the steppe to cool his anger.

Half an hour later they rode out, heading north, the four of them still bound astride their own horses, the Cossacks carrying the baggage.

Stanley said, 'Don't tell us you are escorting us all the way to Moscow.'

'We might get a fair reward. Then again, we might just head to the market in Kharkhov and see what these trinkets and women's fabrics of yours fetch there.'

'Kharkhov. That's heading dangerously near to Tatar lands, is it not?'

Stenka, abruptly converted to a love of porcelain, growled through clenched teeth, 'No Tatars are taking these plates off me.'

As they rode away, Nicholas looked back and saw the pale

broken fragments in the long grass. Crafted in China with ancient skill, shipped across half the world to Egypt, to Constantinople, to Venice, across Europe, to England and the court of the Great Queen. Then sent back again with her ambassadors to the Court of Russia, only to be taken and shot to pieces by some barbaric horseman in the wilderness, and left in pieces on the treeless steppe like shards of unseasonal snow. What a fable of the futility of human endeavour! Nicholas brooded, becoming philosophical. It must be the ache in his tethered arms, the hunger in his belly. And these broken bits of porcelain would remain here, immune to time and decay, long after all of them riding away were dead.

13

They rode for long days, and though the Cossacks spoke little to them at first, gradually they came to identify them. Stenka Timofeivitch the chief in his fine blue shirt, a proud son of the Don. His father was a true Cossack though his mother was a slave girl from the River Kama. Yet what did a man's mother matter? 'Women are only good to shell peas and feel hens for eggs,' said Stenka.

When he took off his shirt to bathe in the river, they saw his left shoulder bore an ugly brand. 'The Mark of Cain,' jested Stenka. He had a loud roaring voice when angered, made his prayers to all gods and none, though called himself a True Son of the Church, and was as likely to swear by Allah as by Christ. He liked to cry 'God is merciful, but Stenka is not!' before falling on any of his men that enraged him, punching them to the ground and cursing them where they cowered. None dared oppose him, all would follow him to the death. He had killed more than sixty men, they said in admiration.

The small dark horseman who had first stumbled on them was Ivan Koltzo, superlative rider, and though small, he could outdrink the Devil. He had seen his mother and two sisters burned to death in a blockhouse by Tatar raiders. There was Chvedar the renegade priest, said to be impervious to sword or bullet, who performed mock religious ceremonies for a glass of vodka. One-eyed, ugly, bony, lanky, quick with his fists, notorious lecher, given to nakedness when drunk, he trimmed his beard with the same knife he had used to stab a fellow priest to death. For comic entertainment he sometimes dressed as a woman. There was Andriushko, hulking, sweet-natured, lazy, with only seven fingers. He talked polyglot gibberish when drunk, and smoked a fine gold-and-ivory inlaid pipe. And there was Petlin, gossip and eavesdropper, fawner and flatterer. He could read and write, though Ivan Koltzo said, 'Riding a cow does not make you a Cossack. Reading books does not make you wise.' Petlin wore a chainmail habergeon, and was fond of killing dogs.

What a crew, thought Nicholas. Our new comrades. Hardly knights or gentlemen, though he fancied they could handle themselves well in a fight.

One evening he quietly asked Stanley, 'How many Cossacks are there like these?'

Stanley shrugged. 'Nobody knows. Cossacks are not a race of men, nor a nation, they have no state, no government. The word only means "free man", wild man of the untamed steppes beyond Moscow's government. Maybe there are five thousand, ten thousand. They shift about, they build no cities, they vanish like the wind. They are as much nomads and bandits as the Tatars, their hated enemies with whom they have so much in common.'

'But if Moscow comes under attack – would they defend it?'

Smith said, 'Not a chance. They owe the Czar only the vaguest allegiance. Anyway, that is not how they fight. They are mounted raiders, not steady soldiers. Imagine trying to discipline a horde like this.'

'Stenka rules them sternly enough.'

Stanley looked thoughtful.

Hodge coughed. They glanced round. The one called Petlin was closer than they realised, smiling over at them and whetting his dagger.

He said suddenly, 'You have been among the Turks.'

None of them answered quickly enough, denied it vehemently enough. He nodded. 'Yes you have. Perhaps you work for them. Perhaps you are Turkish spies. The Cossacks have fought the Turks for centuries. We hear of great movements afoot. And spies moving among us, through Russia, preparing the way.' He spat on his knifeblade and wiped it. 'It is impolite of you not to tell us the whole truth. And it will be ill for you if we discover treachery. We Cossacks hate traitors.'

Stenka rode alongside Nicholas. 'This England is ruled by a great king?'

'No, a great queen.'

'A?'

'Queen. A female king, a king's daughter.'

'England is ruled by a woman?'

'It is.'

Stenka stared at him, jaw lowered, and then he began to smile, and then to laugh. He laughed so hard the tears rolled down his face and he had to drum his fists furiously on his knees to stop himself again. When at last he had dried his eyes, and called back to all his comrades that England was ruled by a woman, to general hilarity, he said, 'In my country, we have this joke. A new bride says to her husband of a week, Why do you not love me? He says, I do, my heart's desire. Then, she says, Why have you not beaten me?'

Nicholas couldn't quite see the point of the joke but he laughed politely.

'This England.' Stenka shook his head. 'It will never amount to anything, ruled by a woman.'

'We shall see,' said Nicholas.

They were sitting in the wearisome noonday heat in a shallow valley, cross-legged in the dust, chewing the gobbets fed to them by the men of the Don. Smith suddenly spat his mouthful of meat and gristle into the dust between his boots and stared east.

Petlin's eyes narrowed. 'You do not like the meat we give you?' he said softly. 'We can give you other things to chew on if you prefer.'

This Petlin was a great danger to them. He had hated the four strangers from the start, perhaps because his chief Stenka had taken to them so easily. He demanded of Stenka continually that their throats be cut and their bodies left for the kites and the steppe dogs, until at last Stenka rose in a fury and spat in his face and then beat him almost senseless. After that, Petlin only hated the strangers all the more.

Smith ignored him now, eyes fixed on the east. The grass shimmered in the haze. Then he said softly to Petlin, 'I think you should get down on all fours before me.'

Petlin stood and drew his dagger. 'What did you say?'

Smith said, 'Ingoldsby, see that dust cloud? Use your younger eyes.'

'I see it.'

'Don't think you see things on the steppe that we do not, English dog!' said Petlin angrily. 'We know every stream, every spring, every ridge and rise and swale. We know why the dust may drift west even in a west wind. Because over that ridge where you are looking, the wind rises and curls back on itself a little and brings a rise of dust.'

'No,' said Smith. 'That dust is not raised by the wind. There is not enough wind today. It is constant and it is too much. That dust is raised by the hooves of many horses.'

Petlin stared a moment longer and then he was indeed down on all fours before Smith in a trice, as he had suggested. Ear to the bare ground. It took him only a second or two to hear the sound reverberating through the black earth. And then he was on his feet and running to Atman Stenka.

'The Tatars! The Tatars are coming!'

Stenka looked up, edge of a dagger brought up to his mouth laden with stew. Then he was on his feet and striding, roaring out orders. As he rolled and struggled to his feet himself, cursing his bonds, Nicholas could hardly believe men could move so fast. Whether it was courage or sheer terror of the Tatars that drove them, hard to say. Ivan Koltzo booted over the cooking cauldron and kicked the shallow fire wide in a shower of sparks. A plains fire might help: a pall of smoke, the horses panicked. He wrapped the burning hot cauldron in a tough canvas and loaded it up. The twenty or so Cossacks were soon mounted, bows across their shoulders, old muskets, arquebuses, some priming wheel-lock firearms even as they dug their heels savagely into their ponies' flanks.

'Keep together!' roared Stenka. 'And you, Andriushko, heave our guests up on their mounts, they need a—'

'Cut our bonds!' Smith bellowed back even louder. 'We've been fighting the unchristened longer than even you, Stenka Timofeivitch! Loose us and give us back our weapons, for the love of Christ!'

Petlin rode around, goaded by this spectacle even more than by fear of the oncoming Tatars, that dustcloud not half a mile off now. 'Do not trust them, Atman, this is all a trick. They may even be in league—'

He was abruptly cut short by a furious Smith heeling his pony in alongside the startled Cossack's and headbutting him hard in the face. Petlin reeled back lengthways along his pony's back and only just succeeded in pulling himself upright again without losing consciousness altogether and falling off.

'Ride west with the rest, Petlin the sour!' yelled Stenka. Then he rode at Smith. 'How many Tatars have you killed?'

'Tatars, Turks, they are cousins of the blood! And I have killed more Turks than you Tatars!'

'You lie! I have killed more than sixty.'

'I have killed more.'

Stenka glared across at Stanley. He trusted the blond giant more than this bellicose bull of a man with his reddened eyes.

Stanley found it all rather braggardly and tiresome, and he really thought they should be going soon. 'I never counted,' he said. 'But he has fought the Turk for three decades, and killed a few score. You should set him free. All of us. You need us.'

Stenka spurred his horse around once more and cried out, 'Andriushko, cut 'em loose! They've nowhere to ride but with us anyway, or the Tatars will have their hearts out on stakes by sundown!'

Andriushko quickly sliced open the coarse hemp bonds and all four gasped as they moved stiff arms and wrists. Four days like this. Four days being fed at dagger-point, four days without washing, four days shuffling bare-arsed over the grass after using the great privy of the Scythian plains ...

'Now ride!' cried Stenka. 'Make for that rise across the gully!'

It was nothing. The gully a thin watercourse gouged through the black earth, no more deep nor wide than the height of man. A paltry barrier, mere entertainment for a Tatar horseman to vault over. Then a shallow rise of twenty feet or so. But it was the only feature in this otherwise featureless landscape: not a tree, not a rock, a mound. Nothing. The worst terrain imaginable in which to defend themselves – let alone from attack by a Tatar raiding party.

14

Nicholas's arms were so stiff, his hands so numb from the aching captivity that he could barely hold onto his reins. He trusted to the grip of horseman's thighs, keeping low, face almost buried in his pony's flying mane. He had the mad thought of holding onto that mane with his teeth. They raced over the plain westwards for the watercourse, Smith riding faster and coming upon the Cossacks carrying the baggage, shouting out for their weapons back. Andriushko was behind them. Nicholas looked back and cried out. Andriushko's horse had stumbled – one of them was doomed to in this wild galloping flight – forefoot in some burrow or marmot hole, and Andriushko came rolling over its neck to land senseless on the ground.

'No!' Stanley pulled his pony up short and drove it round, and Nicholas followed. It might be that the Cossack's horse wasn't badly hurt and they could still bring him back ... and then they saw the first dark shapes emerging out of their own dustcloud. The Tatars.

'Jesus have mercy,' whispered Stanley as they reined in hard. Though the ferocious warriors of the East would be upon them in perhaps two minutes, yet they held their skittish mounts as best they could, the ponies' flared nostrils smelling the danger, their riders' fear – and took in a long curving line of horsemen, like some old woodcut of the Mongol horde of the Great Khan. How they had come upon them like this was sheer bad luck, but the Easterners soon realised this was a party of Cossacks, and the hunt was on. How many? A hundred and fifty, two hundred ... Riding down their ancient enemy this hot summer day, the old sport of the Asiatic steppe.

Broad faces with high windburned cheekbones, crouched low along their ponies' backs. Their arms mostly the bow and arrow, here and there the gleam of curved scimitar of the Saracen pattern, and what looked like long bullwhips. The earth thundering, the dust rolling along with their thunderous course, narrowed eyes almost closed against the dust, and even at this distance, Nicholas thought he could see their wolfish grins. And Andriushko lying senseless ahead of them.

The gentle giant of a Cossack was lost to them.

'Ride!' shouted Stanley bitterly.

Meanwhile Smith had got their bundle of weapons back and was rolling from his horse still at the trot. Stenka had taken to the rise and was marshalling his men. They could not outrun the Tatars, not with their baggage, and Stenka was damned if he would surrender those precious plates of China. A cross-plains gallop that might endure half an hour would only end in the ponies collapsing to the ground with bloody lungs and burst hearts. No, the hell with it. They would take to the rise and in those two or three precious minutes before the Tatars fell on them, they'd charge their guns and let them have a full volley. They were outnumbered ten to one, of course, so to stand and fight was madness. But by the blood of Christ, let the fight come. God stood with the mad often in this mad world. Stenka had seen it.

With a good volley the Tatars would lose ten men, their ponies would rear and reel in indignant rage, and then they would wheel away, releasing a fatal shower of arrows before coming to rest a safe distance off, foam-flecked, panting. And then they'd come back in again, and again . . .

The Cossack band tumbled from their winded steeds and let them breathe a moment standing, and then forced them down, whinnying furiously. They crouched behind them, the ponies' foam-flecked bellies rising and falling like forge bellows. Urgently they primed their guns, powdered the pans of ancient muskets and looted Ottoman arquebuses and the occasional German handgun only a little less weighty and barely more wieldy. Ivan Koltzo raced among them distributing more powder and ball. Others shook their heads and waited with bow and arrow whose simplicity they trusted far more.

The Tatars were breaking wide into a crescent, the ominous arc of the bull's horn, widely outflanking them to come up the rise from three sides or even all four – but then Stenka saw with astonishment that the two foreign knights, his late captives, had already dismounted at the edge of the gully below. They pulled down their horses, the beasts whinnying furiously at being thus separated from the rest of the herd at this moment of high terror for animals so highly nerved, and then both dropped down into the gully, a natural trench in the plains, but as much a trap as any animal pit. Stenka clenched his jaw grimly. So that was it. They were traitors after all, had even brought this upon them, and now waited below to join the Tatar band as they rode in ...

He strode over to where Hodge and Nicholas lay, drawing his curved dagger ready to cut their throats in two swift movements, at the same time bellowing out, 'Shoot those two dogs below first!'

'No!' cried Nicholas, raising his arm. Stenka grimaced and seized his hair and put his blade to the youth's throat and glanced up once more and then saw a strange sight.

The two traitors were priming guns too, leaning out of the gully to face the oncoming horde. What were the sunstruck fools doing?

'Smith!' cried Nicholas. 'Stanley! Get back!'

Stenka changed his mind. They were not traitors. But they were damn fools, and fools die. 'The arrows fly overhead, you fools!' he called to them. 'They come down like rain!'

But his words fell on deaf ears. Smith and Stanley were otherwise occupied. Still panting, they held themselves as still as they could and Smith propped his jezail on its wooden tripod through the long grass and sighted down the long gleaming barrel of Indian wootz steel. Stanley stood beside him, head held a little higher. Lookout.

What were they thinking? For all their heroics, Nicholas knew they were never yet suicidal. But two hundred Tatars or more came galloping down on them ... He could see their red banners fluttering from long spears, their ponies' nostrils flared, he could see that they wore padded and quilted coats for protection, very few with armour, and most had narrow moustaches and pointed beards.

They would hammer down upon the two crouching knights, with one good shot between them, in another minute or two.

Smith sighted and waited, his breathing slowing, his grip on the long lethal musket steadier all the time. Stanley's keen blue eyes roved back and forth across the dust-clouded Tatar line, as if looking for something specific. Then he murmured, 'Got him.'

'Sure?'

'Sure. One of the few with some kind of steel helmet, morion shape, gold torc of some kind around his neck. Grey beard and hair. Rider to his right with a fringed red pennant flying from—'

'Got him,' said Smith. Squinting, turning the jezail a fraction, levelling, accounting for wind, little account today, and the natural fall of the musket ball. Just half an ounce of lead, so small a thing. If he fired at two hundred yards he'd aim just over the head. At one hundred, he'd aim for the helmet but there was a risk the ball might glance off, leaving the rider with little more than a headache. At fifty to seventy yards though, he could aim for the forehead, just below the helmet's rim, and the ball should take him clean between the eyes. They only had one chance.

Three hundred yards.

Then Stanley, eyes moderately better than Smith's though not his marksmanship, looked again at the rider with the red banner.

They were cantering in easy now. Some were raising their short, immensely powerful recurved bows, arrows pointing skywards. Black rain coming.

Two hundred yards.

Stanley saw the Tatar chieftain in his steel helmet turn to his left and seem to speak, and the one with the banner smiled and nodded. He was younger, the chieftain was grey-haired. He saw that they both looked . . .

A hundred and fifty yards.

'Take the rider to his left,' said Stanley.

'Hunh?'

'Trust me. To his left, that is our right. Forget the chieftain. Take the one with the red pennant.'

Smith had never mistrusted Stanley's judgement. He grunted and moved the muzzle of his jezail a fraction and from the Tatar host came a great war cry as they closed in.

A hundred yards.

Smith increased the pressure of his forefinger on the trigger and breathed out and relaxed and – eighty yards – fired. It seemed almost instantaneous. The rider with the red banner slipped and fell from his horse without a noise amid the oncoming din and roar, and the next instant the chieftain gave a great cry and reined in and the host of the Tatars stumbled and slowed to a bewildered trot. Some even came riding round across the front of their own line towards their beloved chieftain.

The older man was down off his horse and tearing his steel helmet from his head and kneeling in the dust beside …

Stanley nodded. 'It was his son.'

Stenka rose up in disbelief at the sight, then raised his sword arm. 'Fire!'

And forty Cossacks loosed musket balls and arrows down onto the confused and milling host below them. There were shouts and some fell from their horses, more confusion, angry cries, others already cantering back out of range.

In the watercourse, the moment he had fired, Smith began to reload his jezail, his hands almost a blur. Muttering to himself, 'Just take him, take him as well, and we could be saved without a fight. Cut off the head of this hydra and it'll never regrow …'

He lay low, aimed, closed his finger on the trigger and fired. The chieftain moved and stirred and glared back. A fine-looking old fellow, broad cheekbones and eyes of an eagle. Quite an enemy to have there. Hell and damnation, how could he have missed? Then there were at least a dozen Tatar horsemen standing or riding their horses in front of him, surrounding him, shielding him with their own bodies. Smith reloaded in less than a minute. The jezail could take it. Cheaper muskets needed time to cool after almost every shot, like cannon, but another wonder of this steel viper was that he had never known her overheat, no matter how hard he worked her. Even in the inferno of Malta.

But there was no chance of another shot at the chieftain. With that mysterious unspoken unity which made a Tatar war party such a fearsome body of fighting men, they pulled around as one and headed away east, the chieftain with the dead body of his son across his own lap. They left not another dead body behind on the plain, they took all for burial. Only a few corpses of horses remained for the carrion birds.

The dust settled behind the vanishing horsemen of the steppe, and the Cossacks slowly stood to their feet and stared after them, barely able to believe their luck. Nicholas and Hodge stared too, and Smith and Stanley relaxed a little, Smith dropping the hammer of his musket carefully down again. They saw that one or two of the horses were not yet dead but pitifully wounded, lying on their sides, slowly stirring their stiff legs in the air. One trying to stand, whinnying, unable, its left hindleg shattered beneath it. Ivan Koltzo went out to them with his long knife.

And then they saw that the Tatars had left one other thing for them. Thrust into the parched earth before them was the spear of the slain son, its blood-red pennant still hanging from the shaft, stirring gently in the hot wind.

15

They didn't linger. They rode hard all that day, northwards, over grass steppe until at last as dusk fell they came to a land of shallow valleys and thin trees, thorn brake and birch, and they took shelter there. Any Tatar would be able to follow their trail virtually blindfold, but it was as far as they could go. The horses were tired and they desperately needed watering. They would rest here the night and hope to sleep as best they could.

Once dismounted, nevertheless the Cossacks crowded around the two knights, clapping them on the back and jabbering praise. Even Stenka gruffly acknowledged they had probably saved their skins – for now – and he eyed Smith's gleaming jezail with envy.

'You are men of mystery,' he said. 'But for now I suppose we must believe you are not in league with the Tatars.'

'Are you not going to bind them again?' said Petlin. 'This is folly. We still know nothing of them. They have lied to us. Now they have raised the whole Tatar nation against us, and what have we to show for it? A few China plates, which they say are valuable. I say, give me that musket of yours, stranger, and be done with it.'

Smith just smiled, and shook his head very slowly.

Petlin strode forward as if to strike him, and Smith's huge fist enclosed Petlin's raised arm, as if to snap it like a twig. He gave a jerk and Petlin reeled to the ground. He let him go. Petlin spat in the dust and cursed foully, and nursing his wrenched arm, strode off into the gathering dark. The rest laughed.

'You'll not be bound again,' said Stenka. 'You are not our

prisoners. But you are not our brother Cossacks either. Yet you may ride with us further, for now.'

'You are not going east to Kharkov?'

'We are not.'

'Then ... north?'

Stenka nodded. 'North.'

They watered the horses, shot some wild duck and a young deer, cooked millet cakes and ate. A little later a shadowy figure reappeared out of the gloom. Petlin, still nursing his arm and his wounded pride. Except – this shape was too big for Petlin. They drew their swords. And into the firelight stepped Andriushko.

There was great rejoicing. 'Andriushko, you simple bear! You ride a horse like a woman, and fall off like a grainsack! How the devil did you get here?'

Andriushko said he had found a stray and panicked horse out there alone, by some miracle, and called it to him. Being a horse, easily lonesome, it had come to him, and he had mounted and followed their trail.

'How did the Tatars not find you and string you up for archery practice? How are you still living? Are you a ghost?'

He grinned and rubbed his head. 'The Tatars galloped right over me. I lost my senses and saved my life. Now I'm a ghost with a terrible ache in his skull. Must have landed badly.'

'But we must give thanks!' cried Chvedar the defrocked priest. 'Let there be a Mass, and let us chant the ancient hymns of the Mother Church to praise our God for returning to us so mysteriously our beloved Brother in Arms, Andriushko, devout Christian, Whoremonger and Drunk.' He passed around a leather flask of the grain spirit they called vodka. 'The blood of Christ.'

The four Englishmen sat out this ramshackle blasphemy of a spectacle, watching with half-amused fascination. Chvedar handed out millet cakes, hot from the stone. 'The body of Christ.'

That at least could not be accounted heretical. 'But can you use this vodka of theirs instead of wine?' asked Nicholas.

'A theological grey area,' said Stanley.

'Bloody savages,' said Hodge. 'We'd be just as well off among the Tatars.'

Chvedar was already drunk himself. '"Eat, drink and be merry,"

86

said our Lord Jesus, "and drown your earthly sorrows in vodka, for the Spirit is with you." The Gospel of Saint Inebrius.' He crossed himself. The Cossacks guffawed. Chvedar their crazed priest. He lifted his robe and made another sign of the cross over his bare buttocks. Smith shook his head. 'The Mother of God protect you this night,' said Chvedar, 'as the Tatars stalk us all around, yellow wolf eyes in the darkness, daggers in their hands.'

'A great comfort, Father Chvedar,' said Stenka.

'May She gather up the host of the Tatars in her loving arms and raise them up to heaven – and then drop them all down again into the burning mouth of hell, like so many maggots. For the Wrath of the Lord is kindled against them, and we are the instruments of his vengeance. The Cossacks are the chosen people. Has He not blessed us with guns and horses and vodka? Surely God the Father is our refuge, and He will crush our enemies beneath his feet as grapes are pressed in the winepress.'

'Like scraps of the Scripture regurgitated by a Bedlam beggar,' said Smith.

'Enough piety,' said Stenka. 'Pass the flask, Father Chvedar, don't drain it all down your own gullet.'

Chvedar drained it – maybe a pint of the fiery spirit in one draught, and then stood, blear-eyed, swaying. He belched mightily, looked as if he might be sick, swallowed it down, and then very slowly drew his filthy robe over his head and stood naked for them. His body bony and white but for the red weals of his battle scars, a surprising number for a supposed priest, his manhood long and flaccid, skinny shanks and huge splayed feet. Then he laid his robe by the fireside and lay down upon it and fell asleep with mouth agape.

What madmen had they come among?

They moved on before dawn. Even the last of the moonlight seemed malevolent, the vast and empty plains only emphasising cruelly their pitifully small numbers.

Petlin joined them again, slinking in like a fox as they rode out.

'The Tatars are trailing us,' muttered Smith.

'I know it,' said Stanley.

'Do you trust Petlin?'

'Less far than I can spit. But he would not league with the Tatars.'

'How many more days to Moscow?' asked Nicholas. He imagined a mighty fortified city, battlements and towers, monstrous cannon – please God, just over the next rise, the next ...

'Days?' said Smith. 'Weeks.'

This country. A great emptiness. Plus some Tatar horsemen intent on killing them in the worst way they could devise.

'Why have they not attacked?'

'They want the right time,' said Stanley.

'There are so few of us,' said Nicholas.

'I don't know. They like to torment the minds of their enemies. It is our punishment, already begun. Refuse to be punished. Do not fear them.'

'All very well. But I do fear them. I don't think they'll treat us too well if they take us alive.'

Stanley said bluntly, 'Don't be. Whatever else happens, Brother Nicholas – don't be taken alive. We have killed the chief's son. They will have plans for us.'

'And these Tatars could teach even the Turks a thing or two about torture,' said Smith with his usual cheeriness.

Towards mid-morning they came upon an ominous sight. A huge circle of bleached bones. Near the edge of the circle was a dark spillage of fresh blood, and a trail leading away into the tall grass. They reined in and looked on in silence. A grim augury. Ivan Koltzo slipped from his pony and knelt and touched his fingertips to the blood and held them beneath his nose.

'Taur,' he said. 'Wild ox. It has gone away wounded, we might track it.'

'And these bones?' said Stenka.

Ivan shrugged. 'They are old.' He stood and nudged them with the toe of his boot. 'Some massacre. This one – this could be a human thigh bone. I do not know for sure.'

Nicholas and Hodge exchanged glances. Nicholas pictured the slaughter. A Russian wagon train, perhaps ten years ago, or even a generation since. A family travelling south, a band of Cossacks, perhaps even a band of hopeful German settlers, with their cattle and their sheep, riding out across the plains to found a homestead beside some peaceful river. And then set upon and slaughtered in this desolate spot by Tatars or bandits of some kind, and not a cross to mark them. Who knew? Yet it could equally well have been a Tatar party slaughtered by Cossacks. Such bones, bleached as these, had no tribe, no nation, barely even distinguishable as animal or human.

He felt almost paralysed with foreboding. They all did. Even now they felt a huge circle of Tatars closing in. There would be no glorious stand, no heroics, no fight. They would be efficiently captured, tortured, flayed, perhaps buried alive beside an anthill with only their heads protruding above the earth, eyelids sliced away by the Tatar women and their delicate knives. What had they done?

Then they started. Very far off, a single shot rang out. Ivan Koltzo was up on his pony instantly and heeling the animal towards the distant sound.

'A lone hunter,' said Petlin. 'Trailing the wounded ox.'

Ivan Koltzo did not look back. 'Pray it is,' he said. And he was gone, horse and rider vanishing into the tall grass as utterly as a diver beneath the surface of a lake.

They waited. And waited. Nicholas felt the Tatars closing in around them. Topknots, wide faces, high cheekbones and burned red cheeks, thin moustaches, long quilted robes, and their small ugly ponies with their stocky legs and huge heads and mighty barrel chests ... Oh, to have no imagination, to be a stolid block of a man. He felt chilled, even thought he might scream. Yet he could be courageous enough in battle. Always it was like this. If you could but fight, could but see and know the enemy, however numerous, could busy yourself with loading muskets or bulking up walls and gates, or even carting barrels of water around the lines – but this impotent stillness shrivelled your heart away.

Flies buzzed. Sweat trickled. Not a breath of wind.

Some minutes later Andriushko, sitting tall on his horse, saw a movement in the grass and gestured to them fiercely. They laid their hands on the hilts of swords, on guns, though without hope. A horseman appeared: Koltzo. They stayed tense, urgently trying to read the expression on his face. It did not look good.

'My brothers,' he said softly. 'We are done for.'

They subsided in their saddles. Well, thought Nicholas. That is it. Never again will we see—

Koltzo said, 'There is no escaping our fate. Tomorrow we will awaken with headaches from hell.'

Stenka frowned. 'Speak plainly, brother. This is no time for riddles.'

'The gunshot.' He waved. 'It was that lunatic Yakublev and his men.'

'You mean—'

'I came upon them. Yakublev and his party. There must be four hundred of them. Only two weeks ago they captured a merchant ship on the river and their summer raiding is done. They can carry no more. We dine with them tonight.'

Stenka and Andriushko both fell upon Koltzo simultaneously, belabouring him with a kind of good-natured, desperate relief.

'You devious rat!' yelled Andriushko. 'I almost shat my breeches there! Plucking our nerve strings like that, God damn your eyes!'

16

The Hetman Yakublev was a distant kinsman of Stenka Timofeivitch, or so they both believed, of the mighty Host of the Don Cossacks; and they were invited, nay, ordered to join in tonight's feast. The wounded ox had been brought down, several antelope, numberless quail driven into nets. Tonight they would set the plains alight. Tomorrow they would retreat to the safety of their island home on the Don.

They cantered through the long grass, howling with triumph. With such numbers they were surely safe from a Tatar attack.

'One thing,' called Stanley. 'Do we tell them we are hunted by the Tatars?'

Stenka gave a curt laugh. 'Of course not. We might be less welcome guests.'

'Is that just?'

'Just? Whatever keeps me alive in this evil world is just. Hah!' And he spurred across the steppe.

The camp of the chieftain Yakublev was a festive sprawl of tents and wagons. In the tents and under canvas awnings sat many a silent female captive or slave girl patiently awaiting her fate, while the wagons were heaped with fantastical piles of loot from the summer raiding: everything from Ottoman carpets to chests of silver coins to Indian cloth of gold, jade, turquoise, sacks of salt from the Caspian, Tatar yak-tail standards and drums, a barbaric long pole with the gaping jawbone of a horse nailed to the top. Two captured caravans from far-off China carrying musk, satin and silk and candied rhubarb, barrels of whale oil from the far north, black gunpowder, shot – and most dangerous of all, Armenian brandy.

Stenka and Yakublev embraced like long-lost brothers, drank cup after cup of brandy and roared with laughter about nothing. Eventually the spirit moved Stenka to confess to Yakublev their small difficulty.

The drinking stopped.

Yakublev stared hard at Stenka. 'You slew the son of a Tatar chieftain? Which tribe?'

Stenka indicated Smith and Stanley. 'These fellows who travel with us did the slaying. And it was a brave act. It saved us awhile.'

'But you do not hand them over? Though they are foreigners?'

'We do not. We have fought together.'

'Hm. Noble.' Yakublev pulled his long moustaches. 'Now you come among us, you may draw a whole Tatar nation after you.'

'I admit it.'

Yakublev looked troubled.

Stanley seized the moment. 'Listen to me,' he said, stepping forward.

Yakublev eyed him from beneath lowered brows. Then he said, 'Speak, foreigner who has put us all in such jeopardy. There will be no washing the blades clean between Cossack and Tatar now.'

At last Stanley decided the Cossacks must be told. They must be trusted.

'There are much greater things stirring,' he said. 'The whole Tatar nation is coming together, supported by the Turks, under the command of their great general, Devlet Giray of the Crimea. You have heard of this.'

'We have heard rumour of it. It is not our war. They ride against Moscow.'

'We have it from the highest sources. All the Tatar nations, backed and financed by the Grand Sultan himself. They are riding north for Moscow, yes, and they will burn it to the ground. They will enslave all they do not kill, and destroy the power of Russia once and for all.'

Stenka himself and his Cossacks and Yakublev and his captains stirred, looked troubled. This impromptu festival of brandy and loot had suddenly turned into a council.

'What is this to us free men of the steppe?' said one of the bearded captains. He sounded almost angry. 'What is Russia to us? We have fled Russia and the reach of Russia to live here, free men.'

'Is Russia not your Holy Mother? Is Czar Ivan not your Holy Father?'

'Some Mother!' cried another sarcastically. 'Some Father! We Cossacks have chosen to be orphans!'

Much cheering and laughter.

Stanley persisted. 'So it matters nothing to you if the great Christian power of Russia is wiped off the earth? If these steppes, the great forests, all the way to the White Sea, are swallowed up once more into a Tatar and Turkish Empire – a Mohammedan Empire? And do you truly think this new Empire will let you roam free over your steppes as before?'

'What is it to you, stranger, this fate of Russia?'

'Because we are Knights of Malta, sworn to defend Christendom. Russia is a part of Christendom. There is no other reason.'

He spoke with such simple sincerity they could not but believe him.

This fair Knight went on, 'If the lovely monastery of St Nicholas outside the Kremlin walls is burned to the ground, its holy monks slaughtered, is it nothing to you? While you feast and celebrate here, look! Under the very Icon of St Nicholas himself, patron saint of wanderers? Has he not protected you well? Is this how you repay him?'

Nicholas clenched his fists. A hit, a palpable hit! An argument as finely calculated as the trajectory of a well-aimed cannonball. Now all the Cossacks, from the chiefs and captains downwards, looked awkward, hunted. Yes, the magnificent Icon of St Nicholas in its great silver frame that went everywhere with them on their summer raids, it had guarded them well in their skirmishes and looting. Did they not owe the Saint a debt? And now Moscow was to be razed by unbelievers, and this fair-haired, red-cheeked Knight of Christendom was come among them like some early Rus or Viking Rurik, urging noble crusade. Just as they were about to settle down amid the plenty and riches of their fortified island home on the Don, with their loot and their lovely captured women, for a long, drunken and pleasant summer of it ... Life was hard.

Then the angered captain who had spoken earlier stepped forward and pulled up his shirt, exposing a ragged, ugly scar: as if some madman had tried to cut into his belly and take out his liver whole.

'This is what Mother Russia did to me!' he cried. 'This was the work of those vicious dogs, Czar Ivan's Oprichnina.' A murmur went up at this accursed word. He jerked his head furiously, eyes blazing. 'Why do you think we fled here to the steppes, we Cossacks? To escape the cruelties of Mother Russia. Not one of us here is free from scars, beatings, flailings and tortures at the hands of the Czar's dark servants. And now you ask us to ride and fight and likely die for him!'

'Then fight for Russia.'

'We are men without a country, we acknowledge neither king nor master, we are free men! The Czar may rule in Moscow, but the Cossack rules on the Don.'

'You could be the noble bodyguard of the new Russian Empire, you could win great glory protecting this new rising power, you would be her elite soldiery, like knights of old, guarding her vast borders with your ferocious heroism, so that Russia would become great because of you.'

Stenka called, 'Pass the bottle!'

Loud cheers and jeers. Stanley waited. At last he said quietly, 'Then do not fight for Czar Ivan, or for Russia. Fight for St Nicholas and for God.'

There was no jeering then, only a long silence. At last Yakublev said, 'These festivities are over, and I fear I smell Tatars on the wind. Come with us, brothers. To the island. We must at least stow our summer loot.'

The groaning wagon train of Yakublev and the Don Cossacks rolled east to the banks of the mighty river, Stenka and his men acting as outriders in case of Tatars. But they saw nothing.

It was a great operation to transport the wagons and horses and captured goods on huge rafts, poled across the river to an island the size of several English parishes, with hills and woods and freshwater springs and a permanent wooden settlement defended only thinly by wooden watchtowers. Nicholas saw the gleam of yellow eyes in the reeds as they poled out, but they were only wildfowl. No Tatars would cross a river or come by raft or boat. They were safe here.

That night they feasted again and celebrated their summer raiding, and the women danced with joy to see them returned. Andriushko got so drunk he rode on a bucking bull, and sang,

If you drink you will die,
If you don't you will die,
So join with me, drunkards all
And raise your glasses high!

The unmarried men had their slave girls and some of the married men also tried to introduce their pretty young captives into their households with wide-eyed innocence, only to feel the terrible wrath of their wives. But over it all there hung the shadow of some grievous decision to be made. Stanley urged Stenka constantly that they must ride for Moscow, and the Cossack chieftain looked silent and troubled.

Nicholas felt torn between admiration and disgust for these wild men of the steppe: in Shropshire they would have been mere gangs of predatory bandits, hunted down and hanged – but here he could not help but envy the feral, untamed energy and joyous lawlessness. It was exhilarating to be among men so free – free as no men before or since – who still rode a measureless and unfenced steppeland that no one even owned. These Stenkas and Ivans, they would fight all their lives, drink, wench, gain scar after scar and die young. Very few of them would see forty. They would leave few good deeds behind them, many widows and orphans. No one could admire them, but they lived by their own code of fierce loyalty, and with a burning bright flame every day of their short wild lives. He could see why men rode south into the empty steppeland and turned Cossack. He could see it very well.

At night before they became too drunk they told tales: grim anecdotes of raiding and blood feud, or travellers' tales of the land north and east over the mountains, the land of Sibir, where tribal peoples lived clad in furs before the Spirit Gate of the Sky, and the spirit flames that lit the sky in green veils, lighting the frozen white world at midnight. There were people who lived in holes in the ground, and sucked the blood of dogs, and slept six months a year in dens of ice. There were ancient peoples who hunted and crawled through perpetual night, diabolical spells worked by beautiful women, and *vourdalaki*, vampires, and on the Island of Bones there were elephants' teeth dug up from the frozen earth of a size you could barely conceive.

And in the tents the women sang lullabies to their infants: lullabies of ancient hatred.

Sleep, my child, and dream – your father
Takes his arms down from the wall,
Rides out to kill the godless Tatar
And all his Kindred, all

Nicholas drank too much sweet Armenian brandy and had troubled dreams. He rode into Moscow on a huge black-haired elephant, bellowing with Biblical wrath, and when the elephant turned its head he saw it had a human face. A gaunt, haunted face, with deep-set eyes and haggard expression.

When he awoke the next morning he knew something had happened. He went groggily to find Hodge.

Hodge said, 'A Tatar rider came to the riverbank at dawn.'

'Alone?'

'Aye. You slept through it.'

'I am a drunken sot.'

Hodge did not disagree. 'He came with a message.'

'Saying?'

'Saying that if the men who slew the chieftain's son were handed over, there might yet be washing of blades clean between Yakublev's Cossacks and the Tatars.'

'But Yakublev would not?'

'He would not.'

'What the devil saved them?'

'Last night it came out that we had fought at Lepanto and Malta. The Hetman Yakublev had barely heard of Malta, so Stanley gave him a rousing account, but he knew of the great sea battle against the Turks. When he heard that we were there, and heard the full story of it from the knights, he declared them great warriors and as good as blood brothers of the Cossacks.'

'Hm. Lucky.'

'So the Tatar said he had doomed his entire people. And when they had finished their other wars they would return and wipe the Host of the Don from the earth for ever.'

'Quite a threat.'

'It is.'

'And Yakublev has decided to ride for Russia.'

'Well.' Nicholas belched stale brandy breath. 'By the beard of the Prophet and his ten tiny toes.'

Hodge cuffed him. 'Idiot. Get up.'

Riders were milling about in the early morning, sun gleaming on odd bits of armour, breastplates, purloined Persian shields. All was confusion. The mist was thinning from the river and women were weeping and singing songs.

Not with ploughs
Our black earth is ploughed
But with sharp Tatar spears;
Our black earth is harrowed
By horses' hooves
And watered with Cossack tears.

Other women were too angry to speak or sing. Their men who had only just returned were riding out again on some madcap campaign against the ancient enemy, the Tatars. For many months. There was even talk of riding all the way to Muscovy. The fools.

'Get your horses!' cried Smith.

'Are we – are we riding?'

'The Hosting of the Cossacks!' cried a crazed-looking zealot with an eyepatch, long robe hitched up absurdly above his bony knees. It was Chvedar. He whirled a long sword dangerously above his head, cantering to and fro among the smoky wooden huts. Children stared at him, a few burst into tears. From the riverside came shouts of boatmen, clunking of rafts, whinnying of many horses.

'To war the Cossacks will ride!' cried Chvedar. 'For St Nicholas and Lepanto against Turk and Tatar, for Great and Little and White Russia and our Holy Mother of all the Russias! For the Lord of Hosts is with us, Christ and his Holy Mother—' at which point his horse stumbled over a squealing porker and Chvedar rolled from the saddle and lay winded on his back, his robe unseemly hitched. Women laughed raucously.

'He was lucky not to land on his own sword,' said Nicholas.

'Is this really a Crusade?' said Hodge. 'Stinks like a tinker's privy to me.'

'I remember reading of the first crusades,' said Nicholas. 'They began in chaos too. But God is with us.'

'If you say so.'

They went to get their horses.

17

The vastness of the country as they rode north was at first astonishing, and then tedious, and at last dispiriting. No matter how long they rode, the terrain remained exactly the same the next day as the day before. As if no progress was made at all. Would they ever reach Moscow of the White Walls, the Kremlin of the Red Towers?

But they were joined along the way by more brother Cossacks, some at last persuaded of the holiness of the cause, although others more confused. Nicholas heard one say, 'We will bring home some rich loot from Moscow, will we not?'

Stenka roared at him, 'We're not sacking Moscow, you dolt, we're defending it!'

'Defending it?' He looked most disappointed. 'Why would we do that, brother?'

They came from the Volga, from the Wild Lands and the borderlands, from Saratov and Kagalnik and Siech. At last the Cossack column raising such summer dust as it rode must have numbered as many as three thousand.

'And how many Tatars, did we hear in Constantinople?' murmured Stanley.

'Remember Malta,' said Smith, 'and do not think in terms of numbers. Or we'd be lost.'

'We're already lost,' said Hodge.

The only useful intelligence that came to them as they rode filtered through the ranks from some rider who had it from a cousin who had been trading down on the Moldavian border. He said that the

Turks had recaptured the great city of Tunis on the African coast.

Smith looked black. 'Don John of Austria had it in the palm of his hand.'

The Cossack shrugged. 'I heard it fell again.'

'So despite Lepanto, the Turks are conquering in the Mediterranean once more,' said Smith bitterly.

'They are still exhausted,' said Stanley. 'It is one small setback, no more. Tunis is just a lair of Barbary pirates.'

Smith grunted.

'But maybe enough for the Turks to feel secure on that frontier again. To turn their attentions to other frontiers ... Northwards, for example ...'

Smith sullenly heeled his horse.

'It never ends, does it?' said Nicholas.

Stanley shook his head. 'Not till Doomsday. It never ends and we never win. We just keep fighting for what is right. But it will never be done. Not in this world.'

At last, after many weary days' riding, twelve or fourteen bone-aching hours a day, the landscape slowly began to change: more woods, rivers, cooler air, and they began to pass more farmsteads, and then villages and cultivated fields and orchards. The smoke of village hearthfires, glint of church roofs, gold crosses, steeples, the whitewashed walls of manors, waterwheels clacking to the peaceful trickle of slowly moving streams.

They were drawing near to their destination.

'But two more days,' said Stenka. 'I remember this country here well. Two more days and your eyes will see Moscow.'

The huge column made its approach known far off, the ground rumbling, dust rising from the dirt roads, and people running inside, dragging their children, bolting the doors at this terrifying sight. But Yakublev gave the order to raise high the Icon of St Nicholas, and he told his men to sing hymns. Somewhat uncertainly they followed Chvedar in singing psalms of dubious provenance, and the villagers understood they were Christian, at least. News of their coming then seemed to spread before them, and sometimes women in headscarves would come forward and cross themselves and give them bread and cheese and apples and plums. Men showed them where they might best fodder the horses and they gave their word not to ride over hay meadows or damage crops.

'Have you heard news from Moscow?' they asked. 'Have there been Tatars on the roads? Is all well?'

The villagers looked afraid at the very name of Tatar. But no, there had been no raids this year. There had been other troubles aplenty – but no unbelievers from the East. 'Are the Tatars coming again?' 'Have you heard tell?' 'Friends,' they pleaded, plucking at their reins, 'tell us, for the love of God. We cannot survive another year of Tatar raiding. We will starve to death this winter.'

Their hearts went out to them. They were tongue-tied. It was Stanley at last who said gently, 'The Tatars may be riding again. We have heard rumour of it. But look.' He waved back over the mighty column, stretching a mile or more down the road. 'We are come to fight for you. You need not fear.'

The villagers wept and tried to believe him.

It was late afternoon and they rode through dappled birchwoods and decided to camp there the night. Tomorrow they might make it to the gates of Moscow if they departed early and rode hard. This might be their last night of freedom for a long time. After this, they were in the iron grip of the dread and beautiful city.

Nicholas rode off a little way from the camp, needing silence. He stopped beside a sparkling woodland stream running over small moss-green rocks, and prayed, and thought of his family, and watered his horse. Then he knelt on one knee just upstream of the gentle beast and washed his hands in the crystal water and cupped them and drank. His horse nickered. He drank more. His horse raised her head, water dripping from her soft mouth, and snuffed the surface of the water. Flicked her ears. Nicholas stopped drinking and glanced upstream. A trail of rusty water from the iron-rich earth. No ... He spat and stood swiftly to his feet. Fool. Never drink without walking the bankside a good hundred yards down.

There was a dense holly bush, a sharp turn in the stream, and then splayed across the muddy bank, a slain man. He lay on his back with his head under water, but what made Nicholas sicken and instantly draw his sword was the foul mutilation done to him. His breeches were pulled down to his ankles and at his groin there was nothing left but a garish red wound. Nicholas turned aside to spew, mere streamwater, his belly was so empty.

Sweet Jesus.

Some village cruelty, some ancient feud. Never idealize the peasants. Those who gave them apples just this morning were the same who would take up their pitchforks in an instant and run bloody riot, killing Poles or Jews or whoever took their fancy. His father used to say, 'When the aristocrats rule, the peasants suffer. When the peasants rule, everybody suffers.'

Or maybe this sorry corpse was a man who ravished another's daughter, the ravisher here quietly castrated and drowned by her brothers in a sunlit birchwood ... But somehow he knew deep down that was not it. This was no simple village feud. There was something sickening and evil here. He sensed with some old battle instinct that there might be more bodies lying slain hereabouts, and his mare was stepping her hooves and trembling now too with deep discomfort. He patted her flanks. 'Easy, girl. Easy.' He took her reins. Suddenly he did not want to be alone here at all. He wanted to be back with Hodge and Smith and Stanley. Perhaps throwing up some defences round the camp. Could it even be that somewhere in these lovely summer woods, small ponies were moving with delicate hooves, and silent, narrow-eyed riders ...

And then he saw them: but they were no Tatars. They were like something out of a nightmare, and he could not even mount up for frozen fear.

Dark wraiths among the light green trees, black riders, sun-dappled. They seemed to suck in the light. At their head came one on a black horse and he wore some kind of crude animal mask carved out of wood. He carried a long whip, and a sword at his side, and roped to his saddle was a severed dog's head, clotted with black blood. Coming horribly slowly through the trees towards him in a broad fan were five or six more, similarly dressed, and again as in a nightmare, he could not move. He knew they had been watching him all the time. They were about to kill him too, as they had recently slain the poor soul on the bankside, but they hesitated a moment because they were not sure he was truly a worthless village peasant, there was some air about him ... He stood speechless beside his restive horse, sword drawn but loose. He could not flee.

He knew who they were now. He hoped desperately that before they trotted across the stream and cut him down, he would have the strength to mount his horse and fight back and take at least one of the devils with him.

The one in the animal mask at the head of the group reined in across the stream. The mouth of his mask was carved as if baring its teeth in a savage grin, and the eyes of the rider glittered through the shadowed eyeholes as if in similar amusement. He spoke in a dry cracked voice, very deep, icily unpleasant.

He was too numb to take in what the rider said. But he spoke enough of the language now to shout back, 'Friend, Christian – we have business in Moscow!'

They laughed, the leader's laugh a muffled growl behind his mask. 'We choose our friends. There is more than one of you?'

He said, voice quieter now, more controlled, 'There are three thousand Cossacks under Hetman Yakublev, not a mile away. I am surprised you have not heard them, or smelt them.'

'Smelt them? Do you think we are dogs?'

He in his barbaric animal mask, severed dog's head at his side. Nicholas already thought them much lower than dogs. He said nothing.

Another of the riders had already trotted over the stream and was standing up in his stirrups close behind, throwing a rope up over a low branch.

Nicholas cleared his throat, painfully tensed, gripped his sword hilt harder, and said, 'I know you. You are Czar Ivan's Oprichnina. I ride with the Cossacks, but I am of a party from the Court of Queen Elizabeth of England.' He sat straighter in his saddle. 'Her Majesty and your Czar have had exchange of letter and gifts, and we bring more. I do not think your Czar and Lord would be altogether pleased if you lynched me now.'

He could hear the rider behind him continuing to haul the rope, the sound of it rasping over the bark, the rider knotting it around the branch to his satisfaction, throwing a hangman's knot of seven or eight coils at the other end with practised hand. Nicholas glanced back. The rider tugged it hard and smiled at him. Another of the riders' horses calmly cropped the sweet green streamside grass.

At last the leader said, 'You interest me. What gifts have you brought?'

'They are for Czar Ivan's eyes, not yours. But there are fine silver plates, precious cloths, and a portrait miniature of our Queen.'

'Does it flatter her?'

He felt his temper flare, despite the situation, and the hot blood of generations of proud Ingoldsbys, who had served their ruling monarch from Otterburn to Poitiers. For all his evil looks and hellish accoutrements, this dark-cloaked figure before him was really just another over-promoted thug on a nice horse. He remembered what he learned at Malta, at Lepanto: that the cure for paralysing fear is a kind of wild scorn, an aristocratic contempt, for danger, for life, for the Angel of Death himself. They can but kill me.

'That is no business of yours.' He swung up onto his horse and pulled the reins tight, the horse's head jerking up with his own, chin jutting, defiant. 'And do not think I am some helpless village peasant who can be castrated and murdered for your amusement. Now tell your thug here to take this rope down again, before I cut it down myself, and maybe him with it.'

The animal mask stared long and hard at him, the eyes burning, boring into him. Committing him to memory. Then he said, voice harsher than ever, 'I wish you safe passage to Moscow, friend,' and pulled his horse around. The hangman cantered back over the stream to join them and in a moment the whole dark troupe had vanished away into the trees.

18

Nicholas looked up at the rope they had left behind, like some silent threat. It was a stout piece. He scrambled up on his horse's back and untied it and looped it over his left shoulder. Then he rode back to find his comrades, feeling madly exultant. That sweet savour of victory! Though not a blade had clashed, not a drop of blood had been shed, yet that was a true skirmish back there, one against six, and he had triumphed! Great God it was a sweet feeling! In the heart and the blood and, shame on it, every one of a man's organs. He had just looked into the face of evil, and treated them with disdain, and survived, and now he knew that their enemies were as much these gloating black-cloaked devils as the Tatars themselves, and they were already in one tormented country and one hell of a mess. But as his blood pumped and he spurred violently and his good horse galloped and jumped tree trunk and stream as exultantly as he, his only thought was, God but it is sweet, this life of danger! I had almost forgot it, dutiful Shropshire squire that I was, but now – bring it down on me like rain!

He came galloping back into camp grinning like a crazed thing, and reined in so flamboyantly his mare's front legs splayed out and her hooves skidded forward in the dust.

Stanley was sitting on a tree trunk, trying to stitch up the sole of his boot with a thin strip of leather sliced from his own jerkin. It wasn't working. 'Invigorating ride? Not had enough time in the saddle lately?'

'Most invigorating, thank you. A pretty woodland, and then an interesting talk with some riders of the Oprichnina.'

Stanley laughed. Smith glared at him. Hodge looked puzzled.

'They were insulting towards our Queen Elizabeth, and then they hung a rope over a branch to lynch me. But I reproved them in no uncertain terms, and they rode off like chastened schoolboys. Nevertheless, I think we may encounter them again.'

'You have a vivid imagination, Brother Ingoldsby,' said Stanley.

Hodge narrowed his eyes. 'Are you telling tall tales?'

He slipped from his horse. 'I am not. Every word is true.'

Stanley laid off stitching and looked at him hard. 'You ... this is the truth?'

'It is.'

Smith gave a rare smile. 'You just ran into the Oprichnina?'

'All as I said.'

They absorbed this unexpected news and then Smith roared with laughter and stood and, though Nicholas tried to avoid it, seized him and gave him a bear hug. Smith's bear hugs hurt.

'Devil take you, Ingoldsby! Born survivor, ex-galley slave, escaped from Algiers gaol, swum the channel to Elmo, shot by musket fire, shipwrecked, and now narrowly escaped a lynching by the Oprichnina! You've had almost as many narrow escapes as I, and still but twenty-eight, is it?'

'Twenty-five.'

'The devil.' Smith shook his head. 'You should have been a Knight of St John after all.'

'I couldn't live with the—'

'The chastity, I know, I know.'

'So where are these Oprichnina swine now? How many? Where are they travelling?'

Then he told them about the slain man, the grotesque mutilation, and he felt chastened that he had felt such exultation so soon after, that it had meant so little to him. We all have the strength to bear the sufferings of others. What cynic had said that?

'The savagery of these black-cloaked thugs is beyond all reckoning,' said Smith. 'How can we serve this Czar Ivan—'

'We are not serving Czar Ivan,' said Stanley, 'nor any prince of this world. We are serving the Christian Ideal. As always. You think our allied captains at Lepanto were all saints? Come, Brother John, you know better than that. Even Don John himself, our gallant commander there, notoriously loves his whores and hardly lives a life of virtue.' He looked down and began to stitch his battered boot again. 'Few men are saints, and very few in war. And we know that this Czar Ivan is a tyrant and rules cruelly. But in Russia this is usual. They hardly know or expect any different here.'

'Well,' said Smith, 'we can but pray that we run into these damned Oprichnina once more.'

'I very much fear we will.'

They rode out the last day before dawn with summer stars still bright, Altair and the lovely Vega in Lyra. The four rode near the head of the column with Yakublev and Stenka and his men. They would travel for a good hour before stopping to eat some coarse millet bread.

They were riding a pale sandy track when Ivan Koltzo stopped and looked down. 'Many horses have passed this way.'

'Recently?' said Stenka.

'Within a day.'

'They are not …?'

Ivan Koltzo shook his head. 'Big horses. Heavy. Perhaps fifty of them, well-laden.'

Stanley said, 'We will go ahead. If you hear two shots in rapid succession, come quickly.' He was already drawing the two German handguns he carried at his waist, and putting a pinch of powder in each.

They went ahead some few hundred yards, spreading wide, looking far into the forest left and right. Yes, there was something. They could not say what. Something nearing them. Like the old witches' rhyme, *By the pricking of my thumbs, Something wicked this way comes* …

And then the track broadened and there was a clearing in the trees and a village. Or what remained of a village.

They closed up together instinctively and reined in and stared. Smith unsheathed his sword. They surveyed the scorched earth in silence, the blackened, still-smoking cottages, the wisps of smoke rising in the peaceful summer air. There were cattle lying slaughtered, cut open, guts fed upon by squabbling crows. There were beheaded chickens, trampled sheep and stuck pigs. And there were dead people.

The Oprichnina had been through here on their punitive raid or *chevauchée*. Already Nicholas understood, they all understood, that there need be no reason or rationale for their cruelty. It was recreational. This village was just unlucky. Word of the slaughter would spread, and other villages, whole provinces, would hear of it and take note. Do not rebel against the Czar. He is God's Anointed, and he afflicts you for your sins. Pay your taxes. Obey. This savagery was committed deliberately to oppress the people, to assert the power of Ivan IV Vasil'evich over every human soul in the land of Russia.

Hodge said quietly, 'You would think the Tatars had already been.'

'Aye,' said Stanley. 'Yet this is what the Russians do to themselves. This is surely more work of the Oprichnina, who you must remember do not officially exist, though they are seen riding beside the Czar on every State occasion. Such is the madness of the State. And they may rape, torture, plunder and slay with absolute freedom. In their black robes they are devilish mirror-images of some black monkish order. We have heard their leader, the very worst, one called Maliuta Skuratov, even keeps trained bears, to hunt naked women through the forest and tear them in pieces for his amusement.'

Nicholas stared about and wondered once more, what terrible land had they come to?

Corpses hung from the trees. Some had been lynched, some hauled up by their ankles with their throats cut, bled like pigs. Their throats and faces and the ground blood-dark beneath them. Some of the slain were very young. There was a big pitchfork with three long tines, its haft driven into the ground, and on each tine was jammed a severed human head. At the foot of an old mulberry tree was an infant's naked body. Its head had been dashed against the trunk.

An old woman sat on the earthen step of a cottage with her head completely hidden under a black widow's veil, shaking violently. Smith dismounted and led his horse towards her and laid a huge hand on her bone-thin shoulder. He said quietly, 'Mother, do you hear us?'

She did not respond.

'We are not the men who did this. We are come ...' and he tailed off, feeling stupid and helpless. He was going to say, We are come to set this right, but that was absurd, obscene. This could not be set right. It was done and could not be undone. Anger rose in him. 'I am sorry.' He left the woman still sitting, still shaking.

'God damn.' Fire burned from inside him. 'God damn these savages! We know who did this!'

'Calm yourself, Brother—'

'So, Ned Stanley,' said Nicholas, angered too, wrenching at his reins, punishing his poor mount for the vileness of men. 'Tell me, we have ridden all this way, under command of our Queen to deliver gifts to this Ivan. Gather what information might be useful. No more than that. And now we are supposed to be fighting for him? This is our cause, these are our allies?' He waved his hand over the scene of horror. 'We fight with these, against the Tatars? Maybe the Tatars are less cruel themselves, for all their unchristened hearts!'

'Necessity makes strange bedfellows,' said Stanley grimly.

'Don't give me maxims!'

Cossacks gathered round to watch. Amid this scene of horror, the young Englishman's rage was a dramatic and splendid thing, and though the language of the two arguing was foreign, they understood the import well enough. Did an old Cossack not once observe, 'If you serve Holy Mother Russia, she will devour you'?

'We fight for the Christian Empire of Russia,' said Stanley patiently, 'not the men who did this. Fight for the people, the villagers themselves. Can you not see that?'

'And we will fight the Tatar alongside these black-robed devils? How can we pollute ourselves so as to join arms with such vermin?'

'First let us defend Moscow,' said Stanley. 'The future is always uncertain.'

Nicholas turned away. It was a sick war, a civil war, always the worst. Where was the clean nobility and the clearness of it? This was no Malta, no high crusade against barbaric invaders of an innocent country, but something far fouler. And they were becoming trapped in it.

'I tell you!' said Stenka. 'I tell you how it is, young English. It is simple. First we destroy the Tatars. Then we destroy the

Oprichnina. Destroy them both! Stenka Timofeivitch swears it.'

'You cannot destroy the Oprichnina,' said Yakublev. 'That is foolish talk. They are an entire professional army, and the close guard of the Czar himself.'

Stenka scowled. He was right, of course.

'Tell us,' said Smith, pulling his horse up before the old woman again and speaking through gritted teeth. 'Tell us, Mother, where have they gone?'

'Wait,' said Stanley more firmly now. 'We present ourselves at Ivan's court, having just attacked a troupe of his own personal bodyguard? A fine plan that is.'

The old woman stirred under her veil. Nicholas had the terrible fear that beneath that covering might be two lightless and bloody sockets for eyes – or they had sliced out her tongue. Some such horror which she hid for misplaced shame. Then she mumbled her answer.

'They have gone back to hell.' The words hung in the air. 'Back to their master the Devil. What do I know? Or the next village, God have mercy on their souls, the next valley.' She gestured with a skinny arm. 'Through the woods, a few miles' ride. If they have gone that way you will see the hoofmarks,' she said. 'And the blood.'

19

They rode through thin birch forest and there were many hoof-marks, and the summer sunlight was beautiful on the pale green leaves and on the soft dappled forest floor. Butterflies flittered through the glades as they rode, speckled woods, or flashes of red and purple wings high in the old oaks. Birdsong and the sound of a startled deer in the undergrowth – and then a high, human scream.

Stanley's wise caution was powerless then. All argument was ended with that scream, which set Nicholas, nerves already jangling, spurring his horse into a canter towards the sound. Hodge naturally went after him, and so the knights after them both. Seeing this, Stenka went after his new brothers-in-arms, and then his Cossacks too. Yakublev roared out, forbidding any more of his men from going after, but by that time two or three dozen were already galloping towards the place of meeting.

'Cover your faces at least, for the love of God!' cried Stanley. And as they rode they fumbled with kerchiefs and tied them roughly over mouths and noses. Then Nicholas, urging his willing bay mare into a gallop, erupted out of the trees into a wide clearing, blood pulsing in his ears, deaf even to the cries from Hodge and Smith and Stanley yelling at him not to go out alone, to attack in a line, he would be trapped . . .

He took in the scene in an instant. A broad sandy clearing, the Oprichnina camp, black tents. Men standing about or sitting, gaming, drinking, dozing. Maybe fifty in all. A naked girl bound to a tree for amusement over on the far side of the camp, already shot with one arrow in her shoulder. Exhausted, filthy with mud, hair plastered to her cheek with sweat as if she had already been chased though the woods like prey for mile after mile, hunted down like a hare. Stripped and doubtless raped and now finally tied, to be shot to death with arrows. Good target practice.

Her head hung down, her lips moved as if in prayer. Around her a group of men in black. Nicholas saw eight, five still mounted, including the one in the animal mask. Three standing a mere twenty feet from her – some archery – one about to shoot. Another casually relieving himself against another nearby tree. Her death so trivial.

The bowstring was drawn back. He would be too late.

As he erupted across the sandy clearing he roared out the first battle cry that came to mind – God for England and Queen Bess! – and the foreignness of the words had its effect. The archer about to shoot the girl turned round and stared, mouth agape, bowstring slackening in his fingers. Other men around the camp lurched to their feet, unarmed, puzzled, and took in this lunatic on a galloping horse, sword swinging. It made no sense. No one attacked the Oprichnina. Ever. They were unassailable. Then behind the lunatic – loosely masked, they now saw, like a bandit – came more of them. This was serious. They began to reach for weapons.

The masked lunatic, howling his strange execrations, swung his sword sharply and it cut straight across the throat of a tall thin fellow stepping forward to halt him with a pike. He collapsed like a puppet and the lunatic rode over him.

Nicholas rode straight for the girl. The archer hadn't even the presence of mind to turn his arrow, already nocked, against him.

'Shoot him down, you idiot!' one of the mounted men was screaming, pulling his own horse around, reaching for his own sword. But he wore no sword. None of them did. They were in camp, there had been no need. They pulled back, one or two of them even broke away and took cover in the trees, and then Nicholas descended on the paralysed archer, sword swirling, and took off the top of his head. The archer turned, dazed, and dropped his bow and fell. He lay there, watching the fight, life ebbing slowly. He felt no pain. He rolled over, clawing at the ground, and the last thing he saw was the bound girl looking down at him. Her face was quite expressionless. He thought that was how the Angel would look on Judgement Day. And then he died.

The knights raced after the madcap Ingoldsby. Four horsemen together had closed in around him, unarmed as they were. One used a branch to fend off his swordcuts, and another hefty fellow seized him round the waist and took them both to the ground. Nicholas lay dazed, the sword gone from his right hand, the weight of the brute upon him, his breath hot and foul. Then he saw the flash of a dagger. Not even time to grab a handful of dust ... He craned up and bit the brute on his fat, pustular nose. He howled and rose up. A second's grace. Then the brute stabbed down with his dagger, eyes closed in pain, and the blade went into the earth an inch from Nicholas's side. Nicholas slammed his arm into the outside of the brute's elbow joint and he howled again, letting go off the dagger. Nicholas turned his head, grabbed the dagger by the hilt, pulled it free and stuck it in his assailant's side. Well-padded, not enough. He stabbed and stabbed again, unable to see, trying to find some vital organ. Wet sides. The fellow's hands at his throat, gargling in his face. Then he jerked and the strength went from him. Nicholas shoved him off in disgust, rolled in the dust and came to his feet, backing into the edge of the forest, bloody dagger extended before him, trying to take it all in.

It was done. In that short time, half of the black troop had been killed. The other half had jumped on unreined and unsaddled horses and fled into the trees. The Cossacks were hunting them like deer. It was imperative that none escaped.

He swiped the sweat from his forehead and blinked and looked down at his hands, his side. Drenched in blood – but whose? He knew of old that even lethal wounds could hurt barely at all. He moved carefully, bent double, stood upright again, leaned left, right, a strange ritual. No, nothing. His worst injury was a bruised arse where he fell from his horse with the brute on top of him. The patient beast stood nearby, waiting for him. Christ, he was lucky, again. Time to thank Him later.

He stepped swiftly over to the girl and sliced through her bonds. She stared ahead, still expressionless. He glanced down. No sign of blood. The only injury, the arrow stuck in her shoulder. The last bond cut, she fell forward into his arms. At a range of twenty feet, the arrowhead had passed almost through her slim shoulder. He could see the dark metal protruding under the skin, just above her shoulder-blade, like some foul boil. It would be best to break off the shaft and push the arrowhead on out. Work for Stanley. All Knights of St John were expert physicians, and Stanley as deft and gentle a battlefield surgeon as any he'd ever seen.

He bore her over to one of the ruined cottages and found a clean enough blanket and laid her down and went to find Stanley. Her eyes followed him as he left her.

'I will find you help,' he said. 'Rest awhile.'

She said nothing.

Already the Cossacks were dragging the corpses of the hated Oprichnina, their tents, gear, everything into the centre of the clearing and piling them onto a heap of dry, resinous pine brushwood. No fewer than four of the thugs they slung onto the pile wore the sign of 'Stenka's cross' on their torsos: one swordcut across, one down.

They piled more on top. They would burn everything, leaving nothing of these wretches' earthly remains but a smoking black pit. 'After all,' explained Chvedar, 'their souls are gone to a smoking black pit for all eternity – why not their corrupted bodies likewise?'

After some time the other Cossacks returned from their pursuit through the forest, bringing back a sack of severed heads.

'How many?' demanded Yakublev, seizing the sack and glancing within. 'Half a dozen. Curse them.'

'They are cunning,' said Ivan Koltzo. 'We can track them, but they have already headed back to the City ... the outskirts ... we could pursue no further.'

Stanley lowered his head, settled his hands on his pommel, breathed. This was bad. Smith too was turning over in his mind just what they had done. Attacked and slaughtered the Czar's own elite soldiery, a day's ride from Moscow. Clever. And now they were about to ride into Moscow themselves, and bid good day! Smith glanced left and saw the proximate cause of their troubles now running over to them. Ingoldsby. All his fault. Hectic of complexion, bright-eyed, his father's son, reckless dreamer, chivalrous to women as a storybook knight, though no celibate. Yet Smith almost smiled, against his will. He could not blame him. Such absurd gallantry as this Ingoldsby's, against impossible odds and in the very face of death, was just what the Knights of St John lived for.

And he was covered in blood.

'From your vigour I would guess that is not your blood there, Brother Nicholas.'

He shook his head. 'The man I killed. It was ugly.' Then he realised they were all looking at him pointedly. He flushed, tried to say sorry for his impetuosity, mouth working, and failed. Stanley saw it too and grinned. He understood precisely.

'No, you're not sorry,' he said, cuffing him. 'Nor I. It was the least they deserved. But I have to say, Ingoldsby, I really don't think you will ever make a very subtle ambassador for the Court of St James. And we are now in quite a predicament.'

'We're in a heap of shit,' said Hodge. 'We're right down in Beelzebub's own privy.'

Nicholas looked rueful. Then he told them the wounded girl lay in yonder cottage and needed Stanley's attention. The knight dismounted and strode over to her at once. Nicholas turned to Ivan Koltzo. 'One other thing. Was there a rider you hunted who wore a wooden animal mask – or had it tied to his saddle maybe?'

Ivan Koltzo nodded. 'Their captain. And it was our brother Dmitri who rode against him, but his horse stumbled as he came alongside and this fellow thrust him clean through and our brother Dmitri died. The rider escaped. A true swordsman, and perhaps a nobleman too.'

'Noble?' said Nicholas. And laughed.

He went and watched Stanley work. It was always a good thing to see. His huge gentle hands turning her, touching the arrowhead through the stretched and reddening skin, murmuring to her. Of course she wanted to die, but this red-cheeked, flaxen-haired giant of a man was a comfort to her, she could not deny. He said they could give her brandy but alas they had no opium.

She said, 'Do it. Bearing my child hurt more.'

'Where is your man? Your child?'

Her eyes shone with tears and she turned her head away to the blackened cottage wall.

The devils.

He sent Nicholas to order men to bring in wild garlic, fresh streamwater, boil more water and to dig down below the sandy soil of the heath and find two good handfuls of dense clay. Boil the garlic lightly then boil the clay in the water and bring all to him immediately. And any spiders' webs they found, clean of flies. The silk was perfect for staunching wounds.

Nicholas ran and gave the orders and returned.

The knight held brandy to her lips. At first she refused, as if wanting to suffer the more, but he forced the neck of the flask between her lips, the masterful physician who knew best what his patient needed, and made her drink. Then he slid his right hand under her shoulder, raising it a few inches off the blanket, and took hold of the arrow shaft very lightly in his left hand.

'Now,' he said. 'Shout when I shout. Don't scream, shout. Bawl. Do not feel pain, feel anger.' And a mere second later he roared out over her like an enraged bear, she raised her head and bellowed all her grief and rage to the black burnt rafters, and simultaneously he gripped the shaft hard and thrust it down smoothly through the back of her shoulder. The arrowhead emerged in a gout of dark blood. She continued to roar in her pain, but feeling more anger than pain as he had said. He propped his knee under her shoulder, and then in a blur of speed and astonishing deftness that Nicholas had witnessed so many times before, he gripped the remaining shaft in both hands, clenched side by side, snapped off the flight in his left hand, plucked loose splinters from the break, gripped the arrowhead beneath her once more and pulled it clean. Glanced at it and flung it away. He rolled the girl onto her side, wound uppermost.

The steaming pots he asked for were brought and set down beside him, and he packed a hot compress of the dark green leaves on both sides of the wound, holding her powerfully so that she did not flinch under its touch. He held it there for many minutes, though his arm must ache, and then drew it away. The wound still oozed blood. He applied another compress, then another, repeating the process eight times in all until he judged the wound had bled out most of its poison and begun to clot. Then he applied the spiders' webs they had collected, and another thin layer of wild garlic leaves, and finally the hot clay, smoothing it over. It dried to a firm crust in moments. At last he was satisfied and sat back.

'That will do,' he said. 'You must keep very still. Lie on that side and sleep now. Do not roll over. Nick – give her water to drink.'

Nicholas held a flask of fresh water to her lips and she drank a little. She never spoke another word and her eyes remained so indifferent it frightened him.

20

It was a grim place to stay the night but they decided they must. Most of the Cossacks slept out on the heathland some way away, but a few kept to the ruined village, including the four Englishmen. Stanley wanted to stay near the girl.

Stenka shared his brandy with Nicholas, watching a red sun go down through the darkening pines. Then he took back his flask again and eyed him. 'Fools die,' he said abruptly. 'We Cossacks have many good sayings, but the briefest and best is, "Fools die." You were a fool today.'

Nicholas burped. 'Everyone dies. And I do what I choose, even in your country.'

Stenka grinned and clapped him on the back. 'So best to die nobly, a noble fool, for the life and honour of some peasant slut? Ach, we'll make a Cossack of you yet! Sometimes I like a fool!' And to Nicholas's embarrassment, Stenka Timofeivitch suddenly embraced him and planted a kiss on each cheek. 'Young Englishman, I salute you!'

Stanley fell asleep, sitting propped against the burnt wall of the cottage, and when he awoke at dawn the girl was gone. He and Nicholas and Hodge ran into the forest, calling. It was Nicholas who found her, swinging from a tree. She had hanged herself in the night. And – the cruel, the laughing Fates of the world, those old hags – she had hanged herself with the very rope Nicholas took down from the tree before, the rope of the Oprichnik. He took her down and laid her on the ground and knelt and wept. Stanley wept also, and thumped the ground in rage.

Later they burnt the rope and dug a grave and buried her and put a cross at the head of the grave and said a prayer over her. Even Stenka, standing beside the sorry spot with his sword drawn as if ready for vengeance, tip to the ground, bowed his head and wept. It was no shame for a Cossack to weep at such a thing. It was as if the silent nameless girl, the young mother, had been a symbol of something they had all lost. Lost innocence, perhaps. Only a few years before she had still been a little girl running through the forest, wondering at it all, all life before her. And she had grown up and married and lived to see her man and her child slain before her eyes, and had killed herself in grief.

The priests said that such suicides could not enter Heaven. But Stenka thought, If God is just, as they say, she will enter Heaven, as surely as any saint. He saw a white bird taking flight for the country of Heaven, the girl healed and reunited with her parents and her man and her child. Surely it must be true. If God was just, if the world was not a mere idiot's tale and a bloody charnelhouse, surely better must come hereafter.

They rode on that last morning until midday, and then the main body of the Cossacks set up camp on a thinly wooded heath some five miles from the town, eyed by suspicious villagers. Messengers were already riding to the city in warning. Only a small party would go on from here: the four Englishmen, Stenka, and Andriushko. The two Cossacks dressed down specially for the occasion, amid much grumbling. They wore clean white shirts that covered up their battle scars and Stenka said sourly that he would try to look civilized. 'Like a fat city-dwelling burgher with a wife like Tamburlane,' he said.

As they were about to ride out, there was a hubbub in the camp and then Yakublev trotted hurriedly over to them, as sombre as they had ever seen him.

'Brothers, make haste. Impress upon the Czar Ivan that it is coming. It is no rumour.' He looked about him. 'A party of riders has arrived in the camp, distant kinsmen. They say the Tatar host has crossed the Oka river to the east. They are maybe three or four days from Moscow.'

'Three days!'

'Let me talk to them!' cried Smith, kicking his horse.

'No need,' said Yakublev with stentorian firmness. 'It is as they say. The Tatar host is three or four days off, and as we have always feared, their numbers are beyond counting. Our kinsmen reckoned at least fifty thousand. They also saw siege cannon, ox-carts groaning with good supplies and powder – and tall men marching in good order. Too good order for Tatars.'

'Janizaries,' said Smith.

Yakublev inclined his head. 'Get you to Moscow. We Cossacks are committed to this now, doomed though we are, and every moment counts.'

And so they galloped out, and came to Holy Mother Moscow.

At first sight over a flat plain, Nicholas's thought was, This is a city we can defend.

There were outlying houses, a river, strong stone walls, and then they came to mighty wooden gates, standing wide open, and were admitted with little delay.

'Have you heard of the coming of the Tatars?' Stanley asked of the guards.

One shrugged. 'The Tatars are always coming.'

'This time in great numbers, and in earnest.'

The guard looked at him blankly, as if he didn't want to hear.

Riding on in, Stanley glanced back and all around. The gates were sturdy enough, but there was no sign of stones or timbers for bulking anywhere to hand.

They trotted up narrow streets, among wooden houses, some with elaborately carved doors and eaves and gable ends. Hurried as they were, Nicholas took in hastening people, the flame of oil lanthorns in dark taverns, pretty maids with fair hair and high cheekbones, gold cupolas on the skyline – and a faint atmosphere of sullen oppression.

This grew heavier when Andriushko reined in his horse and glared down a dark alleyway to the right.

'What is it?'

'Down there,' said the Cossack, 'was where I was almost whipped to death by four of the Oprichnina. Ah, happy memories.'

They rode silently across a wide square busy with market day, where Manchu and Persian merchants traded from fringed stalls. They saw suntanned warriors in silk shirts and furs, blind bandura players with hanging scalplocks, a troupe of Polish actors performing a miracle play, Finnish minstrels singing their ancient myths of Maria the White Swan-Girl and Baba Yaga. Smith and Stanley looked grimmer by the moment ... This was no city readying for attack.

'Maybe Czar Ivan has paid off the Tatars already,' murmured Nicholas, 'or has the gold for it.'

Stanley shook his head. 'Do not even mention his name in public. Nobody dares.'

They took directions for the English House, and were greeted formally and politely by a Thomas Waverley, and an older Thomas Southam, and Robert Greene: sober merchants and embassy men, determinedly neutral, interested only in peace and trade. The last men to confide in that they had just yesterday slaughtered a party of the Czar's Oprichnina. But another enemy was coming.

The merchants invited them to drink, to dine with them, but they brushed them off in their haste. They must speak first. Waverley winced with displeasure.

'A Tatar army is three days off,' said Stanley. 'They mean to burn Moscow to the ground. Have you not heard?'

The English merchants' attitude was evidently that of the city in general. Waverley said, 'Tatar raiders are always coming. There is endless threat and bargaining. The Imperial coffers are vast, the wealth of this country is already immense. The barbarians will be paid off and ride home. Do not excite yourselves. You have come on Royal business, we hear?'

'I tell you,' said Stanley, his voice rising, 'this is no ordinary raid, this is a full-scale invasion. They will destroy Moscow.'

'Moscow is their pot of gold, their paymaster,' put in Robert Greene. 'Why would they destroy it?'

'And how do you know this?' said Waverley. 'Have you seen this great army yourselves?'

Damn their complacency. 'We have not,' admitted Stanley, 'but we have good report of it.'

'Rumours, conjecture, exaggeration. All part of the negotiations, in fact.'

'And we know the Ottoman Court is involved too. It is far larger than an ordinary Tatar raid. Turkey wants back Astrakhan, command of the Black and the Caspian Sea. It fears the rise of this new Russia to the north.'

Waverley looked ironic, amused. 'You have heard this from the Grand Sultan himself? You have dined with him lately, perhaps?'

Stanley bit his tongue. Hell and damnation. It would be better not to tell these merchantmen everything. They were not untrustworthy, but their view of the world was limited indeed – like a money-grubbing mole's.

Smith blurted out, 'Can the city not at least prepare for a possible attack? Even if it does succeed in paying them off? Surely the Imperial Court must be aware of an army approaching in such numbers?'

Waverley said smoothly, 'You must understand that this is a vast country, no England. His Imperial Majesty's intelligence network, his Oprichnina—'

'That's his intelligence network?' said Nicholas. Waverley raised an eyebrow at such rude passion. Stanley laid his hand on Nicholas's arm.

'The Oprichnina,' continued Waverley, 'are not perhaps as sophisticated as my Lord Cecil's in England. There is, if it is not undiplomatic to say so, a great deal of ignorance in this country, of what is what, and indeed of who knows what. Often it seems nobody knows anything. Nobody even knows what nobody knows.'

Hodge harrumphed. 'You may be speaking good English now, but that sounds like Russian, or double Dutch. Not plain sense.'

Waverley eyed him. 'Many people feel it is better to know nothing, to say nothing, and to remain as unobtrusive as possible.'

He added that it was well known the Russian defensive line lay perilously close to Moscow, stretching between Nizhni Novgorod and Tula, and it was often pierced by Tatar raiding parties. He spoke eloquently and soothingly of how they followed the black roads and the secret trails over the steppe, camping in birchwood clearings, no more than ten or twenty miles from Moscow and yet often their approach still unknown or unreported in this immense, thinly peopled country.

'Aye,' said Smith sharply. 'In fact only a day's ride away camps a Cossack force of some three thousand.'

Waverley paled slightly. 'Cossacks?'

'Loyal allies,' said Smith. 'We rode in with them. They come to fight for Moscow.'

'Cossacks,' repeated Waverley. 'This could be merely escalating hostilities. The Cossacks and the Tatars are deadly enemies.'

Stenka finally snapped. 'We know they are deadly enemies!' he roared at the quailing merchants, and gesturing at Andriushko by his side, 'We two are Cossacks! And that's why we make such damned good Tatar-killers! That's why these English brought us here, you whey-faced, pigeon-livered, ducat-counting cotquean!'

Stanley stepped in front of the red-faced chieftain. 'Our pardon, gentlemen, it has been a long journey and we are weary. A glass of wine, perhaps, would restore us all.'

'Wine might only inflame your passions more,' said Waverley coldly.

Stanley smiled. 'And then perhaps, if you might introduce us at Court.'

'Court?' echoed Waverley. He looked them over as if inspecting bedlam beggars. 'The Imperial Court?'

Nicholas spoke up. 'We are under direct command of Her Majesty Queen Elizabeth, and we come bearing gifts for Czar Ivan.'

'Gifts? Ah!' Waverley relaxed a little. Gifts, overtures of friendly intent, better trade agreements … and Her Majesty. 'Yes indeed. Then after you have washed and dressed afresh, perhaps, we may go to the Court. But,' he added, 'an audience with the Czar can take time to obtain. Days, sometimes.'

In three days it would be too late. But for once they all managed to restrain themselves and obsequiously bowed their heads.

They washed, shaved, dressed in fine clean clothes laid out for them in their guest chambers, and ate a hurried meal. Black ryebread and thinly sliced mutton. Nicholas could see Hodge about to comment, so he got in first. 'Not as good as Shropshire mutton.'

Hodge harrumphed. He always commented unfavourably on foreign food.

A maidservant came in with more bread, face modestly lowered, dark curled hair worn long over the shoulders, bright young eyes and rosy cheeks, her slim figure evident in a plain green dress, matched with some rather dainty shoes. Nicholas stared. Something within him lurched.

'Eat,' said Smith gruffly, jabbing him. 'Concentrate. No time for that now.'

'Is she – is she a maidservant?' he whispered.

Smith chewed and swallowed. 'Daughter of the house. One of Waverley's own, I think.'

'They have their families here?'

'Some of them. This is the English House, a little square of English soil, in law.'

'Don't they know the danger they're in? Why haven't they sent them away?'

Smith shrugged. 'Eat. Things to do.'

He glanced back at the girl as she left the room again. She reminded him of someone, and it filled him with fear more than pleasure. She reminded him of Maddalena, his first love, on Malta.

After their brief meal, they were indeed introduced to merchants' families. There was a rather blowsy, flaxen-haired Mistress Ann Southam, not at all what you would expect, and a shrewish Mistress Greene, and three children of the Greene family, Jane, eleven, Robert, nine, and Cecily, five. Thomas Waverley had lost his wife to a fever some years ago, but he had a daughter of seventeen years, raised by her beloved nurse. Slender, bright-eyed, in a plain green dress. She curtsied, blushing. Her name was Rebecca.

21

The two Cossacks agreed it would be better for them to remain at the English House for now, so Thomas Waverley conducted the other four out into the streets, and towards the towering dark red walls of the city within a city called the Kremlin: the Fortress.

They passed by Imperial Guards in white brocade trimmed with fur, holding long silvered axes, standing under banners of the black two-headed eagle, previously of Byzantium and before that of Ancient Persia. Enquiry after enquiry of palace guard and seneschal led them at last to the west door of one of the Kremlin's magnificent cupola-topped churches. It was now late afternoon, and within, a choir was singing.

'His Excellency is at worship,' said their guide in hushed tones. 'Please follow me.'

Ivan was known to be devout.

They entered into a church as vast and dark as a cave, and took their seats amid a congregation of elaborately dressed ladies and noblemen who remained rigid, not one turning to look at them. When his eyes became accustomed to the dimly candlelit interior of the church, Nicholas's eyes began to make out magnificent coloured frescoes of white-bearded saints, blazing golden icons, distant gleams of lanterns through a forest of pillars reaching skywards, like low stars seen through trees at night, and the air was filled with intoxicating incense and the hot smoky oil of gleaming brass lamps. The music of the choir was powerful and profound. As a boy he had often heard the choir sing in the abbey church in Shrewsbury, but it was nothing like this. His soul stirred. He began to see this was a country of great beauty and depth, as well as great fear and wildness.

Finally he saw that before the choir, with his back to the congregation, there stood not a black-robed priest of the Orthodox Church, as might be expected, but a tall, thin figure in a long, elaborate robe, dark midnight blue but covered with gold embroideries. Nicholas could only glimpse his face sidelong when he turned: high cheekbones, sunken cheeks, a long straggling beard, reddish but shot through with grey, for all the world like some old storybook wizard, some woodcut of Merlin himself. This bizarre figure was conducting the choir with a long black baton.

The hymn came to an end and a priest took up reciting the liturgy in Old Slavonic. The figure before the choir turned round. Immediately all the assembled noblemen and women bowed their heads so as not to look directly at him, but Nicholas continued to spy from beneath lowered eyelids. There was something chilling, even horrifying in that haunted face.

No, he was not old, no more than his mid-thirties perhaps, yet already his expression was one of haggard gloom. His skin seemed grey and wrinkled, his eyes deep-set and brooding, the only light in them one of quick suspicion as he looked out over his assembled nobles. His hair was already scanty, his lips thin and clenched, his brow deep-furrowed, and though tall and bony and strong-looking, he was also stoop-shouldered and hollow-chested. And then Nicholas realised that Czar Ivan IV Vasil'evich – for it could only be him – had not been conducting the choir with a long baton. It was a spear.

For a moment he wondered if, had one of the choristers sung a wrong note, he would have been instantly impaled. But he dismissed the idea as an absurd fantasy.

Later on, he would not be so sure.

The church service lasted for two hours. Smith stamped his feet as they stood for yet another psalm, impatient as a bull in the stall. Finally it came to an end, and the Czar with a long retinue swept from the church and vanished.

Stanley seized their guide. 'We must speak with the Czar in haste. We have urgent news of the movement of Tatars. For God's sake, man, we cannot wait!'

The guide looked troubled and disapproving. He detached himself. 'I will see what can be done. There are many levels of court etiquette ...'

Smith raised his face to the high iconostasis and closed his eyes and prayed to St John himself.

St John must have heard his prayer. Three hours later they were being ushered into an antechamber, then another more grand, servants carrying the boxes and crates that they had brought so far over sea and steppe. Only Nicholas himself carried a gift personally, the miniature of the Queen, discreetly covered in a white linen cloth.

He took in a palace of armour and spears on the walls, daggers glittering with jewels, Polish and Tatar cavalry sabres captured in the wars. Silent chamberlains in ermine pelts, a courtyard with two falconers, one with a hooded hawk, the other with a giant Berkut eagle used for hunting wolves. Cabinets of brilliant deep red and blue Venetian glass, silver goblets and crested gold plate on crude trestle tables, silk pillows on rough-hewn benches, priceless cloth-of-gold tapestries nailed to bare wooden walls. Savagery and splendour. Wealth had only just come to this country; and civilized conduct not yet.

At last they came into the most magnificent chamber of all: magnificent yet oppressive, with a low, heavy, gilded ceiling, blood-red walls and massive squat pillars similarly painted in diagonal bands of red and gold. The sense of danger and oppression was only emphasized by both sides of the blood-red chamber being lined with heavily armoured men, standing as motionless as iron statues, holding long gleaming halberds. The thick rugs beneath their feet, too, were all blood red. If any visitors did displease the Czar and had to be cut down where they stood, reflected Nicholas with grim humour, at least it wouldn't leave any difficult stains.

And on a gilded throne at the back of the chamber sat the gaunt figure they had seen before. He now wore an ankle-length golden dalmatic, with gold slippers beneath – too much gold – and sat so still and hieratic, eyes fixed unblinking upon them, he might have been a carven idol.

A servant led them grovelling forward, bent almost double. The four walked upright, but at least kept their eyes lowered.

Another court official stepped forward and declared in ringing tones, 'Ivan the High Prince, Caesar Augustus, by God's grace Emperor of all Russia, Grand Duke of Vladimir, Moscow and Novgorod, King of Kazan ...'

Caesar Augustus? Nicholas was thinking, as the list went on and on. How does that work?

Finally the recitation of Ivan's titles ended, and the official waved his hand over the new arrivals.

'Visitors from the Court of England, Your Excellency. They have brought gifts.'

The glowering idol on his gilded throne remained terrifyingly still. It was indeed unnerving, thought Nicholas. He had stood before Elizabeth herself, one of the most formidable rulers in all Christendom – but this was worse. Elizabeth did not deliberately try to create an atmosphere of cold fear. Yet though from his deeds, and those of his barbaric servants, Nicholas could already class him as an evil man, it was also true that like all leaders of men, all kings and captains he had known, Ivan IV Vasil'evich possessed a damnable charisma.

He remained still, silent and expressionless as the gifts were presented: the porcelains, the linens and fine stuffs, the lengths of creamy Bruges lace. Hodge was getting annoyed. After all they'd been through an' all. He wanted to bow and tug his forelock and say sarcastically, So glad they please you, Your Majesty.

Bloody Czars.

At last the gifts were all displayed and then taken away and the court official raised an eyebrow at Nicholas. He stepped forward and unveiled the exquisite miniature of the Queen, a small oval of Her Majesty against a dark background, her pearls and pale skin gleaming.

'An image of my beloved Queen, Your Excellency. Queen Elizabeth of England.'

At once the idol came alive. Ivan leaned forward and snatched it from Nicholas as eagerly as a child. He surveyed it with bright eyes.

'This is she?' His voice was low, strained, hoarse.

'It is, Your Excellency.'

'And it is true to life?'

Nicholas said evenly, 'It is.'

To his astonishment he said, 'You are her cousin?'

'I? No, no, I am no royalty, I am but a baronet, Sir Nicholas Ingoldsby, her loyal servant.'

'A nobleman?'

'Not a lord, no, but a, a ...' He did not know the Russian.

Ivan cried, 'A boyar! An English boyar!' He leaned forward, dark eyes burning and fixed on Nicholas. Already he could sense this Ivan's furious energy, his wild and unpredictable changes of mood, his crackling power. 'Tell me – step closer, step closer, you please me already, Englishman, your gifts and your manner both – tell me, are you as treacherous and disloyal to your Queen as my boyars are to me? Eh?'

'I would lay down my life for my Queen, Excellency. All Englishmen would.'

'I like this England! Are there other Russians in England now?'

'A few merchants, in London. Traders in fur.'

Ivan sat back. All ceremony was gone from him, he even seemed relaxed for a moment. 'If only Russia were more like England,' he murmured. Then he leapt up. 'Tell me your name again.'

Nicholas told him. Ivan could make nothing of it. He roared out, 'Bring me a translation.' A hare-eyed clerk dashed forward and fell to his knees. 'Get up, you drivelling fool, and tell me what his name means.'

The clerk found that Nicholas's father was Sir John, and finally decided, trembling visibly, that in Russian, this Englishman's name would be Prince Nikolas Ivanovitch of the Golden Town.

'Then so I declare you!' said Ivan. 'Your gift is a noble one. Tell me' – and once again this extraordinary figure stepped close to him, a little too close – 'what do you make of our country?'

Stanley willed, Tread very carefully, Brother Nicholas. *Think*.

Nicholas breathed and said, 'I and my companions find it most interesting.'

'Interesting? And vile?'

'Vile? No, Your Excellency, not vile.'

Ivan rubbed his beard, eyes searching the carpet, brooding. 'Vile as a rotting corpse. It is the Lord's affliction for our sins.' He then grasped Nicholas by the arm, his new confidant, and led him aside a little so no one else could hear. Nicholas glanced again at the Czar: that expression, those dark, damned eyes. Yes, horrifying. That was the word. He breathed as slow and deep as he could, to stay calm.

'It all depends on God what your destiny may be,' Ivan was saying softly, musing, distant. His grip on Nicholas's arm like a vice. 'God Himself is not rational, he loves the violent in nature and detests the lukewarm and the Laodicean. Does He not say in Holy Scripture that He will spew the lukewarm out of his mouth? He damns to eternal torment the timorous and calculating. Everywhere in nature you see ferocity rewarded and gentleness savagely punished.'

It was a monologue, the confessional of one accustomed only to speaking, not listening.

'When I was a boy,' said Ivan, laughing a ragged, tortured laugh, 'a happy, innocent child, living in the eternal innocent sunshine of the Kremlin, in my days of innocence and Eden! – I had a little pet bird. One day out of curiosity I held it tight and kissed it and it cheeped merrily and then I pulled a feather out and it squirmed in my hand, and I pulled another and it squirmed more and more ... In the end I cut its belly open ...'

Nicholas exerted all his self-control not to pull away. Ivan was so close to him physically yet so distant, stinking breath and far-off gaze.

'I cut its belly open, wondering all the while if I should be struck down by Heaven for my cruelty. But it never happened. The little bird was in my hands, my power. I cut its belly open and pondered a while and then the little bird died and I threw it out of the window, as many a man and woman has been thrown out of the high windows of the Kremlin to land mortal in the dust below.'

He nodded gravely, looking hard at his new English friend.

'This is the world God in His Wisdom has made. Better to cut the throats of ten thousand innocent men than leave one guilty man alive. To cut out infection, it is wise also to cut out a wide circle of flesh around the wound. Do you understand?'

Nicholas nodded, understanding nothing, desperate only to get away. There was something both deranged and evil here. And this was the man they had come to serve, to fight for if need be. He remembered the words of the man down at the riverside fair. *He is the Devil Incarnate, come to earth to torment men for their sins.*

Abruptly Ivan dropped his arm and took in the audience chamber once more.

'Who are these companions?'

They gave their names. Ivan looked pleased. He liked Englishmen. For now. At least they were not Russians, like his people – and himself.

'You reside at the English House? And you came with Cossacks?'

Even Stanley was momentarily startled.

'Some three thousand Cossacks,' said Ivan, 'camped now not ten miles off?'

So it was in Russia. Nobody knew anything, but more dangerously, nobody knew what anyone else knew either. This Ivan obviously had some spy network, however unreliable. Stanley confirmed it was true about the Cossacks. 'And loyal servants to Your Excellency, every one. They come for the defence of Moscow.'

'They know of a plot against me?'

'The Tatars.'

'The Tatars?' he echoed with disbelief, and again Ivan brooded awhile. They would become accustomed to these long, silent, threatening gulfs in conversation. Then he said, 'These Cossacks are welcome. They must be hungry after so long a journey. We will send them grain.'

Immediately Stanley thought he must send Stenka back with the grain, to warn them to test it on an animal first. Ivan could easily have the whole lot laced with poison.

Ivan sighed and added, in characteristic non sequitur, 'Oh, how my people suffer.'

Stanley seized his chance. 'Yet their suffering will only be magnified, Excellency, if Devlet Giray of the Crimea and the Tatar Host come against you. All that we have heard, even with intelligence from the English House at Constantinople, tells us that they mean wholesale invasion.'

Ivan waved his hand, as if entirely uninterested in this immediate and severe threat to his people. He was still thinking of this Elizabeth. 'The Tatars would not dare,' he said vaguely. 'They would not stand against the might of the New Jerusalem that has already taken Kazan from them, and now Astrakhan. They are mere barbarians of the steppes.' He resumed his place upon his gilded throne and addressed them once more as a High Czar, a distant being of another order. His voice became louder. 'We are a great new Empire, under the protection of Almighty God! My commandments are obeyed from the heights of Caucasus to the Aral Sea, to the red deserts of Samarkand, to Novgorod the Great! They pass over the black roads of the steppe, the black earth of the Don and the Volga like the wind. By my commandment the great bell of Novgorod now hangs in the Ouspensky cathedral, here in the Kremlin, and its tolling protects all who hear it. Those unchristened Tatars would not dream of riding against Moscow of the White Walls. No.' He shook his head violently. 'It is not the Tatars who are a threat to us—'

Stanley took the risk and interrupted. 'We know for a fact the Tatar Army is not far off, with Janizary units too, perhaps a hundred thousand. They have already overrun your frontier garrisons on the River Oka—'

Ivan overran him likewise, not listening. 'It is the people of Russia themselves who threaten us, day and night, without rest. It is those all around us. Look.' He nodded at the guards along the walls, staring blankly ahead; at the court officials, eyes bowed, mouths dry with fear. 'It is they. It is the boyars. It is my own treacherous, cowardly, deceitful, devil-born Russian people. It is they who league with the Tatars and destroy us from within!' Suddenly he was up and pacing and shouting, the change terrifying in its abruptness. 'My ever-treacherous people plot continually against me, they return me evil for goodness, hate for my love ...' He clenched his fists and thumped them against his chest, and Nicholas saw to his astonishment that there were tears in his eyes.

Just as suddenly, he switched off. 'Come,' he said, 'you must be hungry. Let us dine. You shall be my guests of honour.'

Was he quite mad? wondered Nicholas. How did such madmen survive as leaders of nations? Yet they did. Even Caligula, rapist, sodomite, who fornicated with his own sisters in public – even he lasted four years. And Ivan was no Caligula. He was far more cunning.

They processed after him to the banqueting hall.

22

Aware that every word of theirs would be heard and understood, even in English, Stanley spoke with care. 'A most interesting audience.'

'A ruler of great majesty,' said Smith, bitterness veiled.

'Our gift of Her Majesty's portrait in miniature was well received,' said Nicholas. 'Very well received. And he is a most philosophical ruler. A deep thinker.'

'You speak the truth, Prince Nikolas Ivanovitch,' said Stanley gravely. Smith gave a quiet snort. 'Yet there are courts,' continued Stanley in code, 'where to be too well received, to be a favourite of a more unbalanced ruler, is to be in great danger. Better to go unnoticed.'

'Aye,' said Smith grimly. And they had been well noticed.

'You know what I thought at first?' said Hodge. 'Him sitting there at first so grim-faced and unstirring?' Smith should have clapped his hand over Hodge's plain-spoken mouth, but it was too late. 'I thought he looked like my old man on the privy when he can't go.'

Nicholas would have laughed, but he was still chilled, even frightened by the crazed things Ivan had said to him in private. He longed to tell Stanley. But what was the point? None of it made sense. It was just that now, Nicholas felt sure they were in the Court of a truly evil ruler.

They waited, Smith drumming his knife with impatience, nearly an hour before the Czar once more made his entrance, and all bowed.

Now he wore a conical hat in the Persian style, trimmed with black fox fur, a long white gown, and Morocco boots embroidered with pearls. The four Englishman were summoned to sit on the high table with him. Down below sat long tables of boyars, the arrangement something like an Oxford college.

At the end of the high table sat a man slightly apart, in plain dark robes like a cleric, with clever but predatory face, spectacles perched on his lean nose as he peered down short-sightedly at his food. Then he glanced up and caught Nicholas staring at him, and seemed to smile a faint, wintry smile.

'Who's that?' whispered Nicholas.

There was enough noise and clatter now at the table for them to speak to each other without being overheard. Just about.

'That must be Elysius Bomelius, I think,' said Stanley. 'We must tread very carefully around him. He's as clever as he looks. A Dutchman, I have heard, or perhaps a Westphalian – he also trained in England. A lifelong student of alchemy and the magical sciences, the Czar's personal physician, and also, some say, his Poisoner-in-Chief. He has a great hold over the Czar's mind. Ivan believes he can see the future.'

'But only with his specs on,' said Hodge. 'Pass the bread basket.'

Besides humble bread and salt, there were richer dishes: roasted swans, spiced and roasted cranes in saffron, cock pheasant with ginger, pikes' heads with garlic, hare stew with kidneys and ginger; and to drink, plentiful Rhenish wines and malmsey, and also heady Russian liquor, kvass and vodka. Yet it seemed to them a banquet of the insane. Outside in the villages was a tormented and starveling people, and at any moment, Nicholas could imagine a howling and uproar from the streets, growing louder and louder, like an approaching storm. And then the great double doors of the hall bursting open and the Tatars standing there, at their head some huge reincarnation of the spirit of Ghenghiz Khan himself, grinning ferociously, hands on hips, his thick leather belt hung with dozens of skulls of slaughtered Christians ...

But they dined as best they could, and drank likewise. Nicholas's cup emptied frequently. Stanley said, 'That won't help. With the coming storm, you're going to need all your wits about you, not a hangover.'

Nicholas thought back to Malta, to the prickling fear and dread they all felt at the coming of the Turks. But this was worse: less clear-cut, more muddled, their role more uncertain.

A servant brought them four golden cups of a spiced negus. Nicholas reached out for a cup but the servant insisted politely on handing them round one by one.

At last, slow and stately and red-eyed and almost blind drunk, the Czar stood and was led away to his private chambers, where his personal retinue of three blind old storytellers would tell him stories until he fell into a troubled sleep.

A small, dark figure followed him, almost scampering. It was Elysius Bomelius.

The four were reunited with the waiting Thomas Waverley, politely envious of their privileged banquet, and then at the door, a tall, handsome nobleman turned and bowed to them. Dark eyes; dark, burning eyes ...

'Prince Maliuta Skuratov,' he said smoothly. 'You are most welcome, ambassadors of England.'

Nicholas felt a sickening lurch. It was him – was it not? The black rider in the wooden animal mask. He himself had been scruffy and unshaven then, with a beard of many days, and now was clean-shaven once more. And when they rode in on the Oprichnina camp, they had hurriedly tied on face-cloths, thanks to Stanley's timely command. Would this Maliuta Skuratov recognise him? He felt stripped bare. The nobleman's eyes seemed to bore into him.

'You did not find your journey dangerous?' he said softly.

'One or two common thugs and bandits,' said Nicholas before Stanley could intervene. 'Nothing to worry us. We gave them short shrift.'

'And now we are here, safe within the far-famed walls of Moscow,' said Stanley. 'As personal guests of the Czar himself, no man will harm us. Loyal as we are to his cause.'

Maliuta Skuratov's eyes glittered and he smiled, drawing on black gloves of thinnest leather. 'Quite so,' he said. 'Sleep well tonight in the English House. But do post sound guards at your door. We live in uncertain times.'

*

'That was him,' hissed Nicholas as they hurried along the dark streets, led by a linksman with a lantern.

'Quickly, quickly,' said Thomas Waverley, glancing back at them. 'We should not linger out this late.'

Yet Stanley did the opposite. 'All of you, when I drop my right hand, halt.' His hand dropped. Their footsteps fell silent. And somewhere behind them in the darkness, they heard one or two more pattering footsteps before they too halted.

'We are being followed. Walk on quickly now. And I hope you trust your guards, Master Waverley.'

'Of course, of course,' said Waverley. 'Everyone is followed in this city. Do not worry.' He himself looked more worried than any of them.

As they neared the English House, Stanley stopped again and darted into a town garden that had run to seed, the house itself derelict and dark.

'What the devil are you doing, sir?' hissed Waverley.

Stanley appeared to be kneeling amid what was once a herb garden, like a man looking for a lost ring, and then he stood and went over to a large tree and then came back with a bunch of greenery in his hand. 'Picking flowers,' he said brightly. 'Homeward!'

Stenka and Andriushko themselves slept on the floor across the doorways of the English House, much to the merchants' disapproval.

'If you are butchered in your beds tonight,' explained Stenka cheerfully, 'at least it'll be over our dead bodies.'

Thomas Waverley looked pale.

Nicholas dreamt that they were crossing a wide, wide river over the thinnest ice, and under it he could see fires, spears, and roaming wolves in the ice-blue caverns. And the Wolfmaster himself was Ivan, tall and lean and black-robed, eyes burning like fire under the ice, spear in hand, conducting them down deeper and deeper, into a place of burning. And then he awoke out of his troubled dreams. 'Hodge,' he groaned. 'Hodge!'

Hodge woke and lit a candle and raised it and stared at Nicholas's face. He looked deeply shocked. Then Nicholas knew he was really ill.

Hodge went running down the corridor to get Stanley.
Nicholas lay back, feeling like he was dying.

23

He was already half delirious by the time Stanley and Smith and Hodge were around him again, candles being lit, Stanley pulling up a stool.

'That Maliuta Skuratov,' said Stanley urgently, 'did you shake his hand?'

'Can't remember,' mumbled Nicholas, 'don't think.' His tongue felt thick and dry in his mouth, his head hammered, sweat poured from his forehead. Worst of all were the cramps. He felt like a chirurgeon had sliced open his belly, delved in with both hands and was twisting his guts into elaborate knots.

Waverley hovered anxiously behind them. 'Shall we all be poisoned? Is it the plague? Tell me it is not the plague!'

'I think not,' said Stanley through gritted teeth. 'Wake up your kitchens, get me boiling water. Smith. You know what I picked …'

Smith was already out of the door. He returned with the bunch of greenery in a vase which Stanley had mysteriously foraged from the garden earlier. Sprigs of oak leaf, huge horseradish leaves, feathery yarrow …

'Not just fortuitous, I take it?' said Smith.

Stanley shook his head. 'Precautionary.'

A wide-eyed maidservant appeared and Stanley rattled off orders. Were there bilberries or cranberries in the kitchen?

'Cranberries, yes, sir.'

'Smith – to the kitchens. You know what I want.'

Though they were absolute equals as Knights Commander of St

John, Smith obeyed again. If anyone should take charge over a sick man, it was Sir Edward Stanley.

Nicholas groaned again, heaved, arched his back. Stanley's own mouth was dry with anxiety. This was bad. He started forcing him to drink warm water, fresh-boiled and half-cooled. Pint after pint after pint.

'Will he live?' asked Hodge with quiet desperation. 'What can I do?'

'Stay near him is best,' said Stanley. 'Keep talking. He'll hear your voice.'

Smith returned with various steaming bowls and mugs. Stanley mixed up grim-looking green potations that smelt of bitter field herbs and wet woodland, and forced Nicholas to drink again. He gagged, choked – and drank more. He prayed that the astringent tannins of oak leaf, the mysterious healing properties of dark-coloured berries and yarrow leaf would do their work.

Yet still Nicholas struggled – and then his breathing began to worsen, his chest rising and falling in shallow heaves as he desperately tried to suck in air. He could drink no more.

'Do something!' cried Hodge. 'He's going!'

It was Smith then who leaned forward and raised one of Nicholas's eyelids – pupil dilated, as Stanley had already found – but then he raised the other eyelid as well. 'See!'

The other pupil was normal.

'The devil! I think he's been poisoned twice,' said Stanley. 'Hodge, my pannier in my chamber, bring it!'

Hodge was back in seconds, almost tripping in his haste. Stanley rummaged in his pannier for a small leather pouch, explaining as much to himself as to them while he did so. 'A most cunning poisoner. The obvious signs were all of a stomach poison, which could have come from bad meat, bad water, bad luck—'

'But did you see the way the servant handed us out those cups of negus at the end?' said Hodge. 'They meant to get him.'

Stanley stared. 'Damnation, I think you're right, sharp-eyed Hodge. We do have enemies.' He was shaking a yellow powder from the pouch into another cup of warm water and swirling it about. 'Our cranberries and our oak leaf and such have powerful effects against stomach poisoning. But underneath that concentrated rottenness he was dosed with, something else is working too. The devils. It is that which would have killed him.' Stanley was more confident now, praying inwardly. O Saint Luke, the doctor evangelist, and Saint Benedict, patron saint of those who had been poisoned. Let him not die, he prayed. His time is not yet. He is sinful but he is young.

He held the cup to Nicholas's bloodless lips and trickled the liquid into his mouth. 'Drink in between breaths, Brother Nicholas. Drink.'

With great self-mastery, barely conscious of where or who he was, but hearing that deep, reassuring voice, Nicholas raised his burning head off the pillow and swallowed and breathed fast and shallow and swallowed again as he was bid. Every part of him was in pain, his lungs most of all now, burning up – but his mind was blissfully far off from that, in white cloud. He drank more. He was gone.

'What a game of wits it is,' said Stanley.

Hodge looked sour. A game of wits and medical cunning played over his poor shivering sweat-soaked friend's mortal body.

'Worry not, Brother Hodge,' said Stanley. 'We are not heartless, but light-hearted. Can you not hear his breathing steadying already? We are in control now, thanks be to God for the Queen of Antidotes – the rarest herb of the Americas, carried in my pannier day and night.'

'It was snake venom,' said Smith.

'My thinking exactly,' said Stanley. 'Our dear Ingoldsby was poisoned in his stomach, but also by snake venom. Truly devilish. This Elysius Bomelius has my sincere admiration. But now Ingoldsby here has working in him a herb called ipecacuanha. I wonder if our little friend Bomelius knows about this one? Fresh from the New World, the most powerful antivenin our Order of St John has ever seen work.'

'They make us welcome here, don't they?' muttered Hodge. Then suddenly overcome he blurted out, almost in tears, 'Will he be damaged for life in his organs, Stanley?'

'Be not anxious, Brother Hodge. If we have treated him fast enough, there will be no lasting damage. He is young and strong.'

'But why Nick?'

Stanley shook his head. 'Perhaps it was meant for all of us. I do not know. Here, you make him drink.'

Hodge continued to make Nicholas sip on the potion, trickling it in mouthful by mouthful. 'Be strong, Nick,' he said softly all the while. 'Breathe slow and deep, you will mend. And then we'll get that bastard.'

At those words, Nicholas's right hand clamped into a fist and he punched down weakly on the bed. Then they knew he would mend. Stanley laid his head on Nicholas's chest. His heartbeat was returning to normal.

'He'll live then,' said Smith, even more gruff than usual to hide his joy. 'I'm off to bed. Hodge, stay with him.'

Nicholas awoke after daybreak to find Hodge, having been awake by his side until nearly dawn, now fast asleep. He grinned and stood slowly and flexed his limbs. Not bad. He stared at his tongue in the glass. Peculiarly yellow. Could be the poison, could be the cure. He was weak as a kitten, and still abominably thirsty, but all things considered ... not bad.

He leant on the window sill with his brow against the lintel and looked out over the city. Church bells ringing, wood-fires burning, bread baking, shouts from the river, the summer sun coming up warm over the measureless continent to the east, all the way to Cathay ... His heart stirred. In the dusty streets below, people abroad, washing faces and hands at corner pumps, the hung-over drenching their heads from wooden pails at the sides of wells, scolded by the old women for the waste of it. Nicholas grinned. These old Russian babushkas were a fierce tribe.

Two exotic-looking merchants on horseback, a noble lady hidden in a fine sedan chair going by, a horde of children following after a ragged barefoot priest, an old man pulling a camel – a camel? – and then the prettiest gooseherd of a girl he had ever seen in his life, driving before her a good forty cackling snow white geese, herself almost as fair. It would be vulgar to whistle down at her. Who was he, Sir Nicholas Ingoldsby, Bt, or some bricklayer by St-Mary-le-Bow? Yet by God she was pretty. He willed, but she never looked up. He would never see her again nor speak to her, let alone—

Fool. Amorous fool.

Yet it was a peaceful scene. Could an army really be coming? Did it make sense? Surely it was probable the Tatars would simply accept a pay-off and ride back to the Crimea with a few chests of gold?

Then round the corner came an eruption of horsemen, some five or six, and the geese reared up flapping their wings, orange beaks wide and indignant, then scattered, the harassed goosegirl trying to round them up again.

'Hey!' he shouted out. Pointless, he was not even heard.

The six horsemen slewed to halt. Immediately below. At the very door of the English House. And they were well-armed.

Nicholas was already running to shake Hodge awake where he lay on a low campbed – 'Buckle up, we've got visitors' – and then yelling out for Smith and Stanley. His yells were almost drowned by a furious hammering at the door. He seized his sword and ran to the top of the stairs barefoot. In the hall below, Stenka and Andriushko were already on their feet and glaring at the quaking door. But they had no weapons to hand.

Another figure appeared fleetly at Nicholas's side. It was the girl Rebecca in a white nightshift.

'Back to your room,' he snapped.

'I don't take orders from guests in my own house,' she snapped back.

The door was juddering violently.

'Believe me,' said Nicholas. 'We are your best hope now. Not men such as your father—'

'And I'll thank you not to call my father a coward!' Her dark eyes blazed.

He had seen that hot dark look in many a fair face before. Ah, how he loved a maid's fieriness. Such promise and passion in it!

'It is sober merchants and men of business such as my good father who earn the gold which makes England great. Not swaggering, unshaven adventurers like yourself and your companions. Who manufactures your powder, your swords, your armour? Do they fall ripe from trees?'

He grimaced. There was some truth in her answer. But still, that door was about to come in ...

'I am sorry,' he said. 'But really, you should ...'

At that instant, Rebecca's beloved English nurse, old Hannah, appeared in the corridor too, bustling and tutting. 'What are you doing out here in your shift, girl!' she cried. 'Back to your chamber, tut-tut, where is your maiden modesty before strangers? And you, sir, what is this, what is this? Put away that unmannerly naked sword, this is the English House, not a backstreet tavern!'

And then there was Thomas Waverley too, tucking his shirt into his breeches – and Smith and Stanley both racing past them all, swords already drawn, and taking up a fighting stance at the top of the stairs.

'Is there a safe room for you?' demanded Stanley.

'There are extensive cellars,' said Waverley reluctantly, 'well-built, for our wines. But I do not—'

At that instant a panicked servant scurried across the hallway and flung back the bar. The doors crashed open and two or three of the dismounted riders came striding in. They eyed the drawn swords of the men on the stairs, unimpressed. Soldiers, Nicholas surmised at once. Not Oprichnina. Proper soldiers.

'To the Kremlin with you,' said one gruffly, with fine military succinctness. 'The four emissaries. Czar's own orders.'

24

They dressed hurriedly.

'How d'you feel?' said Smith. 'All ready there with your sword drawn. I was impressed, seeing you were nearly dead five hours back.'

'A little frail,' said Nicholas. 'But we Ingoldsbys are made of stern stuff.'

'You're still pale,' said Stanley. 'And we want you looking especially hearty, for the sake of ... the joke. Play the role well, and it will be most amusing if your poisoner is there at the palace to see us this morning. The healthier you look, the greater will be his surprise – and the evidence of his guilt.'

So with some mirth they mashed the last berries and applied a thin layer of juice to his cheeks for colour, and Smith gave him a light slap or two to stir the blood. Nicholas took a step sideways.

'Gently, Brother,' said Stanley.

Smith guffawed.

Nicholas shook his head clear again and looked at himself in the glass. 'Like an Italian catamite,' he muttered.

'No chance,' said Smith. 'Not nearly pretty enough.'

'Aye,' agreed Stanley. 'It'd be a lonesome old sodomite would want any of you.'

'Sometimes,' said Nicholas, 'for Catholic monks, your wit is low indeed.'

Czar Ivan was striding up and down frenetically in a small, shadowed courtyard, nothing like the grandeur of yesterday. He rubbed his long, bony hands.

'Ah, my Englishmen, my Englishmen!' He sounded pleased, and gave absolutely no sign of surprise to see Nicholas. He even clapped him on the back. 'My Prince Nikolas Ivanovitch. It will be a famous victory, and such glory will surely win the heart at last of this Elizabeth of yours, will it not? The marriage will take place in the Ouspenksy Cathedral, conducted by Patriarch Grigoriy himself—'

An elderly, soberly dressed secretary nearby made a movement, as if to prompt him.

'Yes, yes, developments.' He glowered at them all. 'Your Cossacks are at the western gate. They will be needed. The Tatars are coming. They sent emissaries by night, but they have rejected all our offers of peace. They have demanded the return of Astrakhan. The scoundrels! We do not fear them. We will defend Moscow against them with all our iron Russian will. You are no ordinary ambassadors. You fought at Malta and Lepanto. You two,' he nodded at Smith and Stanley, 'are Catholic Knights of the Order of St John.'

They drew breath. No point denying it now.

Ivan went on. 'You are men of sublime military powers. You defeated the Turks at Malta, you will mastermind the defeat of the Tatars at Moscow. Oh this will be a glorious victory! The Tatars ride against us, with Ottoman support it seems clear, for many reasons – for Kazan, for Astrakhan – and also because they now say we are leaguing with Catholic Christendom! Their evil Khan, Devlet Giray, knows of your presence among us.'

Their minds reeled. How ...? Nicholas felt a sensation of sinking ever deeper. How did they know? He wondered about the Sultana Safiye, about the lovely Esperanza Malachi – but he knew in his heart of hearts they would not have betrayed them. Yet did this mean that their presence here in Moscow had triggered the final Tatar attack? No, they knew of the planned obliteration of Moscow long before. Nevertheless ... they were ever more closely entwined now with the fate of this strange, isolated city and its crazed yet cunning ruler.

'God himself has warned me of it,' said Ivan, fixing Smith suddenly with blazing eyes. One of his usual non sequiturs. 'I see the outcome. My wisest counsellor of all' – they guessed he meant

Elysius Bomelius – 'sees it. He swears. No surrender. We will triumph. The Tatars will be stricken with plague within a week, they will die in their thousands below our white walls. We have seen it all in a dream sent by the Lord God of Israel. The Tatars will pay for their cowardly attack on our beloved Oprichnina in the woods some days ago.'

Confusion on confusion.

He raised his eyes piously to heaven. 'How terrible it is to attack the Lord's Anointed! We reign as Czar by the Will of God Almighty and not by the restless will of men. They can only be of Satan. We have read of it in the Book of Isaiah, in the Homilies of St John Chrysostom …'

He returned to earth. 'You will command along with my best generals, Prince Andrew Kurbsky and Prince Michael Vorotinsky. They at least are loyal to me and return my fatherly love. You are now my counsellors. The rest all hate me, and they hate my Oprichnina for their undying loyalty to me.' Then as abruptly as he addressed them, he turned and swept out of the courtyard, calling back only, 'To the walls, English knights! To the walls of Malta once more with you, and victory!'

And so the Czar had changed his mind. They would never understand why. Neither would he.

Before he could hurry after his master, the elderly secretary was detained by Smith's heavy hand.

'What prompted this great change?' he demanded.

The secretary looked nervously after Ivan, vanishing away into darkened state room after state room, and then said quietly, 'News that the Tatars are merely days away. And they do mean to sack us.'

'We told him as much ourselves!'

'Hush, hush!' He looked around nervously.

'But where is the militia?' asked Stanley. 'We have seen nothing.'

'There is a small force under Prince Vorotinsky,' said the secretary. 'But the major part of our army, the Streltsy, is in the west, fighting in the Baltic States.'

Stanley looked down, shaking his head. Ah yes. He had heard of the Streltsy, Ivan's own trained brigade of musketeers. They were not ill thought of. But they were far off, caught up in fighting that interminable and unwinnable war with the Poles and the Livonians.

Ivan wanted to add Baltic sea ports to his growing empire, but Russia was no match for the Poles in arms. Russian soldiers were dying in their thousands there – while to the east, their own capital lay open to the ancient enemy . . .

'And,' said Stanley, 'the Oprichnina?'

The secretary shook his head rapidly. 'The Czar's own bodyguard. Their sacred oath is to protect his life, not the city or the people, not even the priests or the churches. Only the Czar.'

'Come,' said Smith savagely. 'Let us have a good tour of this city. Before it burns.'

They turned away, but Stanley called back, 'Oh, and do give our kindest regards to Dr Elysius Bomelius when you see him.'

The secretary looked puzzled. 'I will.'

'And do assure him that we are all four in the most superlative health, as you can see for yourself. No doubt it was last night's excellent dinner that so fortified us.'

Still more puzzled, the secretary nodded and hurried away.

The high walls were about the only consolation to them. Even at the gates there was no material to hand, no bulking, no neat pyramids of cannonballs or guns for replying to the guns of the enemy, and no gunners to fire them either. It was unreal. They walked empty walls from stone watchtower to wooden watchtower and met not a soul, until they found one old drunk slumped in a corner.

'On your feet, soldier!' Smith shouted in his ear.

He staggered up. He had an incredibly large and inflamed nose. 'No soldier,' he muttered. 'Came up here to escape my brother Yuri. Was going to cut my balls off.'

Smith wondered if the old drunk would make a useful member of a citizen militia. But his eyes were so bleared and cup-shotten he could hardly see, and his hands shook like aspen leaves in a gale.

Smith sighed. 'Clear off the walls and keep off.'

Stanley was looking south and east. Nicholas looked after him.

'What is it?' said Smith.

'We are in such deep pigshit,' said Hodge. 'Can I leave now? I'd quite like a long walk westwards, if only—'

'Nothing I can see,' said Stanley. 'But did I not hear . . . aye, my ears are deafened by years of gunfire and cannonfire. Ingoldsby, tell me you hear drums. Or rather, tell me you don't.'

'I can hear my own stomach bellyaching and rumbling from last night's adventure.'

'I'm not surprised. But is there anything else?'

Nicholas strained to hear. The day was very still and hot, little wind blew. The air very dry, sound did not travel so well. And he didn't want to hear either. Then, on a light breeze … yes, maybe a deep faint drumming as if out of the earth. He strained his eyes. He could see no dust. But behind the shallow hills and over the sandy plains that stretched away from the city, yes – they were coming. He simply nodded, his blood running slow and cold. How could they all survive this? Why was he here, and why now?

'Quickly then,' said Smith. 'There is so much to see and we only have a few hours. Cathedrals and fine buildings are not so magnificent when burned to the ground.'

Finally they came upon a small band of men with a handsomely dressed officer in gleaming breastplate and helmet, and down below in a square, perhaps a couple of hundred city militiamen in cheaper breastplates, red ballooning breeches, carrying long pikes. Among them, they counted up a total of eight muskets.

'Enough to fight the Tatars off for, oh, I should say a good two or three minutes,' said Stanley cheerfully.

The officer stepped up to them briskly, unsmiling, bearded, eyes blue and keen. 'Prince Michael Vorotinsky, commanding officer. You are the English knights?'

They bowed.

'Why have you come here to die?'

It was not a flattering welcome, but a reasonable question.

'We came in embassy from the English court,' said Stanley, 'and from our base in Malta, hearing that our Christian brothers in Russia were to be attacked. But I admit, we did not anticipate a situation so desperate.'

'Desperate?' said Vorotinsky. 'Too optimistic a word.'

They walked on with him. He told them that Moscow's only real strength was its great distance from anywhere else – 'and General Winter. Any invading force that becomes trapped by the onset of our Russian winter is doomed. But it is high summer, and the Tatars know well the winters of Central Asia, and ride fast, and ...' He waved his arms helplessly. 'They will be here in a day or two. We will fight and die, loyal to the end. But Moscow will fall.'

'We will call in the Cossacks,' said Smith. 'We have a day and a night, at least. There are three thousand of them.'

Vorotinsky grimaced. 'Cossacks? What good are they in a siege? They are skirmishers, riders of the steppe. They will never submit to hefting timber and building walls. Might as well teach geese to play chess.'

Stanley smiled. 'Let us see. In any siege, the longer the city can last, the weaker the besiegers become. Moscow has fresh water, grain, many resources, has it not?'

'Aye,' said Vorotinsky. 'Just no army to defend it.'

'And guns?' said Smith. 'For the love of God, show us where your guns are.'

'Guns?' said Vorotinsky with a strange smile. 'Yes, we have great guns. Mighty and powerful as any in the world, I think. Come, I will show you.'

He led them into a strong, square stone tower. The geometry was poor: an incoming cannonball would do far more damage to it than to a modern, Western-style round or octagonal tower. But in time, the knights knew, gunpowder and cannon would put an end to such old stone walls and towers altogether. Castles belonged to the past: proof against arrows, but not against the explosive power of phosphate and saltpetre.

Then another tower, then another. Each had a solid wooden gun platform, and within were sound and impressive guns called The Vixen, The Wolf, The Thunderer – and at last they came to one mighty piece that made them gasp.

'This,' said Vorotinsky, 'is the Czar gun.'

Smith said, 'What weight of ball does it fire? Eighty pounds? A hundred? Can the platform take it? And where the devil are they?'

And Vorotinsky said, 'They are not.'

'You mean ...?'

'Nor are there gunners to work them.'

Their hearts sank.

'Our beloved Czar,' said Vorotinsky, not hiding his contempt, 'was concerned that the Czar gun, and the others, might be turned around.'

'Turned around?'

'To face into the city. To destroy Moscow.'

'Why? By whom? The Tatars?'

'By enemies, of course. Enemies all around. Perhaps even enemies within.'

Stanley rested his head on the cool bronze. So mighty a piece of work – had she ever been fired at all?

Vorotinsky said, in his elliptical way, the way people must speak who fear to be too directly understood by hostile listeners, 'But then consider the Streltsy. Fine musketeers, with fine German muskets nowadays, yet still so badly commanded they lose every battle. The worst enemy of Russia is always Russia. Her only strength is her capacity to see everything destroyed – everything – and be undefeated still.'

Smith was still brooding over the Czar gun. He laid his hand against the side of the enormous barrel. It was a monster as great, even greater, than any of the guns the Ottomans could bring to a siege: those guns known and feared across Christendom, those guns which could bring down the walls of any city they were turned against. Had they not even brought down Constantinople? Guns with names like The Breath of Allah and The Angel of Death. But this Czar gun was as good as any of them, cast by the finest German engineers, and could match if not surpass the quality of anything produced in those vast glowing furnaces on the Bosphorus.

They stared around this square tower, studied the platform it stood on, stomped their boots. Their thoughts were much the same. If this monster ever was brought into use, what size of charge? How much power would it need? Pounds of it with every shot. A good five minutes between every firing. And you'd pray it didn't erupt backwards with such force against its own blocks and its restraining ropes that it burst free – a terrifying image – smashed backwards through the wall and hurtled to the ground. It might even bring down the tower itself, a very dragon of self-destruction. How suitable it was called the Czar gun. But then imagine the shot! A ball of a hundred pounds, a hundred and twenty, hurtling through those Tatar cavalry ranks like some iron thunderbolt of the gods. Curving in long and low, it could slay a score of horsemen in an instant, and send a hundred more flying into each other in terrorized chaos.

But no. It was hopeless. The Czar himself had spiked the Czar gun, and there were no gunners, no powder and no shot with which to use it. It was a magnificent bronze monument to German engineering and nothing else besides.

Prince Michael Vorotinsky bade them farewell and sent them away with one of his aides. They found Stenka and Andriushko and rode out of the western gate of the city for the makeshift Cossack camp.

'Where are outriders, your scouts?' asked Stanley.

The aide said, 'There are none. For fear they will ride away and join with the Tatars, and then betray the city to them.'

'Is that likely?'

The Russian shrugged sullenly. 'Anything is possible now.'

25

They spent the rest of the day overseeing the citizen militia drilling, and beginning to make meagre preparations for siege: setting up water barrels on street corners for fires, laying out piles of wet sheepskin, timber props for the gates. It was pathetically little.

That evening they ate at the English House, a grim and subdued meal. The merchants were quiet, anxious, and somehow resentful. Nicholas could tell that they blamed the new arrivals for this unpleasant turn of events. In a way they were right. The embassy men still could not believe that the army of Devlet Giray would ride in and sack Moscow. They could not understand the urge to destruction when there could be trade and prosperity, and they certainly did not wish to hear about the military preparations for siege. It was all too ridiculous.

The daughter of Thomas Waverley, however, wanted to know. She asked boldly, 'If the Tatars do attack, will the city be able to hold them off?'

Nicholas looked at her. Trying not to feel drawn to her. Just a schoolgirl. Just a young girl who looked a bit like Maddalena, and yes, had admirable spirit. And was, admittedly, pleasing to look at.

'Daughter,' scolded Waverley.

But Stanley waved his hand. 'The walls are strong,' he assured her, 'and there is a civil defence force of several hundred. We also have our friends the Cossacks.'

Thomas Waverley snorted.

Rebecca said, 'But the Tatars number thousands.'

'True,' said Stanley. 'But a force attacking a well-walled city needs to outnumber it by ten or a hundred to one. I believe this city can withstand a long siege, and send the Tatars home empty-handed at the end of summer.'

Waverley banged his goblet down hard. 'That it should come to this. All quite unnecessary.' Already he was planning to open direct negotiations with Devlet Giray, as a neutral representative of the Great Queen of England, and have the English House declared a Tatar protectorate.

'Have you seen many battles?' purred a woman's voice to Nicholas's right, as the conversation continued around them.

Mistress Ann Southam seemed an unlikely wife to her husband, an Englishwoman who behaved more like a Frenchwoman. She wore her dress cut rather low on her full bosom, and talked in a husky, insinuating voice that sounded not quite sincere.

'I, well, some – I am no Knight of St John, just a fellow traveller, on Her Majesty's business.'

'But you have scars on your hands, I see.' She reached out and touched the back of his hand with light fingertips. 'And another on your brow.'

'I've been in a few scrapes. Nothing to boast of, I assure you.'

She looked at him from under lowered eyelids, as if they were already involved in some amusing conspiracy together. He glanced around. The men were now debating animatedly.

'What age are you?' asked Mistress Southam.

'Twenty-five.'

'So young – little more than a boy!' She bit lusciously into a leg of chicken. It was absurd. He did not ask her age, naturally, but she must have been at least ten years his senior, perhaps fifteen. Hard to tell beneath all the white lead and rouge. He downed his glass of red wine, heart thumping. Only last night he had lain at death's door, croaking to be let in and be done with it all. How he had bounced back! And she was striking, in her way. Even if her most attractive feature, perhaps, was what wits and gallants joked was always the most attractive thing in a woman: availability.

'Brother Ingoldsby,' came a voice down the table. It was Stanley. 'Some cool fresh water? Good for the head.'

Nicholas took the ewer, avoiding Stanley's eye.

*

He lay hot and full of wine on his bed and wondered what tomorrow would bring. But the night was not done yet. He heard the latch raised on his chamber door and a figure slipped inside. In the dim moonlight, a full figure in a cream-coloured shift.

'No, really,' he said, rising from his bed, 'this is not right, this will only cause trouble tomorrow ...'

But already she was embracing him, pressing him down onto the bed again, climbing on top of him, kissing him with hungry lips, and all thought of tomorrow left him.

In the morning he opened his chamber door to check the corridor, and all was clear. Ann Southam squeezed past him, breathing hotly in his ear as she went and patting his bottom, and was back in her chamber in a trice. Very practised. Tch, you would have thought she had done this before. But surely not.

He was just closing his door again when he realised a figure was approaching: neat slippered footsteps, girlish gait, the swish of a dress. It was Rebecca. Had she seen? Nicholas could not shut his door, he was strangely paralysed. She looked as proud as a princess just insulted by some unwashed peasant, flushed with indignation, and swept past him with all the shy haughtiness of her seventeen years, not even turning her head. She must have seen.

As she reached the top of the staircase she turned back to him.

'I am so glad to see that you are fully recovered from your sickness, Master Ingoldsby.'

He could think of nothing intelligent to say, and turned dolefully back into his chamber. That old trollop, Mistress Southam. Now look what she had done. Then he despised himself. That old trollop. How dare he? Had he fought her off manfully, had he struggled for his virtue when she embraced him, pressed herself against him, when she planted her red lips on his and pushed him backwards onto his bed? Hardly. And now that lovely maid despised him for a cheap lecher, an indiscriminate fornicator with other men's blowsy wives – which he was. He looked in the silvered glass upon the chamber wall and said sourly to himself, You cock-eyed fool.

It was time to bring in the Cossacks. Though it would cause great tension in the city to have three thousand wild horsemen within the walls, they could no longer delay. They must take the risk and ask for their help.

They rode over a flat terrain, sandy soil, empty farmland and now depopulated villages, wide open to attack by horsemen of the plains. Timber was plentiful here, wooden barricades might be made, enough to break up a charge – but there was no time. All they could hope to do was barricade the city itself.

They found the Cossack camp a few miles off. It was indeed makeshift – as though the horsemen were ready to shift at any moment, with barely a minute's notice. Most had not even set up their tents, but slept on reed mats on the ground under the summer stars. The packhorses were already half laden.

Stanley found Yakublev. The Cossack chieftain listened to him expressionless, brawny arms crossed over his bare chest.

'Timber, props, brushwood for burning, anything you can drag into the city ...' said Stanley, tailing off. Around him the Cossacks sat cross-legged, drinking, smoking clay pipes, chatting. Some called out obscenities. One shouted,

'Find women to cut wood for you! That is women's work, not men's.'

'Though when the topknots come,' sneered another, 'they won't find your brushwood much of a barrier. They just crossed half of Asia!'

That was Petlin. Smith felt his right hand bunch into a fist at the very sound of that wheedling, whining voice, but he controlled himself.

'You will not help us?' he said. 'As you promised you would? Is a Cossack promise so light a thing? Then why in God's name are you still here?'

'We are ready to ride at a moment's notice, have no doubt,' said Yakublev. 'We will not enter that city – it is doomed, I see it burning already, and any that stay in it are doomed with it – but we will not abandon you either. A Cossack promise is for ever, and no man calls Yakublev a promise-breaker. We are your allies still. We may be able to skirmish with the Tatars, in our time-honoured way. We may be able to pick off their outriders, sow confusion, fall on their van—'

'And get yourselves some good loot,' said Smith bitterly.

'Of course,' said Yakublev. 'We are not paid soldiers of the Czar, and Cossacks must eat.'

'And drink,' said Petlin.

'We came to fight for God,' said Yakublev, 'and perhaps for Holy Mother Russia. But we will not throw ourselves onto that funeral pyre that is Moscow. Which is all you are doing here. And you, Stenka, Andriushko, my brothers – surely you are not going back?'

Stenka hung his head. There was silence. Then slowly he walked over and stood beside Yakublev. Andriushko followed him. Stenka's broad cheeks burned with shame and anger. But this was right. 'I am sorry, my English brothers,' he said quietly. 'You know I am no womanish coward. But the Hetman is right. Moscow is but a brand for the burning now. We do not owe it our deaths, and we cannot fight the Tatar from behind high walls. That is not the Cossack way. You should know it too, and you should ride with us. As the saying is, "To fight another day."'

'Think of the Athenians,' said Petlin, the reader. 'I have read it in a book. You know the story. They abandoned their beloved city before the oncoming Persians, and took to their wooden walls, their ships, under the guidance of wise Themistocles.'

'Moscow is not beside the sea, in case you had not noticed,' said Smith. 'And she has no ships.'

'And her leader is no wise Themistocles either,' muttered Stanley.

'Then the people should flee into the countryside!' said Petlin. 'To their forests vaster than the sea itself! In the city they will all burn.'

'We must stay,' said Stanley simply.

Petlin shrugged. But all Stenka's anger rose up at this cruel, one-sided war, this doomed and stupid city. 'Why, for the love of God and his Virgin Mother?' he roared. 'Ride with us! You are my brothers, it hurts my heart! Why do you stay?'

To save the noble new Christian Empire of Russia from being overrun by the Mohammedan horde? That was why they were here officially, but somehow that grandiose explanation now stuck in Stanley's throat. He said, 'I cannot explain. But we must stay.'

Stenka turned to Nicholas. 'You, young English hothead who rode alone against the Oprichnina like a drunken man – you are not of the Knights, I know you are not.'

'I ...' Nicholas couldn't explain either. Men so often did not know their own motives. He could only say, 'If they stay, I stay.'

'And if he stays, I stay,' put in Hodge. 'See how it is? We're stuck to each other like tupping dogs.'

'Ahh!' Stenka gave a great cry and raised his face to the sky. Then after a while he breathed more calmly and shook his head. 'Well, God go with you, and may you by some miracle survive. The Cossacks will still be riding the free steppes, and you may ride with us too again some day.' He turned away and seized his horse and mounted up.

It seemed to be taken as a general signal, for then the rest of Stenka's band mounted up, and Yakublev gave the same signal to the rest. Within five minutes the remainder of the baggage was tied to the packhorses, the fires were stamped out, the empty pots and flasks smashed in the ashes, and with a mighty clattering of hooves, the three thousand Cossacks rode out and were gone.

The four and their sullen aide sat a while longer in silence, watching the dust gradually settle behind the departing host. Then they pulled their mounts around and rode back to the city. Ahead of them, they could see a constant, thin stream of people, refugees from the villages, pouring into the city through the south gate with their paltry belongings on mules and in barrows.

Near the western gate, Hodge jumped down and picked up a dry stick and remounted.

Nicholas looked at him. 'Don't tell me ...'

'Timber, for bulking the gates,' said Hodge. 'Wouldn't want to have had a wasted trip.'

Even Smith laughed. The darker the times, the more desperate the jesting.

Should they report to the Czar? They decided not. What was there to report? When he heard the Cossacks had gone, his wrath would be terrible. Tense and filled with cold dread, they entered the doomed city once more.

Yet what they saw that afternoon began to give them hope. Prince Michael Vorotinsky and his deputy, Prince Andrei Kurbsky, had been busy. They had bulked the gates with mighty four-wheeled ox-carts laden with stonework, simple but effective.

They had organized a citizen militia in each district of the city, and every street that ran under the city walls had its own female troop who were to be ready with buckets and beaters for fires. They had assessed the city's food and fresh-water supplies, and they were very good. Vorotinsky had also rounded up any in the city who had any medical knowledge whatever – there were perilously few, and the Orthodox priests disdained such matters of the body. They certainly would not dream of tending a female patient. But Vorotinsky assembled a few midwives who said they knew how to staunch blood at least, and to comfort the sick, and he found a mendicant friar who knew his herbs, and a few others. He appointed them the Czar's Own Physicians to the People, and the title immediately made them stand a little straighter and take their work more seriously. He established them in a field hospital towards the south of the city, in a granary, scrubbed with saltwater from top to bottom and prepared with pallets and blankets.

'What about the Czar's own physician, this Bomelius?' asked Smith.

Vorotinsky looked sour. 'His talents lie in other directions than curing men, I think.'

'And what about the guns? Can they be brought to fire?'

'We are trying.' He began to ride off again, set on more tasks of organization.

'The Cossacks ...' Stanley cried after him. He had to be told.

Vorotinsky stilled his horse and his shoulders bowed a little. He did not look back at them but only said quietly, 'I know. I saw them ride off as I stood on the walls. But in truth, I never expected different.' And he heeled his horse and rode on.

'This Vorotinsky – another Jean de la Valette?' murmured Stanley.

'There'll never be another Valette,' said Smith.

'Even I'd second that,' said Hodge.

'But still,' said Stanley, 'troubled straits bring out the finest in some men, though the worst in others. Most go through their whole lives mere ordinary citizens, mediocre, plodding, law-abiding – but when great danger threatens, great darkness falls over the kingdom, suddenly they are free to become the heroes they may have been all along.'

'Aye,' said Smith. 'As the saying goes, it takes hard times to make a hero.'

They wondered. Could this Vorotinsky be the saviour of Moscow after all? For the first time they began to have hope, faint hope.

'A hero's someone who gets killed young for a lost cause, isn't it?' said Hodge.

In the late afternoon the indefatigable Vorotinsky found them again and said there was a good crowd of people gathered in the square before the Church of the Ascension.

'I want you to speak to them,' he said.

'Us?' said Stanley. 'We are foreigners, Westerners, Catholics. The ordinary people of Moscow have no great interest in us.'

'But tell them about Malta. That will interest them.'

Then Stanley understood.

He stood on the steps outside the west door of the church, the others alongside him, and addressed the small crowd. Vorotinsky told them to listen well, and to pass on what they had heard.

He spoke to the people calmly and confidently, as leaders should, especially on the eve of a battle with the odds so hard against them. The people listened. They had not heard such calm authority in a long while. The blond giant, he spoke Russian with an accent, but at least he spoke Russian and not some unholy foreign tongue.

These two powerful-looking knights, these Englishmen, they had been at the island of Malta, at that siege a few years back that had already entered folklore, and they had triumphed over far greater numbers of unchristened Turks, in just such circumstances as these now. The people thrilled to hear the story. They had fought at Malta, all four of them on the steps there, defeating an Ottoman army thirty thousand strong when they were but seven or eight hundred. It was a magnificent tale, and the people listened spellbound. They began to murmur among themselves that all things were possible in God. Some even became boisterous.

'We will drive these wretched Tatars into the ground!'

'Death to the Golden Horde!'

'We have defeated them before, we have taken Kazan, we are a great nation, they are but stinking horsemen of the east, what have we to fear? We are true Christians and Russians!'

Then their own noble Prince Michael Vorotinsky spoke to them too. Prince Andrei Kurbsky went over to the north of the city and addressed more gatherings of people likewise. They said, Do not be afraid. Do not fall prey to panic. A siege is hard work, so keep working. Carry water, beat out fires, carry ball and powder to the walls, tend the wounded. The Tatar army is coming for sure, they have rejected all our offers of peace, and yes, they will attack us. This is now certain. It is also true that they come in very great numbers. Yet to defend a strong walled city with far fewer numbers is not impossible. Far from it! You have heard the story of Malta. So now let the story of Moscow ring out as glorious in the annals of the world!

The people erupted in tumultuous cheering.

'I'd like Devlet Giray to hear that,' murmured Stanley.

'Brother,' said Smith. 'Morale is everything. I am truly beginning to have hope.'

'I too. I think we can do this. We can defend this city.'

26

They oversaw more work at the walls for the rest of the day, and at dusk they went back to the English House. Despite the small successes, again an air of foreboding seemed to weigh down more heavily upon the city as night came over them from the east. People bolted their wooden shutters and crossed themselves as they rode by, though many now kept their shutters bolted across their windows all day, living in darkness but for tallow candles and rushlights. As if that would be their defence against the Horsemen of the East.

'I cannot believe there are still no outriders permitted to tell us where the Tatars are,' said Nicholas.

'We'll know soon enough anyway,' said Smith.

When they came into the main hall, Thomas Southam and Robert Greene were talking together with a manservant, the stalwart Edward Ballard, and seeing the four enter, they fell silent. They felt only just about welcome still in this trapped house.

They were eating a light supper in the gloom of the hall, no longer accompanied by the rest of the household. Nicholas had not set eyes upon Mistress Southam since last night, and was rather relieved.

Smith tore his bread apart. 'If we could but use those guns,' he muttered. 'Czar Ivan must relent. Just a few shots ...'

'That would hardly destroy an army of fifty or a hundred thousand,' said Nicholas.

'No need to destroy it,' said Stanley. 'These are Tatars, not Mohammedan fanatics like the Bektasi, nor the highly disciplined ranks of the Ottoman Janizaries, obedient unto death. Like the

Cossacks, these are light horsemen, skirmishers, chancers. Coming before the walls of Moscow, one thing they would not expect, would hate, would be a long protracted siege. That is not the Tatar way.'

Smith added, 'If they saw our guns roaring out in defiance, if they made no progress, brought down not a single gate in, say, the first week, and if the Cossacks were riding about behind them, harrying them, cutting communications ... then they might well pull back. The siege might well be abandoned. That would have been our hope. No need to destroy them, merely dismay them. But for now we have only the citizen militia and their muskets. If Devlet Giray and his khans scent our weakness – or maybe they have already scented it, have snuffed the wind across the steppe that has told them Moscow is weak. Doubtless they know very well that Russia's only professional fighting force, the Streltsy, are in the west, doubtless they have access to all the military intelligence of the Ottomans and know the position of every company in Livonia—'

'So there is little hope after all?' said Hodge. 'Despite all those stirring speeches today?'

Stanley smiled gently. 'There is always a little hope.'

'Why do we stay?'

'We just do. For the doomed people of Moscow, who must defend themselves, and for this English House, a little square of English soil.'

Aye, thought Nicholas. And the people in it. These are our people now. Forget that mad Czar in his gilded palace. He is nothing.

For what are Kings, when regiment is gone,
But perfect shadows in a sunshine day?

He was going to his chamber when the girl appeared at the end of the corridor. She carried a candle in a small dish that illuminated her face from below in a soft light. She looked so beautiful. She could not die.

She came towards him and slowed, her heart beating furiously. She had sent her nurse Hannah down to the evening market to buy fresh berries, so that she might meet him ... like this ...

He stopped in front of her.

'Will we,' she whispered, 'will we be safe?'

He looked at her and his heart burned and he could think of nothing to say, for no, they would not be safe. And with nothing to say, all he could do was take her swiftly in his arms and kiss her, and she returned his kiss. It was all so sudden, it was clumsy, like the first time, and she dropped her dish and candle with a clatter and he put out his foot and rubbed the candle out, and still no one came. They pressed back against the wall, he was hard against her, and she was returning his kisses with such maiden ardour, their breath warm and mingling, and then the door behind them opened and they were in a chamber, her chamber, her white bed, and his hands were roving, her eyes were half-closed, she was gasping—

'No!' she gasped at last.

He stopped. His head cleared. No, indeed. What was he thinking?

She pushed him away and straightened her hair, rearranged her dress, tried to control her breathing. Thrilled and shocked all at once.

'You wrong me, sir,' she said, with a sudden affectation of primness.

He stood and bowed meekly. Now was not the time to argue, and especially not the time to point out that she had seemed just as enthusiastic as him until a moment ago.

She said, her voice still absurdly prim and now trying to sound older than her years as well – how he loved her for it! – 'I suppose at least your future bride can be assured that you are very skilled and experienced in all the arts of love. Even if in the arms of other men's wives.'

'I swear, I … I …' he stammered, aiming to be charming and self-effacing, 'I was an innocent victim of that Mistress Southam, she took of advantage of my youthful innocence. I swear I have never lain in the arms of any other woman in my life, I was a hapless victim of her womanly wiles—'

He was so obviously lying, smiling his charming smile while he spoke, playing some sort of game with her, and he was so handsome too with his fair hair and clean jaw and his mysterious scars of battle, that she thought she ought to slap him at this point.

So she slapped him. He still smiled, then he seized her around her slim waist again and kissed her again, and she held his kiss for

163

a few more rapturous seconds, their lips parting ... Then she pulled away from him.

'Please quit my chamber,' she said. 'I am not like your other women.'

Great God she was not.

He was gone without another word, gallantly and annoyingly obedient, leaving her open-mouthed and with her heart on fire.

The Czar himself had also been busy that day, in his whirlwind and omnipotent thoughts. He had seen great things, and come to great decisions.

Feeling a day of beautiful inwardness and insight come upon him, such as the saints themselves experienced, he had the lamps in his chambers extinguished, the candles snuffed out. He felt the Darkness of God come upon him. Daylight through a single high window of coloured glass was all that illuminated the gaunt figure below, striding back and forth in the visionary gloom. The Czar paced in his palace of shadows. He was discomposed by all this sense of activity in the city, and the arrival of more people flooding in from the country villages round about, with their goats and their chickens, their handcarts and their diseases. Why were they here? What were they plotting? Fleeing, it was said, from the Tatars. Let them flee. It was all most uncleanly. He himself had had two baths already today. And he had heard news of great speeches being made in the squares. What was going on? He did not care for it.

His mind worked furiously, his thoughts trailed down winding and deep-shadowed labyrinths. He did not believe now that this was simply about fighting the Tatars. He, Ivan, and he alone, saw through such deceits. Men were wicked from the day of their birth, there were always black secrets, bloody deeds plotted, mutterings and treachery. Twice he had received requests from Vorotinsky today to allow the guns on the walls to be armed, and also for scouts and outriders to cover the surrounding country. Why? Why? Something was afoot. He had forbidden it. He saw further, through the foul window of appearances to Ultimate Reality.

He gazed hard into a looking-glass.

I am alive yet I am filthy, ugly – a huge sore, a corpse already in the grave, I stink in the nostrils of God, O slay me, my God, that my land may be redeemed by my own precious blood, slay me, my father, my God ...

For it was only by a miracle of God that he was still alive today. He tried to make better sense of it. Clearly there had been treachery for the Tatars to get so close. Then who? His Streltsy were gone to the west, damn them. They must fight. God would help him, yes, God! He stared at a servant hovering terrified before him, holding the ewer of wine he had ordered but two minutes earlier. He struck out with his iron-tipped staff, the servant fell, still clutching the ewer. It smashed on the floor, the servant lay still, the wine was red, blood-red. A sign from God his loving Father.

Blood-red the wine in the hands of the people!

He had always been blessed with second sight, a great and solemn and terrifying gift. So then: let the Blood of the Lamb be shed for the sacrifice. A sickly patient was bled by the physicians for his health. Then – he turned about on the spot, his long robe swirling, arms wide, face raised to Heaven – then let the Russian people on the eve of this great battle be bled, that they may find strength in the battle to come ...

It was all perfectly logical.

He flung open the door and roared for his own physician, who came scuttling. He demanded that special mixed wine that Bomelius made up. Full of special herbs, and strong in alcohol, it brought happiness and visions but also tremendous energy. Bomelius smiled, bowed, scuttled away and returned soon after with a tall decorated cup of the sacred draught. The Czar drained it in three gulps. Bomelius took the cup and vanished.

He dropped his staff, leaned on the wall. His head thumped, his vision swam. Belly sweetly burning. Then his vision slowly cleared again and he felt the potion begin to work. He stood tall, stretched his arms wide once more, breathed in the swimming air, felt his chest expand. He was so tall, a mighty warrior before the Lord. He breathed in more deeply, his head thumped harder, but not painfully, rather with the exhilarating Drumbeat of War. His veins flooded with fire, he could laugh aloud like a madman! He could ride from here to the Great Wall of China and not tire!

Now there was much to do. He clapped his hands together. Had he not become master of the Kremlin at eleven, with not a friend in the world to trust? His childhood one long, trembling, lonely terror in the dark, one unending bloody nightmare of screaming, stabbing and throat-slitting? The leading boyars had even had his beloved horse assassinated! And his beloved sister, who had also been his nurse and suckled him in infancy, imprisoned in a fetid dungeon, her health ruined ever after.

One day he had seen a man killed in his very chamber by two drunken, raging boyars, and thrown out of the window. He had seen girls raped from an early age, but that was nothing. God had kept his eyes pure through it all. He had taken comfort in ancient wisdom, in old manuscripts of the monks in Church Slavonic, which told him of Czar David of Judea, beloved of God, and of the war chariots of Czar Solomon the Wise. He had read of the histories of Byzantium and Greece, they had haunted his dreams, and he had grown cunning and wise in the ways of men. And he had discovered that he was blessed and visionary.

He heard serving women gossip when they were many rooms away, he heard bells under the river at midnight, ghosts weeping among the gravestones in the cathedral, he walked through a pine forest and the trees all bowed down to him. Yes, Moscow would be the Sixth Empire spoken of in the Apocalypse of St John, and the Third Rome. The Mohammedans, those sons of Satan, they had conquered Jerusalem, and then Constantinople, but they would not take Moscow. Here, here, the true Christian Church would take its last stand.

Yes, it was the Apocalypse come down! It was all so clear now. His head was filled with heavenly voices, instructing him, inspiring him. He was the appointed Scourge of God, and his people were to be scourged by the Tatars. He paced, fists clenched, one held to his chin. His veins ran with molten gold, gold as an icon. Let us go forth, yes, let us face the enemy, the enemy in our midst, that is it. Have we not seen? His people feared him, for they knew he was no ordinary Czar, but a visionary and a holy man. Perhaps even the Prophet of God! No mere earthly monarch like that red-haired English slut Elizabeth, he had turned against her, she had not agreed to marry him. He reeled with the insult of it. Did she not recognize who he was, his holiness? May she be ravished by wild bears. She had been toying with him, he knew it, she was interested only in playing him along like a hooked fish, for her sordid trade agreements. Those English envoys ... His heart welled up with sudden hatred for that purse-mouthed miniature they had brought. What did that red-haired slut know of Great Empires, of vision and destiny and the New Jerusalem? She was not Anointed of God, as he was. And he saw now where the danger lay. It lay all around. It lay in this City of Sin, this Moscow. It lay at his door.

It lay at his door.

He snatched up his scabbard where it hung over a chair and drew his sword and flung open the door and glared at the guard standing outside.

The guard fell on his knees. 'Majesty ...'

Ivan raised his sword ready to drive it down into the fellow's neck. The fellow shook and pleaded for mercy.

'Dost thou bow before the Lord's Anointed?' he roared.

'I bow, Your Majesty, I bow!' he cried, scrabbling contemptibly on the ground as if for purchase.

'Dost thou see in my hands the New Jerusalem, Golden like the Sun?'

'I do, Majesty, anything, I am loyal, I would never—'

'Silence!' Ivan lowered his sword. It was hopeless. This dung-dwelling peasant could not be expected to share in the Visions of the Holy. He buckled his scabbard around his long black robe, sheathed his sword, and said, 'Take up the traitor servant in there and cast him into the river with the Gadarene swine. If he is not dead already, see him executed.'

'Majesty, I ...'

And then he was gone. For there was much to do.

27

After dusk, unknown to the knights or their two young companions, a servant went out from the English House with the best horse from the stables. He carried a letter from Thomas Waverley himself, addressed to none other than the Great Khan, Ruler of Asia and Scythia, Lord of the Faithful, His Excellency Devlet Giray. It was a request for safe passage for a party of English neutrals.

The servant was the trusty Edward Ballard, whom the four adventurers had previously seen talking with Southam and Greene. He came to the south gate of the city, bulked and barred, but a small postern gate left clear, barely large enough for a horse to pass through. He dismounted. The guards stood before the gate with pikes planted in the earth, unmoving.

'From the English House,' he said. 'Let me pass.'

'A strange hour to be riding out of the city,' said a voice from the shadows of the guardhouse.

'English business,' said Ballard stoutly. 'We have protection and free passage by Order of the Czar.'

'In time of war,' said the voice, 'all such orders are rescinded. Needs of the State.' And the speaker appeared from the shadows. Ballard felt a chill pass over him. Oh no.

He wore a long black cloak like a Dominican monk, but unlike such a holy man, he wore a long sword at his side, and a dark eye-mask pushed up on his forehead. In his hands he carried a whip.

Oprichnina.

Instinctively, Ballard drew near to his horse, groping for the stirrup, ready to remount.

'Stay!'

He hesitated.

'What are you carrying?'

'Carrying? Nothing.'

The Oprichnik smiled. 'Come, I do not think you are just riding out for a romantic moonlit ride. To appreciate the surrounding country. With the Tatars riding so close?'

A second, taller Oprichnik emerged lazily from the guardhouse, still picking his teeth, and said, 'Unless perhaps you wanted to meet up with the Tatars?'

'I, I ...' His hesitancy was fatal. The Oprichniki were onto it immediately.

'Strip him down,' they ordered. 'Find it.'

They knew as if they could scent it like wolves. They looked at each other and smiled. What bungling amateurs these English must be.

Some streets away, in the very heart of Moscow, a sound like a dim roar went up, and overhead the dark sky began to burn with a dull orange glow, as if a huge bonfire had been lit.

Ballard, forced to his knees and stripped of cloak, doublet, shirt, craned around terrified. What the hell was that? What was happening? The Devil walked abroad tonight in Moscow. And this plan of Waverley's was a stupid mistake, he had always thought so. But what could a servant say?

The second Oprichnik pointed towards the hubbub with his little toothpick. 'You hear the festivities? The Great Cleansing? For it is the Eve, and the city must be cleansed, you know. You have heard of the Bonfire of the Vanities that they had in Italy, in Florence, some years ago? That too was overseen by a monk and a holy man, was it not? Brother Savonarola?'

The other smiled. 'And we too are holy men, we Oprichniki.' He planted his boot in the small of Ballard's back and shoved him down flat in the dust. 'And we too must have a great bonfire. Strip him naked. Everything.'

The guards tore off his breeches and underclouts with added brutality, to show their zeal. They found the letter. The second Oprichnik took it.

'I can only read a little of the barbarous English tongue and

169

the uncouth Roman lettering, but I see that it is in Russian too, and also Turkish. How very learned. And I see the name Devlet Giray here. This letter is a plea from the English House to the Tatar Khan, I see. A plea for mercy?'

Ballard said nothing. The Oprichnik kicked him ferociously in the side and felt the familiar, sharp crack right through his own heavily booted foot. At least one rib, perhaps two or three. It was always a thrill to find how easy it was to break a man's bones inside his body, with just one well-aimed kick. Extraordinary.

Ballard howled and rolled onto his side, clutching his splintered ribs.

'Push him flat again,' ordered the Oprichnik. 'Now, English dog. Tell me you have conspired with the Tatars, or I will kick you in just the same place again. This time you will howl like a hundred wolves. And remember that broken ribs can pierce lungs, and then you die fast.'

'It is so, it is so,' gasped Ballard, his speech going in his terror. 'It is all so, we confess it, Father. Forgive me, forgive me ...'

The Oprichnik rolled the letter up tightly and handed it to one of the guards like a baton. 'Here. You give it back to him, in a safe place.'

The guard guffawed and knelt behind the naked wretch and shoved the letter home. Ballard howled again, weeping more with shame even than the excruciating pain in his ribs.

'Sling him back on his horse,' said the Oprichnik. They untied their own black horses, dogs' heads jouncing from the saddle, and mounted up. 'To the festivities!'

The other leaned down and spoke softly in Ballard's ear where he lay across the horse, his chest in flaming agony. 'For it is for such as you, Tatar-lover, that the festivities are being held.'

'Shall we take the English House too?' said the first.

The second considered and then shook his head. 'All in good time. They are not going anywhere. Let them stew. We will soon be coming for them.' He reflected. 'But go and make sure they know.'

Nicholas and Hodge were standing at the window staring out into the dark Moscow night. A wind had begun to toss the treetops about. There might be a summer storm coming.

And then Hodge said, 'Orange glow there. Seems a funny time to be having a bonfire.'

A horseman came up the street. A dark horseman. Instinctively, Nicholas and Hodge stepped back into the shadows. The horseman reined in before the door below and hammered on it with the butt of his whip. After a time, shutters opened and Thomas Waverley leaned out, demanding to know who disturbed the peace. Then he saw the horseman's dress.

'Bung it up and listen, you dog,' said the Oprichnik. 'Your man is taken, with your letter to Devlet Giray. Your treachery is exposed.'

'Sweet Jesus,' murmured Nicholas.

'The letter, the letter,' babbled Waverley, 'I know of no letter. Come within, enter our house, have some of our—'

The Oprichnik spat on the door. 'You will stay inside. All of you. We will deal with you anon. Any of you found on the streets, your lives are forfeit. Although in truth,' he smiled unpleasantly, 'it were best no foreigners were out on the streets tonight anyway.'

And then he was gone.

Fury erupted in the English House.

'You sent your man out like a lamb to the slaughter!' bellowed Smith. 'Carrying a letter to the enemy Khan in his cloak like a village simpleton! What were you thinking, man? Do you realise what they will do to him now?'

Thomas Waverley babbled some more, about that being no mannerly way to speak to one's host. But it was a little late for that.

'And now you have condemned us all! Soon this house will be surrounded by the murderous Oprichnina, while the city is surrounded by your friends the Tatars, and we will be caught in the heart of a double siege! A wise plan indeed, Master Waverley!'

'Smith, Smith,' said Stanley, 'not so loud—'

But Sir John Smith, Knight Commander of Malta, face flushed with blood and bull-neck bulging, was beyond calm. He rounded on Robert Greene and Thomas Southam as they too appeared in the upper chamber, still half asleep and blinking.

'And you two, did you know of this cockaninny plan that's doomed us all to a slow death? Tell me you did not.'

They looked at the ground and mumbled 'all for the best,' 'desperate straits,' and other phrases. Yes, they knew.

Smith slammed his fist on a small three-legged table and it nearly broke under him.

Rebecca Waverley was there too, and Ann Southam, more womenfolk and servants. Through the open shutters, from the heart of the city, came terrific sounds of uproar. Everything was erupting in chaos around them.

'Father, is this true?' Rebecca said quietly. 'You offered alliance to the Tatars?'

Waverley snapped, 'So it is, and if you had more knowledge of the real world, my girl, you would better understand why.'

'But this is treachery,' she said.

The humiliated Waverley turned on her, since he hardly dared turn on Smith. 'How dare my own daughter question her father so!' and he made as if to strike her. In the blink of an eye, Nicholas had taken one swift sidestep and was standing close by her side. He stood three or four inches taller than Waverley, but it was more the look in his eye that gave the merchant pause. Waverley's trembling hand slowly fell.

'Even if she is your daughter,' said Nicholas softly, 'you do not strike women. Not in my presence.'

'Nor in the presence of the knights,' said Stanley. 'It is not something we favour. Any more than we favour treachery.'

At that repetition of the dread word treachery, it finally seemed to dawn on Waverley what he had done. Suddenly defeated, he sank down upon a stool, white-faced, and muttered, 'What have I done? I thought to save all our lives, but sweet Christ, what have I done?'

The other merchants looked at the floor. Robert Greene pressed his forehead to the wall and closed his eyes.

Smith surveyed them with contempt. He could only think of the manservant Ballard in the hands of the Oprichnina. Even his tough, battle-scarred old heart went out to that poor, damned man.

'You should all think most on what you have done to Edward Ballard,' he growled. 'I just pray that he dies quickly. As for you, sirs, you had best pray, and pray hard, that God forgives you all for the savage doom you have sent him too.'

At that, Waverley buried his face in his hands and wept. Then his daughter knelt beside him and put her arms about him. He was her father still.

'Come,' said Stanley. 'Out of the room.'

No sooner had they stepped out of the chamber into the hallway outside, than more pandemonium erupted down below. The Devil indeed rode through Moscow tonight.

A Russian servant girl had come running to the back door, babbling in terror, and was now spreading her terror very successfully among the servants in the hall. They ran downstairs. She talked wildly, raising her grubby white apron to her face, crossing herself, gesticulating. The servants were listening wide-eyed. More of the household gathered.

'The Czar himself is to lead the procession, they say, with a great cross!' she babbled. 'A great silver cross with Christ golden upon it, and a buffoon riding a bear, you never saw such a thing, and they say there is to be a great cleansing, and the traitors among us are to be found out and put to the test, the Jews and the Persians all drowned in the river, and all the while people say the Tatars are drawing near, but they say first we must be made strong through burning ...' And then she broke down and sobbed into her apron, the madness of it all too much for her.

Stanley understood immediately and his blood ran cold. The special Russian word for it was pogrom. It was a strange aspect of human nature, that when people felt threatened from without – invasion, famine or plague – they turned upon some imaginary enemy within. During the Black Death, maddened mobs had turned upon Jews or Lollards for scapegoats, killing them in the most unspeakable ways, as if to drive out the sickness in their midst. But the real sickness was in men's own hearts.

Smith turned on the company. 'Are we all within doors? All the English household?'

They summoned every last person throughout the sprawling townhouse and one was missing: old Hannah.

'Wherever is the old dame?' muttered Waverley. 'We cannot go out after her, not amid this madness.'

'She went out to the evening market!' cried Rebecca. 'Is she not back yet? I only wanted fresh berries, it is my fault!'

'The fires are burning at the market!' said the Russian girl. 'There is talk of turning over the tables of the moneychangers, of driving forth the Jews to the Moskva River ...'

'To your room, girl,' Waverley ordered his daughter. 'Do not worry, Hannah will be found. They will not harm an old woman.'

Rebecca fled upstairs with a cry.

'Does Hannah speak any Russian?' demanded Stanley.

'Not a word,' said Waverley. 'Despises it as a language of savages.'

'Then the moment she is apprehended and questioned,' said Smith, 'they will know her for a foreigner, and then ...' He drew his hand across his throat.

'But you cannot go out after her in this!' said Waverley. 'I remember the mob rioting in London, but gentlefolk who stayed indoors were quite safe. It was only on the streets that—'

'Not everyone is safe here,' said Stanley. 'One is still out.'

'She has been the girl's beloved nurse since infancy!' cried the Russian girl. 'She is like a mother to her!'

'She is a serving woman,' said Waverley coldly.

'And we cannot get out anyway, surely,' said Robert Greene. 'The house is being watched back and front.'

'I think not,' said Stanley. 'I doubt if they have troubled. Where have we to run to? And whatever is taking place this night, whatever Witches' Sabbath, no sane person would want to be out in it anyway.'

'Quite so,' said Waverley. 'Come, let us have a glass. Call my daughter down again. Let her not be alone.'

Moments later – 'Sir, Mistress Rebecca is not in her room.'

They searched the house. The kitchens being emptied of servants, she had slipped out that way. They counted the horses in the stables. All present. She had gone on foot, as unobtrusive as possible in her dark grey cloak. Too young to understand the danger, or how bestial a mob may be.

'My daughter!' cried Thomas Waverley in his grief. 'My only child! Her dark hair! They will take her for a Jewess!'

Then why the devil wasn't he already out looking for her this instant? thought Nicholas, running to his chamber to get his sword.

'She at least speaks some Russian,' said Robert Greene, 'does she not?'

Smith and Stanley were buckling on too. 'To the stables!' Waverley was saying this was madness, Greene was saying they must exercise caution, let us not be hasty. But the time for their merchant advice was past.

'Hodge,' said Stanley, 'you remain here.' He clapped him on the shoulder. 'Remember this is English soil, old comrade. It will agree with you.'

Smith said, 'Organzie the servants as best you can, stout sticks and staves at the door. Stop that Russian wench caterwauling and putting the fear of God in 'em all. Tell any that come to the House in no uncertain terms that it is English, favoured by the Czar himself. Deny all knowledge of that damned letter. Hold firm. The mob has no real plan, no real determination, and can be turned aside by firmness. And if you have to fall back – take to the wine cellars.'

'And the Oprichnina? If they come?'

Stanley's mind raced. What indeed? He pictured them all trapped on a desolate plain, between a line of Tatar horsemen to the south, and to the north, a monstrous, red-mawed bear. 'We will be back soon. Stand fast. Hold firm.'

Waverley was not yet done. 'I'll not take orders from servants, even in extremis! I am still master of this House!'

Smith lost his last shred of restraint. It never took much. He seized a fistful of Waverley's doublet-front and pulled the merchant towards him, until their faces were but an inch or two apart: a study in contrasts, the merchant whey-faced, scanty-bearded, looking into the blood-red face of Mars himself. Waverley went up on quivering tiptoes. 'Do as Hodge says,' Smith advised him softly. 'You are no longer master of this house.'

Then he dropped him and they were gone.

28

Nicholas was mounted up and out of the stables. No good ordering him to stay. He was already, on such slim acquaintance – Stanley could see it plain – half in love with the girl Rebecca. Well, he thought with a sour smile, at least unlike so many of his other conquests, she wasn't half-whore. Though sired by a world-class dolt.

The other two were saddled up in less than a minute and galloping out through the stable-yard arch into the street, the servants bolting the gates firmly behind them. They reined in and listened a moment. Distant shouts and cries, the sky full of eerie light and soaring sparks, everything humming and prickling. Waverley's pale, silent face looking down on them from an upper window. But otherwise they were not watched. The Oprichnina were busy elsewhere tonight.

Then Nicholas saw it. Nailed to the front door of the house, concealed from Waverley's view above by the portico, was the head of Edward Ballard, his mouth an open, gory hole. They had knocked out all his teeth.

Stanley swiftly rode over and pulled the ghastly trophy free of the nail and hid it under his cloak. They rode up the street and he stopped on the narrow bridge and dropped it into the stream below. An ill burial. They could do no other. He prayed for the poor man's soul.

He said to them, 'Our own lives are in danger here with every breath, but we must pray that Christ and the darkness will protect us. The girl cannot have got far, and we know where she is heading.

Hannah also will be between here and the market. For God's sake do not be recognized, do not let your faces be seen by those devil's black horsemen. Keep to the shadows.'

'There are many shadows in this city,' said Smith.

'Speak only Russian. Do not even try to explain that we are English and under protection. A mob inflamed with murder pays no heed.'

Nicholas had no helmet. He tied a kerchief over his nose and mouth, and they urged their horses on, towards whatever evil ceremony or foul Walpurgisnacht was taking place in the heart of the accursed city.

They passed by refugees, huddled, half-starved, bareheaded, sitting like beggars and madmen in a graveyard under hides and soiled blankets. They cried out feebly for food and water but what could the three riders do? Down the street, the wooden houses of the citizenry were all firmly barred against the desperate country people, flooding into the city for succour. A cruel regime makes all its people cruel, thought Nicholas. The infection of callousness starts at the top.

The evening market lay in the north of the city, beyond the river and the main square. They must find her. They must. O, God, where was she? Mary shield her. Nicholas kept the outward calm of his older comrades, but his heart thumped with a painful dread. Where in this garish hell of a city could she be? Seeing such an eruption of the mob, would she not seek refuge in some kindly household, some monastery? But was there one safe place for her in the city? Was there any such kindness? He rode tall in the saddle, looking down every side street, surveying the dark houses and stables for the outline of a girl crouching, trembling. Such innocence must be saved. He felt it all the more acutely, knowing his own innocence was so long gone. She was a symbol to him now. Oh, if he could but shield her from the horrors to come, the atrocities of the Czar and the onslaught of the Tatar. A maid like her should not see them – but she would. What could he do, one paltry horseman, against such a storm of history? She was out alone now amid this, all he could do was find her, protect her, and try to weather it together. He dreamed as he rode, searching the darkness with a night-hunter's eyes, that they would eventually ride away together, somehow, flee this accursed city, out into the sweet green countryside again ...

The shouts of an inflamed crowd filled the air, and they carried their swords drawn, rested bare against their right shoulders like Spanish hidalgos, reins in their left hands. Rode tall and confident and haughty, so the mob would take one look at them and step aside, doffing caps, bowing, remembering they were but lowly serfs and peasants.

They rounded the corner, and there was the arched stone bridge over the Moskva – meaning *dark or troubled waters*, Cecil had said – and it was densely crowded with people watching some torchlit spectacle on the water below. Brutish faces gleamed, mouths open and roaring like a crowd at a bear pit. Many were so drunk they could barely stand, breathing gusts of venomous grain spirit over each other, held upright only by the tightly wedged jam of their neighbours.

The three reined in at the edge of the crowd. Some glanced at them uncertainly but most ignored them.

'If we force our way through it will attract a deal of attention,' said Stanley.

'What else can we do?' said Smith. 'Swim our horses across?'

Nicholas was standing up on his saddle, a little precariously. He said, 'I'd keep out of the river if I were you.'

They rode through to the wall of the bridge, crying 'Soldiers of the Czar!' and the drunken crowd shuffled and shoved and barged and made way. They looked down. Spectators were roaring with glee and with relief that it was not they who were suffering down there.

The slow-moving river was illuminated for several hundred yards by bankside bonfires and flaming torches, as for some glittering royal pageant on the Thames: the gilded royal barge, brass trumpets flaring, regal magnificence, all of the guilds and citizens of London out to cheer Her Majesty, Gloriana, down to Greenwich in her splendour ... but here things were done differently.

Here the torches were lit to illuminate the ceremony of the Oprichnina driving whole families wailing down into the river. The mob all around him was cheering them on, like some game played on the Styx or Acheron or one of the rivers of Hell.

Mothers floundered out into the deep mid-channel of the river, cold even in summer, and began to sink in their long skirts. More were driven into the water behind them at spearpoint. They cried out and rolled back, faces lifted out of the water, thrashing, struggling for breath. Then more of the Oprichnina pushed out among them in wooden longboats, and with long poles and boat hooks started clubbing them about the head or stabbing them with fishing gaffs and dunking them back under until they came up no more. They and their admiring spectators on the bridge found it all high entertainment. Nicholas felt physically sick.

'Here's another, here!' shouted down a woman just near Nicholas, gesturing wildly. 'Look, you missed her!'

And the Oprichnina came over in their boats. 'Back down below, little fish, where you belong!' Their wit was scintillating.

On the bankside just below the bridge now there also appeared a procession of Jewish elders in long robes. They went with dignity, eyes closed, praying the ancient prayers of King David. At the edge of the river they were clubbed across the back of the head and fell forwards into the water. The Oprichnina then dragged and kicked their unconscious bodies out into the river like so many animal carcases from the slaughterhouse, to be carried away by the Moskva, eastwards down to the Oka and then the mighty Volga and the sea.

One of the elders raised his head just before the blow of the club was delivered, and said in a voice that carried like the voice of a high priest over the water, 'But hear me, though my people have not leagued with the Tatars, yet they are coming!' By the flickering torchlight, Nicholas even thought he saw the bearded elder smile. 'We have heard it. Tomorrow the wrath of God will come upon you for what you have done to his people, and the horsemen will come like fire and whirlwind. Your proud towers will be laid low, your walls will fall like dust, and you will be utterly consumed.'

And then the club sounded with a sickening hollow thunk across the back of his close-capped skull and he fell forwards.

Further along the crowded bridge, more people were being thrown over the parapet: old women, slaves, whole families.

'What is their offence?' demanded Nicholas of the red-faced fellow near him with the thick white moustache.

'Traitors to our beloved Father the Czar!' cried the fellow. 'Jews, foreigners! Have you not heard?'

Nicholas glanced back the way they had come and there in the middle of the street was a single rider on a black horse, in a long black cloak, dog's head hung from his saddle. The horseman seemed to be regarding him steadily through his wooden animal mask with that horrible lupine stare, eyes burning through the dark eyeholes.

Stanley had seen him too. He turned his face away. 'Cheer,' he snapped.

'What?'

'Raise your arm,' he said, doing so himself. 'Death to the traitors, everlasting life to the Czar!'

Another splash, another roar, another dull clubbing. Though it sickened them to their stomachs, both Nicholas and Smith saw he was right. May God forgive them. They raised their arms and cheered as another innocent was forced under.

'And we are fighting soon to save this city?' muttered Nicholas. 'Why not just let it burn?'

'This mob is but a thousand strong,' said Stanley rapidly, beneath the roar of the crowd. 'A thousand more Oprichnina. Enough to make a massacre. A city in boiling chaos is like a pot of boiling fowl. The scum rises to the top. Look around you – discreetly. Our friend still sits behind us. These are the worst of the people. The men are brutes and criminals, the women worse, the sourest, wanting vengeance on life itself for their own hardships. Look at the raddled old whore down there, rejoicing to see the beautiful young Jewess drowned. But most good folk are safe in their houses, as scared of all this as any. As is intended. There are many thousands of refugees from the country here too now, you saw them in the graveyard. They are not murderers and savages, they are a lost and suffering people. There are children and infants who do not deserve to die or be sold into cruel Tatar slavery. The Knights do not fight for mankind because they are innocent or perfect, but because they are mankind, and loved by God.'

Nicholas remained silent, heart wrenched. He felt a horrible powerlessness at so much passive suffering, so draining, so miserable, until he almost began to feel shame at being human. This was so far different from a noble cause like Malta, or a great maritime crusade like Lepanto. It would help if the fight could begin. But who to fight? Trapped in this squalid antechamber of hell. Let the girl be found at least, sweet Christ. Then let them just get home.

Suddenly a different shout went up from the mob, some word going round that the great festival in the square was about to commence, with the Czar himself as master of ceremonies. They began to surge north over the bridge and through the streets towards the great red square of St Basil's Cathedral.

'Come!' cried Smith. 'Push on through! Make way, soldiers of the Czar! Make way, you scum!' And he heeled his horse forward through the people, freeing his boots from his stirrups and kicking out left and right. The people soon made way.

Nicholas glanced back. Their dark observer was gone.

29

They forced their way through the crowd with as much speed and braggadocio as possible, Smith leading. It was his forte. One glance up at that red-eyed, bull-necked figure, something like a centaur crossed with a minotaur, bellowing in thick Russian and waving a bare sword to boot, and most people gave him plenty of room. As they got ahead of the crowd and came towards the great square of St Basil, they forced their horses into a canter, veering and swerving to miss various obstacles. There was an elderly man lynched and hanging from a wall like a withered fruit. And there were more bodies strewn in the streets.

And then they heard a voice ring out behind them. 'Those three! They are not to be trusted! Bring them down!'

Suddenly all pretence was gone. They spurred their horses into a crazed gallop and veered away from the flood of people streaming towards the centre, wrenching their reins and slewing right into a darker street between high wooden houses. Heart racing, mouth dry as dust, Nicholas saw a great burning firework fly across the sky overhead. How they were celebrating their pogrom!

The streets went by in a blur, shouts and cries, screams and odd musket shots. The city was in chaos, half the people were drunk, and it was all to the Englishmen's advantage. No one knew what was going on. Another great flaming ball of a firework, fired with such carelessness that it caromed into a steep rooftop opposite, tiled with wooden shingles like all the houses in Moscow, dried pale grey in the summer sun. Almost instantaneously a house fire broke out.

'That'll really help!' cried Smith. He might not have been joking.

Nicholas rode with his sword trailing low, ready. Someone staggered forwards out of the shadows and took a swipe at his face with a blazing torch. He wasn't sure if it was only an accident but he struck it away with the full force of his blade. Someone cried out, already behind him now, and he rode on. The street curved around, the high close-packed ramshackle wooden houses seemed to teeter over their heads, and yet another firework exploded onto a rooftop nearby.

'Are you thinking what I'm thinking?' said Stanley.

'That I am,' said Smith.

'What?' cried Nicholas.

Smith grinned insanely. 'Those are no fireworks.'

No time to explain. Ahead of them the dark street was burning with the infernal orange glow of another house fire, and they galloped round, meaning to get past before it was too late. The Muscovites seemed intent not only on exterminating all Jews and foreigners tonight, any Persian and Tatar merchants unfortunate enough to be in the city, but on burning down their own city as well, to flush out the vermin and the enemy within. Such madness. And amid this growing madness, there were more and more chances for the English party to survive, if they could but seize them. But they must find the girl and old Hannah. Defeating the Tatars now seemed no more than a hollow jest, a distant dream.

But the orange glow wasn't a house fire. They came round a corner and pulled up their horses so violently they reared and screamed, teeth bared, throats stretched taut. Ahead of them was a burning barricade of logwood, timber and smashed wagons. To prevent any wretches from trying to flee the festivities in the square, presumably. Burning everywhere. What need for the Tatars? And it was manned by a line of ugly-looking brutes armed with wood-axes, pruning hooks, hayforks and all the other clumsily murderous ironmongery of the peasantry-at-arms.

As always in moments of extreme danger, time slowed and Nicholas had time to think and plan – though he knew now it was really his brain racing urgently ahead, to ensure his own survival. This was no line of soldiers, just thugs. Untrained, one line deep, none behind. As he came crashing through, mounted, above them, there would only be a single man in range of hurting him on either flank. So all he had to do as he vaulted his horse over the barricade – all! – assuming the animal did his bidding, conquered its own primeval and thoroughly pragmatic terror of fire, and didn't get itself skewered in the chest by a pitchfork – all he had to do was avoid a slash or a stab on each side, and cut the two fellows down in the correct order: first the more dangerous, then the less dangerous one. And all this to be judged and executed while in the air, clenching his mount, leaning fore then aft, and praying not to be pitched over onto the ground as they landed. For then he would be quickly despatched where he lay.

No more time. The heat of the barricade burned his face, the brutes moved and readied their weapons, seeing these three ferocious-looking horsemen ride down upon them. Nicholas kicked his poor beast – and it shied violently at the leaping flames, reared up, screaming that terrible whinnying horse-scream. He held on. Smith and Stanley were over already and down the alley, not yet realising they had lost him. The peasants regarded this flailing spectre, began to crowd around him, though keeping their distance as he slashed around him mightily with his sword. He must pass. He must pass! Then they were swarming around him like wasps around an invading hornet, and he was slashing and cutting at them – these very people they had supposedly come to defend.

With one last terrific heave he pulled his horse around, delivering a wide semicircle of a sword slash with it, and men went reeling backwards clutching opened faces. He spurred his horse back up the alley, took in another cluster of people ahead of him, wrenched his reins left so hard his horse's rump skidded down into the ground, rear legs buckling, up again, sprang forward – another alley, another, under the inner walls of the city now, more fires, blurred faces, he was alone.

He cantered on, sometimes shouting out idiot Russian for good measure – 'Long life to the Czar! Death to wicked foreigners!' – almost laughing in his wild elation. It was becoming dreamlike now, as combat often could, and he began to feel absurdly invincible. Not good. No one was invincible.

He pushed up in his stirrups, stared about, glanced down every alley – and then there was another crowd of people across a street ahead, their backs to him. He craned over their heads. A terrific explosion went off somewhere in the heart of the city and women crossed themselves and cried out they were betrayed. The city was in the grip of near total hysteria. The Czar's madness had spread over all.

He looked over the crowd of people, standing with solemn and murderous intent, and saw beyond them, trapped in a blind alley – the scene rushed towards him, magnified, intensified – the huddled figures of a girl and her aged nurse. The old woman in a grey serge dress and white apron, the young girl in a dark grey cloak, face buried in fear against her nurse's side. Behind them, still another fire burned.

Rebecca looked up and saw some horsemen behind the mob. Oprichnina no doubt. She was already praying to Christ to receive their souls. Two of the mob began to walk forward with their long staves, another was putting an arrow to a primitive woodsman's bow. One shouted how pretty she was, though she was no Russian.

They shouted, 'Death to the foreigners, death to the Jews, death to the Jewish whore and her bawd!'

Time slowed and Rebecca saw the arrow revolving slow but flying fast. Hannah stepped in front of her and the arrow found its mark with an ugly thump high in the nurse's chest. She gasped, the thick grey serge of her dress and her white apron gradually stained red, and then she staggered. Far, far away, people were shouting. The girl behind her flung her arms about her beloved nurse and screamed, and they stood like that together for a moment, as if there was still hope. And then Hannah's head fell forward on her chest and her weight dragged them both to the ground. The girl fell upon her howling.

Feeling a warm flood of power, the bowman nocked another arrow to the string.

Nicholas galloped round in a frenzy, however painfully his horse's hooves must fall on the hard-packed summer earth, and found the entrance to the dark passageway he had glimpsed ahead.

The arrow flew and clattered uselessly wide. The bowman nocked another but another man batted him down. The mob walked nearer, grinning now. The alley was dark and there were many doorways. Why trouble to kill this Jewish whore? Why not just rape her to death?

And then out of one of those dark doorways, against the orange firelight that burned at the dead end of the alley, there stepped a single horseman, black silhouette against the flames. The men stopped, puzzled, muttering. 'Oprichnina ...?'

Nicholas sheathed his sword a moment and got quietly down and calmed his horse. Then he looked up at the ranks of the soot-smeared, sweat-streaked mob, and said, 'Not Oprichnina, no. Englishman, and Christ be thanked, not damned Russian like you.'

They stared a little longer, motionless, dumbfounded. Very swiftly he turned to the girl, kneeling in the dust, clinging to the dead weight of her nurse like some shivering monkey to its mother. He prised her fingers apart. She was exhausted with grief. He laid Hannah down on the ground and pressed his fingertips under her jawline, then closed her eyes with a sweep of his hand. He slipped his arm round the girl's back and his other arm behind her legs and lifted her up and laid her across his left shoulder.

He was aware without looking that they were starting to run towards him now, an animal roar, angry blackened faces in the firelight, faces bestial, contorted beyond reason or plea, bent only on slaying. He laid the girl across his horse's withers and keeping the nervous stepping beast between him and the mob, set his left foot in the stirrup and ... could not remount. Only then did he know he had been cut across the thigh by some filthy peasant blade. He still could not feel it. The devil. He stood as tall as he could, grabbed his saddle, tried to vault up, his thigh muscle screamed red and hot, he failed again. The horse began to pull around in its terror, the animal roar of the mob in its flattened ears. Nicholas's sword still sheathed. The girl as if asleep across his horse. Please God. He breathed deep and heaved once more and was clumsily across and pulled himself upright and swiftly round and found his stirrups and drew his sword and cut wide. Then there was one fellow with the telltale look who came first, a fellow who must be taken down, and he wrenched the horse right and drove his sword forward unexpectedly over the girl's body and down into his throat. Pulled back his sword, the fellow came with it, fell gargling against the girl's dress. He wrenched his sword free, spurred violently. The rest of the mob came on. Among them, he saw a fat woman with a sickle and a boy with a dog on a rope.

He made for the narrow passageway just as two big armoured horsemen appeared. One of them was slathered in blood across his gleaming breastplate and pauldron. The two horsemen nodded and rode out into the blind alley and took up their positions, like bronze equestrian statues facing the mob. The boy rode away down the dark passageway with the girl.

The two horsemen sat their horses with swords ready but in utter silence, their visors down. Like gleaming metallic gods. The mob numbered more than a hundred, and yet, and yet … They slowed and came to an angry, frustrated halt, some twenty feet before the two silent figures guarding the passageway. There was a moment's pause. And then, very slowly, one of the horsemen shook his head.

30

Nicholas trotted away with the girl barely stirring. After a while he pulled into the shadows under the wall and shook her, as if shaking her awake. He made her sit up behind him, arms about his waist.

'You are not hurt yourself?'

She shook her head. Face tear-stained, eyes red.

'My pity upon your nurse. She died to save your life.' He tore a strip off the bottom of his shirt.

'I know,' said the girl very softly. 'It should have been me. I sent her out to the market.'

'She was old, you are young,' said Nicholas. He bound the strip of linen tightly but not too tightly around the cut in his thigh, as he had seen Stanley do many a time.

'You are hurt?' she said.

He flicked the reins. 'Hold tight now. We face a short but eventful ride.'

They must head back to the English House. Hardly a place of greater safety now, by any definition. But where else was there? It was the only choice. If only they could escape the city altogether soon. For this wretched crusade was surely over and done.

He rode feeling the girl's head upon his shoulder, sometimes her trembling body. He rode with his sword hanging loose at his side, bright in the firelight, past gang after gang of leering faces, hands reaching out to touch, to whistle or comment, or sometimes merely staring, eyes blank with slaughter. But he batted them aside and not one touched them. They passed through them unscathed like

Shadrach and Meshach through the flames of Babylon.

Not far behind them were two heavy-armoured horsemen. No one dared to leer at them.

And then behind them, in chilling silence, abreast across the street, a troop of eight Oprichnina. They carried long spears. The man at their head wore an animal mask. They rode at the same pace as the three, not attempting to overtake them. As if herding them forward towards some deliberate fate.

Stanley looked ahead. The great red square, riotous shouts, the bonfire of the vanities.

Before they came to the square, there were two more dark alleys, one left, one right.

'Nick,' said Stanley softly. 'Do not look back. When we get to the alleys there, you break left. We break right.'

'Can we not stay together?'

'No. They will pursue us. Get the girl back to her father. Ride like the wind.'

The dark alleys came nearer, and the wild shouts from the square. And then without even a shout to warn their followers, they broke.

Nicholas galloped his horse down a horribly narrow alley, it jutted left – and straight into a small courtyard, still hung with washing from a hemp line. They were finished.

He slid from the horse, teeth gritted for the throbbing pain in his thigh, worsening by the minute now. He bade the girl stay mounted, and told her to look to the wall. She stared down at him, wide-eyed.

'Look to the wall!' he shouted and shoved her round, then turned and stood before horse and girl.

Two Oprichnina came round the corner and stopped in the entrance to the courtyard. One of them wore an animal mask. His eyes glittered. Could it be …? Yes, he feared so. The eyes of Maliuta Skuratov, who had hated him and hunted him from that first day beside the stream in the birch forest. He did not know why. Because he had not been sufficiently afraid of him, perhaps, as a grovelling peasant should be. But Nicholas Ingoldsby was no grovelling peasant, he was a hereditary knight, son of a Knight Hospitaller, and an Englishman to boot.

He glanced about in desperation. Had he been alone, and not so badly cut, he might have tried climbing up that creeper there, into a window ... If if if.

The unmasked of the two Oprichnina was smiling. He said, 'You are the English.'

He said nothing. His left hand felt empty. He remembered what the knights had taught him. Use anything, throw anything. You can kill a man with a sharp stick or a soup spoon if you must. He slashed out with his sword and cut down one of the pieces of washing and seized hold of it. The riders laughed.

'He fights with washing. How very English. They are all women.'

He saw in a flash what would happen to Rebecca if they killed him and took her captive, and he thought of the knights' other lessons. Do not delay. Attack at once, in silence, and with all ferocity. Attack like a madman: not just with a wild ferocity, but irrational, unpredictable. He took in the thick brutish eyebrows of the unmasked rider, the scars on his cheek as if made by the fingernails of some too-young girl he had raped, the rotten black teeth. He saw him and his fellows jeering and swiving, jaws sagging, stupid, while Maliuta Skuratov looked amusedly on. Then as suddenly as someone striking a match, the old furore came upon him, the crimson madness, the lust for battle, controlled – only just – by the sense of killing only those he knew as evil. For God was a God of battles, the Lord was a man of war, and fighting was a heady wine – he was racing at them now, seeing a low stone post nearby, aiming to get his right foot upon it and launch himself upon the right-hand rider, Maliuta himself – and sweetly drunk it made you, so drunk you did not even regard your own wounds while you fought. Had he not seen that gallant Italian knight Lanfreducci still fighting at Malta when he could hardly walk, and laughing in the face of the Turks until the moment he died? Lanfreducci was watching him now, looking down from the gold court of heaven.

He flung the square of washing in Maliuta's face, placed his foot on the post, launched off and barged into him in mid-air from the side. He hung from him with his left arm clenched around the startled rider's neck, flailing with his sword but was too close to use it. The horse bucked and began to topple sideways. At last he mastered his sword, holding it at an extreme angle and driving it sidelong and deep across Maliuta's back. The Oprichnik commander roared in pain, his horse sidestepped whinnying into the neighbouring horse, Nicholas's arm still bizarrely clenched around his neck as if throttling him, hanging down with his feet almost touching the ground. Yet the wounded Maliuta was his best shield, and as the horses barged together and the second rider, utterly baffled by what was happening, struggled with the reins, Nicholas thrust his sword forward behind the first, a long low clean thrust that went straight through the second rider's belly. God, the stench, the instant privy stench of ruptured guts.

He moved faster still then. He dropped his sword, pulled himself up onto the horse with both hands, thigh fire-hot yet causing him no pain now. He wrestled briefly with the wounded Maliuta before him and then rolled him clumsily to the ground, turned on the second but he was already dead, slumped forward in his own stench, red and brown leaking over his saddle and down his leg. He slipped off the horse again, drew his dagger and knelt over the prostrate Maliuta Skuratov, who was twitching horribly, wriggling, trying to move away from him but as if paralysed. He had cut him across his back deeper than he had thought. Perhaps his spine ...

'Please, please,' said Maliuta, his voice high with fear behind that horrible mask, 'in the name of God, let us not be brutal as Russians are brutal ...'

'I will treat you,' said Nicholas, 'far better than you have treated others. I will not torture you, I will not burn you nor shoot with arrows so that you suffer but do not die—'

'Thank God, thank merciful God, let me confess ...'

Maliuta's hand had slipped under his cloak as he spoke. His legs seemed paralysed but he could still stab.

It was wrong to torment one dying – a Turkish trick. Make it clean.

'But nevertheless,' said Nicholas, 'your life ends here.'

'I must confess!' cried out the wretched Maliuta. 'I must not die unshriven!' Then his hand flashed upwards, holding a dagger, and Nicholas thrust his own dagger hard into his assailant's forearm and the dagger dropped. Maliuta shrieked and clutched the wounded arm across his chest.

'You will never be unshriven,' said Nicholas, 'nor ever forgiven your sins.' He reached down and shoved the mask off his face and his vision seemed to swim, his face prickle with cold. Beneath him lay Elysius Bomelius.

'You,' he said at last.

'I.' He was gasping, shaking. 'You have sore wounded me, we have been enemies, but now for the love of God and the love of Catholic Europe, let us two find unity in our—'

Nicholas pressed his left hand down hard on Elysius's forehead and drew his dagger swiftly across his scrawny neck and he gargled and died. He cleaned his dagger on Elysius's robe.

He went to the second rider sitting a dead weight in his saddle, pulled him down and rolled the heavy weight of his corpse into a corner. Then he sank back against the wall, mind reeling, and closed his eyes a moment. Red fog and exhaustion and the shakes and the blood pumping to the beat of a frenzied drum, and the thought struck him hard as a bullet, that they were indeed fighting on two fronts.

He realised he had been cut across the forehead, he had no idea how or when, and the blood was leaking into his eyes. He pressed the back of his hand against the wound and it made the imprint of the cut enough to tell him it was not wide or deep. He tore off another linen strip. He was running out of shirt. At this rate he'd be half naked by the time they got back to the English House. Keep jesting. Get through hell by jesting. He tied the strip around his forehead and pushed himself off from the wall.

With some revulsion he picked up Elysius's demonic animal mask and tried it on. It fitted. He shoved it inside his jerkin for now. The second horse, damn it, and the horse's saddle were too befouled to use. Poor beast. He remounted the first horse and took up the reins and finally looked over to the girl, to say she could turn about now.

She was staring at him with horror-stricken eyes.

He shook his head. 'I told you to look to the wall.'

'You have killed them both,' she said in a haunted whisper.

'That I have. Before they killed me, and did worse to you. Come. We must ride out. Put up your hood.'

But she could not, he saw. She was almost paralysed with horror. And there were more horrors to come this night, that much was sure. How else could he protect her? Struck now with deep exhaustion, he slid a final time from the horse and remounted in front of her, awkward, thigh muscle taut, skin crusted and cracking with dry blood.

She was trembling.

Innocence was more rare than rubies in this world, and must be protected.

'Close your eyes,' he said. 'Bury your face in my cloak. Do as I say this time. Do not look out. Or you will never sleep easy again.'

And he – he would ride through hell with eyes wide open.

Yet still she looked revolted by him, this killer of men, this madman. The courtyard was filled with blood and the stench of ordure and two corpses, and he had knelt beside one of them, there before her very eyes, a wounded man, and had cut his throat with a single draw of his dagger as if he was killing a chicken.

He reached back and placed his hand on her head and drew it against his cloak. He kicked the tired horse, its own large brown eyes as if filled with horrors too, and said again, 'Close your eyes,' and they rode out of the courtyard.

From a window above, a child watched them go.

At the entrance to the passageway were two more hulking Oprichnina.

Nicholas could not fight again. He bowed his head. They were foredone.

31

The two thugs barged them backwards into the courtyard once more. They sat their horses before him in the gloom, dimly lit by reflected street fires and the burning night sky, and then pushed back their hoods.

Smith and Stanley.

Nicholas was too tired to rejoice. 'You.'

'Us. It is our only hope of getting through this. Here.' And they tossed him another black cloak, a heavy black whip, and even a severed dog's head on a short rope, the rope threaded in and out of a hole knocked in its skull. Hodge the dog-lover would not like this. He grimaced and tied the ugly parody of an heraldic emblem to the pommel of his saddle.

And from his jerkin he drew a wooden animal mask.

Stanley drew breath. 'You killed him? Maliuta Skuratov?'

Nicholas shook his head. 'Prepare yourself for a shock. It was Elysius Bomelius.'

They stared. 'The physician?'

'Or poisoner, depending on your point of view.'

Smith said slowly, 'He has been the secret head of the Oprichnina all along?'

'More than one wear such masks,' said Stanley. 'And Maliuta Skuratov still lives, and still wants us dead. But we salute you, Brother Nicholas. It is never pleasant to take a man's life, but that was good execution done on that wretch. I just wonder if he might have told us anything useful under questioning.'

Nicholas shrugged. 'I don't think his word was ever reliable.'

'No. We also found on one of the dead a roll of paper. A letter.'

'Not ... not Waverley's letter to the Tatars?'

'Just so. Still in his robes. We burned it.'

'And you ... you killed all who pursued you?'

'There wasn't much room for manoeuvre down that alley,' said Smith. 'They had no idea, crowded each other. It was a straight hacking job.'

Nicholas felt the girl's arms tighten around his waist. He was glad she hadn't witnessed Smith's straight hacking job. And he still could not believe the luck of the letter ...

'You think the news of it never got back to Ivan?'

'Not yet.'

'And now the very Oprichnina who arrested Ballard, all those who actually knew about it, are slain?'

'Let us hope so,' said Stanley. 'Then we may just have a needle's breadth of a chance of escape from this circle of hell. Keep close now. Maid,' he added, 'we will ride straight back through all that mayhem, to the English House, to your father. You understand?'

She nodded. Face already hidden, eyes closed.

Nicholas drew on the wooden animal mask and tied it round the back of his head, then drew up his hood again. He prayed the evil spirit of Elysius Bomelius would not somehow infect him. Did they not say he practised alchemy, magic? But the eyeholes were perfectly placed. See and not be seen. He felt strangely invulnerable. Yes, the perfect accessory for any secret and all-powerful State servant.

They rode out.

All the other streets were barricaded. There was no way back but through the great square before St Basil's, and the heart of the festivities.

They would never forget what they saw that night, though they would try often enough. A vision of a mad king's nightmare, or of some medieval doom painting perhaps, with the Devil and all his horsemen loosed upon Moscow. The square was lit by many torches as if for a play, and many more bonfires. There was a gallows all set up ready in one corner, and over another fire was a huge cauldron of boiling water, and a kind of vast frying pan, as if from the kitchen of a giant. The crowd surged back and forth, crying out their love of the Czar and their hatred of traitors. The three had never seen such madness.

'Russia's greatest enemy is rolling towards us,' said Nicholas tightly from behind his mask, 'and even now the Chieftain of the Russians is busy sentencing to death hundreds of his own people. For which they applaud him.'

Then out of the gates of the Kremlin rode the infernal procession itself. There was a buffoon riding an ox – for this killing was after all a comical business, as Ivan the Visionary saw, and a grand jest of God. Ivan sometimes tried to explain to his closest confidants, under the deep inspiration of vodka, that all human sufferings were but the jests of God. And then came the Czar himself.

The three riders were holding their horses tight, pushing on through the crowd, wanting only to be away from this garish carnival, heated by the raging bonfires around them – and yet they could not help but stop and look, and their blood was chilled. Ivan was dressed half as Czar, half as a member of the Oprichnina himself. A tall red conical hat, richly bejewelled, a long golden coat fabulously studded with emeralds, a quiver full of gilded arrows over his shoulder, a bloody dog's head at his saddle, and in his hands, arms outstretched like Christ on the cross, a sceptre and a whip. It was all the more terrifying for being both nightmarish and comical.

'Make way!' bellowed Smith. 'Out of our way there!'

The crowd moved apart for them, but it was damnably slow. Let them not be noticed, please God. Let them not be suspected.

They came to the edge of the square and the exit was heavily barricaded. Even Oprichnina could not escape.

A half-naked man was tied down upon a wide wooden bench and a thick, taut rope lowered over him. Nicholas held the girl's head and pressed her face against his shoulder. The rope was drawn back and forth over the man's belly, and very slowly he began to be cut in two. His cries were so terrible that after a time even his executioners could not stand it, and shoved a gag in his mouth.

Upon a platform before the Kremlin walls stood a clownish figure in his tall jewelled conical hat. He seemed to be wearing a rare smile.

'Do you not find the sentence just, good people?'

They roared back that they did.

They made a man kill his own father, then killed him for being a patricide. People were impaled. Women were tied to stakes and whipped, and then set upon by trained bears. No one ever asked what their offence might have been.

Rebecca put her hands over her ears but she could not drown out the sounds entirely, the screams or the harrowing cries, half agony, half despair. Nor could she block out that smell of burning human hair and flesh. But with eyes closed she imagined she was riding blindfolded through some ancient and barbaric city before the time of Christ, perhaps Rome, or Nineveh, and she prayed that they would somehow ride clear, though she knew they were no less sinners than any who suffered here. Then she ceased praying for their own safety and prayed instead for the poor people who were being so vilely treated and killed all about them. May God have mercy on their harrowed souls.

'Enough!' said Stanley angrily. 'We must get through!' And they pushed on into the crowd, bellowing out in Russian, 'Business of the Czar, clear the way there!' Then people called back, 'God save Ivan the Dread!'

Nicholas pictured the Czar seated on a golden throne atop a pyramid of slaves, and those slaves a people unawakened, silent and inert, regarding their Father the Czar with awe and love no matter how cruelly he might treat them. A ruler must be Dread and Terrible, or how should his people respect him?

The clown came down from his platform and took a copper jug himself and poured boiling alcohol over the heads of traitors or boyars he had long disliked, and set light to their beards and watched their heads burn like plum puddings! The air made a funny roaring, whooshing sound through their gaping mouths and noses as their skulls blazed up. The victim of torture reveals his true self beneath his struggles and desperate cries, Ivan had long understood, so he observed closely the final throes, but he was disappointed to learn but little here.

Amid all this festivity there sounded a distant boom. A monstrous, muffled boom, a thunderous bellow from the plains beyond, a crack, a mighty splintering ...

Smith looked around at his comrades with baleful eye. 'Saved by the Tatars. Now there's an irony.'

'They have come?' said Nicholas. He felt the girl behind him shiver. 'Those are the Tatar guns?'

'The Tatars never used guns,' said Smith, 'or but few, and none that size. Those are Ottoman guns.'

'But indeed they have come,' said Stanley, 'and are already trying our gates. Break down that barricade, you there! They have come with Ottoman guns. Some very ...' Now he kicked out wildly, not caring, lashing with his whip. 'Big ... GUNS.'

Another leader of men also sat on a wooden platform that night, beneath a canopy of resplendent crimson and gold. A leader in a different mould to Ivan: shrewd, cautious, of fine judgement, scrupulous personal habits, an abstainer from alcohol but an enthusiast for women, a rider of brilliant horsemanship and a military commander with perfect understanding of the fighting tactics of the steppe. The Great Khan of the Crimean Tatars, Devlet Giray: most elusive and perhaps most intelligent ruler in all Asia.

Now he stroked his fine oiled moustaches and smiled. From his vantage point, in his sprawling camp upon the Sparrow Hills, barely a stone's throw from Moscow, he could not but be amused at the scene spread out before him under the warm night sky of midsummer. His Ottoman artillerymen had lobbed a few incendiaries into the city, with happy results, but it was his spies and lookouts galloping back to the camp who had brought the strangest, the most absurd of all reports. At the same time as Devlet Giray was probing and testing, trying to ascertain Moscow's defences, her guns, her ability to mount a cavalry sortie from the gates – none whatsoever, as far as he could tell – the Muscovites themselves were also setting fire to their city.

Devlet Giray smiled again and shook his head. Christians. Perhaps they were punishing themselves for their own sins again. What could one make of such crazed idolaters and drunkards as the Russians? Yet they had also visited humiliations upon his people of late, at the capture of Kazan and Astrakhan, and when they put their bovine minds to it, by the stars could they fight. He who underestimates his enemy will fall to him.

Still, Devlet Giray summoned his generals and his subordinate khans about him, and while he drank springwater they drank arak and toasted the fall of Moscow with much jubilation.

'To the final extermination of Rus!'

'Death to the infidel – and long life to his gold in our panniers!'

'And his fair-skinned daughters in our beds!'

'I'll take his wives,' growled another. 'I prefer them with more fat on 'em, like I prefer my meat.'

That was old Tokhtamysh Khan, whose son was killed lately in battle with the Cossacks. In his seventh decade and still a keen collector of concubines for his tent.

Devlet Giray raised his hand.

'But remember,' he said, 'this is not just another raid. A few dozen houses burned, a few churches torched. Muscovy not so long ago was barely a city, defended by nothing more than a wooden stockade. She was nothing compared to the great cities of the south, Bokhara and golden Samarkand, Astrakhan of the Volga, the fortress of Azov. But now look at her. She has great walls of stone, she has a strong regiment of musketeers, though we attack now because we know they are far away in the west. Her fool of a Czar has left her undefended. But still she must be brought down, and not by horseman and bow. She must be razed utterly so that she does not rise again.'

They nodded solemnly.

'But then look how they burn their own city tonight in their revels. Apparently they are seeking out traitors in their midst. One of my men signals to my lookouts from a tower on the walls, and no one notices.'

Old Tokhtamysh said, 'You would think it was their secret desire to be conquered. Like a woman. And they themselves have done half the work already!'

Devlet Giray arched his fine black eyebrows. 'Yet within her walls, and aside from her many idol-filled churches, Moscow is still largely a city built of wood. It is a fine hot summer. Do we really need a long siege to take down her walls and towers and put her people under the yoke?'

'We do not,' said Tokhtamysh. 'But fire or no fire, my men and I ride in, even into the flames. We have first right of blood. My son was slain. The Cossack party who did this came to Moscow. We know this. I saw the men who killed my son that day.' He touched his fingertips below his right eye, and then drew them across his bare throat. 'And I will know them.'

32

Even the knights had thought it. Smith had muttered, 'You would think Ivan was in league with the Tatars, almost.'

Stanley said, 'He is mad, but not that mad. Though it sticks in my throat to say so – he is, for all that, a devout believer. What God will make of him at the Judgement I dread to think. But Ivan would not league with any Mohammedan force. He sees himself as a Christian king still.'

'God help us all,' said Nicholas.

Now they raced back through streets eerily quiet and deserted. In the far distance they heard another muffled boom, and instinctively Nicholas ducked as he rode. Malta again. But no force of Knights upon the walls to fight back, no Jean de la Valette to lead them.

Galloping over the bridge, he tore off the hated animal mask and threw it into the river below. Even if it had afforded disguise and protection, he would do without it now. It carried an odour of evil.

They came skidding to a halt before the English House once more. Smith hammered at the wooden gates into the stable yard. A window shot up in the house and Nicholas's heart warmed to hear those familiar stubborn Shropshire accents.

'We'll not have any of you buggers in here! This is the English House, and the English House it will remain. Now shog off with ye!'

Stanley could not help but grin. 'Well held, Master Hodge, well held. Would that all Moscow were as stoutly defended!'

'I thought you were those damned Oprickniks. Those cloaks you're in.'

'Safe disguise.'

Hodge and the servants began unbarricading the gates from within. They had barricaded well. It took a while.

Nicholas slipped down from his horse and helped the girl down after him. She seemed calmer now, very tired. She said quietly, 'I did look.'

He was blank.

'In the square there,' she said. 'I did look, though you forbad me. I saw those things. I need to understand. I am young, I understand nothing. You think I am stupid.'

'I certainly do not think you are stupid,' he said. 'But I do think you are young.'

'You were at Malta,' she said. 'At sixteen, I hear.'

As if in mocking reminder, another boom sounded, and this time it was followed by a high roaring.

'Incendiary!' muttered Smith. 'Watch for it.'

And like a shooting star, a missile larger and clumsier than any cannonball came flaming and tumbling overhead. Clumsily shaped, more like a haybale – for that was indeed what it was. Yet it flew well enough, propelled by some rope-powered onager or trebuchet beyond.

Smith was itching to get up on the walls. 'Come on, Master Hodge, let us inside!'

'All in good time!' replied Hodge. More huffing and puffing, more moving of heavy oak furniture.

And then immediately after, another such missile, lighting up the night sky like a giant firework. It crashed heavily into a wooden rooftop only two streets away and immediately the hungry flames began to roar upwards.

'Moscow,' said Stanley, 'is really going to burn tonight.'

'How come it flies so well?' asked Nicholas.

'Huge trebuchet to shoot it,' said Smith, 'very high trajectory. A heavy weight jammed inside it, maybe even a cannonball to give it momentum. The whole thing soaked in heavy oil, naphtha, honey, any old ingredient of Greek fire – she'll burn up very well. And of course,' he added, his voice dropping even lower, more bitter, 'not a soul to resist, shoot back or douse the flames.'

'What of Vorotinsky?'

Stanley shook his head. What indeed? They had not heard one Russian musket shot from the walls. And of course, the guns faced the wrong way ...

Come on, Hodge.

Nicholas turned back to Rebecca. She was shaking again. He dared to take her in his arms. Like an older brother, he told himself.

'Yes,' he resumed, 'I was at Malta. At sixteen.'

'And I am seventeen.'

'You are a maid.'

'Maids can bear children at seventeen, and younger. You think there is no blood and pain in that?'

He said nothing. From the heart of the city he seemed to hear a sound like the roar of the sea.

'I saw,' she said. 'I saw enough in that square. The cruelty of men is a bottomless abyss.'

He did not disagree.

'But – but I thank you for what you did in the courtyard. Killing those men. You saved me after all.'

Suddenly a wild-eyed figure appeared at the end of the street, shoeless, hat askew, carrying a sack on a stick as if ready to set off on great travels. 'The Tatars,' he cried, 'the Tatars are coming!'

'Yes,' growled Smith. 'We know that.'

Then Nicholas, and Stanley too, understood the approaching roar. It was the Moscow mob in full panic and running crazed riot, understanding at last that now was not the time for their festivities. The Tatars were hammering at the gates, they were hurling incendiaries over the very walls, and the city was virtually defenceless.

The roar came nearer, and then at the end of the street appeared a great surge of people, maddened by fear. And the Englishmen were standing in their path, as if in the path of a buffalo stampede.

'Hodge!' Smith kicked furiously at the door. 'Get this door open NOW!'

'The damn gate-bar has jammed!' cried Hodge. 'We can't open it!'

'Then let us straight into the house!' Smith put his shoulder to the door and started to heave. Stanley joined him. It did not give. The tide of people was almost upon them. Nicholas was about to lift the girl back onto his horse but the poor creature began to rear, eyes wild and white. They crammed into the doorway, horses pulled in close, swords drawn. Oprichnina in appearance still, but who knew what protection that might still afford? Maybe they were the enemy too now.

They heard cries of '*The Tatars are at the Gates!*' and '*Christ save us!*' A maddened, blood-crazed mob of housewives and wailing children and apprentices clutching axes, and they watched in horror as an old goodwife came tottering out of her door ahead of them and one stout apprentice simply cried out, 'The Tatars!' and swung his axe and cut her down, and they surged on. Where were they going? Out of the south gate, straight into the arms of the enemy?

Nicholas got ready to fight them off, hundreds of them, shouting out that they were Oprichnina, but it was futile. The mob would kill anything that stood in their way.

Suddenly Smith was back on his horse and wrenching it about and letting it rear, spurring it, bellowing, panicking it further, and then its forehooves came crashing down against the stout front door and it burst inwards and he rode through straight into the hall. Nicholas thrust Rebecca through and then he and Stanley followed, dragging their horses after to cover them. They turned on the threshold and someone flailed wildly in the doorway, blocking it, he only had one eye, and Stanley planted a boot high in his chest and shoved him back into the raging human torrent. Whether he lived or was trampled, they would never know. They flung shut the doors again, one hanging badly loose, and Hodge appeared behind, panting, with some manservants and began shoving furniture close to again.

They collapsed in exhaustion. Waverley and Greene were standing on the stairs, gazing aghast. Then Waverley saw his daughter and she ran to him and they embraced and wept.

'I thank you, gentlemen,' said Waverley through his tears. 'My daughter ...'

Stanley waved a hand. It was nothing, really. Nicholas thought he might have made more of it.

'Are we ...' stammered Robert Greene, 'are we all lost? What is to become of us? Do we face lives of Tatar slavery?'

'They are not in yet,' said Stanley. 'But they soon will be. They mean to burn the city first, I think, and then ride in and scoop up what remains for booty.'

Greene crossed himself and bowed his head. 'My children ...'

Aye, it was hard for those with children. What was to become of them indeed?

They left their horses trembling and sweating in the hall, one of the grooms calming them and rubbing the foam from their flanks with wide sweeps of his hand. Foam spattered upon the black and white tiles. Waverley looked disgusted. This house would look like a common stable before the night was out.

Smith read his thoughts and laid his hand on his shoulder as they strode past him. 'Do not be anxious,' he said in the words of Christ. By less obvious way of comfort, he added, 'The house will probably be burned to the ground soon anyway.'

The merchants were in despair. Everything was against them. Had it come to this? What were they to do?

Smith turned sharply. 'On which note – your cellars are made of brick, are they not?'

'Naturally.'

'Show us.'

The English House had two large, vaulted red-brick wine cellars, stacked high with barrels of malmsey and Canary wine.

'Be ready to remove yourselves down here. Have the servants bring down wet sacking, buckets of water, plenty of cloths.'

'When do we move down here?' said Waverley, quailing.

His young daughter said, 'I think we will know when it is time, Father.'

33

They went up to the first floor chamber. Nicholas glanced from the upper window. Was that God's benevolent dawn that was breaking, or just man's malignant fire? An oppressively red summer dawn, as full of foreboding as a puritan sermon. His heart beat, his mind raced with all the old eve-of-battle thoughts. Let me not die. Let those I love not die. But how can we live? Let me not show cowardice. I am still young, O Lord. And she is younger. Christ, save her. Make my sword arm strong, for her sake.

Stanley drew Smith's attention to something further off. A burning house in the next street. They watched. The flames that had roared up in the still night, the sparks spiralling above them – they had begun to veer and tilt, the sparks to dance more wildly and fly sideways, over rooftops not yet ablaze ... The wind was getting up. As if Devlet Giray's own prayers had been answered, not theirs, and the ancient, malign Tatar gods of the sky had commanded the wind from the steppes to rise up and do their bidding.

'To the walls,' said Smith curtly. 'But you, comrades, stay here. Ingoldsby, you need that leg wound seeing to.'

'We are with you,' said Nicholas. His jaw jutted a little, his mouth set in that old stubborn line the knights knew so well of old.

'You are not.'

'That I am. I am no knight, nor Hodge, and not under your command, but under that of the Queen of England. If we want to go to the walls, we go to the walls.'

Stanley sighed. 'That leg will get worse.'

'It's fine. It just needs a splash of that Russian grain spirit.'

'You are leaving us?' said Waverley.

'We will be back. Move down to the cellars soon. Take nothing with you that might burn. And pray.'

Stepping out into the street and looking up, Nicholas realised it was only the city burning that made the sky red. It was still night. A cursed long night for a summer night. They wet their neckerchiefs in a water trough and tied them about their necks again. Ready to pull over their mouths when the smoke should start to thicken, which it would soon now.

There was a group of six militiamen huddled miserably at the top of some steps. Only two had muskets. They were drinking from a shared flask. Stanley demanded to know where Prince Michael Vorotinsky was. They gestured sullenly.

Nicholas held his hand out for the flask and they passed it. He took a burning draught and then poured another splash over his thigh wound. They stared at him. He passed the flask back. They grunted. They'd all be dead or enslaved by dawn, what did it matter? Even a waste of good vodka did not matter.

They found Vorotinsky at the base of a gun tower. He greeted them with subdued courtesy, and his white brow was tight with despair. He gestured inside the gun tower. They went in and looked and came back.

Smith said, almost disbelieving, 'They have been turned around.'

Vorotinsky nodded. 'Czar's orders.'

'To face into the city.'

'Aye. The enemy within.'

'Even now, when the enemy is so visibly and plentifully without.'

'Ours not to reason why.'

Out in the darkness, among the Tatar lines, they could hear the familiar sounds of gun platforms being built. Ottoman or Bulgar carpenters working peacefully on fine timber, constructing good strong catapults and trebuchets. Smith peered into the darkness, lit by occasional pinpricks of torches, flickering now in the rising wind. Beyond the flames of the city, damnably dark, a clouded night. But in that darkness, plenty of activity. They stared and stared. Nicholas thought of Priam on his lofty ancient walls, hearing in puzzlement the work of the Achaean carpenters, and then the sound of the wooden horse rumbling close ...

As doomed as Troy the night before she burned.

'You have wet all the house roofs, spread sacking, rugs?' said Smith.

'We have done what we could,' said Vorotinsky. 'They are going to rain down more incendiaries, are they not? As much as cannon fire?'

'Evidently. You can just make out the steep trajectories out there. A few big cannonballs to batter in the gates, but mostly high arcing catapults and trebuchets to toss in burning loads over the walls.'

'Bales of hay and straw,' said Stanley. 'I thought it might have been plague victims they would be lobbing in, diseased body parts, the putrid corpses of rats ... Such things have been known in the Mongol Wars, and since ancient times. But plague still needs days or weeks to take hold, and can be as much a menace to the besieger as to the besieged. He comes to round up the defeated for slavery, only to fall to their diseases too. No, Devlet Giray wants fast results. The Tatars are rapid skirmishers. They like to fight with fire.'

'My city is to be brought low by a handful of straw,' said Prince Michael.

They were silent. Nothing to say.

And worse still, nothing to do. It was agony for all of them.

At that very moment, the darkness out there on the plain burst into life and everything was illuminated. For with marvellous coordination and discipline that was surely Ottoman, not Tatar, torches were set to the entire line of catapults and their thickly oiled loads burst into life. The watchers on the walls drew breath. There must have been forty of them out there.

There was a single pistol shot and then the ropes were released. They heard the huge ropes thrum in unison as their mighty pent-up force was released, and the forty bales arced up in a long, graceful line, blazing more furiously as they sailed through the night air, their arc perfectly calculated, the wind reckoned, and came in right over their heads.

'Now that's what I call a firework display,' said Hodge.

And then all forty came hurtling down upon granaries, barns, woodstores, churches, and narrow street after street of dry timber houses. A few simply exploded and scattered into bits in the middle of squares, adding to the general panic. They watched, and within only a minute or two, Moscow was alight with a dozen more in-extinguishable fires, the wind fanning them into ever greater and more ardent life.

And then there were no more incendiaries. Not all night.

'I think Devlet Giray has further plans,' said Stanley.

They spent the last hours of darkness trying to help douse the flames, but the damage was great and the terror of the citizens much greater. When dawn broke they walked through a grey ashen cityscape through weary drifts and plumes of smoke, down streets where half the houses were nothing but smouldering heaps of earth. There were dead and charred bodies carelessly hidden under coverlets and canvas, though barely a shot had yet been fired. Nicholas felt that dreamlike unreality of war again, intensely. Through this ashen landscape, women were still heading off to the early morning market with their baskets over their arms, to the square before St Basil's where only last night, many dozens of people had been tortured to death for their edification. He saw a group of headscarved housewives gossiping with each other, won-dering about what would come of it all, grim-faced, yet still hoping ... and immediately behind them, a mound of slaughtered bodies under a horse blanket. Slaughtered not by the Tatars, but as part of last night's celebrations.

A strange, disconcerting lull – deliberately disconcerting, of course, nerves fraying like old rope, the temptation to simple sur-render growing by the hour. Another trick of Devlet Giray's. Your enemy's fear and uncertainty are two of your most potent weapons. The Tatars were in no hurry, were fine-tuning their trebuchets and resting their guns, watching the sullen city smoulder behind its walls and reckon its own damage and their power over it. Why go to any great effort when you could have Moscow for nothing?

And then a messenger came to the south gate and was taken to Vorotinsky.

The message he bore did not even greet Ivan or any by name. It read with un-Oriental curtness, 'You have no defences. You see what we can do. There is no need to take down your gates, your walls. Moscow is a city of wood, and we will burn you to the ground. But of our great clemency and mercy, we invite you first to acknowledge our suzerainty over Kazan and Astrakhan, and then to surrender and submit yourselves to slavery. Let that be punishment for your insolence, and be thankful that we exact no more.'

In trepidation they rode with the messenger to the Kremlin. They didn't think the Czar was going to like it. He might very well kill the poor messenger on the spot.

'Surrender and submit ourselves to slavery! The people of Russia are my slaves, not those of that unbelieving dog of a slant-eyed Tatar, shit on his mother's grave!'

He picked up a wooden stool and hurled it against a wall. Ivan was a strong man, especially when maddened with rage, and the stool smashed apart. They stood well back. Then he snatched up his heavy iron-tipped staff and began to whirl it about like some deranged wizard. Stanley thought the Tatar messenger had a fifty-fifty chance of dying in this chamber. But the Asian warrior stood impassive, arms folded, obedient only to his Khan, a magnificent figure for all one knew of the Tatars and their rapacity, and quite evidently contemptuous of this childish tantrum of the Russian Czar.

'Every last man, woman and child in Russia will die before we give way one inch to those Christless savages! I will tear that horse-fucker Devlet Giray limb from limb, I will drink his blood straight from his open throat!'

He seized a bottle that stood on a table and drained it in one. Hurled it to the floor. 'And where is my cursed physician? We need more tonic! Find him!'

A terrified servant said they had not found him yet, they were searching all the palace but he appeared to have—

'Are you saying he has gone over to the enemy?' cried Ivan, his voice almost a shriek, and he raised his iron-tipped staff high and prepared to bring it down on the idiot's head. He knew how it would feel, the satisfying power of it, he had done it so many times before. The bony clonk and crack, the skull splitting open like an egg, the oozing of brain, the funny startled look in the fellow's eye, and then the light going out. Him falling to the floor, clumsy and dead. And then the tiresome wiping clean of his staff ...

'No!' cried out Stanley. 'Excellency!'

Ivan must have heard something through his red madness, for the staff swerved at the last instant and crashed down upon the table, gouging a huge chip out of its surface. The servant was close to fainting.

'Go!' Stanley bellowed at him. 'Find Bomelius!'

The servant fled.

Momentarily exhausted, Ivan let his staff drop to the floor. His rages always exhausted him, though the accompanying violence was exhilarating. He needed more tonic. Where was that Bomelius? He had gone over to the enemy. He knew it. He was beset by traitors and foul sinners.

He stared at these people before him. Who were these impertinent strangers? He knew them not. They offended him, distracted him from his Holy Work. He was like Christ scourged, panting, drenched in sweat, eyes burning beneath his brows. He felt the heat of his own beloved burning city in his blood. How he suffered! He was Russia, Russia was him. They were one. And he was holy as Russia was holy, beyond sin. But there must be sacrifice.

His thoughts tired him. He called for a chair and sank down.

'No surrender,' he muttered. 'We will never surrender. Let there be death before slavery. The Tatars may not have Moscow.'

They sent back the messenger to Devlet Giray, saying they would fight on. Then they spent a grim morning overseeing the militia. Three hundred now. Eighty muskets. They concentrated them at the south gate. It was absurd. But perhaps there was still some faint hope that sheer stubbornness, sheer refusal to surrender, might wear the Tatars down ...

'Or plague in the Tatar camp,' said Smith. 'That would work. Pray God sends them boils and pestilence.'

Towards evening they returned to the palace. Smith was prepared to beg Ivan, to his face, to let them turn the guns around and man them. If Ivan tried to smash him on the head for his impertinence, Smith was beginning to think he might fight back, and hang the consequences.

A chamberlain shook his head. 'The Czar has departed Moscow.'

'De ... Departed?'

'He rode out of the north gate with his close guard an hour since. The Tatars made no move to arrest him.'

Maybe the Easterners reckoned the city would fall to them more easily with the Czar gone. Or they reckoned to capture Moscow first, and then mop up Ivan later. They stood stunned. The chamberlain turned away.

'A cheerful people,' muttered Stanley.

'You'd be cheerful,' said Smith more loudly, 'with a Czar who spends his time oppressing and torturing you, and then bolts and runs like a rabbit the moment danger appears over the horizon.'

'Dangerous words,' said Vorotinsky, 'dangerous words.'

'Then let them arrest me,' said Smith. 'Let those bastards of the Oprichnina come and try.'

Stanley called after the chamberlain, 'Where has he gone?'

'I cannot say.'

The time for caution was over. Stanley felt the relief of knowing that it was all in action now. He stepped close to the chamberlain and laid his hand very heavily on his shoulder, gripping just tightly enough to make his meaning clear. 'Tell us, sir. We need to know.'

The chamberlain bit his lip. 'The Czar has fled with the Czarevich and his children and his treasure and his faithful Oprichnina, to his palace at Alexandrovskaya Sloboda. He may retire further off yet if danger still threatens, or seek refuge in a foreign court.'

'Did he talk of England? Refuge there?'

The chamberlain said quietly, 'It has been mooted.'

Then Nicholas laughed, sensing too that the time for caution and diplomacy was over. 'What an idiot!'

Devlet Giray still seemed to be practising diplomacy, or at least negotiation by pressure and threat. A stream of refugees from the outlying country came across the plain, and were allowed to pass unmolested through the Tatar lines and up to the gates, where they were admitted.

'An act of mercy,' people muttered.

The refugees brought tales of whole families dying on the roads in the east, in villages and towns laid waste. People ate grass and the boiled bark of trees. The citizens began to talk of giving themselves up.

'Mercy!' stormed Smith. 'You fools! The Tatars have half-starved them first! Now they drive them into the city, to swell our numbers, so we have more to feed. They bring empty bellies, disease, and most of all these tales of suffering, to break your spirits! You dolts. That is the nature of Devlet Giray's mercy. He is a commander of infinite cunning.'

It was as Smith said. The refugees spread terrible tales of burned-out monasteries, the infidels drinking from the sacred vessels, plucking ornaments from holy images to wear as barbaric jewellery. They put hot cinders in the boots of monks and made them dance. They stripped young nuns and raped them laughing, cut off their noses and threw them down wells.

Another people might have found some resolve in such tales of atrocity, but the people here were already too demoralized and broken by their own oppression. A spokesman came to Vorotinsky saying that many of them wanted a truce.

'Never!' cried Vorotinsky. 'The Czar himself commanded us to fight to the last.'

'Then we will all die, all the city.'

'So let it be,' said Vorotinsky. 'We are the people of God, we do not fear death.'

34

As dusk fell they stood on the thinly manned walls and saw a sight that chilled them.

'It'll warm us soon enough,' said Nicholas.

Gun after gun was drawn up to face the south wall, and catapults and trebuchets now of every size. Incendiaries as before, but now they would rain down unceasingly until the whole city was one vast fire, and there were other more evil devices too. Greek fire pots, of subtle design, strong enough to withstand being hurled from a catapult, well wadded, and double-skinned. Some could even be fired from cannon, packed tight with rags and straw, so that they would not shatter but erupt from the barrel at high speed. Once launched into the air, the rags and straw naturally fell away and the fire pot streak high into the sky, to fall on the rooftops and into the streets of Moscow.

Soldiers in the German Wars called them Pandora's boxes – for they contained all the sorrows of the world. Nails and sharp flints and stones, thick black oil from the Caspian shore, naphtha, sulphur, even sugary date wine to make the burning mixture stick to any surface it landed on. Such a mixture could even stick to the sides of galleys and continue to burn below the waterline, as Nicholas himself had seen. It stuck to living skin and continued to blaze, so that people ran screaming through the streets like human torches . . .

Devlet Giray had promised to burn Moscow to the ground, and now he meant it. He did not want any more testing or skirmishing, or talk of truce. He had lost patience. And he did not intend to lose more than a hundred men in this siege.

'I hope to God they have taken to the cellars,' said Smith.

'I trust the whole city has,' said Stanley. Indeed it was eerily quiet now, the streets deserted, even the emaciated refugees taken in and hidden.

'What do we hope for?' said Nicholas abruptly. 'Truly? We will all burn.'

'There will be chaos,' promised Stanley. 'In chaos there is opportunity, as they say in Cathay.'

Nicholas had just discerned the first star in the sky, towards the south-west – Venus, Goddess of Love, ah, heaven's irony! – when the first guns roared out. He managed a sour grimace, and then the bombardment erupted with full strength.

Reeling, deafened, blinded, men shouting, a few scattered and impotent musket shots from the walls, Vorotinsky's voice somewhere, hoarse and desperate. Through the mirk, a huge gout of black smoke and flame from one of the biggest guns, then a titanic roar and down below, the ominous sound of the entire south gate shivering and buckling, already splintering at its hinges, bulking behind collapsing back into rubble.

'Below!' cried Smith. 'Vorotinsky, send me some men with pikes. Bulk her up again!'

At last it seemed the citizen militia were galvanized, by the sheer noise and terror of it if nothing else. There was no time left to reason.

Even as they raced down the steps, they heard the distant familiar thrum of catapults, and the strange, fiery roar of forty incendiary bales tumbling through the air above them and crashing down upon the city.

And then, almost immediately, another big gun roared out and another eighty-pound ball slammed into the reeling gate below.

Nicholas had his sword drawn already. This would last about an hour. And he was ready to run back to the English House at any moment.

Hodge nodded. 'With you.'

Even as they scrabbled about behind the double gate, throwing crude lumps of rock back onto the pile, a team of militia trying and failing to put up a long timber prop, another monstrous gun was readying out there on the plain, lined up and calculated by the expert gunners to strike in exactly the same place as before. The glowing linstock lowered to the pan, then the gunnery team crouched down, hands over their ears, eyes closed. The dread pause, the hollow fizz – and then the bronze beast erupting backwards on its carriage against its restraining ropes, vomiting forth another stone or iron ball in a trumpet of smoke and flame.

'Get back, Smith!' roared Stanley.

This shot was so perfectly executed, the south gate simply surrendered before it, the loose bulking of rubble and timber behind it blasted to smithereens. As the smoke and the white dust gradually cleared, they saw the gate hanging clean off its hinges. The mighty ball had gone straight through the timbers of the gate and on into the city, half-demolishing a nearby house. From within they could hear desperate cries and screams.

A figure hauled himself up from the rubble, white with dust but for a red stain down his forearm. Smith. He raised and lowered his sword. Still working.

Then a huge cheer went up from the Tatar host, and at a single nod from Devlet Giray on his platform, the grim-faced generals raised their rods of command and a large party of cavalry began to gallop in across the plain, making straight for the ruptured south gate. Such confidence. They would enter the city through a single breach, not even troubling to break down two or three sections so that they could attack on several fronts at once. They knew. There was no soldiery here to speak of, and that wretched Czar was already fled, they knew exactly where to. They would pick him up later and make him pass under the yoke. Perhaps remove his eyes or his ears. They knew that his main army was tied down in the west. They knew everything.

A troop of some twenty pikemen came trotting down from the wall.

'Line up before the gate,' bellowed Smith, 'pikes at the ready! We must hold them! They cannot gallop in over rubble!'

The musketeers on the walls also levelled their guns at the oncoming horde with trembling hands, but one was so young and inexperienced he lowered the muzzle of his long musket too far and the ball, inadequately wadded, simply rolled out of the barrel and fell to the ground far below.

Vorotinsky strode back and forth on the walls. 'Reload, you dolt! No firing until I give the command! I want every shot to count!'

Nicholas and Hodge stood near Stanley. It was absurd, desperate, so let them fight with added desperation. Let them fight for that little square of home territory that was the English House, and that blithering idiot Waverley, Greene and his wife and three sweet children, old Southam and his slut wife, and of course for that girl. If the Tatars broke in and took Moscow – though how could they not? – all would perish or be enslaved.

And it needed little imagination to picture where Rebecca would end up. Nicholas saw it all with grim, cold fury. Repeatedly raped and then sold into slavery as a fair captive to some khan. Kept on if she fell pregnant and bore a son, but if she did not, turned out onto the steppes to die. And anyway, by thirty she would be accounted old in the eyes of her Tatar lord, and finished. Among the heathen of Asia, women were good only for bearing strong sons. If she gave him a daughter she would be disgraced, while he turned to fresher and younger captives yet, nubile virgins, those in the very first flush of womanhood. Twelve or thirteen was the age thought ideal by the devout Mohammedan. Their devil's scripture itself, the Koran, pictured paradise itself as little more than a celestial brothel full of such compliant and ageless maidens.

He gripped the hilt of his sword, teeth clenched. Then let them try and take her.

'Here they come!' cried Smith.

The Tatar horsemen appeared in the gate, pressing through thirty abreast, and half the militiamen broke and ran. There was no order. Nicholas took in a mass of wild, jostling steppe warriors, fur hats as common as helmets, pointed kalpaks, slim long-handled axes shining and whirring, cruel lances, and much-favoured recurved bows. Some horsemen wearing war paint across their broad cheeks in bands of red, yellow and blue, some fighting naked to the waist and covered in tattoos and strange symbols. Some wore their raven black hair in long ponytails down their backs, their squat Asiatic horses hung with amulets and animal skulls.

They were a long way from Shropshire.

He dodged a blow from an axe and seized one horse by the reins and dragged it forwards over the rubble so that it stumbled and its rider slashed about clumsily, unbalanced, and he managed to drag the rider down and kill him. Stanley was crouching behind a fallen horse, blasting another rider down with his hefty handgun. Smith broke his sword and seized a pike and then broke that in half too, and was reduced to swinging it about him like a half pike, surrounded by horsemen ...

But all the while the incendiaries kept falling, and the greatest noise now was the blazing inferno behind them that was Moscow. Stanley glanced back. 'Nick – you and Hodge, back to the House! Cover your mouths!'

'You too!'

'We'll follow!'

A stroke of luck came to them then. With the usual chaos of battle, an incendiary came down short and the huge, blazing bale tumbled straight into the back of the troop of Tatar horsemen before them. Immediately horses reared up screaming, and there was the stench of burning horsehair and Tatar riders flailing about with whips.

'Fall back now!' cried Smith.

They fled through burning streets, ducked low under the searing blaze of wooden houses, wet their kerchiefs again in a trough and ran on, half choked. At the end of the street, they had glimpsed Tatar horsemen, already ecstatic with battle madness, apocalyptic laughter, riding into the fire, killing everything.

The four had long since pulled off their steel helmets. Men's heads could boil in them. The city was burning away to nothing before their eyes.

The noise of the firestorm roaring was more terrifying than anything, a continuous roar of such astounding volume that they could no longer hear each other, even when shouting. They were choked, blinded, the smoke burning blacker, the pitch roofs melting, dripping molten tar down around them ... Ahead, Nicholas saw Smith drop to his knees and Stanley haul him up again. Was this the right street? Night and black smoke, like crawling through a cavern of hell. Nicholas's lungs were seared, his eyes were red and inflamed and filled with tears, he could hardly see. They must get back to the house soon or they would choke and die here . . .

People ran back out of their burning houses, making for the river, or even climbed down ropes into wells. Many were burned. The four staggered now, not ran, past twisted shapes no longer human, charred bodies of dogs and cats, corpses unidentifiable and emaciated, the fat melted off them and puddled in the intense heat. Children like cinder dolls, and falling perpetually through the darkened air like strange snow, bright flaming motes, flakes of wood from the rooftops, scraps of cloth from the burned dead, carried up high by the heat of the flames and cooled and then falling back down into the city, silent and ashen white.

Nicholas glanced back at one point and a gust of wind parted for a moment the dense curtains of dark smoke, and he saw a sight he would never forget. To the north, at the heart of the burning and dying city, he saw the great red walls and towers of the Kremlin, its gold onion domes, seemingly untouched by the fire that was destroying the people it ruled over. An old Russian story.

Then there were Tatars ahead of them, surrounding a woman and child. She sank to her knees, and they crowded in and speared her and the infant where they knelt. One horseman slipped from his saddle with a long curved knife in his hand, ready to take scalps.

Smith bellowed out. A deranged figure still covered in white dust, red eyes blazing, still clutching a shattered pike in his mighty fist. Then the Tatars were riding down upon them, through the very inferno. Nicholas had never known so crazed a fight. Stanley had managed to keep and load his heavy German handgun, a clumsy matchlock, but no need now to have a smoking matchcord ready. He simply ripped a smouldering board from the side of the house and touched it to the pan and let it smoulder and then aimed two-handed. The big ball hit a Tatar horseman full in the chest and he reeled back. No more time to admire. Stanley thrust the gun home under his belt and they turned and ran, crouching low. The Tatar horsemen were momentarily slowed, unsure how many more guns waited for them round the corner, and then a change of wind blew a thick pall of smoke sidelong and enveloped them.

They could hear the Tatars' coughing and choking even above the roar of the inferno.

'Attack!' cried Smith, running out.

Four of them, already half-suffocated, helmetless, not a loaded gun between them now, already carrying three or four injuries as well – against twenty or more fresh horsemen? Smith was wrong this time. Stanley brought him down with the kind of flying grapple you would see in a village football match. Hodge shouted out, 'Get back in here, you bloody idiots!' The two knights rolled in the dust a moment and then the smoke began to clear. The Tatars were riding down on them.

'Here they come!' cried Nicholas. 'Back!'

They backed down a narrow alley and fought a desperate rearguard fight all the way. Stanley wielded a burning timber at one point, Smith used a wooden well-cover as a shield, the kind made of thick oak planking that usually took two men to lift. With incredible deftness and speed, Stanley managed to reload his handgun amid this mêlée and aim and take down another warrior. Nicholas saw his right shoulder explode in a red mist. Another warrior caught him off guard, trapped him against the wall with his horse, levelled an arquebus almost in his face, fired before Nicholas could duck – and misfired. In a trice Nicholas seized the arquebus by the barrel and pulled it from the startled horseman's grasp and – an arquebus could weigh a hefty twenty pounds – shoved it back like a ram straight at the rider's kneecap. A hideous crunch, an animal howl. The horse sidestepped, Nicholas dropped down against the wall and ducked beneath the horse and closed up with the others.

'The back of the house! There!' cried Hodge.

An arrow glanced off his shoulder, the point missing his ear by a whisker. 'Bugger you!' he hollered back.

And then Stanley glanced upwards and cried out something but the air was filled with noise and they didn't hear. A burning house was coming down on them like a blazing red sea on the chariots of the Egyptians, drowning them and the Tatar horsemen in flame. They dropped everything and ran.

They crouched in a burning doorway, once the back entrance to the English House, and looked back. Nothing but flame. Stanley's right cheek had been burnt, a mottled and angry blister like a poached egg showing through the black charcoal dust that covered his face, all their faces. All were half-choked, half-blinded, their eyes streaming. How had they seen anything in that fight? But they still lived.

And even over the sound of the inferno, Stanley thought he heard a horn. A brazen horn or maybe a ram's horn, made to carry over the steppe ... He raised his hand. It came again. Smith heard it this time. They looked at each other.

'What?' said Nicholas, desperately hoping. 'What is it? More Russian forces? Streltsy?'

'Alas, not that,' said Stanley. 'But it may just be – our friends Stenka and Yakublev causing trouble.' He tightened his kerchief over his mouth one last time. 'We must go.'

They tore off doublets and shirts and wrapped their hands and pulled aside glowing timbers, crouched, crawling like serpents, under a low roof of smoke, and got through the stone-floored kitchens and came at last to the oak door to the cellars, still soaking wet, thank Christ. Stanley hammered on it and shouted in English, and a moment later they heard a fumbling on the other side. The ceiling of the kitchen over their heads gave a huge crack. The English House was burning from the top down, like many of the houses, lit by incendiaries from above. Those fine first-floor chambers, the bedrooms, the wood-panelled corridor, the attics, already consumed in the violence of the fire. If the House had burned from below, it would have been long gone by now.

The volume of the roaring flames increased, overhead, all around. The smoke was sucked up and away by it, but breathing was no easier, the heat almost enough to make them pass out. Nicholas crouched against Hodge, the cloth pressed to his mouth, wondering if you could inhale air so hot, your lungs began to roast from the inside. And then the door was open and they were stumbling blearily down a spiral of stone steps, the door bolted behind them. They came into a red-brick cellar lit by one candle, and a circle of terrified faces. Little Cecily Greene began to cry.

The denizens of the cellar saw four unearthly figures, coated in white dust and black, red-eyed, bearing wounds about them, one with a filthy bandage around his thigh, another with a horribly blistered cheek, one with a long cut in his forearm, the black-bearded one. Two them were down to torn shirts, and two, the blond giant Edward Stanley and the young Ingoldsby, were naked now to the

221

waist, drenched in sweat, the torn remains of their shirts bound around their hands. Even by the single candle, the serving women, and Mistress Ann Southam too, could not help looking over the magnificent torso of the giant, strong as an ox, the biceps bulging, and the lean muscled chest and arms of the younger one, the handsome boy – and to think the giant, at least, was a Catholic monk, and sworn to celibacy! Even in this grim cellar, a city burning down around them, they could not help but think it was a crying shame. Though they had already heard some household gossip about the other. Men. Really.

And then a girl's cry, and a slim figure rushed towards them and threw her arms around Nicholas. She stood back, her face smudged from his. Flushed, anxious, yet eyes sparkling with tearful relief.

'Aye,' he said fatuously, awkward before this audience, conscious he was bare to the waist and the women were observing him closely. 'We made it.'

Her father coughed. He knew from the frightful look of the four, and knew it with some irritation, that they truly were strong fighters, unafraid of battle, and he resented it.

'Your appearance is terrible,' he said.

'Aye,' said Stanley, touching his hand to his blistered cheek. 'It's quite a warm summer night out there.'

'And I always thought Russia was supposed to be cold,' said Hodge.

Waverley did not comprehend their humour.

The four sank back with that utter exhaustion after battle that they knew so well. The others continued to stare at them, Waverley and Robert Greene and Thomas Southam and Mistress Ann and the several serving men and women, as if they were creatures come from the burning pit.

At last Waverley said, 'Well, let us thank the Good Lord for your deliverance.'

Bit early for that, thought Smith. Have you seen what it's like out there? But he manfully held his tongue.

35

Unheard by the fearful gathering in the cellar, but as Stanley had heard earlier, horns were sounding here and there in the south of the city: Tatar horns, echoing one great horn sounded from the nearby heights. It was the order to pull back. Because any battle now would be fought outside the walls – where the Tatar horsemen fought best.

Devlet Giray had surveyed the blazing city from the heights of the Sparrow Hills with considerable satisfaction. All was accomplished as planned. And they had said that the age of the steppe horseman was done! That the future lay with those dull drilled regiments of musketeers, like the Streltsy or those of the Turks! But where was the dash and the exhilarating gallop, the heroism and the glory in that?

But he could now see from his vantage point that the city before him was burning wildly out of control, and its fate was no more in the hands of any mortal commander, but subject only to the Will of Allah. He had no desire to lose any of his best men, always the first into any captured city, in that firestorm. There would not be any great loot from this molten inferno, but they had taken a good few hundred slaves, so let it be. The capital of this upstart Russian power was all but laid waste, and their entire empire could now be retaken bit by bit, with no resistance.

They should make for Kazan and take it. He might return to Moscow next year – and take up residence in the Kremlin for a while, with a slave called Ivan Vasil'evich serving him his coffee or his iced sherbet! That would be amusing.

He watched more slaves being whipped into the camp, women of Moscow with faces still covered in smuts and ash from the fire! He smiled at them. Some of the young Russian girls, with their pretty fair hair in braids and their high cheekbones and their pale blue eyes, were enough to drive a man wild. Perhaps a few for the Sultan on the Bosphorus, to flatter him, but not too many. That peace-loving scholar couldn't be much of a one for swiving. Instead there would be a happy apportioning of these pretty blonde kittens among his generals tonight, a few to his bravest warriors, and much grunting and thrashing in the tents thereafter. He laughed aloud, a harsh, abrupt laugh. War was sweet!

And how he was looking forward to composing his next missive to that lank fool Ivan! A terror to his own people, but his enemies' best ally. He had it in his head already. Devlet Giray would mock him for his rank cowardice, demand he swear fealty as a vassal, humiliate him utterly ... It was all about scornfully trampling your enemy in the dust, taking his gold, and ravishing his women until they clung to you through the long night, wrapped their lissom limbs around you, and sobbed that they would never leave you even if you were to give them their freedom.

Oh, by the ten thousand names of Allah, but war was holy and sweet.

He saw one of his men raise his whip to a stumbling girl, and called out, 'You there! Stay your hand.'

Victory made you benevolent, tender-hearted. You even began to dislike seeing slave-girls whipped! What a comedy. He looked closely at the girl. Head bowed, cheek flushed, breasts like small apples, something in the way she walked ... A young fawn of a girl, and virgin still, or he was no judge of women.

He jerked his head. 'Take her to my tent. Have the women attend to her.'

Far out on the plain behind the vast Tatar camp were drawn up the baggage wagons, beside the slave pens filled with hundreds more captured village girls, strong young men and pleasing children. The wagons were laden with loot taken from churches and monasteries along the way, guarded by well-armed eunuchs. Those geldings were thought to be more honest. Why should they seek to enrich themselves? They had no heirs to inherit their wealth. And from this rearguard had come a message of some panic.

Accursed Cossacks again.

A messenger came running, breathless, saying they had been seen on some hills not far off, many hundreds, perhaps thousands, eyeing the baggage like vultures eyeing carrion, knowing the main Tatar host had been drawn into Moscow, and looking for easy pickings. They might be down at any moment like lightning, like a wolf on the fold, and away again with the best loot before the Tatar host even knew of it.

But then some of the Cossacks had fired a few arrows down onto the baggage camp. As if they wanted to make their presence known.

It was then that Devlet Giray had taken one last, good look at Moscow burning. Almost pitiful, its lack of resistance. And yet did it not say in the Holy Koran, Garments of fire have been prepared for the unbelievers. Boiling water shall be poured upon their heads, melting their skins and bursting their bellies. They shall be beaten with rods of iron, and when in their agony they try to escape from that Burning, my angels will drag them back down, saying, 'Come, taste the torments of Hell-fire!'

Blessed be the word of Allah.

That was when Devlet Giray turned away and gave the order to pull back out of the doomed city, and the great ram's horn sounded.

'And reinforce the guards at the baggage camp.'

They had been crouched in the cellar for no more than twenty minutes, the four comrades doing their best to tend and rebandage each other's wounds, when the brick-vaulted ceiling over their heads gave an ominous crack. Glancing up, Smith caught a faceful of dust cascading down, and saw an ugly black crack open up across the corner of the vault. Already the temperature in the cellar was far hotter than they had expected, to their silent dismay. The men's and women's faces were dripping with sweat, their clothes plastered to them, even their eyes reddening in the heat. Greene's children had their faces buried in their mother's skirts. It could not get any hotter down here or they would be in danger of burning alive. Old Thomas Southam was beginning to struggle for breath, head down, hands clenched into fists. Ann Southam, for all she was his trollop wife, held him close and talked to him low and reassuring.

But only moments after the ominous crack above, the temperature in the cellar seemed suddenly to rise, and from above their heads they could hear a tremendous, muffled roaring, like some caged wild beast behind a curtain at a fair.

The three children of Robert Greene began to scream. Thomas Southam's gasping got worse, and Waverley paled and cried, 'We are trapped like swine in a slaughterhouse! We will burn alive in here! This was a dreadful mistake, I tell you, a dreadful mistake, we should never have—'

Rebecca held his trembling arm. 'Hush, Father, it is better here than outside, believe me. Had you seen the Tatar horsemen and what they did ...'

Waverley groaned. They were doomed.

'Lie down as low as you can,' said Stanley. 'All of you, flat on the floor, face down. Children, breathe only through your noses, keep your mouths closed, so you—'

But he was interrupted by another, far louder crack overhead, and suddenly the volume of the fire's roaring increased fourfold, a storm right above them. The temperature was becoming near unbearable. Old Southam laid his hands flat out on the stone floor of the cellar and whimpered pitifully for air. But it was thinning fast.

'The fire above is sucking it out of here!' said Hodge urgently. 'Like a log fire sucking air up the chimney.'

Smith nodded grimly. 'He's right. The cellar has served us well enough until now, but it is beginning to kill us.'

Stanley looked around in desperation. It was just possible that the back street was now burned out and quieter again, and the Tatars had been called back ... And yes, they were roasting alive in here. Timbers heaved and cracked over their heads, the great oak posts and joists of the House burning back, the heat hellish. If a floor fell in from above it might smash through the ceiling and all would be crushed.

'I cannot breathe,' gasped Southam, clawing at the floor, 'I cannot breathe, God save me!'

And then Mistress Greene suddenly reached out for her husband, and went limp.

'Do something!' cried Ann Southam.

'Sir,' said Smith, 'blow air into her lungs! Shake her! Waverley, how thick are these walls?'

'I do not know,' said Waverley. 'Thick, and half-buried too.'

Stanley said, 'Is there no coalhole down here?'

'No,' said Waverley, 'the other side of the house.' He waved a limp hand. 'There is a scuttle for the delivery of wine barrels but—'

'Why did you not say, man?'

'The door is locked and I have no key!'

'How strong is the door?' cried Smith. 'Let me at it!' He got to his feet and immediately sank to his knees again as if felled. The heat trapped just below the ceiling was enough to knock a horse senseless.

'Open another vent, the fire may just roar up the fiercer with the rush of air,' said Hodge.

'A risk we must take,' said Stanley.

He and the other three crawled into the neighbouring cellar, hotter still, tying their kerchiefs over their mouths once more. Smith stabbed his pike through a small tun of Madeira and it flooded the floor. They heard some wailed objection from Waverley behind, something about Crown property, but it made little impact. They wallowed in the sticky puddle, dipped their kerchiefs in it.

'This'll either make us drunk or save us,' said Stanley. 'There's the door, Brother John, have at it. The hinges look weaker than the lock to me.' He called back. 'The rest of you, crawl to us! Keep low!'

At that moment there came a terrible noise from above – it sounded like a timber of oak was being twisted around like a blade of grass by some maddened giant, some Nordic fire-giant – and then it was as Stanley had feared. A huge fall above smashed through the cellar roof, and immediately half-buried it and the flames roared up.

Nicholas was back in amid the inferno in a trice, pulling Rebecca through, Ann Southam, she herself dragging at old Thomas, but then he stumbled and fell ... It was chaos, Smith bellowing, smashing at the iron hinges of the scuttle door, smoke suddenly blinding them, Hodge and Stanley groping also, unseeing, for desperate hands held out to them, burning, burning ...

A heavy wooden clatter and the door was wrenched off and they crawled out of the scuttle one by one, choking, blinded, hearing pitiful screams and cries behind them. Came out on all fours like dogs into a back alley and lay gasping, coughing up lungfuls of smoke, their very tongues burned and tingling, lips charred. Someone vomited. Stanley's voice still shouting, 'Get away, get away, keep moving!' then turning and crawling back in to rescue any still alive.

Afterwards, Rebecca remembered crawling and then stumbling onward down an ashen lane, half fainting. Heaps of blackened timber, a crooked black hand reaching out to her from a heap of ash, and then a small stone stable, blackened without, miraculously untouched within. The randomness of fire. There was even straw inside, unburned even in this blaze, and a russet pig standing in the corner, eyeing her. She huddled close to Ann Southam, who she had little cause to like, and they looked about them, and at each other's ashen and stricken faces, and then the women began to weep but with no noise. The last thing Rebecca had heard as she crawled out of that cellar was her father's voice crying out, the last thing Ann Southam had heard, the quavering voice of her husband.

No more were rescued. The last fugitives fell into the little stable like broken men. Stanley looked back at the English House. No more would come out alive. None. It burned more violently than any other around, but perhaps it was a wonder it had stood so long.

He bowed his head and he too wept.

Robert Greene was burned to death in there, and Thomas Southam, and the fool Waverley, and Mistress Greene too, and the three children. The whole family wiped out. Stanley named them in his heart. Jane, aged eleven, Robert, aged nine, and Cecily, but five years on this earth. He named them before God, and begged God's forgiveness that he had failed them.

Then there was a heavy, familiar hand on his shoulder.

'Let us go on,' said Smith.

But they were defeated. In every way. 'Go on where, Brother?'

'At least to the riverbank. Wash our wounds.'

'The river is choked with corpses. Some good that will do our wounds.'

Even Smith was lost for words a moment. It was true. They had awoken to find themselves still in hell. Then he said, 'A fountain, perhaps, a well. We must find water. The Tatars are gone.'

Slowly, liked dazed or dying creatures, holding each other, they rose up and walked out into a ruined city, a wilderness of ash.

Fires still burned fitfully, here a small chapel, behind them the accursed English House. There were corpses, pools of smoking human fat. Slaughtered pigs and mules. The severed head of a single militiaman, burnt black and stuck on a spike of timber like a rotten fruit.

'Take care there,' said Stanley indicating. Another pool, dark grey. Molten lead from a roof. A cat half-burned, still alive, dragging its back legs, mewing pitifully. Smith knelt swiftly beside it and gave it its release.

Half the city was gone. In the north, fires still burned. And in the centre stood the walled fortress, the cathedrals and the palaces of the Kremlin, hardly touched.

'I never thought we would head there for refuge,' said Smith. 'But now ...'

Stanley nodded wearily. 'Bomelius is dead. Ivan is gone, with his Oprichnina. It may be a place of refuge, until we can find a boat and get away from here. Downriver, or northwards, to Archangel, and home.'

England or Italy or Malta – anywhere but here.

Smith nodded. 'We should go.'

36

They stepped cautiously into the wide square of St Basil's, strewn with dead bodies, overturned wagons still smoking, spears stuck in the ground, smashed barrels, even the detritus of Ivan's own festivities. A huge overturned cauldron, and in cruel mockery, a gallows still standing undamaged, ready to execute more Muscovites for any treachery. They passed by, swords drawn.

'This feels dangerous,' said Smith. 'Too open.'

'Agreed,' said Stanley. 'Quickly, to the Kremlin Gate.'

They came to a low postern gate in the wall and Smith hammered on it. Stanley stood at the rear, turned, ready. Something was not right. Something was coming.

A Russian voice sounded within. 'No admittance!'

'Servants of the Czar!' said Smith. 'Let us in. The Tatars have been called back. There is no danger.'

'No admittance,' repeated the gatekeeper. 'Czar's own orders. The Kremlin is not Moscow.'

'It's not?' Smith said sarcastically. Then, lower voiced, 'Man, we have a whole bag of gold here. It's yours if you open this door. We know the Czar is not within. Your fort must be almost empty.'

There was a slight hesitation, and then the voice repeated, 'No admittance.'

In exasperation, Smith stepped back and looked up at the height of the walls. Impressive, but one might almost improvise some grappling hook and rope, and just climb in ... Were there left more than fifty guards within that vast complex of churches and palaces?

Then Stanley said, 'Smith,' and he looked round.

In utter silence, a last troop of Tatar cavalry was clustering in the mouth of an alleyway across the square. No wonder it had felt bad. Here they were. Twenty of them, savage-looking brutes, the last of the scavengers, saddle-panniers overflowing. Several bloody scalps between them, hung from their horses' barbaric trappings.

In an instant Smith was hammering thunderously on the postern gate, bellowing with all his might.

'Press back against the gate!' cried Stanley. 'They may ignore us, they have their loot, and the horn has sounded!'

Nicholas pushed Rebecca behind him and stood before her. Hodge stood before Ann Southam, and Stanley before them both.

The Tatars hesitated. One indicated. They had seen the two fair-skinned women. Especially the younger one. And then they came cantering.

They reined in, a tight circle around the trapped little group.

The leader of the troop said harshly, 'Hand them over. We may not cut your throats after. If you refuse, we will kill all six of you and ride on.'

Ann Southam began to wail. Rebecca hissed, 'Silence, madam. Not now.'

Stanley shook his head, playing for time, already calculating. The smaller fellow to his left – he thought he could take him down and mount his horse. Once on horseback he could cause some mayhem. Of course he could not take them all, but they were mere pillagers, stragglers and cowards, the dregs of any army, and might yet be driven off. If only the damn door behind would open ...

'Not worth it,' he said, both voice and sword steady. 'You will lose good men if you come closer, and besides, your order of retreat has sounded. Back to your camp with your loot.'

The leader gave a thin smile. 'Ah,' he said. 'Your ardour to protect this mare and this filly tells me they are good fucking!'

'You savage!' shouted Hodge, and spat at him.

The Tatar leader raised his spear, and at that instant Ann Southam rushed out from behind Hodge and threw herself on the ground at his feet. The others gaped.

'Take me, sir!' she cried. 'Take me! My husband is slain, I am a poor widow, I have nothing. Take me, but leave the others. I am ... I am obedient to your every wish.'

The Tatar leader looked down at her curiously, then jerked his head. 'Bind her.'

Two horsemen dismounted and tied her arms tight behind her. She hung her head. Stanley checked the unmounted horses, and by an eye movement indiscernible to any but Smith, indicated he would take the skewbald, Smith the grey.

'Very well,' said the Tatar. He dangled his spear loosely again, dominant, amused. 'Old venison sometimes has good flavour. But you know what we say among my people. Happiness is to ride a strong horse all day and a young girl all night.' He waggled his spearpoint almost playfully now at Rebecca. 'Let us have the other one too, and we will all go our way in peace and, what do you say, Christian forgiveness?'

A moment of silence, and then pandemonium. Simultaneously, Nicholas rushed at the leader, so fast he was past his spearpoint in a trice, and clutching the shaft in his left hand so he couldn't use it, whilst thrusting forward hard with his sword. Horses whinnying, rearing, riders pressing in. A club whirling through the air. A scream from Rebecca. Mistress Ann Southam knocked to the ground. Smith and Stanley both up on horseback, and then one of the dismounted Tatars with unbelievable speed and ruthlessness, drawing his long knife across the skewbald's back legs, bringing the poor creature slumping to the ground with cut hamstrings. Smith rolling in the dust, fighting to get up again, hidden by horsemen. A bellow of pain from Hodge. Nicholas pulling back his sword from under the leader's quilted coat, quite bloodless, and then a blow to the head that made his eyeballs reel in their sockets, his very brain go ice-cold. He slithered down, half-senseless.

A minute or two, he was lying in the dust, barely able to move. There were Tatar voices. His senses slowly returning, limping, but his skull filled with ice, his innards clenched up, near to vomiting, and everything seen through a silvery early-morning mist. Others lay on the ground near him. He saw Hodge not moving at all, perhaps dead. Oh God. Stanley dragging himself up, three spears pressed down into his back, pushing him down again. A warrior leaning over Smith with a long curved knife in his hand, grasping his thick black locks in his hand, pulling his head up from the dust, slipping the knife under his grizzled beard, his throat ... A shout. The warrior looking up, setting his mouth in disapproval, but obediently dropping Smith's head back down with a clonk. Standing, thrusting the knife back under his sash-belt.

The leader still mounted, unhurt. Nicholas's sword thrust had missed entirely. Seated behind him, skirts pushed up, legs bared, gagged, blindfolded, and her wrists tied, Rebecca. Nicholas heard his own cry, as if very distant, and struggled to rise but could not. His gorge rose. His hair was sticky with blood.

After Ivan's senseless cruelties, the ruin of Moscow, the burning of the English House, the deaths of their countrymen – when they felt utterly defeated and it seemed it could get no worse – it had got worse.

The leader rode around them as they lay in the dust. He wanted them left alive so he could have his amusement.

'See!' he cried. 'Look! How prettily she sits behind me. Akish, God of the Sky, there will be good fucking tonight!'

His men gave a raucous cheer.

'And the old mare, she will serve a dozen of us by tomorrow dawn, I have no doubt, and still be begging for more!'

Ann Southam was tied behind another warrior. Her eyes blazed, but she was gagged. A faithless wife she may have been to old Southam, but she had proved herself brave just then, brave and self-sacrificing, more than any of them. But it had not worked. Bravery often won nothing in this harsh world but its own glory.

'And you have taken all these wounds for nothing, look.' The leader spat. 'You fools. Now we ride away with your women, and you lie in the dust like sickly dogs. Remember what comes to you if you dare to fight the Tatars. You suffer. Only be grateful you have not died. But I, Zamurz of the Nogai Tatars – I am feeling joyous and merciful today. Perhaps,' he grinned one last time, teeth white as a wolf's, 'perhaps because I know I shall have such sweet fucking tonight!'

And with many a harsh cry and a cloud of dust, they spurred their tireless little steppe horses and were gone.

Nicholas could not move. None of them moved. From their injuries or from their despair, it was hard to say.

*

But the sun rose relentless as ever, and it was yet the summer sun and rose equally upon all as the hand of God had ordained, and they needs must crawl as best they could and find shade. Hodge was still senseless, but his chest rose and fell, and so they dragged him staggering and crawling – Hodge was no lightweight – across the square and they found shade beside that grotesque, man-sized cooking pot in which only two nights ago, Ivan had laughed to see his suspected enemies boiled alive.

They lay in silence and gazed out upon ruination, and amid the ruination, the mocking finger of the gallows.

At last Smith croaked, 'We must find water. Tend wounds.'

Stanley sat cross-legged, head bowed. 'Aye,' was all he said.

They had failed in every way. They had failed to protect innocence in this guilty and blood-stained world, time and time again. Everything was lost.

They did not move. An hour passed, more.

Smith was thinking if he died, he did not mind. No Knight of St John feared death, but he feared creaky or palsied old age, feared ending up back in Valletta an old, powerless, enfeebled shadow of his former self. He would very happily die in battle, he was in his fifth decade, and at night he was a mass of aches and pains from three decades of battles. But now he needed to be very strong indeed. Find the very last reserves of willpower, when there was nothing left to fight for. But there was. Nicholas and Hodge, their old comrades and beloved friends, they were young, and they needed tending.

He dragged himself up and the sunlight on the bright square was blinding. His throat was almost too parched to let him draw breath. He closed his eyes, took one tottering step, like an old woman. And then he heard more horses' hooves.

'Are they coming back?' muttered Stanley.

Smith looked towards the sound. They could not fight any more. Perhaps they would all be slain here. Well, all men must die. But their two friends were young.

Careless clattering of hooves, many in number, riding without fear. And then into the square rode a wild-looking troop of steppe horsemen, many moustachioed, most half-naked, magnificent physiques turning coppery in the summer sun. And heavily armed with pistols and muskets and daggers and long curved swords.

They reined in and the leader smiled down.

'Ah,' he said. 'At the very heart of the fight, my old Inglisz friends. You look like you have taken a little battering or two.'

It was Stenka. Even Nicholas stirred. He had almost forgotten the Cossacks, thought they had ridden away long since, back to the empty wilderness of the southern steppes.

Stenka dismounted. 'I am glad I was not here.' He looked around at the devastation, and then said, 'My braves,' and embraced each of them. 'You have walked through hell. I salute you. This is an evil world.'

'It's not over yet,' said Stanley.

Stenka looked at him. He saw a very strong man, very nearly broken. 'Here,' he said, pulling a deerskin flask from his belt. 'Water. You look a little thirsty. Afterwards, vodka.'

'Afterwards,' said Stanley, 'sleep.'

37

As they rode out of the ruined city, survivors were at last emerging here and there from cellars, knowing by some sixth sense that the Tatars had gone at last, the worst of the fires were over. Everyone wanted water – and to begin burying the dead.

Some stared at the passing Cossacks and crossed themselves, or held out their hands. The Cossacks gave generously, water, a few sacks of grain they had brought in, even a steppe gamebird or two. But they could not feed a whole city. Their work was done here. The steppes were calling.

'We have sent scouts far and wide,' said Stenka. 'The main Tatar army is already long gone, south and east of the Sparrow Hills. We are safe now. They are heading home.'

'Not for Kazan?' said Stanley.

Stenka looked thoughtful. 'Or maybe to take Kazan. It will not be hard.' He waved around. 'Russia is done for.'

'We heard the order of retreat. That was you, harrying the rear?'

Stenka grinned. 'The baggage wagons, and the slave pens. We got little for it, but we lost hardly a single man.'

It was something.

They camped out on the plains, where it felt clean, where the dry summer grass smelt sweet, where fire had not raged nor blood been spilt. It was a warm but clear night, little wind, the starry sky above with all its enchantment. They ate bread and roast meat and drank water and a little wine, and bandaged each other's wounds. Chvedar the renegade priest himself splashed vodka generously over them against infection, intoning some words of Church Slavonic, saying, 'I anoint you in the name of Christ. Take this holy chrism and be healed, my beloved children, fresh from slaying the Amalekites before the Lord.'

It was impossible to know whether he was being mocking or serious.

Hodge's wound was the most spectacular. A Tatar had clubbed him with a ferocious iron-studded club, aiming for a crippling or even killing blow to the spine. But Hodge had twisted away from it just in time, and the mighty blow had landed on his hip bone.

'Lucky it didn't split your kidneys,' said Smith. 'Tell us if you start pissing blood.'

'Now be very brave,' said Stanley. 'This is really going to hurt. Nick, give him a stick.'

Hodge chomped down.

'I need to press down right on the heart of the bruise,' said Stanley. 'To know if your bone is broken beneath.'

Hodge closed his eyes.

'And if it is?' said Nicholas.

'Then it won't heal without rest. Weeks and months of it.' He nodded to Hodge. 'I'll be quick.'

Hodge arched and gagged against the stick, hollered, eyes watering, as Stanley for several seconds pushed hard and probed directly upon the fantastically mottled flesh where the club had landed. Then it was done.

Hodge was weeping, to his shame. That had hurt. He spat the stick from his mouth and yelled out. Nicholas held him. Hodge glared at Stanley, despite himself.

'My apologies, friend Hodge,' said Stanley, smiling faintly for the first time since the fire. 'But I bring you glad tidings. The hip bone is steady. Not moving or grating, not broken. Strong bones you have there. You've just got one almighty bruise. We can get a salve on it tomorrow if I find some herbs.'

'Well held, Matthew Hodgkin of Shropshire,' mumbled Smith through a mouthful of roast fowl. 'Taken on the arse, like a man.'

'If I didn't hurt so bloody much,' said Hodge, 'I swear I'd be up and stick that chicken down your poxy throat.'

'No pox for me,' said Smith, 'since I've never been with a whore,

237

unlike some. And it's not chicken either. Partridge. Here, let's see that bruise.'

He squinted by firelight and whistled. 'That's going to colour up lovely. Pretty as a Cornish sunset.'

Hodge pulled his breeches up again. 'Glad it pleases you. That blow to your arm hurt much, does it?'

'A fair bit.'

Hodge grinned. 'So sorry to hear it.'

Nicholas lay awake under the stars, for all his exhaustion. They would heal well enough here in the Cossack camp, and then ... ride home? But how could he? She still lived. And he could not abandon her.

Hodge knew his thoughts, as ever.

'Second time she's gone missing, eh?' he said clumsily.

'She is young,' said Nicholas, abrupt, savage, then turned away and talked no more.

Hodge cursed himself. Idiot. That had not sounded well.

He gazed into the firelight, took another mouthful of water and then vodka and sluiced it down. It was foul on the tongue but good for the soul. Aye, she was young, that girl. And pretty. A very pretty maid indeed, Rebecca Waverley. But now she was in the hands of the Tatar slave-drivers, and many miles away, and so too was that Ann Southam, who had been so brave for their sakes in the city, and what of her? What hope?

Their best hope was that they would find kind masters – surely there were some in Tartary or Araby? The Waverley maid might become some rich merchant's wife in Baghdad or Samarkand or some such outlandish place. She was so lovely to look at, he would love her much, and if she bore him children, especially sons, he would love her all the more and she would be set up for life. And that life might not be too bad. You must be practical about things, thought Hodge, taking another swig. She might keep her Christian faith, if hidden. What else was there for her? Life was strange, a dream journey. You never knew what was next.

But then he glanced sidelong at his old friend and master Ingoldsby and saw the firelight in his tawny eyes and feared, with an inward sigh, that they might yet be riding out on some ridiculous quest for her anyway. Held captive as she was by fifty thousand Tatars.

Two days later there were signs of Cossacks making moves to pack up and leave for the south, when a horseman came galloping into the camp from the city.

Now that the Tatars had moved off, Ivan had returned. He was back in the Kremlin.

'Has he brought his Oprichnina?' demanded Smith.

He had. The entire guard.

'Hardly enough to effect anything,' said Stanley.

Smith brooded.

'And he wants to talk to the Englishmen,' said the Cossack. 'He says you are his military advisors.'

'That we are,' said Hodge, shifting painfully on his bruise, 'and I've got my military advice for him all ready. "You're buggered, mate. As buggered as a blue-eyed choirboy in Algiers jail."'

Smith was on his feet already.

'You're not really going back, are you?' said Hodge.

Smith was buckling on his sword. 'We are.'

Ivan's rage was terrible. And no more realistic than usual.

'They must be punished, those accursed heathen! They must be hewn in pieces before the Lord in Gilgal! Look at my beloved city! How could my wretched people fight so poorly? They are slaves and cowards one and all!'

Vorotinsky was there too. And, in the far corner, quiet and watchful – Maliuta Skuratov. They all bowed with exquisite polite-ness. Ivan ranted again until exhausted. Stanley then suggested he start another purge of his people, to make them strong once more.

Ivan regarded him a moment, panting, his burning eyes more deep-set than ever. He took it as a serious suggestion, not as sarcasm. Then he snapped, 'No, we have not time. The Hour of Judgement is near. My people are beyond instruction and punishment. We might as well whip a pig for being greedy. Vorotinsky, you will lead the attack upon these infidel pillagers and barbarians, and cut them down upon the steppe!'

'Excellency, we have no cavalry.'

Ivan's rage increased. He pulled at his own robes like a small child in a tantrum. 'Then your damned nobles, the boyars—'

'Mostly slain, Your Majesty.' He might have added, By Your Majesty.

'Your own family!'

'What, six of us?'

'Aaargh!' Ivan gave a howl of inchoate fury, fell against the wall, hammered at it with his fists, his face white and pouring with sweat like a man in a fever. They waited. He might faint. But he did not. He was muttering someone's name. 'Bomelius, Bomelius, where art thou? Thou of all my beloved counsellors, thou hast deserted me ...'

At last he calmed himself enough to say, 'What if you had the Streltsy?'

'The Streltsy are all to the west, in the Livonian wars, Your Majesty.'

Through gritted teeth Ivan said, 'No, I have ordered two thousand of them detached. They are marching back to Moscow after us, they will be here in another day.'

Two thousand Streltsy: Russia's only well-trained, modernised troops, often under European commanders of great experience: Swedes, Switzers, Brandenburgers ... They might have made some difference in the defence of Moscow – though they could hardly have resisted the firestorm, even so. But now, Smith and Stanley began to think fast.

Vorotinsky shook his head and said bluntly, 'This is futile. The Streltsy are welcome in Moscow, to help rebuild, to keep order, to guard against further attack when we are so weakened. Even the Poles might come and attack us now. But Streltsy musketeers can't march after steppe horsemen and expect to catch up with them. The idea is absurd. And we remain vastly outnumbered.'

Blunt words indeed. Ivan turned a furious gaze on him. He had had men beheaded as traitors for less blunt speaking than that. But Vorotinsky was unperturbed. He would speak the truth only, and die when he died.

Another voice said, 'We need to lure the Tatars back to us again.'

It was Nicholas.

The older men glanced at him. Then Smith said, his heart beating with the faintest hope, for the first time in many days, 'If there is one thing the Tatars do not like, it is a set battle. And we still have our Cossack friends.'

'Cossacks!' said Ivan with deep suspicion.

'They did good service in the siege,' said Stanley. 'Harried the Tatar rearguard, drew them off, prevented worse damage.'

Vorotinsky nodded. 'It is so.'

Ivan only repeated bitterly, 'Worse damage,' and spat loudly on the flagstones.

Vorotinsky said, 'Two thousand musketeers, and perhaps three thousand Cossack horsemen – against fifty thousand? Well, it sounds a little better.'

'But what are we fighting for now?' said a sinuous voice. Maliuta Skuratov.

'For God and for the Glory of Russia!' cried the Czar.

'And for—' put in Nicholas. Stanley talked over him. Best not to complicate things.

'We have known some difficult odds before,' he said, trying to sound bullish. 'The great thing is planning. And then keeping your head when your plans go completely awry.'

Ivan glared round at them all, mouth working furiously, and then he turned and strode from the room without another word.

He was beginning to have dark suspicions about these Englishmen.

Maliuta Skuratov glided after him.

38

'Listen,' said Nicholas urgently as they rode out of the ruined south gate. 'Listen. I think you've forgotten something.'

Stanley slowed and looked at him, puzzled. 'Go on.'

'How many do you think the Tatars have lost?'

Stanley shook his head. 'Fewer than a hundred. A handful to our ragged musket fire, the skirmishing. More who got themselves trapped and burned to death. In truth, hardly any. As Devlet Giray intended. For his remaining number – numbers are always exaggerated in war, but having seen the extent of his camp from the walls, this host of Devlet Giray numbers not less than fifty thousand, as is said. And fresh from victory razing Moscow, full of self-belief. They will not be expecting any counter-attack, it is true, and they do not form ranks. They remain light horsemen and steppe skirmishers still.'

'So you think the old chieftain still lives?'

'Devlet Giray? Of course. He is an old fox.'

'No, the chieftain on the steppe. Who charged against us.'

The others stared. God they must be weary, thought Nicholas with impatience. My old Knights Companion look almost stupid. He punched Smith's good arm in desperation. 'You shot his son! That chieftain!'

It all seemed so long ago, though it was only a few weeks. 'Aye, of course,' Smith harrumphed. 'Of course I remember.'

'He still lives. And he still wants vengeance?'

'And you want to ride after this vast army of Tatars,' said Stanley, 'and rescue your girl. I understand. I know your heart goes out to her. But Nick,' he said gently, 'life does not always work out as we want it. I think she is gone. I do not think we can ride after the Tatars. I pray she still lives' – he was frank, but it had to be said – 'and she probably does, she would be accounted fair by any tribe of men on earth, God knows. She will be a much-valued slave girl. But she might end anywhere. She might be sent back to Constantinople for the Sultan's harem, kept by Devlet Giray himself, sold to Persia or China. My friend, forgive us, for we failed her. But I do not think you will ever see her again.'

'Listen to me,' said Nicholas, and his voice was urgent, his eyes blazing. They knew that fire, and it was contagious. Dangerously contagious. 'The old chieftain still lives, he still wants blood vengeance on us—'

'On me, specifically,' said Smith with a certain pride. 'No one else could have taken that shot.'

'Well, on you. On all of us. Blood feuds are undying. Now listen.'

The Tatar horde moved east, slow and stately and magnificent as some great male lion over his domain, knowing he is the strongest on the plain, fearing nothing. They covered no more than ten leisurely miles a day, hunted much game, continued to pillage any of the scattered farms they came across. The grasslands were still rich enough for their tens of thousands of horses. They drank and feasted at night, enjoying their slave girls.

In one of the Tents of the Women, there was a stout Tatar woman called Babash, with a round, rosy face, tiny hands and feet, and eyes almost lost in her rolls of fat. She guarded a dark-haired beauty who spoke neither Turkish nor Russian. She spoke a few words in her ugly tongue and then refused to speak more. The other, older woman captured along with this one, buxom and flaxen-haired, had proved more amenable.

Babash pinched this young one's arms and twisted her hair and threatened to send her to one of the generals, and this foreign vixen spat at her. So Babash laughed her high-pitched laugh and sent her to one of the generals, rejoicing to think how he would break her. And the vixen scratched his face so badly that the general sent her back! He was much mocked by his fellow khans for it, but he just shrugged and said he did not want his balls bitten off, and there were easier swivings to be had. Did he not have twenty other new girls for himself anyway? None of them scratched.

Babash would have happily pinched the girl and burned her until she was broken, ready to submit herself to any man. But Devlet Giray himself had heard of it and laughed, and was intrigued that she spoke a language no one understood. He had come and looked at her naked one night – how she had fought as she was held down by six of the women and stripped! – and the vixen had looked straight back at the Great Khan with a burning fury, naked as she was born, and Devlet Giray thought that she was magnificent. Plainly still a virgin and like a ripe young fruit, sweet as a Kashgar apricot. He stroked her hair and ran his hands over her flesh and she yelled at him in her strange tongue, and he reckoned she might be worth as many as fifty horses. Fifty.

Such girls do not come along every day. And much as he loved women, and would have enjoyed breaking this one in and hearing her first little moans, no woman was worth that much. He told Babash to keep her intact and not to mark her or cut her, and he would find a buyer for her soon enough. Babash could certainly protect her from others. Devlet Giray had seen her use her little curved dagger, her fat fist moving in a blur through the air before men's hypnotized eyes. None of his warriors would go against her. Two had died.

So Babash kept close watch on the slave girl, though she remained contemptuous of her. Because she herself had never been that beautiful, nor worth fifty horses, and because she knew that this virgin's spirit was still unbroken, curses on her proud head.

Ivan Koltzo was talking to Petlin. Both were drinking heavily.

Koltzo said, 'I see the way the wind is blowing. Do you not?'

Petlin nodded. 'Aye, I see it. Moscow may be finished, but this is just a battle in the unending war between Tartary and Russia. And in the wind I scent the coming of Grand Tartary, not White Russia.' He drank and swiped his mouth and added bitterly, 'We Cossacks are on the losing side, right enough. We hadn't even the strength to take the best of Devlet Giray's baggage train.'

Ivan Koltzo glanced around to see if anyone was near, then said more quietly, 'But why do we have to be the losers?'

Petlin's eyes narrowed. 'Dangerous words, brother. If I understand you right.'

'But we are free men. If a Cossack is anything, he is free. We do not owe loyalty to the Czar or to Russia. We are free to choose our masters.'

'You would ride with the Easterners?'

'If they are to be the Lords of the Steppe once more, as of old, in the days of the Great Khan and the Golden Horde. If the future is to be theirs ... would you not at least be tempted? Would not any man?'

Petlin said nothing but licked his lips.

'Imagine,' said Ivan Koltzo. 'Instead of a band of three hundred, we ride perhaps as the privileged bodyguard at the head of any army of a hundred thousand. Moscow lies waste, its crazed Czar hanged from its walls, and then all of Asia is ours. A new kingdom arises in the East ... the great capitals of Bokhara, Samarkand ... would it not be a new life for us? Imagine the gold we would have! Imagine the women.'

Petlin smiled and chuckled and shook his head. 'Dangerous words, and more dangerous imaginings. Yet you voice what has been in my heart, it is true. Nevertheless, I do not think I could simply ride away from my brother Cossacks. Not so easily. Not after all these years.'

'Not after the way Stenka has treated you? Not after the way he has preferred those new English friends of his to you?'

'He has not always treated me badly.'

'But he has not shared the booty with you this time, has he? He has shared it with them instead.'

Petlin raised his head and stared at Koltzo. 'What booty?'

The following night, Devlet Giray sat in his council tent with his greatest khans and his chieftains seated cross-legged on carpets around the side of the tent. In the centre, back to back, were roped two Cossacks. They had come riding straight into the camp of the Tatars unarmed, and demanded audience with the Great Khan himself. They had nearly been killed on the spot, for their horses were pleasing to the eye, but they had said with great vehemence that they had news for the Khan, Devlet Giray, that he would wish to hear, and killing them would be a terrible mistake. They had survived by a gnat's wing.

Their news was of some interest: among their own Cossack brotherhood, they said, encamped now south of the ruined Moscow, was also that party of foreigners who had slain the son of Tokhtamysh Khan, when they fought that day on the steppe. They were fierce fighters, and had also fought in the gate of the city, and killed several fine warriors there. They were great Haters of Tatars.

Tokhtamysh said that he always believed it was so, but now he knew it. And behold, the foreign devils were delivered into his hands for vengeance.

Devlet Giray was cautious, but now there was sudden danger. His khans were against him.

'Lord, what old Tokhtamysh says is true!' said one sternly. 'Honour is accounted more among the Tatar people than gold or even life itself. And if these two Christians are to be believed—'

'We are to be believed,' interrupted one of the bound men. He was struck with the butt of a horsewhip but did not cry out. 'And we will lead you to them. The last thing they expect is that you would return and attack them. They think you are gone. Their defences are nothing.'

'—if they are to be believed,' the chieftain went on, 'we must ride out for blood vengeance!'

'And if you do not,' said another, white-bearded, stocky, magnificent, 'then I, Tokhtamysh, will ride out with my warriors and make war myself, for the sake of my slaughtered son. His spirit remains abroad, how can he rest unavenged? I see him on the steppe, still wandering. His footprints are bloody in the moonlight. And you, Great Khan ...' Old Tokhtamysh looked steadily at Devlet Giray upon his throne. 'I, Tokhtamysh, will think you less a khan for it.'

There was a stir among the chieftains, but none said a word in protest, though this was a deep insult. Yes, it was a dangerous moment for Devlet Giray. More dangerous that anything he had faced before the walls of Moscow.

Grasp this moment. Rule this tent and these men, now.

246

He stood swiftly. 'Hear me.' Be lordly, not threatening, not petty. 'Hear me, beloved old warrior, my brother Tokhtamysh. Have we not ridden out together these many years, have we not been horse-brothers, have we not fought and suffered together, longer than many men have lived?'

Tokhtamysh was not angry. Not yet. He said, 'So we have.'

'You know that I love you as a brother, as I love all my people. Devlet Giray hesitates for love of his people, not love of gold or love of womanish peace. I hesitate to trust these two unbelievers.' He looked at the bound pair. Then he thought it politic to kick one of them, hard. 'Why do you betray your Cossack brothers? I still doubt you.'

'They betrayed me and they betrayed my family,' said one of the wretches. 'The tale sickens me, I will not recount it. But I owe them nothing. They who were my brothers are now my most bitter enemies. Unto death.'

'And you would truly lead us to them?'

'We would. And rejoice to see them slain.'

Devlet Giray brooded a theatrical moment longer, stroking his fine moustaches. Impressing his khans with his deep and far-sighted intelligence. Yet now it was action that would bind them under him again, and only action. He must take the risk. They were heady with victory, and all for more war.

He swept his arm high in the air, and said, 'Then I say aye! I say they have been sent by the Sky God Astur, to lead us to another glorious victory!' He laid his hand on Tokhtamysh's arm and added more gently, 'I say we are led by the Spirit, to exact just vengeance, and lay the sad spirit of your slaughtered son to rest.'

The old chieftains erupted in a roar, batting their hands in drumbeat against the taut side of the camelskin tent. Old Tokhtamysh wept and roared loudest of all.

39

Later that night, Ivan Koltzo lay in a wooden cage on the back of a wagon, crammed against Petlin. Though the Tatars had decided to trust their word for now, they were still treated like animals. Petlin managed to sleep, curse him. Ivan Koltzo lay looking out at the stars over the steppes, the wandering evening star a burning eye on the horizon. He was cold and cramped, and the danger was great, but his heart was exultant.

Two days later, on a grey, cool morning on the late summer steppe, the Cossack bands of Stenka and Yakublev, along with a small party from Moscow under Vorotinsky, crested a rise and looked over a steep downland slope towards a wide river.

'So,' said Smith. 'This is where we will take our stand. Only a few days from Moscow, yet true wilderness.'

'This is it,' said Stenka. 'This is where Ivan Koltzo will bring them back, hot for your blood.' He sighed. 'Why are we here? For Russia? Why for Russia? What has she done for us?'

'For gold and glory!' said Stanley.

'Tch.'

A long curving valley, with the steep downland running along its north side, without trees, without cover. The river to the south, and one end enclosed in a natural amphitheatre, with no way out.

Smith said, 'Only a fool would camp there.'

Stanley grinned. 'That'll be us then.'

'I, Yakublev, will ride free with my men as roving cavalry, always beyond the reach of the Tatar, keeping them at bay, keeping them from committing all their numbers.'

'And you, Prince Michael,' said Stanley, 'you will come over the rise to the north with two thousand Streltsy musketeers. If you have time, you may be able to put up palisades. But—'

'But when will you come, exactly?' said Stenka.

Vorotinsky shook his head. 'That we do not know. But we must come. We must.' He spoke with quiet passion, gripping his sword-hilt. 'Moscow is burned, our empire is on the verge of ruin, and we are fighting now for our very survival. We do not simply want to win, we must. The Tatars must not dare to return again.'

Yakublev made an uncomplimentary noise. He had said before he thought this was a madman's plan, with more holes in it than a moth-eaten silk. He would keep his men riding free, and not commit to that trapped valley.

Vorotinsky said, 'Believe me, Cossack, I pray to every saint in Russia that I will be back with the Streltsy – with the Czar's permission. It was only his suggestion that we might have them, remember. And two thousand horses to bring them, or we may be too late. But my fear is, he may have changed his mind, and demand they remain in Moscow for his protection.'

'And what then?'

Vorotinsky did not answer. The Assyrian came down like a wolf on the fold ...

He pulled his horse around and his party with him. 'We go back to Moscow. We will return as fast as we may.' And they were gone in a cloud across the plain.

'Aye, aye,' said Stanley, looking after them. 'And the coming or not of the Streltsy is only one small imponderable among many in our little plan!' He grinned with absurd, boyish happiness at the peril ahead. 'God alone knows how this one is going to work out. Ingoldsby, I do hope you have not made us all fools.'

Nicholas grinned too. Rebecca was coming close, he knew it. She was coming back to him. That was all he felt. That, and the blood-hot danger of coming battle. But this time, unlike Moscow, there was no Ivan in command. There were Smith and Stanley, Stenka and Yakublev, and Prince Michael Vorotinsky. Stony-eyed veterans all. So what if they were still outnumbered ten to one? It was going to work. It had to.

'So,' said Yakublev, 'you will draw the Tatars down into this shallow valley to your wagon circle, hold them off there, and then the Streltsy will come up over this rise and fire upon them and cut them down.'

'It is the new way of war,' said Smith. 'It is ugly and it is mechanical, and a musket volley cuts like a scythe through mounted knights or steppe horsemen alike. Their age is done. This is the age of gunpowder. But do you want to win, as Vorotinsky says, do you want to save a Christian Empire from the Mohammedan, or do you want to look fine and gentlemanly on the battlefield?'

Yakublev looked unconvinced. He had never much thought of the Tatars as Mohammedan. He said, 'And then we will all go home.' He turned to his old comrade Stenka. 'You will be like a goat tied up as bait for a lion. You are happy with that?'

Stenka bleated then roared with laughter. 'Let them come and get Stenka the Goat! See how he butts!'

'And you, young love-struck Englishman,' said Yakublev, nodding at Nicholas, 'you ride with handpicked men and get to the vanguard and the slave pens, and find these two captive whores of yours.'

'Not whores,' said Nicholas. 'We'd say, womenfolk.'

Yakublev shrugged. He could see little difference. 'This is another joke of a plan. After this campaign, the Tatar slave pens are the size of several markets. They have captured hundreds at Moscow. Naturally they will be guarded. How will you find your wh— your woman? By asking around courteously? I do not know how it is going to work.'

'It'll work,' said Nicholas.

The slope was steep to ride down, and certainly too steep for any horseman to ascend. They leaned back hard in their creaking saddles and let their horses pick their way down as slow as they chose.

The wide, cold river below ran in deep channels and over shallow gravel, a tributary of the River Oka, its banks often uncertain, meandering into sedge and rush-grown bog. It made the place seem more louring and forebidding, and the summer sky was clouding over now, growing shield-grey and ominous.

'How much time have we?' said Stanley.

'We do not know,' said Yakublev.

They brought the ox wagons round the end of the valley and

dragged them up. The ground was boggy, the oxen groaned, the huge eighteen-foot whips snaked through the air and bit into their tough old hides. Twelve wagons in all. They hauled them into a circle and tipped them over on their sides with mighty crashing, and lashed them together, leaving one narrow gap for now. Some rode out single file along the riverbank and found what wood they could, washed down from forests God knew how many hundreds of miles distant. They shaped stakes for palisades and made a wider circle outside. Prepared some food and tried to remain in good cheer. But all felt dread stealing upon them. They felt horribly trapped in this worthless and lifeless place. Goats for lions. Was vengeance for Moscow worth this much? Was Russia?

And how long could they stand the waiting? How long would the Tatars take to come back? They had no idea. The waiting was going to be torture. And many more doubts would arise, the men become restive in that inaction. What if Devlet Giray did not like the terrain? It was too obviously a terrain of ambush. What if he changed his plan, like all good commanders do? He must know there was still half a chance his two Cossack informers were duping him. What if they came behind, over the rise, and fired an arrow-storm down upon them from above?. Then they could do nothing but shelter in the cover of the tipped-up wagons and die one by one, stuck like pincushions. What if the Tatar horsemen found the Streltsy out on the open plain, no great horsemen but mere marching or mounted infantrymen? They would slaughter them all.

O, God, they prayed, Have mercy on our folly.

That night was silent and overcast. They lit a sparse fire and the lookouts sat their horses on top of the rise and looked east and shivered though the night was mild.

Hodge was arguing with Nicholas. 'Course I'm coming with you. Unless you knock me senseless first.'

'I just might.'

'Just you try.'

A big Cossack guffawed. Andriushko. 'I'll come with you on your quest of the heart too, little English brother.'

'I don't need anyone else,' said Nicholas. 'Best if I go alone, as fast as possible.'

'I too,' said Chvedar the renegade priest. 'You will need spiritual solace.'

'And a couple of gallant knights,' said Stanley.

'You will be needed here,' said Nicholas. 'I'm going alone.'

Three agonized days passed, and then early on the fourth morning, Nicholas was watching the hills, and suddenly one of the scouts was turning about and urging his horse down the steep hill as fast as he could without breaking a leg.

'Stanley!' he cried.

Stanley had already seen. 'So they are coming.'

They watched the first scout, and then the other five of them all along the skyline, turn and make a dash back for the wagon circle. They were coming, sure enough. No escape now.

'And no sign of the Streltsy?' said Stanley.

No one answered. Hodge muttered, 'Are you sure we've timed this quite right?'

'Aye,' said Stanley. 'Those Tatars move fast, do they not? Guns at the ready, all of you!'

None dared say what they thought. The sky was more grey by the minute. If rain came, all their guns and muskets would be pretty much useless. So too would those of the Streltsy – if they came at all.

The scouts rode in gasping and the last wagon was drawn across. They fell from their horses and said that the Tatars were closing in on the end of the valley, and strung out along the riverbank beyond for half a mile or more. Their baggage wagons and their captives were left far back on the other side of the river.

'How many have come?'

'All of them.'

The smoke of matchcord. One fool letting his gun go off early, the drift of black powder smoke. A waterbird's solitary cry from the river. And the terrible waiting.

Devlet Giray sat his horse and pondered. He must not show hesitation, his khans were taking it for weakness, yet he felt uneasy. The Cossacks had got wind of their coming, and pulled their wagons into a classic defensive circle. Yet he was reassured that they had got themselves trapped in such a place. Otherwise he might still have suspected some kind of ambush.

Then why not simply close up the mouth of the valley, roll their field guns off their wagonbeds at leisure some three hundred yards off, and blast the Cossack wagon circle to smithereens? After half an hour of such treatment, let the smoke clear, then ride in and finish off the few survivors where they lay, deaf and blind as newborn kittens.

Because, said his khans – Devlet Giray smiled a faint, disbelieving smile at their words – because that would not be the old Tatar way. Let this be an honourable victory for us. Let us have a charge!

Yet if he was to be pushed into this madcap second battle, then they must proceed with caution, not typical Tatar wildness. It was caution that had made him and kept him the Great Khan of the Crimea.

His warriors were so numerous, the valley so narrow and enclosed, they could not all attack at once. He would send in a force of only four or five hundred, to ring the Cossacks' wagon circle and finish off those white devils. He eyed the heights to the north. They should be taken too, though the Cossacks were horsemen like themselves, and could hardly make use of such steep slopes.

He heard a rider behind him and turned. Even his heart flamed to see it. Old Tokhtamysh in his Tatar war paint.

At dawn this morning, Tokhtamysh had had his women paint a sun and moon and talismans of power upon his broad cheeks and forehead. He wore neither armour nor quilt, though the day was cool, but rode naked to the waist, for he was looked over by the sky gods, a man riding in just vengeance for the blood of his own son. He carried only a single knife at his waist, and with this he would kill that foreign blackbeard who had killed his son. Then he would rip off the man's armour and his coat and bare his chest to the sun and with this knife, Tokhtamysh would cut out his heart and raise it up and drain his enemy's blood into his mouth and drink it.

'You want to ride arrowhead?' said Devlet Giray quietly.

Tokhtamysh nodded, his mouth set grim.

'You do not need to.'

'The gods have willed it.'

To ride arrowhead meant to ride far out in front of your men, a clear target to your enemy. The position of greatest honour and greatest danger.

'Old comrade,' said Devlet Giray, and curses, he heard his own voice shaking with emotion. 'If you do not return . . .'

'Then I will ride this sunset on the plains of heaven,' said Tokhtamysh. 'With my son.'

The days of such things were past. It was the age of cannon and musket, and professional armies paid their wages by their king. But Devlet Giray knew there was a rare magnificence here still, that they would not see much longer.

'Then ride out, old friend. Ride with Astur the Eagle.'

40

'Here they come!' yelled Stanley. 'Steady now, boys! Make every shot count!'

Nicholas's arquebus was shaking in his hands. He knew at a glance that this old gun he'd been given would be no good at anything more than thirty yards or so, and he could already imagine the deafening bang it would make when fired. The spit and spew of powder, his eyes screwed shut. This was the kind of gun that exploded in your face. As if he didn't have enough to fear.

They could hear them before they saw them, given the curve of the valley. The thunder of hooves, the wild yelling. And then round the bend came a fantastical figure on a squat skewbald, teeth bared, reins bunched savagely short, galloping like fury, the rider crouched low, holding just a long knife in his right hand, arm outstretched. Some fifty yards behind him rode the mass of horse warriors. Many hundreds of them were coming.

Nicholas's trembling did not get any better. He looked down the wavering barrel and it helped him focus. He saw the old warrior out at the front and recognition stirred.

'Smith!' he called. 'It's the old chieftain from the steppe!'

Smith too was looking down the long, elegant barrel of his jezail. 'Got him,' he muttered. He felt an unwonted disgust. He had already killed the son, though of necessity, and now he was about to kill the father. What was it all for? The old warrior, some twenty years his senior, rode bare-chested, without gun or even bow. Just a knife, little longer than a kitchen knife. But Smith knew what it was all about. The old warrior wanted to die, here, now, in battle, leading his men. He was on the verge of becoming sick of his life, sick of his old man's aches and pains, dreading palsied old age, deaf ears and dim eyes, longing for the heaven of his people.

Smith's finger tightened on the trigger and he quieted his breathing and pulled and the wheel lock whirred. Fizz and sputter and the sharp crack, and the ball flew from the beautifully rifled barrel, and eighty yards off, old Tokhtamysh was shot clean through the heart. He fell back and rolled from his horse, and the skewbald came galloping on riderless towards them.

Behind him, five hundred warriors howled and spurred forward.

And then Nicholas began to hear the familiar crescendo hiss of arrows, the muffled thump as they stuck into the ground or the wooden boards of the wagons. Or men. One cried out, another. Two of them hit already, Tatar horsemen sending arrows arcing high into the air from their immensely powerful compound bows even as they galloped, perfectly judged so that they turned and came down again like stooping falcons upon their enemy. Crouching behind the wagons did little good. They'd have been better crouching under them.

'Fire!' bellowed Smith, and every Cossack gun barked out.

Ears ringing, eyes stinging, black powder smoke, men and horses falling, horses screaming, tumbling over fallen horses. And then the horsemen were breaking into a circle to gallop round the wagons. Not even a Tatar horseman could make a horse crash bull-like into a solid barrier. They were difficult, fast-moving targets, pouring arrows down inside the wagon circle or wildly firing with squat arquebuses and pistols. Lead balls slammed into the thick boards of the wagons, wooden splinters few wide, a ball passed straight through and ploughed into the ground. Cossacks ducked and yelled to each other, desperately fumbled to reload their ancient guns, but were slow, too slow ...

'Quicker, my brothers, quicker!' said Stenka, standing broad-chested in the centre of the circle, clutching his sword already, head back, seemingly invulnerable. 'Return fire, or they will soon be in!'

Stanley looked desperately to the heights – nothing – and then knew that he must not look again. They must simply fight on, and stay alive, and hope.

Then warriors who had had their horses shot from under them

came running towards the circle, knives in their belts.

'Men coming in! Take them first!' yelled Smith.

A heavily tattooed warrior leapt up and caught the upper edge of an ox cart and swung himself up and came slithering over the top. Nicholas laid down his gun and drew his sword and seized the huge ironbound ox wheel and tried to pull himself up to meet him. A knife flashed down and he ducked, Hodge yelled out something and a pistol banged nearby. The warrior slammed down upon the boards. Nicholas's head must have just appeared over the top as he looked to see if he still lived, and a second later an arrow swished in low and he distinctly felt its flight feathers kiss his hair as it passed by.

'Down, you fool! Have you forgotten everything?' shouted Smith.

He had not forgotten Malta, but it seemed long ago and far away. He was older now – and slower.

They fought with grim desperation, and only a handful of the most foolhardy horse-warriors, vainglorious adolescents, managed to bring their horses in close, vault from them in mid-gallop and come flying in over the top of the wagons with knives ready in their hands. One landed so clumsily that he cut himself in the belly. Another crashed straight over into the circle and stood and Stenka stood before him with his sword and they fought hand to hand for a minute or more, and the Tatar boy was very good, very quick. And then by one of those evil chances in which war is so abundant, a Tatar arrow came down and sank deep into the boy's shoulder and he dropped his knife and clutched the arrow and stood amazed. Stenka brought his sword in wide and quickly felled him.

It was the arrowstorm that would destroy them. It came down like iron rain, and the Cossacks could hardly move within their circle for fear of being hit. And they were hit, time and time again. Already dead and dying men lay strewn about, the survivors trying to drag the wounded under paltry cover close by the wagons. Their fighting numbers were down from three hundred to no more than two hundred. Another hour of resistance, another half an hour, and they would be done for. Of the Tatar horsemen, they had brought down a few, but many more still rode around. Some even took a rest, turning back down the valley, trotting their horses through the boggy ground to water them at the river's edge, and then coming back fresh for the fight.

Stanley and Smith communicated by signs, but there was little more to say. A miracle would save them.

And then the Tatars threw in ropes, tied at the end with iron poles hammered into hooks, and hooked one of the great wagons and began to drag it clear to open up a breach.

'Bastards!' shouted Hodge. 'Look, breakin' in!'

'And we've got to break out!' cried Nicholas desperately. For they had to get to her, and now. But how could they ever break out amid this?

A band of defenders climbed up onto that wagon and tried to hack through the ropes, a lashed team of Tatar horses straining at the other end a mere twenty or thirty feet away. Hodge leaned out dangerously between two wagons with a smouldering arquebus and released a blast of ball and stone chips at the horsemen, and several were hit, cursing and howling. One of the ropes was cut, but others were flung in now all around the circle. And from beyond that, still the arrows came down.

Another Cossack was struck in the temples by a ball that did not kill him, but sent him reeling around the circle, bleeding profusely, his face a terrifying red mask, and crying out, 'We are betrayed, my brothers! Where are they? We are betrayed by the Muscovites, for what need had they to come to us? They are happy to see the Cossacks destroyed, along with a few hundred Tatars with us. Never trust a Russian. Never!' And then he fell silent when Smith stepped up and clubbed him quiet with the butt of his gun.

Stanley looked down the valley. There was something coming. A distant noise. More horsemen. There was no limit to their numbers.

Devlet Giray was sending in another five hundred, fresh and ready for the kill. He wanted this finished off now. Tokhtamysh was slain, a clean and noble death. Let it all be done with now, let every one of those impudent Cossacks be slain, and they could head home. He glanced up one last time at the heights to the north, thinking they ought to have put lookouts up there. But no point now. It was all done. It was as good as over.

With the five hundred he sent forward, another thousand or more surged along too, wanting to be in on the famous victory over that cluster of obnoxious strangers, and the celebratory scalping. Many of his khans rode with them, eager as boys. He watched them ride off, but he would not join them. Many of his best and boldest warriors went. Far too many. And then still more of the Tatar army streamed down that narrow valley beside the cold lake shore.

As they rode away, Devlet Giray saw that the ground they galloped over at the river's edge was already being pounded into thick mud. Many of them as they jostled together slowed from a gallop to a canter, even to a laborious trot, their hardy little steppe horses sinking now up to the fetlock, snorting with disgust, accustomed as they were to the dry, windswept grasslands of the open steppe. So much for the glorious charge. This would be a famous but a very muddy victory.

He turned to the slave at his side for a beaker of water, and when he turned back, at the edge of his vision he saw some movement on the heights. One of his khans must have posted a troop of scouts and lookouts up there after all. Wise man. And yet ... He stared, eyes narrowed.

'Slave, up there on the hills ... what is it?'

The slave, a Circassian youth, looked for a moment and then gasped and held his hand to his mouth.

Then Devlet Giray knew what he saw. Waving like reeds against the sky, pennons and banners. Gold banners of Saints, and the Crucified Jew ...

Then his voice sounded horribly afraid and weak in his own ears. He clutched at his reins and cried out, 'They are no scouts, they are Russians. Turn back! Turn back!'

He might as well have tried to turn back the river itself.

The mass of eager Tatar horsemen, now closing in on that pitiful little circle of unbelievers at the head of the valley, even squabbling amongst themselves for best position and most scalps, cast never a glance up at the heights to their right. But one or two, amidst their own wild gunfire and the drifts of black powder smoke, happened to look up, pricked by some sixth sense. And they saw with puzzlement the eerie procession of gold crosses and icons being raised high upon long poles against the grey sky, and they glimpsed black-gowned priests swinging censers among long, orderly lines of men, heavily bearded men with heavy muskets. The musket barrels were unwavering, solidly rammed for firing down, expertly balanced upon pikeheads with their butts driven into the ground.

One Tatar horseman, suddenly chilled to the bone and understanding what was happening, stared wildly around and saw his fellow warriors as they really were, a horribly tight-packed, jostling crowd of thousands, all order gone.

'Brothers!' he cried, trying to pull his own horse around and failing in the oncoming tide. 'Brothers, look up! See above! We are ambushed!'

A few looked up, and reined in, but others did not even hear and pushed them on from behind. They heard only the sound of their own wild cries of victory and their guns loosed off carelessly into the sky, saw only the gilded glory of the coming victory. But the warrior trying to stem the tide caught a faint drift of the haunting and demonic sound of the hymns of the Christians, the *'Dies Irae'* and other hymns of judgement and apocalypse sounding over the valley and fading away over the cold waters beyond.

In desperation he started to lay about him with his whip, as if trying to drive recalcitrant cattle. 'Go back, you fools, turn back! It is a trap!' He caught another violently across the cheek and that warrior, incensed, and thinking this fool had lost his wits out of sheer cowardice, knocked him clean off his horse with a mighty punch in the face, and the Tatars pressed on.

41

Devlet Giray felt a growing fury that must find outlet. He rounded on his slave.

'Ride back to the slave pens, and order the guards to stand ready to slaughter every last captive taken at Moscow.'

'Every ...?' faltered the Circassian. He was born a Christian.

'Every man, woman and child,' said Devlet Giray. 'All of them. And the two Cossacks held captive. Kill them.'

But Ivan Koltzo knew this would come, and had already made his move. Once the Streltsy appeared, he knew his hours were numbered.

At the rear of the Tatar party only yesterday, he had taken his chance. He stumbled and fell at the river's edge, and was savagely beaten for it. But as he was being beaten, such was the Cossack's strength of mind, his hardiness, that he was thinking clearly all the time. Even as he rolled and yelled out, he was feeling with his bound hands for the stones beneath his own body, blazing with pain. Then he found what he sought, a flat, sharp-edged stone, and clutched it and folded his fingers around it and staggered to his feet, bleeding from head and cheek and his elbow singing in agony.

But he was nearing his freedom, one step nearer. Hidden in his palm now was one of those grey stones called flints, still used sometimes by the steppe horsemen for their arrowheads, and to powerful effect. That night, thrown in the dust under a wagon along with Petlin, he cut his own bonds, craning in pain with his bruised elbow, sawing for three hours solid. But eventually the bonds gave, and he rubbed his chafed and bleeding wrists, and peered out. The guards slept. So did Petlin.

He would never wake.

Koltzo fell upon the traitorous wretch, gripped him round the neck, and drew the sharp stone hard across his bared throat as if he was no more than killing a chicken. The flint cut like a knife. Petlin opened his mouth and gargled almost inaudibly, a dying man. Ivan Koltzo dropped him and spat on him. 'You were a true traitor indeed, Petlin,' he said. 'But I was a true Cossack.'

He rolled Petlin on his stomach so no blood showed, then he lay down again with his hands behind his back as if still bound, and waited for the first man on a horse to pass by.

He lay under the wagon until long into the next morning, all but ignored, and heard the sound of the battle down the valley. Eventually he took the risk and crawled out and stood and watched, hands behind his back. The rough Tatar camp with its scattered tents was a mile or more behind the post of Devlet Giray, but he could make out the land and hear the thunderous noise of the charge, and he could see the grassy heights. He leaned against the wagon, throbbing with pain but little fear. Ivan Koltzo had lived through many worse situations.

Finally a plump Tatar came ambling lazily by, and stopped and grinned. 'Your friend still sleeps?'

'Aye. Idle dog.'

'He is missing the great battle. You have won our thanks.'

'In truth, it was nothing.'

'Your reward from the Khan will be great.'

'I doubt it.'

'No, truly.'

Then there was movement on the heights, and the Tatar gazed up. He squinted. But Ivan Koltzo's heart leapt. It was working. After all, this whole madman's plan was working. Yet still so much to go wrong.

He vaulted up behind the Tatar on his horse and hugged him to steady himself and cut his throat with the flint. Then he tossed the flint to the ground and pulled out the Tatar's dagger and shoved him off the horse and galloped away before any more of the bewildered guards could understand what was happening.

Koltzo rode out of the camp and wide towards the long shoulder of the hills just as the message came back from Devlet Khan to kill him and Petlin.

'Bring him down!' cried a Tatar captain. 'That man going there! Bring him down!'

Muskets and arquebuses were hurriedly brought to bear on the galloping figure, but there were few finer horseman on that steppe than Ivan Koltzo. He stayed low and swerved his horse back and forth and already he was a hundred, two hundred yards away up the slope. Musketballs zinged past his ears but none struck him, and a small party of Tatar horsemen was finally sent after him, but he had too great a lead on them.

The biggest danger was as he appeared on top of the rise and hurtled towards the Streltsy lines. Would they take him for a lone maddened Tatar?

To face any outflanking manoeuvres, Vorotinsky had of course placed a powerful left horn of his musketeers six deep, to take down any Tatar horseman coming that way. But they would have to be riding uphill, not a Tatar speciality, and he guessed they would not.

Without forethought, Ivan Koltzo began yelling out the Lord's Prayer in Russian at the top of his voice as he galloped. One of the Streltsy captains looked out at this single, crazed-looking figure, seemingly unarmed, and gave the order to hold fire. Koltzo came in and fell from his horse and leaned against its heaving flanks and looked back. A distant band of Tatar horseman was wheeling round and back down the slope.

Panting, he looked to the ranks of men along the heights and his heart burned. Two thousand only, perhaps, but immaculately ranged in four ranks, five hundred guns in each rank. Two thousand best German muskets between them. They had been drilled and drilled for weeks and months on end by their severe Brandenburger commanders, and they were all hardened veterans of the Polish and Livonian wars. And they had just come from Moscow. They had seen what the Tatars had done to their city.

This was a good spot. They were almost unassailable by cavalry. Each rank would fire a volley of five hundred guns. Perhaps a tenth of the guns would misfire each time, but that was still a lethal rain. A Streltsy musketeer could reload and fire in a minute. Thus every fifteen seconds, another fresh rank of five hundred men would step forward as the front rank stepped back to reload, and the muskets bark out again.

Ivan Koltzo swiped his face and grinned and bowed to the captain.

'Ivan Koltzo,' he said. 'At your service.'

Every single one of the last men fighting within the wagon circle was caught up in their last desperate stand when the first musket volley rolled out from the heights. Nicholas heard it, and Hodge, and then Stanley was yelling out, 'Smith! Smith, you deaf ox! Did you hear that?'

Smith side-swiped a fellow with a half-broken arquebus, clutching it by the muzzle, and caught him a whooping blow in the guts. The fellow dropped to his knees and bowed his head. Smith raised his arquebus again and then heard the volley.

Vorotinsky had ordered his musketeers to turn their fire close towards the stricken wagon circle, but ensure they did not hit it. That first volley scythed in, the sound of the gunfire still heard by few above the roar of the fighting, and yet suddenly the Tatar horsemen closing in on that wretched ring found that that their comrades were falling all around them. They began to pull up, bewildered, still crowded on by more behind.

Stanley grinned at the two Tatars that stood to the left and right of him, both clutching bloody swords. Then with renewed energy he took them both down in a blizzard of blows from the sword in his left hand and the broken pike in his right. Seconds later, through eyes blurry with blood, some his own, some that of other men, he looked down at them stretched in the dirt.

A second volley. Dozens more horsemen fell.

He turned on another. Perhaps fifty Cossacks still fought within the circle, and there were at least that many Tatar warriors inside as well now, fighting hand to hand. Yet their mounted comrades outside the circle were slowing, pulling about, no longer trying. What was happening? They stood and stared.

'Hear that?' shouted Stanley. 'You are done. Moscow is paid for. On your knees if you would live!'

One Tatar warrior wavered, holding his sword, suddenly unable to fight.

From all up the valley came a chaos of yells and screams. Wild, despairing screams.

A terrible panic was spreading through the close-packed masses of the Tatar horsemen. They were being fired upon by Russian Streltsy! The best musketeers north of the Ottoman Empire.

There was even another ugly rumour spreading. A much larger band of Cossacks, the Cossacks of Yakublev, were not with the wagon circle at all, but riding behind them, to destroy their rear-guard or burn their camp. And worst of all, they had lost all their beloved freedom of movement, the one thing any wild nomads of the plains hated most. Lost their freedom to fall back, to gallop out wide, to manoeuvre and keep beyond range. They were locked down in a bloody, muddy riverside massacre, under the unblinking, murderous black eyes of two thousand Russian muskets. Another volley, another two or three hundred warriors reeling and falling ... They were imprisoned between the hills and the river, and as they jostled and turned, their horses rearing and plunging, the ground beneath them was mashed to ever deeper and more cloying mud.

Some kicked their horses down to the river's edge and drove them in, but the banks dropped away steeply and soon they were swimming. The current was strong, and horses and men began to founder.

On the heights, Prince Michael Vorotinsky, immaculate on a huge, dappled grey stallion and clearly visibly to all two thousand of the Streltsy in his resplendent bronze cuirass and crested helmet, threw his arm out and directed a volley over the valley to the river's edge. Another hundred or more warriors were cut down, and many more panicked, more jostled and fell, trampled and floundering and then drowning.

It was not the noblest battle. But Prince Michael cried out, 'Remember Moscow! They must not return!' And his soldiers were steeled. Another rank stepped forward, muskets primed.

Within the wagons, the fight at last began to fall off. A few Tatar horsemen rode around one last desultory time, howling and slash-ing the air with frustration. And then they turned and pressed back down the hated valley. A few did try to ride up the steep slope to the heights, but naturally Vorotinsky had this all in hand. Special squadrons, posted earlier, now rose up from the grass and fired down on them and they were driven back.

Stanley leaned on his broken pike, exhausted. 'Cannae, Trasimene ...' he murmured. 'How one must study the battles of the ancients to win the battles of today.'

Smith lowered his arquebus and gave the Tatar whooping at his feet a gentle boot in the shoulder. The fellow looked up, green to the gills.

'Stay there,' said Smith. 'Don't move. And you may live.'

Stenka strode about, checking on his men. He found Nicholas, lying exhausted. He got to his feet.

'Yes,' said Stenka. 'Now. Look, those six horses. They are yours.'

And Stanley too was calling, 'Nick! It is time!'

42

A minute later they pulled open a gap between the wagons and the six rode out in file at the gallop. Smith and Stanley, Nicholas and Hodge, Andriushko and Chvedar, as all had sworn. All six were already wounded.

Vorotinsky looked down and saw them ride out, and ordered his men to suspend all fire at the wagons. Concentrate now on the mass of horsemen in the valley.

They cantered straight into the shallows of the nearby river, not even looking back to see if they were pursued. Stenka and his men had them covered with a last few working muskets. A couple of Tatar horsemen thought they might yet achieve something if they followed, but Stenka dropped his arm and the Cossack muskets rang out and one horseman fell in the shallows and the second turned and galloped away.

The river was alternately gravel shallows and deep channels with strong currents, treacherous going, and they slipped from their horses and swam alongside holding onto the pommels. At last, shaking with exhaustion, they hauled themselves out on the far side, soaked and muddied, and crawled back onto their mounts, streaming with water. The horses were reluctant to do more than walk, let alone gallop. They heeled them furiously.

Their one hope lay in Devlet Giray's attack having been so rapid, so impatient, their rearguard camp would be no more than a cluster of hastily erected tents, perhaps some rough barricades, loose knots of guards. What did the Tatars think they had to fear?

'At the gallop!' cried Stanley. 'In and out like lightning is our way!'

As soon as they came in sight of the sprawling camp, with its slave pens the size of fields, Nicholas picked out a cluster of eight white conical tents, and one taller than the rest, finely embroidered around the doorway. They galloped straight for it. Some Tatar footguards were as much puzzled as anything else by this absurdly small raiding party, and still unaware of the disaster unfolding across the river, though the roar of the muskets from the heights had made them anxious. Now they stepped towards the six riders and cried out a challenge.

They galloped in and cut them down. More guards came running. Smith unslung his jezail.

They slewed to a halt before the most handsome tent and Nicholas slipped from his horse, the others remaining mounted, forming a ring. The tent flap was tied closed with a rope and some complex knotting, as if some treasure lay within. Nicholas wrenched at it in frustration, and shouted out. All around them, clamorous cries giving the alarm.

Inside, a beautiful dark-haired girl sat tied to a stool, blindfolded, but beneath the blindfold her eyes flared open wide at the sound of that voice, her lips parted. A fat woman glared around with tiny porcine eyes and drew a dagger, so small and so sharp it was like something used by a carver in wood.

Nicholas laid hold of the rope and hacked at it with his sword, but his sword was badly blunted from the fighting. Men were running towards them now. Stanley let off a packed arquebus, and then a pistol, and rode forward boldly at the oncoming guards. More yells, jabbering. The thump of a man hitting the ground. Nicholas hacked desperately at the rope but it would not give. And then in a blur so fast he hardly saw it, a tiny knife in a tiny fist shot out between the lashings of the rope and sliced across his arm and he cursed and leapt backwards. The knife in the fist vanished again.

Then Chvedar the renegade priest was at the door of the tent with a brand snatched from a cookfire, and hurling some flagon at the ground. Grain spirit, soaking the tent. He put the brand to the soaked tentskin and it roared up fiercely. Moments later Nicholas could slash the burnt skin to blackened ribbons, and drove on in with sword held flat and straight before him.

Rebecca now stood, blindfolded, hands bound, and at her throat was the tiny little knife, its blade already crimson with Nicholas's blood. Behind her, almost hidden, stood a plump little Tatar woman. Then the woman, eyes almost lost in her rolls of cheekfat, peeped round from behind Rebecca, and she gave Nicholas an unearthly smile.

He knew at once that she was very dangerous. And she was not holding Rebecca to ransom, not merely threatening to kill her if he stepped any closer. She was just about to kill her anyway.

Everything happened at once. He was running towards them, throwing himself at them ... and there was Smith's shout, and the roar of his jezail deafening in Nicholas's ear, a shot with barely an inch of safety to it. But the ball caught Babash in her right shoulder and spun her round and away from Rebecca, the knife still in her fist. Rebecca sank to the ground and Nicholas fell on her.

Babash, though a burning hot lead ball had just gone straight through her shoulder and out of her back, was not finished. Something flashed out from her left hand and thumped into Smith behind, and he grunted and went quiet. Then Babash closed her left hand across the wound in her right shoulder, seemingly not weakened, and advanced once more upon Nicholas and Rebecca to cut their throats.

It was Chvedar who saved them. He came running with a knife in his hand and fell into her. They stood there for a moment locked together, for all the world like some couple in a loving embrace, perhaps about to dance. But Chvedar's knife was deep in Babash's back, and her little knife had cut deeply across his belly. Then they fell together.

Nicholas tore the blindfold from Rebecca's eyes, and drove his sword in between her wrists and wrenched, and it was enough to cut her thin bonds. He held her freed hands and rubbed them and they kissed and wept. But the tent was burning, and they had had enough of burning. He crawled over to Chvedar, the woman lying in a mound across him. She was dead. Chvedar still breathed. Nicholas began to roll her off him but Chvedar whispered, 'No, do not, little brother.' Blood dribbled from his mouth. The dead woman on his belly was all that was keeping his guts in. And besides, he was going now. He could still see the young English gallant and his beautiful girl blurrily through the clouds and the smoke. The lucky devil. He smiled.

'And I, Chvedar,' he whispered. 'Dying like this in the arms of a fat Tatar wench. My life was always strange.' His bloody mouth creased in a faint smile, and he said still more quietly, 'Receive my wicked soul, O Lord.' And then he was gone.

Outside, Smith was still slumped, something horrible and gleaming embedded in his neck. Stanley hauled him up, shouting.

'On your feet, man!'

Even Smith, that great, indestructible Knight Commander of St John, seemed near finished. But Stanley shook him and roared in his face.

'Then get it out,' mumbled Smith, 'get it out.'

Stanley glanced at the wound. It wasn't a knife, more like some kind of metallic star with evil sharpened points. He shook his head. 'Later. Leave it in.'

'It's not artery?'

'Of course not, man!' cried Stanley with a certain pitiless scorn. 'Just blood. Later. Bind it up. To horse!'

Smith crawled into his saddle, while Stanley turned and loosed another wild pistol shot, a huge dag-pistol loaded with slivers and nails and chips of stone that spattered horribly into the enemy pressing in on them. There were horses screaming, men, the burning tent, savage close-quarter fighting, and then Andriushko was shouting at them 'Go! Go! Or you will not make it!' and riding straight at a much larger party of Tatar horseman coming towards them.

Stanley knew this moment. He dragged Smith's horse by the reins and pulled him away, and lashed out and booted Nicholas's horse savagely in the rump and he in turn pulled the horse Rebecca now rode. They turned and fled. They could not even look back, but they knew the scene. There would be Andriushko galloping, sword swinging, towards that troop of twenty enraged horsemen. They would break around him, slowing to cut him down, and he would duck and weave and might take one or two with him. And then he too, like Chvedar, would be gone.

And those he had died to save would already have two or three hundred yards' advantage on their pursuers, and be making for the river and their own camp.

They came back across the river clinging to their horses. Stenka was ready and gave them covering fire again, and the pursuing party halted on the opposite bank. Some leaned and spat. They had lost. But they could see from the carnage among their own main army that there was far more lost this day.

By way of counter-attack, more Tatar horsemen tried to ride up the shoulder of the hills, the way Ivan Koltzo had taken, so they might attack the Streltsy lines.

No!' cried Devlet Giray. 'Do not pursue that way! Pull back, right back now! Save yourselves!'

But again all discipline was lost. The horsemen streamed up the shoulder in their hundreds, and were cut down by the massed ranks of the Streltsy left horn.

More panic ensued when the main body of Yakublev's Cossack horse, three thousand men fresh for battle, sliced in on the jostling, chaotic Tatar horse from the north and picked off more and more, before wheeling free again across the plain: the Tatars' own tactics. Then they came in again – and again ... Like a huge wheel bound with sharpened scythes.

Still the Streltsy musketeer poured down fire from above, and the Tatars were being attacked on two fronts, still pressed back against the muddy river's edge, hardly able to move. The carnage all along that bankside was terrible, the earth itself a sodden brown mash of mud and blood.

At last, all order gone, the Tatar horsemen by some strange uniformity of will simply stopped fighting and fled. Many did not even make it back across the river to their own camp, but simply broke and rode east. Horror-stricken, heartbroken, disbelieving the disaster of this day, longing only for home and for peace. Already the burning of Moscow seemed to many of them a hollow and bitter kind of victory, without honour and without glory.

Devlet Giray himself still wanted to press back over the river, and slaughter all the Russian slaves in their pens. But it was impossible now. Even for him, still with so many men under his command. The Cossacks of Yakublev pressed hard upon them. All spirit was gone. At last he too, with a roar of anger, spurred his horse and rode east.

The vast pens across the river were left silent and unguarded, the enslaved themselves staring out across the plains, blinking the dust from their eyes, hardly believing. Still enslaved in their minds, but free men.

43

They re-sited the camp on the heights in case of counter-attack – and well above the vast heaps of the slain. The Streltsy stayed with them, the horsemen of Yakublev. There was exhaustion and quiet conversation among the tents, and slow, weary, victorious smiles.

The evil star embedded in Smith's neck made a horrible sucking sound as Stanley pulled it free and then bound the streaming wound tight.

Smith closed his eyes. 'I'm getting too old for this.'

Stenka passed a flask. He alone seemed unwearied, eyes sparkling with delight. Nothing tasted as sweet as victory, nothing. And what a victory.

'And it was Petlin's treachery,' he said, 'which made it possible, which brought the Tatars back to us, swearing vengeance on you Inglisz. What a tale. And then got themselves caught up in the one thing they hate: set battle.'

'Petlin's treachery,' said Ivan Koltzo, 'and my own great heroism.'

Stenka laughed and thumped him, and they drank. Then they drank more solemnly to their dead comrades, the hulking Andriushko, and Chvedar the renegade priest.

'I tell you truly,' said Stanley, 'not one of our own high-born, oath-sworn Knights of St John ever died more nobly than these.'

Stenka smiled with tears in his eyes.

Besides them, he had lost another hundred men at the wagon circle, out of all his three hundred. It was a desperate trick, though it had worked. And all Cossacks longed to die in battle. It was the way. Not one of the Streltsy had died. Not one. And Yakublev had lost perhaps another hundred men. As for the Tatars, on the other hand – of Devlet Giray's army, perhaps five thousand lay dead, another ten thousand wounded.

'Ten thousand dead,' said Stenka.

Smith said, 'Maybe. Their losses were terrible.'

'They will not return to attack Russia,' said Stenka.

'Not any time soon, no.'

'Then it worked.'

'Indeed it did. God was with us. He must have been. It was the craziest plan I ever heard.'

There was abandoned loot at the Tatar camp, wagonloads of it, quickly requisitioned and divided by Yakublev and Stenka. The slaves were guarded overnight, to be brought across the river tomorrow by rafts. Many thousands of them. The greatest challenge might yet be keeping them fed and watered on the long walk back to Moscow. Had their mad dash to find Rebecca all been a waste anyway, had Chvedar and Andriushko died for nothing? Would they have found her at the camp eventually, safe and sound?

Stanley said, 'We did not know that. And even now, I do not think so. I think that obese woman who was guarding her was itching to kill her anyway. I think it was timely we went when we did. It was some deep prompting.'

'Why did she want to kill her?' said Nicholas.

Stanley sighed. Smith put in, 'Women. Don't ask me to explain. I understand the ways of whales better than I do women.'

'And we did not even find Mistress Southam,' said Nicholas.

Rebecca herself came quietly and sat with them. Nicholas was amazed at her composure. Would she not have nightmares?

'No,' said Stanley. 'We did not find Mistress Southam. We only half succeeded. God have mercy upon her.'

Rebecca was looking at them, a small frown upon her forehead. And then she held her hand to her mouth to hide her smile.

'I'm not sure it becomes you to smile at the fate of poor Ann Southam,' said Nicholas, sounding rather pompous even to himself as he did so.

'The fate of poor Ann Southam,' said Rebecca, and then sighed exaggeratedly. They were all looking at her now. Even Stanley could not help thinking she was damnably pretty. There in the firelight opposite him, in first bloom, her skin lustrous in the firelight, hair long and shining dark, her big dark eyes … Good God. Remember your vows, man. And you are old enough to be her father, very comfortably.

She said, 'It is tragic. Most tragical and melancholy.' Like an actress.

They were missing something. Nicholas said, 'What do you mean?'

Stanley said, 'Are you hinting …?'

She smiled, girlish, impish. 'Well,' she said, 'it may seem very tragic for poor Mistress Ann Southam, who was after all widowed barely a week or two since. But though I am sure her heart is broken with grief, from shallow appearances at least, she hid her grief very bravely.'

'In what way?'

'Why, as she lounged comfortably in the tent of the Khan Zamurz, one of the greatest khans under Devlet Giray. The one who fought us at the walls of the Kremlin, you remember.'

They remembered.

'Well,' said Rebecca. 'It seems Mistress Ann Southam pleased him very much. They like their womenfolk fair-haired, of course, and though she is older than some, they liked her full figure too. I imagine in only a few more weeks' journeying, she will be reclining again quite comfortably on soft cushions, dressed in Chinese silks, eating sweetmeats and drinking sherbet, waited upon by no fewer than six maidservants.'

'Good God,' said Smith.

'And at evening,' said Nicholas, 'I suppose she and this Zamurz Khan have friendly and agreeable conversation until late into the night?'

She flushed. 'Quite so.'

'Well,' said Stanley, and he raised his cup. 'To the happy future together of Zamurz Khan and his good lady wife, Mistress Ann. A triumph of Anglo-Tatar relations.'

Smith growled an uncouthness.

*

They came back to Moscow and camped some safe few miles outside and sent communication to Ivan. He was delighted with his own glorious victory over the Tatars. The bells of the city rang out – what bells still survived.

Moscow was already being rebuilt. Nicholas and Hodge crept in one evening, anonymous, and saw great activity, and knew that this grim place would rise again swiftly, perhaps more strongly, for all its troubles.

And they heard some extraordinary news, racing back to tell the knights.

'He has disbanded the Oprichnina!'

Smith stared. 'He has?'

'He was disgusted with the way they took no part in the victory over the Tatars.'

'But he didn't allow them to!'

Nicholas shrugged. 'Even so. Many have been executed – in the usual ways, publicly. And among them, Maliuta Skuratov himself.'

They digested this. Then Stanley said, 'Sup with the Devil, you should use a long spoon,' and they grieved no more over the fate of the Oprichnina.

'You are not returning to Moscow to bid formal farewell to His Excellency the Czar?' asked Prince Michael Vorotinsky.

'We are not,' said Stanley. Vorotinsky eyed him shrewdly. Stanley considered and then said, 'Perhaps you would bid farewell to His Excellency on our behalf? Bid long life to Czar Ivan, Beloved Father of his People, Great Leader in Battle, Hero of Rus, who watches over them as tenderly as a mother hen over her chicks.'

Smith said, 'You don't think he'll smell a rat?'

Vorotinsky said, 'All rulers love praise.'

Nicholas added, 'Say too that the services of his most excellent physician, Dr Elysius Bomelius, were much appreciated by his English guests in their hour of intestine distress. A remarkable healer of men. We trust that the good doctor is in perfect health himself, and did not meet with any unpleasant mishap in the Great Fire of Moscow.'

They were enjoying themselves now.

Stanley said, 'And we have no doubt that to posterity, Ivan will be known by a great name, like that of our own great Anglo-Saxon king of England, Alfred. All ages after will know him as – Ivan the Great!'

'Or perhaps even,' said Nicholas, 'given his intense piety and gentle sanctity, like that of St Francis of Assisi himself ... Saint Ivan the Gentle.'

Vorotinsky said, 'This is your English humour, is it not? When you say one thing and mean another?'

Stanley smiled. 'Prince Michael Vorotinsky, do you doubt our sincerity?'

Vorotinsky smiled a rare, wintry smile. Then he held out his hand and they shook hard, with deep respect and affection.

'God bless Russia,' they said.

'Pray He does,' said Prince Michael. 'Russia needs it.'

And he was gone.

It was time to bid farewell to the Cossacks too. Stenka and Yakublev and Ivan Koltzo and the others wept freely and embraced them and called them brothers and swore them to return one day.

And it was with deep feeling that the four bid farewell likewise. Though this war in Russia had hardly seemed a crusade, yet Nicholas knew he would never forget or regret his time among the wild brethren of the Dnieper and the Don. Of all the men he had ever known, they seemed the most lawless and alive and free, riding the vast and windy steppes without fences or owners, without kings or governments, a brotherhood to be envied by any man burdened and settled.

Stenka wiped his eyes at last and sniffed and spat and put his hands on his hips and regained his pride.

'How do you like this?' he said. 'Ivan has sent word to us Cossacks, giving heartfelt thanks, and offering us five hundred Streltsy to join us in an army of exploration.'

'Exploration?' Smith grunted. 'All the world's at it these days.'

'Where?' said Stanley.

Stenka waved his arm with the grandest of gestures. 'Eastwards. The wild frontier. The land of Sibir, the Land that Lies Asleep.'

'You will go?'

Stenka sighed. 'Though we love the steppes and this is our

homeland, yet we are promised many rewards. There is a whole new world to the east – the size of a hundred Russias! It makes my head spin. But what an adventure! Broad-faced Finnish hunters, grease-coated Lapps, Karelians, Chuvash, Mordvinians, the White Sheep Turkomans who hold the strategic corridor of Azerbaijan, and in the broad valley of Perm the Bashkirs herding their fat-tailed sheep; and beyond that, forest people who dwell in trees and worship the reindeer as their ancestors ...'

Stanley smiled. 'You paint quite a picture, Stenka.'

'Well.' Stenka returned to the here and now. 'We will consider this expedition over good brandy. And now, here, see – I give you gifts, from the wagons we captured.'

And Stenka brought forth the most expensive cloaks they had ever seen: four immaculate, gleaming and glossy fur cloaks of black sable.

They gasped. Then the knights shook their heads.

Stenka looked angered. It was a deep offence to refuse a gift.

'Understand, we are monks sworn to poverty,' explained Stanley gently. 'Our obedience to God must be higher than our obedience even to you, Brother Stenka.'

Stenka stared, then suddenly the stormclouds passed and he grinned, and prodded Smith.

'You mean you do not even own that fabled rifled musket of yours?'

'Though it pains me to say so,' said Smith, 'no, I do not. It belongs to my Order, not me.'

'Tch. I do not understand how any man could not wish for possessions. Stenka wishes for every pot of gold, every fine jewelled sword, and every woman in the world! Hah! But be that way, holy knights. You two younger brothers, you will have your cloaks at least.'

Still Nicholas and Hodge hesitated. Such a gift.

'Especially when,' said Stenka, 'you see their origin!' And he turned them inside out with a flourish. Inside, upon the soft skin, was branded the Russian Imperial Eagle. Stenka saw their expressions and doubled up, nearly choking with laughter. 'Aye, what a joker God is, after all! These were stolen from the Czar's own treasury somehow by the Tatars, then stolen back off the Tatars by us – and shall we take them back to the Czar? Shit on his mother's grave, shall we! Here, little English brothers. Take and wear these in happy remembrance of your good friend Czar Ivan IV of Russia!'

They could not resist. It was too good a joke.

44

They camped one last night under the stars, the Cossacks now drinking wildly, and already, after just two days encamped, restless and ready to be off again. To the great and uncharted forests and rivers and ice-bound mountains of the East ... They sang their melancholy songs of longing.

The wild falcon flies
Over the Volga
He stoops not nor bows
To the great Lords below
He drinks the dark water
At the gates of Saratov
At Tsaritzin, Svialsk,
And cries to the river,
'O why are you sad, Mother Volga?'

Nicholas half yearned to go with them. But he yearned as much for something quite different.

Rebecca sat quietly now, overwhelmed, withdrawn, grieving deeply. Her father, her nurse Hannah – she was alone and there was nothing left for her here.

Hodge drank thirstily, still clutching his sable cloak and staring at it in disbelief. 'Do you realise,' he said, 'what this could fetch in England, if you could find a nobleman to buy it off you?'

Nicholas shook his head. It was hard to reckon.

'I'll tell you what it could buy you,' said Hodge. 'An entire cloak of the stuff, in such condition ... from sables caught in a Russian midwinter, you can tell that, the coat's so thick and soft. I'll tell you what you could get for it. A whole farm, that's what you could get. Best land too. An orchard. Barns. My old man wouldn't believe it.' Hodge's eyes were as dreamy and blue as the distant hills of Wales on a summer's day. Already he saw himself master of five hundred acres, sheep of thousands ... his own cider press, maybe! All for the price of one sable cloak. Then he wrapped it very carefully indeed in his own old travelling cloak. Maybe this daft jaunt abroad hadn't been so daft after all, if a nice slice of Shropshire was what had come of it.

Hodge fell asleep, and Nicholas went over to her.
    'You are tired now?'
    She nodded. Her face was streaked with tears. He sat near her.
    'Do you ... Do you have family in England?'
    'I have cousins.' She wiped her face. 'Delighted to see a penniless relative on their doorstep, they'll be.'
    'Your father will have money in his name, with a London bank.'
    'I suppose.'
    'Where are your cousins?'
    'Worcestershire.'
    Worcestershire. Not far from Shropshire. But couldn't he just say ...? He could not. He swallowed. Useless.

They rode south. What had they done? He glanced back one last time at the grim city. He had a vision of Czar Ivan, not just pacing the blood-red corridors of the Kremlin, sunk in madness and cruelty, but bestriding the continent of Europe now from north to south, the Tatars driven back for good, nothing to fear. Thanks to them, Ivan ruled unchallenged, it seemed, from the White Sea to the Black, and now his Cossack Army of Exploration would push east as well, into that vast and unknown land of Sibir. The Russian Bear was awakening from long sleep, opening its red jaws wider, wider ...
    He blurted out his thoughts to Stanley. 'Are we sure we know what we have done? Making Ivan strong again?'
    Stanley grinned, rolling along at ease on his horse. 'Of course

not! We are no cautious, far-sighted statesmen! Only feckless knights errant and adventurers, the last crusaders born out of our time. Always seeking some new crusade against the enemies of the Cross, in a world long since grown old and cynical and become a new money-loving world of merchants and colonies, trading posts and city exchanges. Such a world must regard knights errant and crusaders as absurd anachronisms and old, doddering clowns.'

He still smiled, but his eyes were distant. 'Do you remember the mad, emaciated Spaniard we met at Messina in Sicily, before Lepanto?'

Smith said, 'Aye, I remember him. Don Miguel de Cervantes, wasn't it?'

'Remember how he talked ceaselessly of gallant quests and knights errant and maidens in distress and high and noble adventure, like some teller of old tales to King Arthur and his circle at Camelot? What a moonstruck loon. Yet the older I get, the more years pass and the world seems to grow harder and colder and more gold-besotted, the more I look back at that mad Spaniard and think I will stand beside him and his crazed dreams after all.'

They ambled on a little further then Smith raised an invisible cup. 'Aye, here's to it. Lunatics all.'

And they drank an invisible toast.

They took a river barge down to the Black Sea and found a merchantman to the Bulgarian coast, then a filthy coaster that got them round to Greece, and thence Italy and so more easily home. Nicholas passed the time writing his careful report for Her Majesty. He wrote in measured prose, as befits a man trying to sound sober and wise, but could not avoid suggesting a mixed victory. Muscovy would rise to great power, he judged. A Christian power, yes. The Islamic advance had been held, though the Tatars hardly seemed the most fanatic of Mohammedans. He foresaw many more clashes between Russia and the Ottoman Empire to come. The eventual victor, he could not say. The Ottomans, with their vast resources, populations, wealth, armed forces without parallel in the world, and superb organization – or Russia with her vast and barely explored territories, her redoubtable peasantry, her apparently limitless ability to suffer, to be defeated and yet not broken? It was in the hands of the Almighty.

At Malta there were more farewells, too sad to relate. Stanley hinted they still had business in England, and not the business of assassinating Queen Elizabeth either.

'But times grow ever more complicated,' he said. 'Perhaps one day ...'

That was all any of them could promise, so instead they embraced and wept, and knew they would never have such friends all the years of their lives.

'What we have lived through,' said Stanley, shaking his head. Eyes bright. 'Who would believe it? What we have lived through together.' Then he laid his big hands on their shoulders. 'If I had had children, sons – I would have wished them as you are.'

'Come back one day,' blubbed Smith, barely able to speak. 'Come back to Malta, 'tis not a long voyage, and you will always be welcome.'

Nicholas said they might yet.

'And this maid,' said Stanley, laying his hand on her shoulder very gently, 'you care for her now.'

Rebecca wanted to say proudly that she could care very well for herself, but knew she could not, and embraced Stanley with many tears.

And then they stepped aboard the Genoese merchantman and waved a last time and the two knights turned away from the quay-side into the narrow streets of Valletta and were gone.

That night, Rebecca said softly, 'They were truly like fathers to you, were they not?'

'They were. After my father died.' He smiled sadly. 'Though the education they gave me was ... unusual.'

'Do you still miss your father?'

'I do, and still talk to him daily.'

'I too.' They stood together in silence at the rail for a long time, and then she said, 'So many have died.'

'Aye. But more are being born all the time. Thank God.'

'A great procession,' she said. 'From birth to death. What is it all for? Are we here to be tried?'

'I think so, exactly,' he said. 'To be tried, and almost certainly found wanting. And then to be forgiven.' And he reached out and took her hand, and then she turned to him and they kissed.

A gusty autumn day, the Palace of Whitehall.

'So you do not advise that we should engage to marry this interesting Crowned Czar of all the Russias?'

'I do not, Your Majesty,' said Nicholas, hardly able to believe he was advising his Queen on marriage. Although he knew by the faint smile on her lips that she was not really taking him seriously as a counsellor. But she found the idea amusing.

'Though his wealth and his empire are vast and growing, and he is not a Catholic?'

'Nor an Englishman neither,' put in Hodge.

The Queen smiled upon his interruption. Hodge could do no wrong in her eyes. What next, was she going to knight him or something?

Nicholas said, 'He is not a Catholic, nor indeed ...' He had a sudden flashback to that grotesque moment when Ivan, appearing in the great square dressed in clownish conical hat and gold robe, poured boiling alcohol over the head of a man and set fire to him ... and laughed. He drew breath. 'His Christian faith is a complex one, Your Majesty. He does not always behave as one would expect of a Christian king. I fear your marriage would not be altogether happy. He is subject to a certain moodiness.'

'Indeed?'

'And has a certain fondness for ... well, extreme violence.' He racked his brains for something good to say about the Czar. 'He had a difficult childhood.'

'He is not alone in that,' said Elizabeth sharply. But she disliked direct attention. She looked instead at what the two emissaries were wearing. Finely dressed indeed.

'You know that by the sumptuary laws of our beloved father, it is forbidden for any man in England below the rank of viscount to wear sable.'

She had him there. He stammered, embarrassed, 'I didn't know, Your Majesty, forgive me.'

She stood and said with startling abruptness, 'We wish you to marry. If you agree to marry a good Protestant girl, to raise your children as Protestants, then – well, would you?'

It was no facile answer that Nicholas made. He had thought endlessly about the truths of Christianity on his long adventures, seen so many men kill or die for their beliefs. Yet there could only be one God. A God with many names, perhaps.

At last he said, 'I will live and die a Catholic subject of Your Majesty, loyal to you to the last. But my children – I could raise as Protestants.'

The earth did not shake, the ghost of his father did not appear. Nothing happened.

'If you agree to do so,' said Queen Elizabeth, 'then your first son will be made Viscount Melwardine, in the country of Shropshire. Then he will be able to wear that fine sable cloak, at least.'

His mind reeled. His son, a viscount of England ...! His father would like that very much indeed.

'Is there no girl in the kingdom you can marry? Perhaps we can find you a compliant lady-in-waiting here at court. It is high time, you must be thirty.'

'Only twenty-five, Majesty.'

'You look a lot older. All that foreign sun and those wars, I suppose.'

Unable to argue, mind still reeling, he blurted out, 'There is an orphan girl I have brought back from Russia ...'

Hodge guffawed. 'He hasn't even asked her to marry him yet! Hasn't got the bollocks for it!' He shuffled. 'Begging your pardon, Your Majesty.'

Elizabeth was thinking she wanted to keep Hodge by her side always. But he was a Shropshire yeoman, she could see that, and far too good for the Court. Ingoldsby angered her, though.

'A Russian orphan!' she cried. 'This country is overrun with foreigners as it is, there are hundreds of Jews again in London, Frenchmen, Dutchmen, Flemings ... and there must be a dozen blackamoor servants in the City now, we see them every time we go abroad, to our great distress. And you tell me you have brought back some wench from Russia!'

'I have, Your Majesty.'

'With child, I suppose?'

'No, Your Majesty, I have not—'

'Does she speak English?'

'She does, she—'

'Then send her in.'

A minute later, Rebecca was curtsying deeply before her and shaking visibly.

'Speak, girl. What is your name?'

'Rebecca Waverley, Your Majesty.'

'Ah.' The Queen glared at Nicholas. 'You have a pleasant wit, Master Ingoldsby. You made me think she was a Russian wench, but she is as English as I. And you claim you have not broken her virgin knot?'

Nicholas and Rebecca both blushed together. The Queen was known to be blunt-spoken on matters of the body. She once mocked the Earl of Oxford publicly for letting a fart.

'I swear I have not laid a finger on her,' said Nicholas, not quite truthfully. 'She is as pure as any maid in England.'

'Hm,' said Elizabeth, 'that means little. But at least she is English.'

'As English as roast sirloin and old ale, Majesty.'

'A pretty simile for a maid,' she scolded. 'Say rather, as English as a white rose in June.'

'As you say, Majesty.'

'Rebecca Waverley. Are you the daughter of Thomas Waverley, the merchant at Moscow?'

'I am, Your Majesty.'

'A sad story, you have my sympathies. There is a good estate for you in London, my exchequer will see to it. And as for this aged vagabond here, this Sir Nicholas Ingoldsby – it seems he would be happy to take you to wife, though he is evidently as shy as a school-boy in asking you. Doubtless because, despite all his many years of travel in sunny foreign lands, where the women are notorious for looseness and whorishness, he has never known a woman, or even come close to one. Is that right, Master Ingoldsby?'

286

God, she was nearly as cruel as Czar Ivan himself. 'I, I ...' he stammered.

'I, I ...' she mocked. 'Well, you are either a pure soul indeed, or at least you will have some manly experience when you take this one to your bed. So tell me, girl – what say you to this man beside you? Would you take him as your husband?'

It was not the romantic moment of proposal that Rebecca had dreamed of in her girlish dreams. Her mind was in a dense Thames fog, her body burning all over, yet she heard her own voice say very far off, 'Yes I will.'

'Well then,' said the Queen. 'That's settled.'

There remained just the matter of Hodge's sable cloak. It was impossible to raise one so low-born to the peerage.

'So what shall we do with it, Master Matthew Hodgkin?' said the Queen. 'Use it to cover a milking stool? Wrap a newborn lamb?'

'Please, Your Majesty,' he said. 'I was wondering if, if I might ... sell it. To a nobleman? If it might be sold in the Court ... then I could buy a farm or some such ...'

'Hand it here.'

She examined it. 'This brand within. This came from the Russian Imperial Wardrobe? A gift from Ivan himself?'

'Not, not exactly, Your Majesty.'

'Well, let us enquire no more. Things that take place outside England are of no concern to us, and no doubt barbarous. It is a fine piece. No doubt one of my Court fops and popinjays will give you a good price. The Earl of Leicester, perhaps, or Southampton. We shall see to it.'

There was then an awkward silence while she stared at them. 'Well?' she snapped. 'Be off, be off with you, that is all! We have greater business of State to attend to than fixing up your marriages and selling your cast-off clothes for you!'

Nicholas and Rebecca were married in the parish church of the village by a priest with a tongue too big for his mouth, so that most of Cranmer's wedding service was lost. But they did hear the bit about not satisfying carnal lusts, and Nicholas glanced sidelong at her, but she refused to glance back.

They kissed on the church steps and he shouted for joy, he couldn't help himself.

Rebecca and Hodge both wept.

'No matter,' said Rebecca gently to Hodge. 'You know I have a lovely cousin over near Worcester. She is but seventeen, a lass who loves the fields and the woods, and she would love to hear about your travels.'

'I'll not marry,' said Hodge. 'Not my game at all. I've got my new estate to look after.'

Nicholas and Rebecca hardly left their bedchamber for a week.

And Hodge was married to Rebecca's cousin Sarah by Whitsun.

EPILOGUE

Ivan the Terrible grew steadily worse after the events of this story, ever more inventive and savage in his cruelties, while fantasizing more and more about leading a crusade against the Muslim world. He even sent an emissary to Rome to ask for Papal support, but none was forthcoming.

In 1577, always jealous of Prince Michael Vorotinsky, who had captured Kazan and saved Moscow, he decided the illustrious nobleman and great commander was guilty of practising black magic. The Czar had him tortured by being tied to a stake between two blazing fires and slowly burned. Ivan himself joined in the proceedings, as was his custom, using his iron-tipped staff to brand Vorotinsky's flesh. At last the prince, horribly burned but still alive, was placed in a litter to be taken to the Monastery of Belozersk, but he died on the way.

The renegade Prince Kurbsky, one of Ivan's greatest enemies, wrote from the safety of exile of how Vorotinsky had suffered 'in his innocence at the hands of that drinker of blood', and praised the dead hero for having fought 'from your youth up to your sixtieth year for Christ our God, defending His sheep against the Mohammedan wolf'.

At last, in 1581, in a rage at what he considered her indecent dress, Ivan struck his pregnant daughter-in-law Elena so violently, he caused her to miscarry. Ivan's son, the Czarevich Ivan, confronted him. Furious at being questioned like this, and already harbouring deep suspicions that his son was plotting against him for the throne, Ivan beat the Czarevich to the ground with his spear. Moments later he fell on the youth, who was bleeding profusely from a deep wound to the skull, crying, 'I have killed my son! I have killed my son!' And so he had. The Czarevich Ivan died four days later.

Ivan lamented extravagantly, gave lavish gifts to the monasteries, prayed for forgiveness – but in his own tortuous theology, he also argued that God too had killed his own Son, Jesus Christ, on the Cross, and therefore he himself was only the more Godlike for what he had done. He died, sickly and half deranged, on March 18, 1584. There were rumours of poisoning.

Devlet Giray, great Khan of the Crimea Tatars, died in 1577, finally relieving Ivan of endlessly having to defend his southern border.

In 1581, having pushed eastwards across the Urals, the Cossacks captured the city of Sibir, and by 1607 they had reached the River Yenisey, already halfway across the vast land of Siberia. Russia was no longer a grand duchy, nor even a kingdom. It was an empire.

Queen Elizabeth I of England had many more marriage proposals, but accepted none of them. Some said that she could not, because she was already married to England.

As well as the prickly correspondence with the Russian Czar, Elizabeth also exchanged several cordial letters with the Sultan Murad, and his wife Safiye. Murad once wrote that he believed Islam and Protestantism had 'much more in common than either did with Roman Catholicism, as both rejected the worship of idols', and suggested an alliance between England and the Ottoman Empire. Elizabeth was never going to ally England with anyone if she could help it, but she continued to permit exports of tin and lead for munitions to the Ottoman Empire, and seriously discussed joint military operations with Murad III during the outbreak of war with Spain in 1585.

When Murad died in 1595, the Sultana Safiye made sure her son Mehmed became Sultan, and from then until her death in 1603, she was effectively joint sultan with him.

*

As for those two battle-scarred old Knights of St John, Sir John Smith and Sir Edward Stanley, who can say? It seems unlikely that they would ever have settled down to a peaceful old age, dozing in the Maltese sunshine ...

AUTHOR'S NOTE AND FURTHER READING

The major events in this account are all correct, but for some compression of dates to form a narrative, the crucial ones being the attack on Moscow by the Tatars, its defence by the gallant Prince Vorotinsky, its devastating firestorm, and the subsequent 'Revenge Battle' of the Oka.

Most of the main characters were real historical figures, from Sultana Safiye and her maidservant, Esperanza Malachi, to Devlet Giray, Khan of the Crimean Tatars, to those sinister figures in the court of Muscovy such as Elysius Bomelius and Maliuta Skuratov. But at the heart of it all was Ivan himself: the Terrible. The actual Russian word, *Grozny*, has a more complex meaning than merely 'terrible'. It also suggests awesome, powerful, even magnificent. But I have certainly not exaggerated Ivan's character, and even some of the smallest details in the novel – his conducting a cathedral choir with a spear, for instance, or his torturing small animals as a boy – are taken from history. One only has to skim through the index of one of the most sober and scholarly recent biographies, by Isabel de Madariaga, to get a true sense of the man: *ill-treatment of ... justification for cruelty ... Bible, Antichrist ... and magic, witchcraft ... Kills his son Ivan ... debauchery ... death of...*

De Madariaga's portrait is the most detailed and up-to-date; also highly entertaining, and lighter reading, are the biography by Henri Troyat, and the racy, colourful account by Harold Lamb, *The March of Muscovy: Ivan the Terrible and the Growth of the Russian Empire, 1400-1648.*

Other books I used included *The Virgin Queen* by Christopher Hibbert; *Elizabeth's London* by Liza Picard, and *The Time Traveller's*

Guide to Elizabethan England by Ian Mortimer, all highly recommended; *The Elizabethan Secret Services* by Alan Haynes; the wonderful *Lords of the Golden Horn* by Noel Barber; *Subjects of the Sultan* by Suraiya Faroqhi; and *The Ottoman Empire* by Lord Kinross.

There remains some uncertainty among historians as to whether Ivan really did make that infamous proposal of marriage – *whilst already married* – to Elizabeth I. Certainly he proposed marriage to Elizabeth's grand-niece, Lady Mary Hastings, a proposal which the Queen herself rather coldly rejected on the grounds that Lady Mary would not please any man who was 'a lover of beauty', since 'she has just had the smallpox'. But other letters in the National Archive at Kew imply strongly that Ivan also proposed marriage to the Queen directly, and was rejected, to his great indignation.

And besides, it makes a much better story.